Talia:
On the Shore of
the Sea

Servants of the Moon
and Sun: Book Two

By

Joel C. Flanagan-Grannemann

ServantsoftheMoonandSun.com

First edition Version 1.2 (~28 typos corrected)
Published November 2022

Edited by Jay-Jay Flanagan-Grannemann
TheHyphenatedEditor@ServantsoftheMoonandSun.com

Cover Design by 100covers
contact@100covers.com

DDC: 816.3 Flanagan-Grannemann

Suggested LC subject headings:

    Interpersonal relations — Fiction
    Women soldiers — Fiction
    Soldiers — Fiction
    Princesses — Fiction
    Kings — Fiction
    Queens — Fiction
    Interpersonal relations and culture — Fiction
    Fairy tales in literature
    Fairy tales — Adaptations
    Sleeping Beauty (Tale)
    Sleeping Beauty (Tale) in literature
    Revenge in literature

Please sign up for announcements and updates via email at
list@ServantsoftheMoonandSun.com

ISBN: 978-1-7355384-2-6 E-Book
ISBN: 978-1-7355384-3-3 Trade Paperback

Dedication

This book is dedicated to:

my wife, Jay-Jay (for extraordinary editorial effort),
my mother, Anita,
my dad, Bruce, and
my father, Glenn (may he return swiftly).

Sorry I left the latter two out of the first book.

Author's Note

For your protection,
all Fairy names have been translated into your language.

Talia: On the Shore of the Sea
Servants of the Moon and Sun: Book Two

Table of Contents

Prologue

"Lord Troilus, Lady Perrault, thank you for coming." Tra waved the Iridescent-wing Fairies to chairs. "May I offer you some wine?"

"Only if it is from your vineyards in the north," Troilus replied, sitting down. Behind him at his left, Lady Perrault maneuvered his drooping wing so that it did not catch on the back of the chair.

"Is that comfortable?" she asked.

"Yes, my dear, thank you," he replied, reaching out to take her hand as she took her seat.

Lady Perrault smiled brightly as Tra brought three glasses of deep red wine. Her shimmering silver hair was tightly braided, and hung in a thin line between her wings. She let go of her husband's hand to take the glass Tra offered.

"There is no good wine in the south," Troilus commented, taking a sip. "Only brandy, and very little of that is worth drinking." He smiled. "We sell most of it to the Humans."

"The King buys all he can," Perrault said around a sip. "He thinks it is the best we make."

Tra took her seat across from them and laughed. "Humans have no taste."

Lord Troilus set his glass down and reached over to adjust his left arm. "Cursed crossbow. It hit something, and my foolish Healer still can't fix it." He ran his fingers through his thinning hair.

"She does the best she can," Perrault admonished him. "It was that cursed Leather-wing Medic whose sloppy Healing ruined your wing."

"If I ever find her again, I'll leave her with more than a droopy wing," he swore.

"Leathers are good for some things," Tra agreed, "but they should keep their hands off their betters."

Perrault Sent to her husband, *"So you say, Feather-wing!"*

Troilus Sent back amusement, accompanied by a sharp reminder to his wife that they still needed Tra.

Troilus addressed Tra. "I hear congratulations are in order."

Tra smiled, her hand going to her newly-flat belly. "Only a few weeks old, and her wings are already strong."

"Born in the dark of the moon?" Perrault asked. She swept the three fingers of her right hand over the inside of her left arm, elbow to palm.

Tra returned the gesture and bowed her head. "As is proper."

"And your sisters?" Troilus pressed.

Tra lost her smile. "Both bore healthy children."

Perrault raised her eyes.

"Gren's son is an Iridescent," Tra finally admitted.

"I thought that veil children were always female," Troilus commented, with a glance and Send at his wife.

"She defied me," Tra said coldly. "It was probably at the urging of that Wingless Bastard."

"We men can be useful," Troilus said, but then cut Tra off when she tried to comment. "My son and his husband speak very highly of the three of you."

Tra set aside her anger to preen for her guests. "Thank you, My Lord. We've been working hard to keep our eldest sister in check."

"This foolishness of having Law Masters at all the plantations," Troilus said with disgust. He waved his glass; Tra quickly refilled it. "And she says it's our responsibility to pay for everything. Staff, offices, everything." He made another disgusted sound. "This was all your niece's fault," he accused, pointing at Tra with his glass. "All that time-consuming work, destroyed." He glared at Tra. "How did that foolish child even wind up there?"

"And how did she discover what Summerwind was doing?" Perrault asked, also glaring at Tra.

Under the eyes of these powerful Iridescents, Tra outwardly wilted, and appeared cowed. Inside, however, she raged, and pictured shoving wine bottles down the old fools' throats.

"I misjudged her," Tra finally admitted. "She was supposed to go alone, but all her cursed Ladies and her Guard decided it was their honor to go into exile with her." She took a sip of wine to calm herself. "I will not make that mistake again."

"But we've started in the middle," Perrault interrupted. "This all began well before the exile. You were there: tell us everything," she demanded, setting down her glass.

"Yes, My Lady," Tra acquiesced. She took a moment to gather her thoughts. "It all started when the Prince came to Fae-Treval. He stood before the Queen, tall and arrogant, to announce that he wanted peace. That he wanted the restless peace that had held since the Battle of Brine Hill to become a true, lasting peace. That cheeky bastard called himself 'a simple spinner of Fairy silk' and used that to ingratiate himself with the Heir."

"Some of his creations are beautiful," Perrault admitted. "The dresses he made for the Ladies of the Heir were stunning. He has studied our Fairy styles well. I have seen other Humans, and even Elenites, try to make clothes for Fairies and fail horribly. They just do not understand the needs of the Fairy body."

"He understood the Fairy body, all right," Tra sniped. "He was given quarters, and almost immediately began to seduce and manipulate most of the court's young Feather-wings into his bed. And he brought in more and more of his horrible spinners and hangers-on. Men with wing-fever, but no sense of decorum or honor."

"Which you used to gain a foothold in his house," Troilus reminded her. "You led that Lord Bath around by his manhood, and gained valuable information from him."

"Yes." Tra waved away that fact, since it had been Gren's idea. "We learned a few things, but he used the Fairy girls we sent him, too."

"You underestimated them both," Troilus said in rebuke. "Get back to the story. We have an appointment with the Queen, and we need to know everything that has happened."

"The Prince used his charm and generosity to worm his way into the Heir's affections. He even danced with her at the presentation of Lord Oberon and Lady Titania's children." She shook her head. "I wish my mother were here to see what the Heir has been allowed to do. She would have brought that slut to heel. It was scandalous! Holding him tight, and flying through the air in the sacred turns of the dance." Tra took a sip of her wine to cool her anger.

"So, the Queen had decided to wed her daughter to the son of the Human King?" Perrault asked, in an attempt to nudge Tra to move on with her story.

Tra shrugged. "I don't know that for sure. But Lord Phillip — who led the knights' charge at Brine Hill, which led to the death of the Queen's husband — kept pressing the issue. It was either that, or reparations for the 'harm done to the Human Realm by the Fairy occupation.' We tried to turn our sister from this course, but she wouldn't listen. She kept insisting that if this would bring peace, then we must at least consider it." Tra shuddered. "A half-breed Queen. I would sooner cut off my own wings."

"Was the Heir amenable to, or at least considering, this union?" Troilus asked, frustrated with Tra for continually straying off the path.

"She must have been. She went to Elen and spent a day at his Crafthouse. Spent good silver on his trash."

"Then our allies attacked the town, the Crafthouse, and the Heir. I hope you had nothing to do with that?"

"No, that was Wingless. He needed a lever with Bastile, and showing the Prince that he could attack and do damage at any time he pleased provided that. He heard about the Heir's visit, and chose to attack when she was vulnerable. He seems driven to hurt her personally."

"And it worked! Wingless got the silk he wanted, and the means to make more. That was his goal," Troilus stressed.

"But it drove the Prince and the Heir closer together. He insinuated himself into the Return, and then even further into the court. I tried. . . ."

Perrault cut her off. "You keep saying 'you tried.' Well, apparently you didn't try hard enough. That foul Human stood Vigil for one of our fallen soldiers. He — somehow — was able to light the Pyre. Just how did he manage to do that?"

"I don't know, but I would guess it was the work of that meddling Paramount Miranda. She's always supported the Queen and the Heir."

"Then we need to find a wedge against her," Troilus said. "Ask the Mistress. She must have something to use against that old meddler. We must keep her clear of our affairs."

4

Tra narrowed her eyes, sensing more to his hatred of Miranda. 'This might be a wedge for you,' she thought. "I will speak to her," she responded aloud.

"Good." He waved his hand for more wine. "So, after the Return, what happened?"

Perrault refilled his glass as Tra continued.

"They became closer. My son kept a close eye on them. She took him to the Tower of the Moon, and then to watch the stars. I don't know how that slut kept from climbing on him that night. She was always quick to take others to her bed."

Perrault narrowed her eyes at Tra's continued insults toward Talia. She fixed Tra with a hard eye. "She is still the Heir, and still your niece. I would choose your words carefully. You sound like a Human, insulting our freedom to choose our partners without shame. That word comes to the lips of Human men all too easily."

Tra lowered her eyes. "I apologize, My Lady. Her actions reflect badly on the Queen and all Fairies. I was just reacting to that."

"See that you keep a civil tongue," Perrault chided her.

Tra nodded again, keeping her anger in check.

"Your son was watching them?" Troilus prodded.

"Yes, he and his companions. Sympathetic Fairies who knew the Prince was an enemy, and a defiler of our traditions." Tra smiled. "Then Bastile showed his colors. His hunting party attacked the Heir. But sloppily. Only his own man was killed. But it did finally drive the Queen to expel the Humans. She was weak, and gave them the night to gather themselves, instead of driving them out the gates immediately. My son was going to catch them, but. . . ."

"Wingless interfered again."

"That bastard almost killed my son. His men tried to take the Heir, but failed. That . . . the Heir, took him somewhere, had her way with him, and then sent him back. Just as news came that Fairies had killed the brother of the King. Then the Queen had to act, so she threw the Humans out, but not before letting him insult her and parade his filthy people through the throne room." Tra took another sip of wine before continuing. Her head was beginning to ache.

"Then the Heir was exiled, and for some reason, those naïve children chose to go with her. Summerwind was ready to break her, but the rest got in the way."

Troilus commented, "She should have separated all of them at the plantation, but instead, she allowed them to stay together and create a plan that brought both her and all of our many generations of work down." He smashed his fist down on the arm of his chair, breaking it off. He grabbed the broken piece and waved it at Tra. "We gave you all that Power, and you squandered it. Let it be destroyed. Used it for a petty vendetta against your own sister. You are very lucky the Dark Mother was watching, and killed those Captains and Supervisors before they could talk."

Tra started to cower, but with a sudden surge of anger, stood straight instead. "You squandered it. I used it. I used all that potential from the lost. All those spirits bound to the earth. I created a Shield of despair so thick no hope could penetrate it. Healing was so muted that Fairies died from simple splinters. I used the Power you gave me. And yes, I gambled, and I lost. This time." She stood up. "You think those Captains and Supervisors would have talked? That they would have revealed all our plans, and brought the Queen down on all of us? You're an old fool. Wingless was good for one thing: he can manipulate minds. Most of them didn't even consciously know what they had done. And if they had tried to speak," she snapped her fingers, "they would have been dead before two words could escape."

Troilus glared at the angry woman standing before him for a long beat. Then he smiled. "Good. I thought something like that was likely." He waved the shard of the chair. "Oh, sit down. If you hadn't defended yourself, I would have killed you as a waste of resources."

Tra sat down. She straightened her skirts, and brushed a stray strand of hair back from her eyes. "You would have tried."

Troilus only smiled again, and gestured to his wife. Tra turned, and saw Redfire disappearing as the woman closed her fists. Tra swallowed and nodded. "Well played."

"We do our best," Perrault said lightly, sitting back in her own chair. "We've been playing this game for a long time."

"So, you think you've found them?" Troilus asked.

"Yes. Some of The Nine have been spotted in a small town called Silverflow. Wingless sent his two best Fairies to capture them. We should be hearing from them soon."

"Silverflow?" Perrault asked, confused. "That's pretty far south. What are they doing down there?"

"Chasing ghosts," Tra replied. "Paramount Holly says they're following the trail of the Exile Queen. A fool's quest, but it keeps them out of our business. Another of our agents has confirmed this."

Perrault and Troilus exchanged glances over the head of the oblivious Tra.

"*This could be dangerous,*" Perrault Sent. "*The Exile Queen was our prime foe. She might have knowledge or weapons that these children could find.*"

"*Then we will deal with them. Calm, my love; this is a long game. She doesn't understand that, but we do.*"

"What are your plans for rebuilding our Power?" Troilus asked.

"I have found another place, much more secure. Wingless and his people are providing us with locations of Fairies buried by the Humans." Tra smiled. "We will build our most fearsome engine again. And your army?"

"Rebuilding. It will be ready when the time is right. Excellent," Troilus said, levering himself up with the help of his Power. "Keep a tight rein on your sisters. Especially Gren."

"I will, My Lord. She will be disappointed that she missed the two of you."

"I am not," Perrault said, rising with the help of her husband. "That harpy would burn an entire town to kill one Fairy. I shall hold you responsible if she interferes with any of our plans."

"Yes, My Lady," Tra said, cowed by the Power she saw in the other woman's eyes.

"Now, my love, we must go meet with the Queen." Turning to their host, Troilus reached out and took Tra's hand. He brushed the back of it with his lips. "Till we meet again, My Lady." With that, he took his wife's arm and exited the room.

Tra sat back down. She rubbed at the spot Troilus had kissed. Her hands began to shake, but she quickly folded her arms across her narrow chest.

"They're dangerous," the Mistress of Shadows remarked, as she dispelled her Shadow and took the chair Troilus had been sitting in. "Even more than we knew."

"Your people must follow them. I want to know every secret you can find. He has a wedge, and I must find it."

"As I said, they're dangerous," the Mistress cautioned, picking at the chair's broken arm. "They have a secret store of old Power that is unknown to me. I've sent agents after them before. They've all disappeared."

"Then send better agents. Clever agents. His ego is as big as his manhood is small. Maybe a fawning acolyte? Young? Pretty?"

"Maybe," the Mistress replied, considering. "Or perhaps a pretty Healer?"

☾ ⌇ ☼

"Lady Perrault, Lord Troilus." Luna greeted the pair warmly. "Please come in. I hope the trip from the south wasn't too taxing. It's horrible that you can't use Rings anymore." She tutted. "Such a pity."

"Not to worry, my girl. I'm beginning to enjoy the trips. I get to see more of our beautiful Realm this way."

"Please, sit. I will bring you some refreshments. The Queen will be out soon."

"Thank you, Luna," Perrault said. "You truly do hold our Realm together. What would the Queen do without you?"

"I do not know, My Lady. I hope we never have to find out."

Chapter One
Black Blades

"We can't fly anymore," Talon informed Min. *"We must land to rest."*

"If we must," Min relented. This was the fourth time Talon had urged her to land. Now she would have to.

They landed, and crouched in the grass. There was no other cover.

"I thought I felt something," Min Sent. *"Faint, but there."* She pointed in the direction in which they were headed.

"We'll rest an hour or two. Then, we'll fly."

Talon folded herself into a small ball, and wrapped her wings around herself. Min wanted to do the same, but couldn't. She pulled out the crystal shard Talia had given her, and concentrated. She could feel the Web tying back to Talia. A tiny wisp pointed forward. She tried to follow it, but it disappeared in darkness.

"Curse you," she said, not knowing who exactly she was cursing: Shatter, the Blood Cult, or herself. Min dropped into a meditation. She opened herself to the flow of the Realm, looking for anything that was out of place in this still land. Nothing.

Suppressing another scream of frustration, Min delved deeper, into the sky, the wind, even the small creatures of the grassland: little furry things no bigger than her hand. Curious, they moved, sniffing. Always sniffing.

Min's eyes shot open. "Smell."

"What?" Talon asked, raising her head.

"They can smell."

"Who?" Talon was confused.

"The little creatures of the grassland. They can smell things that are out of place." Min closed her eyes. "I wish Gil were here. She would be better at this."

"What are you doing?" Talon asked, taking a sip of water.

"Asking the little creatures to find Shatter."

She searched out the small furry beings, finding tunnels and colonies all over the land. They travelled both above and below the

9

ground. She followed their movements, and saw the patterns. Except in one place: the creatures gave wide berth to one section of grass.

"There." Min stood up and pointed. "She's there."

Talon stood, too. "That's off the line the Captain said she would take."

"But I know she's there."

Talon took a deep breath. "Then let's go."

☾♒☼

Shatter knew they were coming, but she couldn't move. The darkness had spread across her shoulders and chest. She was on her back, wings spread. The darkness was complete. Her Sight was gone. Only a few spots of light remained above her.

"Mother," she whispered, "give me strength." Her hand gripped her knife.

Two forms loomed over her. Her wordless scream gave her a burst of energy as she lunged at one of them.

"Shatter!" Talon called to her Captain, catching her arm. The knife fell to the ground.

"You're safe," Min announced, catching Shatter's other arm.

Shatter thrashed, not hearing them. Talon pinned her to the ground. Her wordless cries made Min shudder.

"Can you do something?" Talon urged, keeping her weak Captain down. "She'll bring our enemies."

"They're coming," Shatter cried.

"Shatter," Min soothed, "we're here." She Looked at Shatter with her Sight, and fear gripped her. Shatter's upper body was almost completely black. Her wings were turning black as well, with tendrils creeping toward the edges. The cut itself was darkest. That particular patch of blackness was creeping over her entire torso. Min tried a Sleep Spell, but the darkness pushed it away. Min tried something stronger. It slid off Shatter like water.

Talon let go, and hit Shatter in the head. She slumped back, out cold.

Talon stood, and Looked around. She Saw nothing. Her Sight strained, but there was no one near.

Min sat back on her heels and gripped her crystal. *"We've found her."*

Talia replied within two breaths. *"How is she?"*

"Bad. The cut seems to have spread something into her body. It resists Magic. I can't Heal her."

Talia Looked through the Web and Saw the darkness that had taken over Shatter. She Saw tendrils of corruption moving into Shatter's body from the cut, darkness creeping toward her heart and mind. She also Saw a thin thread of darkness reaching out from Shatter, back the way she had come. *"Min, there's something connecting Shatter to this darkness. Is there something in her pack? I sense something like the Geode Web."*

Talon had already opened Shatter's pack. She recoiled. "Feels like rotting meat." She dumped the contents out onto the ground. The bundle unrolled, and they saw the knives.

Min felt sick. *"It's the knives Shatter said cut her. They're like living darkness to my Sight."*

"I can See them," Talia confirmed. *"They're tied to something far away. We must destroy them."*

"But we must study them first: find out what they are, and how they work." Min's mind recoiled at the corrupted lines that formed the blades, and the darkness they carried. She would need more Power and protection than she had here to examine them safely.

"The enemy is tied to them. They're tracking her with them. If you keep them, you'll be caught. They're killing Shatter. Destroy them now!" Talia commanded.

Min motioned Talon to step back, then held her open palm out toward the knives. Silverfire bloomed, and she brought it closer to the blades. They began to smoke and bubble, but the metal held its shape.

"I need your Power," Min commanded Talon. Talon placed her hand on Min's back, between her wings, allowing her Power to flow into Min. The Silverfire grew in strength. The knives twisted under the assault.

"Die, foul things," Talon cursed.

11

Min cupped both of her hands over the knives. Silverfire filled her. She could see the dark bonds begin to break down. With a pitiful cry, the knives lost their shape, and dissolved into a black puddle.

Min sat back. Her mind buzzed, and her hands shook.

"Min." It took her a moment to realize that Talia was talking to her. *"Answer me."*

"I'm all right. The knives are destroyed."

"The thread's broken. You must move. They can't track you now, but they still know where you are."

Talon picked up Shatter. "I can't carry her too far. We passed a small grove of trees. We'll take her there. We can try to Heal her, then race for home."

Talia asked, *"How long till you can use your Torc?"*

"Maybe a day. Depends," Min answered.

"I don't sense anyone near. Hurry, and get to shelter. Contact me when you reach the trees."

"Should I try to take the melted knives?"

"No. Leave them. They'll know we destroyed them. I have enough from your Sight."

"Yes, My Lady." Min broke the connection, and hurried after Talon.

(♒ ☼

Talia opened her eyes to find her Ladies and The Nine all arrayed in a circle around her.

"They found her." The exhalation of held breath filled the room.

"Thank the Goddess," Goldberry whispered.

Flora buried her face in Elanor's chest and wept.

"She's grievously hurt," Talia informed everyone. "Min and Talon destroyed the knives that made the wound. Somehow, they were keeping her from Healing. They're still in danger. Enemies might be close. They're running to shelter." Talia struck her leg in frustration. "Goddess! I wish we could do more to help them."

"We can meditate, and ask the Goddess to Heal her and bring her home," Goldberry suggested, bowing her head.

"Yes." Talia took command, as she knew her mother or her Captain would if they were in her position. She looked around the room. They all needed something to keep their minds from descending into despair. Flora was still gripping Elanor. "Nova, Willow, take Flora below, and stay with her. Try to get her to sleep. When Shatter returns, we'll need her knowledge."

Nova nodded, as Willow moved to help Flora down the stairs.

"Helm, Honor: I want you both outside the door. Harpoon, Silidin, find a place to take watch up the mountain. I want a wide net. If we're discovered, I want ample warning."

They nodded, and left.

"Goldberry, lead the others in a meditation of mercy for our Captain." She turned to Elanor: "I want you with me. I will risk contacting Paramount Miranda. She must know of this."

☾ ≈ ☼

Elanor sat down across from Talia. They joined hands, with the Geode between them. First, they Warded themselves. Then, Talia reached out and found the Paramount's Geode. Despite the hour, Miranda was awake. She responded by bringing up her own Wards, then answering.

"*Lady Talia. Something must be very wrong for you to seek me out at this hour.*"

"*Yes, Paramount. I have just contacted a member of my group. She has been attacked by the Blood Cultists. She was cut by a knife of dull black metal. The wound won't Heal, and blocks her Power from working. It has spread throughout her body. We had to destroy the knives to break a connection to the wound and to something else, similar to a Geode Web.*"

"*Share with me everything you and your Lady saw and did,*" Miranda commanded. Talia did so, and Miranda fell silent as she took in the information.

Finally, she spoke. "*There have been rumors for some time of weapons like these. Fairies killed with single blows. Wounds that would not close, and killed their victims. Always in the hands of*

Humans, or Elenite raiders linked to the Human Realm. If they're linked to the Blood Cult and your Aunts, then there's something far larger going on."

"All died?" With effort, Talia suppressed the worry that had begun to fill her.

"Yes. There's some anti-Magic quality in the blades. Healing doesn't work. The victims' wings turn black at the end. We've never destroyed one before the victim died, though. In truth, we've never even had one. I can only say that she might have a chance." Miranda mentally took Talia's hands. *"You might have to take her arm, though."*

"Like a serious infection," Talia replied, grasping for any hope.

"Yes. I will study what you Sent me. Please contact me with any more information you obtain."

"I will. Thank you, Paramount."

"Goddess bless, Lady Talia."

Breaking the connection, Talia looked into Elanor's concerned eyes.

"Will we be able to save her?" her Second asked.

"I don't know. We'll know more when Min and Talon get to shelter."

(∭ ☼

Talon laid Shatter down in the grass. The trees were thin, and provided little cover. Min set up a Ward, and wrapped a Shadow around the perimeter. "I hope that will keep us hidden," she whispered to Talon.

"We need to ger her stabilized, and on her feet. We can't stay here. We're too close to where she fell. The knives will lead them here."

Min got out the crystal. *"Talia,"* she Sent.

"Here."

"We've found shelter. Meager, but shelter."

"How's Shatter?"

"*Still unconscious. The darkness has retreated to just around her wound. But her breathing is shallow, and her heart doesn't beat with the strength it should.*"

"*Miranda could only tell us a little.*" Talia paused, then forged ahead. Min needed to know. "*All the others who have been wounded by these weapons have died.*"

Min looked at Talon, then down at Shatter. Talon read the look, and put her hand on Min's shoulder to join the Web.

"*We won't let that happen,*" she told them both.

"*No, we won't,*" Talia confirmed. "*Min, treat her wound with Goldberry's ointment. It helped before.*"

"*My Lady, we're not secure here. We must hurry,*" Talon urged. Her soldier's nerves were vibrating like harp strings.

"*I understand. Min, what do you See?*"

"*The darkness is retreating to just the wound, but it's not going away.*"

"*Talon, can you Heal her?*"

Talon tried, but her Power couldn't get past the darkness.

"*No. It's a wall to my Power. If there were more of us, we might be able to force through the barrier, but alone, we two cannot.*"

"*Does she seem strong enough to travel?*"

"*Maybe in a few hours, but not now.*"

"*Talon, you must decide. I have faith in you.*"

"*My Lady, we can take turns carrying her, but that will slow us down. Waiting, she might get strong enough to travel, but the enemy could soon be on top of us.*"

Talia paused again. "*If you take her arm, will that help her recovery?*"

Talon took a moment to consider. Min looked at her with shock.

"*Min, you must put your emotions aside,*" Talia ordered. "*We're trying to save her life. We must do what needs to be done.*"

"*Yes, My Lady.*"

"*It will stop the infection from spreading, and allow her body to Heal. The shock is another matter, though,*" Talon said from experience.

"*Once the wound is gone,*" Min finally said, "*I think our Healing will be enough to help her to her feet. We could be ready to move in an hour.*"

"*We'll have to cauterize the wound,*" Talon added.

Min had a sudden thought. "*What if I try to apply Silverfire to the wound? That might overwhelm the darkness.*"

"*I don't know, Min,*" Talia admitted. "*All of this is unknown. Try it, but be prepared to remove the arm if it doesn't work.*"

"*I will,*" Min said.

"*We must break the connection. You must have all your concentration. Goddess grant you strength.*" Talia was gone.

Min looked at Talon, who had already cut away the sleeve of Shatter's shirt, and was tying a length of cord around the top of the Captain's arm, right below the shoulder. The wound was an angry black line.

"Should we wake her?" Min asked.

"Better not. We'd just have to put her under again."

Min took a deep breath. She held her hand over the wound, and called Silverfire. In her Sight, the fire clashed with the black of the wound. Shatter began to mutter, and Talon had to hold her down. The blackness fought back. Smoke rose from the wound. Talon gagged at the smell.

"Stop," she ordered Min.

Min did, and sat back. "I don't have enough Power. Grant me some of yours," she asked, holding out her hand.

"It wouldn't make any difference," Talon told her. "I can See that it will just burn a hole in her arm, and do more damage. We might have to take it anyway. Best to just do it now."

Min reluctantly agreed. "What do you want me to do?"

Talon stretched Shatter's arm out. She tied a cord around the wrist, and then to a small tree. "Hold her shoulders to the ground. Keep her mind quiet. Be ready to seal the wound with Silverfire and begin the Healing."

Talon stood up and drew her sword. She passed her hand over the blade. It began to glow faintly. "Goddess forgive me." She looked down. "And Shatter, too." She looked to Min. "Ready?"

Min nodded. She was in Shatter's mind, keeping her pain turned off, and her mind asleep. Her right hand was shining with Silverfire.

"On three. One," she raised the blade; "Two," took aim; "Three!" She brought the blade down, severing the arm. Talon pushed the appendage out of the way, allowing Min to press her glowing hand over the wound. The Silverfire sealed it. Min poured Healing and calming energy into Shatter's body. Talon carefully wrapped the arm. In her Sight, she could See Min's Healing flow up the stump of Shatter's arm, gathering up bits of darkness left on her body, and snuffing them out with sharp bursts of light. Shatter's wings soon returned to their natural color.

After a few minutes, Min sat back, her face pale. "She's Healing. With the darkness gone, her own Healing is coming back."

Talon sat down beside Shatter and took her hand. "The sun will be up in a few hours. We can give her till then to rest. Then, we must wake her and start home. It might take us a day to get within range of the Ring."

"What about the Ephemeral Ring?" Min asked.

Talon reached for Shatter's pack. "It's not here," she said, after looking inside.

"We need to tell Talia," Min said fearfully, reaching for the crystal. "If the Blood Cult has it. . . ."

"Wait," Talon interrupted, rolling Shatter slightly. "She had it under her clothes." Talon pulled the Ring out and unrolled it. Min passed a hand over it.

"The Weave is gone. The last trip must have destroyed it. We can't use it." She rolled it back up again. "I'll tell Talia." She closed her eyes.

Talon sat back down, and turned her Sight on Shatter. The Captain's body was gaining strength, and her mind was starting to activate. Talon wrapped her in a sense of calming safety, keeping her body still, and began to wake her mind.

"Shatter," Talon called.

The Captain began to awaken. Her instincts fought against the paralysis of her body and the Calming Spell. Her Power tried to strike back.

"*Captain Shatterstaff. You're safe.*"

Her mind settled. "*Talon. You shouldn't have come back. I told you not to come back.*"

"*Talia sent us. You can blame her.*" Talon Projected a sense of Talia, giving orders and keeping their troop strong. A queen under the mountain.

"*Foolish child.*" Shatter almost smiled. She began to take stock of her body. "*Why have you wrapped me in a Calming Spell?*"

"*We — I — had to take drastic action to save you.*"

"*What action?*"

Talon hesitated.

"*What action, soldier?*" Shatter was fighting through the Calming Spell.

"*I had to take your arm.*"

Shatter strained against the spell, her shock and anger ripping at the Weave. Talon tightened the spell. "*Captain. There was nothing we could do. This was the only way to save your life.*"

"*Release my body,*" Shatter commanded. Talon hesitated. "*Keep the Calming Spell, but release my body.*"

Talon did, and Shatter opened her eyes. Her hand tightened in Talon's grip. She turned her head, and looked at where her arm used to be. Talon had to put more Power into the Calming Spell.

"You had no choice," Shatter both asked and stated.

"Yes. The corruption from the blade was killing you."

"You should have woken me."

Min had come out of her conversation with Talia. "You were in bad shape. The wound was blocking your Healing. You wouldn't have been coherent."

"It was still my choice," Shatter argued. She pointed at the wrapped bundle. "Is that it?"

"Yes."

"Unwrap it, and show me."

"Captain," Talon started.

"Now. And remove the spell. I need all my emotions."

"Shatter, please," Min started.

Shatter looked them each in the eye. "You will take the spell from my mind. You will show me the arm," she ordered. "I will not be put off."

Min reached out, and removed the spell. Shatter winced, as her emotions poured in. She had to close her eyes. "Mother," she grimaced.

Talon undraped the arm and laid it at her Captain's side.

Shatter opened her eyes, and looked down. She reached out to touch her former appendage, but pulled back, her hand clenching. Talon offered her wordless support.

"Cover it," Shatter ordered after a moment, and lay back down. She turned her head to the left, away from the stump of her right arm.

Min Reached into her mind and put her to sleep again. Shatter slipped into the much-needed rest without a fight.

Talon wrapped the arm back up, and went to stand at the border of the Ward. She stretched out her senses. There was nothing near.

"What did Talia say?" she asked after a while.

"She's glad Shatter is alive. Sorry we had to do this alone."

"She'll never forgive me."

"Not right away," Min agreed. "But in time, she will. She's a soldier, and she understands that decisions had to be made. Just don't push her."

Talon turned her attention back to watching. "I hope so."

Chapter Two
Over the Grass

The sun was coming up. Min gently woke Shatter. She sat up. "How do you feel?"

"Like I ran for days, and then lost my arm," Shatter replied wryly. "Did I have anything else with me?"

"No," Talon replied. "Only the Ring, and the pack with the knives."

"And what happened to them?" She looked at Min, ignoring Talon.

"We had to destroy them. The enemy was tracking them," Min informed her.

"Seems like you've been making a lot of decisions for me," Shatter accused with some of her Captain's strength. "We needed those blades, to find out what they are."

"They would have led our enemies right to Talia and the others," Talon countered.

Shatter turned an angry gaze on Talon. "I don't remember asking your opinion, soldier."

Talon bowed her head, and turned away. Min helped Shatter to stand.

"We did what we thought was right," Min told her starkly. "You would have done the same."

Shatter could only grunt. She picked up the bundle that held her arm and put it in her pack. She reached down, and tried to remove the knife strapped to her leg. One-handed, she fumbled with the straps.

"Let me," Min offered, moving to help.

Shatter growled, and pushed her away. "Soldier, I need your long knife."

Talon silently removed the knife and its belt. She held them out to Shatter, who took them and held them, not knowing how to arm herself. Min stepped up.

"Allow me, Captain." She took the belt and fastened it around Shatter's waist, positioning the blade on her right hip.

Shatter gestured for the Wards to drop, and started out.

"Time is wasting," she called. "We must get home."

Min looked at Talon, whose face reflected both sadness and betrayal. She gestured for Min to go next. Min took her hand, and together they followed Shatter out of the grove.

☾ ♒ ☼

It was quiet. The grass was covered in dew. A light breeze came from the west. The beautiful morning seemed to make the horrible events of the night and the preceding few days even worse. Shatter looked around, with both her eyes and her Sight.

"I don't sense anything. Maybe they weren't as close as you thought." She started off at a brisk pace. Talon and Min followed.

Several hours later, they stopped to replenish their water at a spring. Shatter had only spoken to Min, and then only to give a few orders. Her left arm kept reaching to where the right should have been, then pulling back. She would walk for a while, then reach back and touch her pack. Min watched this happen several times.

"*Should I talk to her?*" she Sent to Talon.

"*No. Let her be. She'll have to deal with this in her own way. Talia and Flora will help. There's nothing we can do till then.*"

"Soldier!" Shatter commanded. "Get into the air, and make sure we're alone out here."

"Yes, Captain." Talon took to the air.

She circled, then hovered over Shatter and Min. "*Nothing. No one in sight.*"

"*Good. Stay ahead of us,*" Shatter commanded.

"Pick up the pace," she told Min.

"Yes, Captain," Min answered, as she walked more quickly behind Shatter.

They walked all day, pausing only to eat some of the dried meat Min and Talon had brought. Shatter brushed aside any concerns Min had about her walking too much.

"I would fly if I could," she informed her, "but I can't. I must have hurt something. Shieldbreaker will have to look at my wings when we return."

When it began to get dark, they were still outside the range of the Ring. Shatter commanded Talon to look for a suitable campsite. She found some ancient boulders sticking out of the ground, and they made a cold camp. Without speaking, Shatter ate, then rolled herself in Talon's cloak, and went to sleep.

Min passed her own cloak to Talon, saying, "I'll keep watch. Sleep, and I'll wake you at moonrise."

Talon thanked her, and went to the other side of the camp to lie down. Min cast a Ward, then settled into a spot where she could see both of the others. She took out the crystal, and Sent to Talia.

"*We're camped for the night,*" she informed the Heir.

"*Good. How's Shatter?*"

"*Taking it hard, and taking it out on Talon.*" Min shared the events of the day.

"*I'll speak to her when you return.*"

"*It will be difficult. She's not speaking, only giving orders. I want to talk to her, but Talon says no.*"

"*Just be there. She'll have to work through this on her own. Flora seems to think her arm can be regrown, but it will take time.*" Min felt a reflection of Flora's relief and confidence in Talia's mind.

"*Thank the Goddess.*"

"*Yes. Tell her we'll be ready to go when you return.*" Talia turned to other matters. "*A camp has already been made, and a rough framework has been laid out for the shelter.*"

"*Good. I hope that will make her happy.*"

"*Stay safe, and contact me when you get within range. The Ladies have been pouring energy into the Ring to extend it.*"

"*I will. Goddess keep you.*"

"*And you.*" Talia broke the connection.

Min looked at Shatter, who was sleeping fitfully. Her hand clenched, and her eyes darted under their lids. "Goddess keep us all."

Shatter woke Min in the pre-dawn light. "Time to go," she said.

Talon was already up. She handed Min some dried meat and hard bread. "We need to get moving. Something's coming. Both Shatter and I can feel it."

Min took a bite, and reached out to the web of animals she had used to find Shatter. She could feel the disruption of something moving over the grasslands. Min forced the tasteless food down, and stood up. Her cloak had been thrown back over her.

"You feel it, too," Shatter stated, looking at Min's expression.

"Yes, I do. Something is moving over the grass. It's disturbing the animals."

"We have no choice but to move in the most direct route," Shatter announced, looking at the sky. She found the red star. "We'll move as fast as we can in that direction." She pointed. "Min, keep your mind on the Ring. The moment you feel we're in range, call out."

Min nodded, tightening her pack for the run.

"Talon," Shatter ordered, "take point. Min, at my shoulder."

Min raised her eyes at Talon, who nodded back at Shatter's use of her name for the first time.

"Let's go," Shatter commanded, breaking the Ward, and moving out of the shelter of the rocks. Talon moved a few paces ahead, and Shatter and Min followed. They began to run at a steady pace. The ground was soft, and slippery with dew. The air was tense. Min was glad for the weeks of training with The Nine and the months of hard work at the plantation. Before, she would have been unable to run so far and for so long. Now, it was simply a matter of putting one foot in front of the other, and looking out for rocks.

They ran through the morning. A part of Min's mind was always looking for the Ring. She strained to catch the Song. Behind them, a darkness followed. She began to worry, and her legs began to burn.

They stopped for a few swallows of water and food as the sun reached mid-morning. Talon kept looking behind them.

"Are we close?" Shatter asked.

"I've been listening for the Song, but I can't hear it yet," Min informed her.

Shatter's demeanor was both concerned and nervous. "I want to send you up in the air, but I worry you'll be seen."

"My thoughts, too," Talon agreed.

"So, we must run," Shatter decided, standing. "Goddess grant us speed," she beseeched, and they began to run again, across the grass.

(∭ ☼

At mid-day, the sense of pursuit was strong. Min could sense riders behind them, moving fast. Shatter and Talon could feel them, too. They began to look for shelter, or a place to make a stand. But there was nothing, only more grass.

"If we stand, they'll just ride us down," Shatter Sent.

"If they want to capture us," Talon suggested, *"they'll surround us. Make us surrender."*

"We can't," Shatter stated.

Min and Talon agreed.

They ran on.

Talon suddenly waved at them. Another group of rocks had appeared out of the ground. Shatter waved them in that direction. Min reached out and tried to find the Ring, but it was still too far away. The rocks loomed up ahead. Talon was already on top of them, and waved them on. Straining, Shatter was able to lift herself on her damaged wings just enough to reach the top. Min landed beside her. The rock was weather-worn and pitted.

"We have the high ground," Shatter commented, dropping flat. "But they'll surround us."

The rock was about ten feet in height. The sides were steep, except one: that one sloped up only slightly, and would not be difficult to climb.

Talon got out her bow and strung it. Min had only her sword and knife. Shatter had only Talon's long knife.

"See if you can grab some loose stones," Shatter instructed Min. "I can still throw."

Min reached out with her Power and began to pluck stones from the ground and float them up to Shatter, who gathered them into a pile. Talon propped her quiver at her side, and laid down.

"They'll surround us," Shatter told Min. "And then, if they have bows, they'll use them to keep our heads down, while some try to climb up there." She gestured to the sloped side of the rock. "She can't shoot through your Shield, so you'll have to work with Talon to drop it for each shot, and raise it again afterward."

Min took a deep breath. "You trained us for this," she muttered to calm herself.

"They're coming," Talon announced suddenly. A group of five riders crested a rise in front of them. The leader spotted the rocks, and gestured at them. The party rode on, and stopped right outside bow range.

"We caught you," the leader yelled. He was an Elenite in dirty clothes. He drew his sword. The others were also Elenites, in the same sort of garb. None had bows, but two had sets of short spears on their saddles. "You thought you could run, but we caught you!"

"Come and take us, then," Shatter taunted. "Ready, Talon," she whispered. "Min, try to strike them off their mounts." Min nodded, and prepared.

"We will," the leader promised, as he spurred his mount at them. The two spearthrowers pulled their weapons and followed. The other two moved around to flank the Fairies.

Talon waited two breaths, and then released. The arrow sped, on target, but was deflected by a Shield thrown up by the leader.

"Ha!" he cried, but he was then hit in the face by a rock that had been thrown by Shatter. He hung on, and stayed in the saddle, but lost his sword. Min hit the spearman on the left with all her strength, and flung him to the ground. Talon notched another arrow, and hit the second spearman. He fell.

The leader cursed, and got his mount turned around, back to where his sword was stuck in the ground. The two others were moving around the rocks. Talon took aim.

Suddenly, arrows sprouted from all the Elenites still on choraback. There was surprise all around as they fell. At least ten mixed Leather- and Feather-wing soldiers landed all around the bodies. They notched more arrows, but didn't aim them at Shatter, Talon, and Min. The leader of the soldiers, a Feather-wing, turned over the leader of the attackers. He waved his hand in front of his face at the smell.

Shatter stood slowly. "I know you," she called at the Feather-wing. "I sold you my chora."

"Yes, you did," he replied. He gestured for the rest of his troops to check the other attackers.

"All dead," a Leather-wing woman called out. She and another soldier began dragging the bodies together. A third caught the attackers' chora.

"It seems I was right that there was more to you than you said. Where are the rest of your Sisters?" the Feather-wing leader asked.

"Escaped. I led these vermin off so my Sisters could get to safety." Shatter's wings flared.

The Feather-wing moved closer. Talon took a loose aim at him. He stopped, and raised his hands. "We found the others that you killed. And then followed these that came along after. Dirty Elenites. I figured they were hunting someone, so I followed to be of service."

"And we thank you for that service," Shatter offered earnestly.

"Looks like you had some tough times. I remember you having two arms before."

"I did. Are there any black blades on them?"

The leader looked to his Second, who was stripping the bodies. She gestured to the ground. "Foul smelling thing."

"Be careful," Shatter warned him. "The wound won't close, and resists Healing."

"I will." He cocked his head. "So, what now? You look tired. We can escort you to your Sisters. I don't think there are any more of these pests in the area."

Shatter glanced at Min and Talon. "We're honored, and we thank you for helping us, but we're close to our home. We can get there on our own from here."

The Feather-wing stared up at them for a long moment. "I don't remember an Iridescent with you before."

Shatter only looked back at him. Her wings flared again.

"No matter," he said. "You want your privacy. You can have it. I've removed a stain from these grasslands. I'll take news of these raiders back to the Law Masters and the Queen's Governor. They'll want to see this deadly weapon." The soldiers had stripped the bodies, and were digging a pit for them. "Will you at least eat with us before you go?"

"It's the least we can do," Min said, but Shatter shook her head.

"We must be on our way," Shatter told him. "We thank you again for your aid, and ask the Goddess to bless and protect you and your soldiers."

The Feather-wing gestured back, and a soldier handed him a pack. He looked inside, then held it up for all to see. "Water and rations. I figure you're low." Shatter nodded, and Min floated it out of his hands and up to them. Talon took it and looked inside, nodding.

"Thank you again," Shatter said earnestly. Her wings stilled.

The Second brought something over to the leader. She handed him a medallion on a chain. He looked at it.

"Any idea why they would carry the mark of the Human Realm?"

"No idea," Shatter told him honestly.

"More mysteries." He put the medallion in his pocket. "Well, we'll be here for a bit to dispose of these foul things."

"We'll take our leave, then," Shatter announced. She moved to the edge of the rock, and floated down. Min and Talon followed.

"Goddess guide you," the lead soldier said.

"Goddess protect you," Shatter replied. Together, she, Min, and Talon moved off, leaving the soldiers to bury the Elenite enemy. The Feather-wing leader watched them till they disappeared over a rise in the grass.

Chapter Three
To the Sea

Talon was the last one through the Ring. Gil-Galin's hug almost knocked her down.

"We were so worried," she muttered into her soldier's chest.

"So was I," Talon replied, patting her Lady's back. "So was I." Talon let Gil hold her for a little longer as she looked around the library. The tables and chairs had been moved aside, and the crates were stacked, ready to be moved. Min was still engulfed in a circle of Raven, Elanor, and Goldberry.

Shatter, who had been first through — after Min had refused to go before her — was surrounded by Talia, Flora, and Steel. Flora clung to her left side. Shatter looked extremely uncomfortable, and looked to Steel for help in freeing herself. But Steel only smiled, and hugged her Captain.

Talia finally moved to Flora, and pried her away from Shatter. "Please, Mum — she needs her space just now. You and Shield can look at her wound in a moment."

Flora pulled away, wiping her eyes. She hit Shatter on the arm. "Foolish," she muttered, and moved to a seat Nova had set up for her.

"Steel," Talia requested, "please take the others below, and help with the food. Shatter, Min, and Talon must be starving." Steel nodded, gripped Shatter's hand, and showed everyone out. Elanor looked back at Talia, who motioned for her to go with the others. Soon, Talia and Shatter were alone. Shatter sat down on a crate.

"Good to have you back," Talia said, sitting down beside her. "I was worried."

"I was almost dead," Shatter replied. "And would have been, if you hadn't defied my orders, and sent Talon and Min after me." She looked Talia in the eye. "Thank you." She gripped Talia's arm.

"And you were saved by some soldiers from the town?"

"Yes. They killed the Elenites who were following us." She gripped Talia's arm more tightly. "They had the mark of the Human Realm."

Talia went cold. Her free hand went to her belly. "So, he hunts me. How did he know?"

"We mustn't jump to conclusions, but these raiders were linked to the Humans in some way." Shatter remembered her conversation with the Blood Cult Fairy.

"Best to leave here soon, then."

"Yes. You told Min that a camp was ready."

"We've moved supplies to the ruins, and Raven found a place up the coast for us," Talia informed her, with pride in her people.

"More good news. I wish to see it, as soon as we eat."

"No: you will eat, and then sleep. We'll go check out the camp tomorrow."

Shatter started to protest, but Talia held up her hand. "I'll put you to sleep if I have to."

Shatter relented. "I might be able to fight it off at full strength, but not now."

"Good. Let's go eat."

$$\left(\!\!\begin{array}{c} \approx \\ \approx \end{array} \diamond\right.$$

It was a feast of relief, and joy that all their little family was back together. Talia kept Shatter by her side, and shooed away anyone who lingered too long. Shatter's hand would start to flex, and Talia would send the visitor away, to help somewhere, or to tend to an errand. After the third time, Shatter noticed, and gave Talia a thankful nod as she sent Raven away to prepare for the next day's move. The only one who wouldn't move from her side was Flora. She sat on Shatter's right, and despite both Shatter's and Talia's urging, would not move. She had stopped poking at the wound, but still sat with her hand on Shatter's leg, unwilling to let her go.

"Mum, don't you think you should check on Elanor?" Talia would say.

"No, Mistress, she has it in hand," Flora would reply.

After two such suggestions, Flora leaned over, and looked directly at Talia. "Mistress, I will sit by her side until I decide to move. You cannot make up a reason for me to go."

29

"Yes, Mum," Talia relented. She then gestured to Nova, and asked her to send Steel and Elanor over.

Once the Lieutenant and Talia's Second joined them, Talia addressed the group. "I want to talk with all of you about what happened to Shatter, and what might be coming."

"That second group was Elenite," Shatter informed them. "They were driven. They would have given no quarter had they captured us. By the look of them, they had ridden hard ever since I escaped the first group."

"Something drove them?" Elanor asked.

"I would assume it was the black blade. I wish I could have taken one from our rescuers, but that would have involved a longer conversation, and I don't know if I would have prevailed." She shrugged. "If they act like our Geodes, then there may be more raiders coming in search of us yet."

"But with the soldiers from the town awakened to the danger," Steel put in, "it will be much harder for them to move around."

"There were two Fairies in the first group. The leader and, I would assume, his Second. They could move more easily," Shatter countered. "And they might have aid or sympathy in the town." Shatter paused, reflecting. "The Fairy I killed claimed he wanted to take back power the Queen had stolen."

"This is disturbing," Talia commented. "We've been moving the supplies to the ruins, and now that you're safe, we can fully commit to leaving," Talia added. "But I want to balance safety with speed. I will allow only Elanor and Shatter to take someone through the ruins Ring. It was locked with a powerful Ward. My mother allowed me access. I need to keep the circle small."

"What if we need it in an emergency?" Shatter asked.

"That's the problem. I don't want to remove the lock, but the fewer who know its Frequency, the better." The debate was clear on Talia's face.

"Don't you trust the others?" Elanor asked. "I believe we're all worthy of trust."

Shatter answered for Talia. "The question isn't trust. I trust all of you with my life. The problem is that if someone is captured, they could be made to reveal the location, and take an enemy through."

"We would sooner die," Elanor stated.

Talia took her hand. "I'm not doubting that, but many pressure points can be leveraged. We don't know the full abilities of the Blood Cultists. They might be able to open our minds as simply as we open a bag. Or they could just threaten another."

"'We cannot reveal what we do not know,'" Steel quoted Halfwing. "I do worry about escaping in an emergency, though."

"We have another Ephemeral Ring ready," Talia noted. "And Goldberry will work on getting the first working again. We also have the Ring that Raven and Spearhead found. It's under a broken tower, though, so access to that one is difficult, and it's also very weak. We wouldn't be able to use it with Torcs from the ruins."

"I understand your reluctance, but we need to have an escape route if the new camp gets attacked," Shatter advised Talia. "I would feel better if all of us had access."

"Couldn't we leave an Ephemeral Ring near the ruins Ring and use that?" Elanor asked.

"The ruins Ring is. . . ." Talia searched her mind for a fitting word. "Fickle. It almost has a mind of its own. It might be one of the first Rings. Besides, the two Rings would interfere with each other." She stopped and thought. "I will consider. I understand why we all need access, but I also know why I need to limit it."

"You both protect us and put us in danger with either option, Mistress," Flora confirmed. "Let the wisdom of the Goddess guide you."

"Regardless of what you decide," Shatter added, "this Ring will have to be locked in a similar manner."

"Indeed," Talia agreed.

"What happens if you try to use the Ring, and it's locked against you?" Steel asked. "Fatal?"

"Very fatal," Talia confirmed. "You never return to either place. You become lost in the void between."

"A last option, then," Shatter commented in a low voice. Steel took her meaning, and smiled grimly. It took Elanor a moment, but then she recoiled in shock.

"Yes, it would be," Talia said, in an equally low voice. She then steered the conversation into all the details of moving their troop to the new camp. "It won't be as nice as here. We'll have to struggle to get a shelter up. One good thing: Harpoon says the weather will be mild, with little chance of rain."

"Thank the Goddess for that," Elanor said.

"Yes, and we'll have to build a place to live." Talia looked at each of them. "Captain Shatter, can you use the knowledge you gained with the reconstruction of Riverbend to build a house for my child to be born in? I would have her born within sight of the sea."

Shatter looked at her, the reality of the situation suddenly hitting her. "It would be my honor, My Lady. I will go there with the dawn, and see what I have to work with."

☾ ∭ ☼

After a little further conversation, Steel and Elanor left to prepare for the following day. Flora finally drifted off, and Shieldbreaker brought her a blanket. "Please sit with her," Talia asked. "I don't want her to wake up alone." Shield nodded.

"I would look at your arm," she told Shatter.

"Tomorrow," Shatter told her, getting up. "First, I must sleep."

"First," Talia countered, "I would speak with you in the library." She held out her hand, and Shatter had to adjust herself, after first trying to use her missing right arm to grab Talia's hand. Talia took Shatter's left arm, then touched her own Torc, and took them to the library Ring.

"That wasn't necessary," Shatter chastised her. "We could've flown."

"I wanted you to rest. And I need to give you access to the ruins Ring." Talia put both hands on Shatter's shoulders. "Join with me," she requested.

Shatter did. Talia Showed her the Frequency of the Ring, and Showed her how to unlock it. The simplicity of the Weave awed Shatter.

"That's all?" she asked, opening her eyes.

"Yes, that's all," Talia said with a smile. "You can now go through safely, and take others with you."

"And I can smash the lock," Shatter added, "if I need to."

"That would mean your death, and the death of anyone with you," Talia reminded her, knowing that she knew the consequences.

"I understand."

Talia didn't let go. "I want you to know that when I sent Talon and Min, I told them to do whatever they could to save you. Any action they took was with my consent. Any anger you feel should be directed at me."

Shatter dropped her head. "I'm ashamed of how I treated Talon. She only did what had to be done. I understand that here," she tapped her forehead, "but not here." She tapped her chest. "It will take time, but I'll get used to it."

"Flora and Shield say they can regrow the arm. It'll just take time. I don't want you to think you'll be like your father. You will not be known as 'Shatterstaff One-Arm,'" Talia said, half joking.

"That's not what I meant," Shatter assured her. "I'll regrow the arm. It's a long process, though. I've seen others go through it. Sometimes the limb isn't the same. Sometimes, it would have been better to not even try. That's why my father didn't Heal his wing. I have faith in Flora and Shield to do a good job. But the body is a fickle thing."

"We're all here to help, if they need it," Talia promised. "And we're here if you need anything else as well."

"I know, My Lady, and I appreciate that you spoke to me in private. I must be strong for the others."

"Of course, Captain." Talia let go. "I'm staying here. I have more reading to do. I only got through one of the Exile Queen's chests. There's still much more to review. There are so many mysteries to solve."

"I could stay with you. I don't have a scholar's mind, but I can listen."

"I'd like that." She led Shatter over to her worktable. Two bedrolls lay on the floor beside it.

Shatter raised an eyebrow. "You sleep up here?"

"Most of the time. I read late, and wake early. I feel like there's something I'm looking for, but I can't find it."

"Alone," Shatter stressed, looking at the other bedroll.

"Sometimes Goldberry, or Min, or Elanor, stays with me. Sometimes others. Sometimes Steel. Anyone is welcome," Talia said offhandedly.

"Elanor." Shatter stressed the name.

Talia understood. "We've come to an understanding. Our love must be simple for now. We can't let our passion overpower us. It took her a while, but she understands and accepts that now." Talia sat down, and motioned Shatter to do the same. "She'll always be with me. Maybe one day we can go before the Goddess and pledge to one another. Maybe not. As the Heir, I must be more than a woman. But she'll always be at my side, however the Goddess wishes us to be."

"Good. I was afraid her resentment would drive a wedge between you. I'm glad it hasn't."

"I am, too." Talia shifted to her research. "Now, I was reading about the Exile Queen's grandmother. She was a great Paramount."

$$\text{☾ ♒ ☼}$$

In the morning, Talia gathered everyone in the library.

"I've reached a decision. I will show you all the Frequency for the ruins Ring. This is the lesser of the two dangers. You'll be able to use the Ring. The information will be in your mind. I'll Show all of you how to Ward that information, so that it cannot be accessed by anyone invading your mind. You'll be able to unlock the Ring and, if necessary, you can 'destroy the lock,' as Shatter put it, if you're forced to take an enemy through." Talia stopped. She lowered her eyes.

Shatter stepped in. "By doing this, you will be killed. You'll disappear into the nothingness between the Rings. You'll take anyone traveling with you there as well. This is an option of last resort." She looked around. "I know my soldiers understand that sacrifice."

"We understand that sacrifice, too," Elanor stated. "As your Ladies, we've taken an Oath."

"I do not take this action lightly. I will make sure each of you has strong Wards set in your mind to prevent anyone from taking the frequency from you," Talia promised.

The Ladies looked at each other in confirmation of their understanding of the seriousness of the situation.

"We understand," Nova said. "We know the danger, and the necessity of that kind of sacrifice."

Talia sighed. "Thank you. It seems I keep asking more of all of you."

"Never more than we're willing to give," Steel assured her.

"Now," Talia continued after a moment, "I will take Shatter, Raven, Min, Silidin, Nidilis, Helm, and Harpoon to the new camp. They'll be staying there to set things up. Everyone but Shatter will be starting on construction. It will be tents for us again, until we can get shelter built."

"There's good timber close," Raven advised everyone. "It will be an easy trek, and the Twins are strong with telekinesis, so we can get the logs to the site quickly."

"The rest of you will stay here, and work on getting everything ready to leave." Talia turned to Elanor. "Can you repair the Ephemeral Ring?"

"I think so. Goldberry and I plan to look at it this morning. We'll have a time estimate for you when you return."

"Good. I hope you can repair it quickly. I'll be taking the second Ephemeral Ring so it can be used at the new camp," Talia replied. "For security, we'll still go through the ruins Ring, and then the camp Ephemeral Ring."

"We reinforced the Weave on the second rug," Min reported. "It will take more transits than the first one did."

"Again, good work," Talia praised them. "We have much to do. Those going, do you have everything you need?"

"Yes," Raven confirmed. "Tents and supplies have been packed."

"Then let's go," Talia said, standing.

Flora cleared her throat.

Talia took the meaning. "After quick," she stressed, "goodbyes. We'll all be joining them soon. Shatter will go through first. Then I'll be back for each of you."

Talia moved to the Ring, as the others got up and embraced those leaving. Shatter joined her, and they went through the Ring. The room on the other side was already filled with crates and chests. The history chests had already been moved there. Talia showed Shatter how to open the door. They went through, and up a sloping corridor, till they came to another door.

"This one is covered with an Illusion on the other side," Talia told her. "It's simple to see through when you know the key." Talia Showed her.

"You're filling my mind to the edge with Magic." Shatter wryly tapped her head. "If I had known this would be my destiny, I would have paid more attention during my time at the Tower of Learning."

"You've taken it all in with grace and the ability of someone who grew up there."

"I just have a disciplined mind," Shatter told her. She unconsciously touched the empty sleeve of her mail, which she had let hang from her shoulder. She realized what she was doing, and rested her hand on the hilt of her sword.

Talia opened the door, and the two of them walked out into the morning sea air. Talia took a deep breath, and stepped onto the sand. The tide was out, and the waves broke gently, further out on the beach. Talia took a few more steps, and spread her wings to the sea air. "This is where I belong," she confessed to Shatter. "I feel I've truly come home."

Talia turned, and saw that Shatter was down on one knee. Her hand was thrust into the sand. She pulled it out, and let the sand run out through her fingers. She did it again. Her face held a look that Talia had seen only a few times.

"You're happy, Shatter," Talia gasped, going to one knee before her. "I've only rarely seen that look."

"This is the first time I've seen the sea," Shatter admitted, letting the sand run through her hand again. "I heard stories — the First Fairies, their feet in the sand. I'm just a simple soldier. I never thought

I'd be here." She looked at Talia. "I always wanted to look on this beach. Thank you."

"It's my pleasure. And you're much more than a simple soldier." Talia took Shatter's hand. "Stay here. I'll bring the others in." She stood up, and left Shatter on the beach, looking out at the sea.

$$\left(\!\!\!\begin{array}{c}\approx\\\approx\end{array}\!\!\!\right)\;\text{☼}$$

Talia brought the others through, one at a time. She taught them the Ring's Frequency and the lock. They joined Shatter on the beach. By the time she brought Helm through, Shatter had re-checked their gear, and gotten them into good order for the trip up the coast.

"It took us about half a day flying," Raven was telling Shatter. "Walking might take longer."

"My wings are healing enough to keep up with you," Shatter retorted.

"I would prefer to make the walk," Talia said from behind. "We need to get a feel for the whole area."

"As you wish, My Lady," Shatter replied, smiling. "Now, let's go. Hopefully, we can make it by dark."

They set off, with Raven on point, and Helm as rearguard. Raven led them up the beach. The walking was easier behind the dunes. The sound of the waves and the birds pulled a blanket of calm over Talia. Behind them, the ruins disappeared. The Twins began to sing softly, merging the rhythm of the waves with their steps. Soon, they were all singing, and moving quickly.

At mid-day, they stopped on the banks of a small stream that came down from the hills. "There's another freshwater stream at the camp site," Raven informed them as she drank, then poured water over her head. The weather was milder than they had become used to in the Exile Queen's mountain.

Nidilis moved to take off her ringmail. Shatter stopped her.

"You must get used to its weight. Use your Power to regulate your body heat," Shatter advised her.

"Is that how you do it?" Silidin asked.

"How you keep from sweating?" Nidilis clarified.

37

"That, and training," Helm told them.

"You should take off your outer layer," Harpoon suggested. "That'll allow air to circulate."

The Twins agreed. Min and Talia simply opened the necks of their shirts.

"We should get moving," Shatter hinted, standing. She took a deep breath of the sea air. "This air is giving me energy." The others nodded, and rose. "Let's pick up the pace."

"Sing the Chora Racing Song," Helm urged.

The Twins started with bright smiles. "Run, Lizzie, run. Run, Lizzie, run. Carver's gonna beat you to the bright shining Moon!" Helm and Harpoon joined in loudly.

They set off, running up the beach. The Twins set the tempo, and they sang the miles away.

☾ ∿ ☼

The sun was setting when they arrived at the camp site. They crossed a small freshwater stream that came down from the low cliffs in a thin waterfall. The sand went up to the base of the cliffs.

"The water comes up to the rocks at high tide." Raven pointed to the top of the cliffs. "The view from the top is spectacular."

"And a good view of the surrounding area," Shatter commented.

"There's a narrow path up the cliff," Raven pointed back, "before the waterfall. The cliff front itself is sheer, and hard to climb."

"No problem for our wings, though," Talia added.

"Winds come up from the water, so flying can be tricky," Raven cautioned.

"Looks like a good place from here," Talia told her. "The cliffs continue further on?"

"Yes, and the beach disappears. This is the last place someone can land from the water," Raven observed. The Twins wandered closer, gazing up at the cliffs with wonder. Helm and Harpoon followed behind them.

Talia took Shatter's arm. "I think we can make this a home."

"Yes, My Lady," Shatter agreed. "We'll have to look at the ground to be sure, but it looks good from here."

"So, let's get up there." Talia turned to Raven. "Lead us up: you've been here before, and know the currents. Shatter — do you feel up to it?"

"Of course," Shatter responded, flexing her wings. "Lead the way."

Raven unfurled her wings, and fanned them. "Follow me. I don't know what it might be like. Be ready for anything." She took to the air, with Shatter close behind. Talia followed, with Min and the Twins trailing her. Helm and Harpoon came up last. The winds from the water were light, and they made it to the top without difficulty.

Talia went to her knees, and thrust her hands into the short grass. Shatter began to pace around. She saw the stakes Raven and Spearhead had laid out.

"A little close to the edge," Shatter commented.

"I'd like to be that close," Talia informed her, still sniffing the ground.

"We don't know what storms could come. It would be risky being so close to the edge. Also, enemies could undermine the cliff," Shatter advised her.

"I see," Talia said, standing. "I will trust your judgment. As long as you build me a seat so I can watch the sea." She pointed to a single oak tree at the edge of the cliff. It was far from its sisters, but clung with solid determination to the edge. Strong roots rayed out from the base — both inland and down the cliff face — holding it in place despite the wind and rain. "I will watch the sea under the shade of that tree."

Shatter smiled. "As you wish, My Lady."

"Harpoon," Talia asked, "what do you think of the possibility of storms?"

"I can't see that far into the future, but the currents are pretty calm right now. Nothing is certain," she stressed.

"Good. You've picked a good place." Talia turned to them all. "This is where I will have my child. I can feel all the paths leading here."

She turned back to the sea, and raised both her arms and her wings as the waves crashed, and the sun set.

☾ ≈ ☼

Shatter urged them to set up the tents and settle down for a meal. Min set up a Shield and Shadow Ward over the campsite, while Helm heated up a thin stew, and Shatter, Harpoon, and Raven drew and debated designs for the house.

"It would be easiest to use the trees, and build a log longhouse with a few separate rooms and a large central area," Shatter proposed.

"I'll need a nursery," Talia reminded her, as she sat down beside them. "Also, we need some rooms for privacy. We've had so little in the last few months."

"As soldiers, we're used to that," Raven said.

"As Ladies of the court, we're not," Min informed her sternly.

"We'll do the best we can," Shatter assured her. "But we must focus on shelter first, then go for comfort."

"Will you have enough Fairies to raise this house?" Talia asked.

Raven looked at Harpoon. "We can fell the trees and prep them in a day. Setting the walls and the roof will take longer."

"I'd feel better if we could start moving everything tomorrow. We can use tents and the Shield for shelter for now," Shatter told Talia. "We can Ring back to the ruins and start moving in the morning."

"There should be enough space in the Ring room to store what we won't need right away," Talia agreed. "And there might be some other rooms there that we can use as well."

"Very good. We can return in the morning, and lock down the Exile Queen's mountain. The sooner we're out of that area, the better."

"Do you expect our enemies to find us?" Silidin asked nervously.

Shatter looked at each of them. The worry on their faces and in their body language was plain. "I think it's foolish to think those two groups were the only ones the Three Sisters have sent. The sooner we're away, the better."

"I agree," Talia added. "We must ensure the Spells and Wards there are strong enough to hide the entrances. We'll store everything we can in the ruins, leaving only what we must at the Exile Queen's mountain." She became thoughtful. "We may need a place to flee to one day." She touched the ground. "Then we can bring the rest of our company here."

"Then we should get some sleep," Shatter told them. The Twins were already yawning. "We have much to do tomorrow."

Chapter Four
A New Place of Safety

The day dawned bright. Shatter and Talia shared a quick breakfast with those who would be staying. Raven had already decided where to start harvesting trees for the walls. She unwrapped the axes she had brought from the Exile Queen's armory. The leather grips had decayed, but the silksteel shafts and blades were still strong.

"I wish we had something like a saw," Raven commented.

"I guess that wasn't something the Exile Queen needed for her troops," Talia said around a mouthful of food. "Maybe we should take a trip down the coast to the fishing village. . . ." She looked to Raven for the name.

"Realm's End," Raven filled in. "A grand name, for a small place."

"They ship out fish that goes to all corners of the Realm," Harpoon informed the others. "I remember the town seal. Much of their catch makes its way to the palace."

"Why don't they have a Ring, if they sell so many fish?" Talia asked.

"I sensed that that was a question that shouldn't be asked," Raven said. "I got the distinct impression that they feel Iridescents aren't to be trusted."

"Well, we'll have to be careful then," Talia said, "but we'll need tools and other supplies we can't make."

"I think we can use the same cover story I did before," Shatter told her. "A group of soldiers settling down to make a better life away from war isn't suspicious."

"But how did we get here?" Helm asked. At a look from the Twins, she noted, "They'll wonder."

"Exactly. We'll have to work on a good story," Talia said. "Shatter, you devised the first one, any ideas for this one?"

"I'll think on it, but there have to be other towns close by. They might have Rings. We'll need more information to form a believable backstory.

"Until then, we'll have to make do with what we have," Shatter decided. "The Twins are good with their Power, and I'm sure they can figure out a way to do what a saw does."

"We'll do our best," Nidilis swore.

"Together, we'll find a way around or through." Silidin smiled at Talia.

Talia smiled back, then got up. "Just so. Now, Shatter and I will return to the mountain." She gestured to the Ephemeral Ring on the ground. "Make sure you maintain a Ward and Shadow over that."

"We can move it into a tent, and then Ward the whole area," Min suggested.

"Good. We can't make any mistakes with Rings," Talia stressed. "We know their Power can be traced. Always go through a locked Ring."

"Yes, My Lady," they all replied.

Talia smiled. "There's much work to do, but I have faith that we'll be able to make a place of safety here." Talia made the Sign of the Three. The others returned it. "Min, you have a piece of the Geode." Min nodded. "Contact me if there are any problems, or if you have any questions."

"We intend to begin moving supplies through from the mountain later in the day," Shatter informed Min. "We'll contact you when we're ready."

Everyone stood, as Shatter and Talia stepped into the Ring. "Goddess guide you," Min appealed, as Talia and Shatter disappeared from the campsite, and reappeared in the ruins Ring.

"Mistress!" Flora exclaimed. She turned from a chest, where Shieldbreaker stood by her side. "You scared me."

"Sorry, Flora," Talia apologized, stepping out of the Ring. Behind her, Shatter moved to fold her arms, but settled on tucking her hand into her belt. "What are you doing?"

"Someone packed my second herb satchel. I was trying to find it." She looked at Shield.

"It wasn't me," she protested.

"Whoever it was, we'll need it for Shatter's procedure," Flora said, looking over Talia's shoulder at Shatter.

"We have time," Shatter said. "We'll be busy. It can be delayed until we have better shelter."

"The sooner it starts, the sooner the arm will be finished," Flora told her imperiously. "And the sooner I start, the better the chance of everything going well."

Talia stepped in as Shatter tried to speak. Turning to her Captain, she said, "I think it's important for you to be whole again."

Shatter narrowed her eyes, but didn't protest. "I just didn't want to get in the way."

"No," Flora said, crossing to her, and taking her arm. "Never. We'll put you back as you were."

"Then tonight," Talia said.

"No. It must be done at sunrise," Shield stated. "The rising of the sun will add to the potency of the Healing Power."

"Good," Talia agreed. "We can also remove my Child Ward." She joined Flora, and put her hand on Shatter's right shoulder. "They can grow together."

Shatter took a deep breath. Faced with the two Fairies she was most committed to — even above her wife and husband during this journey — she could only say, "Yes, My Lady. Yes, Mum. In the morning."

"Good," Flora said happily. "Now, help me find my satchel." She pulled Shatter off the Ring, and moved to another crate.

Talia stayed in the Ring. "I must check on Elanor and Goldberry. Do you want me to start sending the others through with supplies?"

"No," Shatter replied. "Just make sure everyone has their personal kit and tent together. Most of the supplies are gathered in the library. I'll have to return, and see how much space they'll take up here."

"Nova thinks there might be another basement or chamber nearby," Shield put in.

"I'll ask her," Talia promised, raising her arm, and traveling to the Exile Queen's mountain.

She arrived in the library Ring to find everyone — except Honor — in a Circle around the first Ephemeral Ring.

Honor turned as Talia appeared.

Speaking softly, Talia inquired, "Are they rebuilding the Weave?"

"Yes," Honor replied. "Elanor and Goldberry remade the Weave yesterday, and now the Circle's getting ready to Power it."

Talia thought about stepping in and adding herself to the Circle, but reconsidered. She didn't want to throw the balance off. She opened her Sight and Watched instead.

The lines of force making up the Ring's Weave swirled in the same pattern as before. Talia Watched as Steel led the others in adding Power to the lines, then snapped the Weave into place. The flash wasn't as bright as last time, and all the Fairies kept their seats. Steel and Elanor looked up and smiled at each other, as the Weave of the Ring settled into place, and its Song returned.

"Bravo, Ladies and soldiers," Talia called out. Everyone jumped, and stood up quickly. Elanor ran over, and embraced Talia.

"You're back!" She kissed Talia on the cheek. Elanor began to tighten her grip, but Talia moved to prevent it.

"I am, and that was good work." She gestured to Goldberry and Steel, but also freed herself from Elanor's arm. *"We'll speak later,"* she Sent to Elanor.

Elanor squeezed her arm in understanding, and stepped back.

"Thank you, My Lady," Goldberry said. "We wanted to get the Weave back as soon as possible."

"It was a lot easier this time." Steel approached Talia, her hands tucked confidently in her belt. There was a tiredness in her eyes, though. Her new roles — and Shatter's absence — were beginning to take a toll.

"Practice," Talia said, as Goldberry hugged her, too.

Everyone gathered around the Heir. "We've set up the camp, and Raven and the others are working on the first steps of building our shelter. We all need to be ready to move. Everyone, gather your personal gear and tents here, and be ready to go." Talia turned to Steel. "Is everything from below packed up?"

"Yes, My Lady," she replied. "All the weapons and the cloth goods are packed, and most have been moved here, or to the ruins Ring. The rest are below, and we're about to start moving them up. We just needed the Ephemeral Ring."

"I don't think we should tax the rebuilt Weave," Elanor put in. "We can float the crates and chests up. One Fairy at the bottom and another at the top should be sufficient."

"Good," Talia said. She reached out, and took Nova's hand. "You sensed some other rooms around the ruins?"

"Yes, My Lady. I was only on the surface for a short time, but I think there are other closed rooms."

"Then let's go find them." Talia gestured to Honor. "Arm yourself and Nova, and we'll go exploring."

"Yes, My Lady." Honor went quickly to the neat piles of gear, and brought back her sword and Nova's.

"And my bow," Talia requested of Steel. She nodded, and soon brought back Talia's bow and quiver.

"Do you want anyone else to come with you?" Steel asked, handing the weapons to Talia.

"No, just the three of us will be enough. The rest of you should get everything ready. Goldberry, are the Illusions ready for the entrance?"

"Yes. I've mapped out the anchor points. Since we've been living here, the mountain has become more cooperative with our Magic."

"I noticed that, too." Talia smiled. "Good work. I'm immensely proud of all of you. There will be more work in the coming days. Hard work. But I know we can handle it. Goddess guide you all."

"Goddess guide you," the others replied. Talia, Nova, and Honor stepped into the Ring, and disappeared.

$$(\; \text{〰} \; ☼$$

Flora was still looking for her lost satchel of herbs when the three appeared.

"Are you sure it's not with your baggage?" Shatter was asking, for what sounded like the fourth or fifth time. Shield hid a grin as she opened another chest.

"I'm sure I looked," Flora said, scratching her head. Her wings flittered.

Shatter saw Talia and gave her a 'rescue me' look.

"I'm taking Nova and Honor to look for another storage space," Talia told the others as she opened the door. She closed it on Shatter's look of betrayal.

"We'll have to go through them all again," Flora was saying.

Outside, the sun was shining, and the sea air was fresh. Talia took a deep breath, and turned around. The only remaining wall ran to the left. Talia could see the place where she and her mother had stood so many years before. To the right, the wall collapsed into the trees and underbrush. Nova pointed in that direction.

"I sense something that way."

"Lead the way," Talia gestured, then fell in behind her. Honor brought up the rear, with her bow out, and an arrow on the string.

They walked for a few minutes. The sound of the sea diminished as they moved through the trees. Birds began to sing lightly. Nova pointed to a large tree ahead of them. As they got closer, they could see that the tree was on top of a ruined building. The sandy soil had collapsed in front, revealing a dark opening.

"Here, My Lady," Nova said, moving carefully down the slight slope.

"Careful," Talia cautioned, following. Honor shook her head, and trailed after.

They stepped across the threshold, into the darkness. Nova conjured a Fairy Light above her. A low growl stopped them in their tracks. Two sets of eyes looked back at them, shining in the light.

"Back!" Honor shouted, shouldering forward, and raising her bow.

"No," Talia said, raising her hand to block Honor. "Nova, raise the Light."

The Light climbed to the ceiling. Two large cats — each about five hands at the shoulder — appeared out of the dark. Their tails whipped and darted behind them. They hissed again, showing teeth. The sound of claws raking on stone filled the small room. The one on the left was black, except for small spots of white around its neck and feet. The other was grey and cream, in odd splotches.

"Sea cats," Honor breathed reverently. "See the tails — they can grab, and hold on. I've seen them hang from rocks to catch fish. Careful: they might be small, but they have sharp teeth and claws."

"Nova," Talia whispered, "move the Light toward the back." She did, and a moving mass of smaller cats appeared in the gloom. They squeaked and meowed at the Light. The second adult turned its head and growled at the kittens. They went quiet. All eyes turned to the three Fairies, shining gold and green in the Fairy Light.

"Lower your bow," Talia ordered Honor. "They're just protecting their children."

"As am I," Honor protested, but she lowered the weapon.

Talia stared at the two adults. The black one stared back at her. Her front paws still moved and scratched the ground, but she had stopped hissing. The other stepped back, her tail whipping.

"A mated pair?" Talia asked.

"No. Sisters. Litter mates, most likely," Honor said. "The males are solitary. They wander in, mate, and leave." She gestured to the kittens. "Those are probably all from the same father. The females stay together to raise the kittens till they can be on their own. Males leave. Females either stay, or go off to find another place."

Talia went to one knee. "I know the story," she said, her left hand moving to her belt pouch. The black cat hissed.

"Let her sniff you," Nova advised. "Then you can offer her food."

Talia held out her open hand. The sea cat hesitated, then moved closer and sniffed. Talia smiled. "Did he tell you lies, too, Little Sister?" She gently pulled a bit of jerky from her pouch. She offered it. The cat sniffed at it, tilted her head, then took it. She licked it, chewed it, then turned and threw it back toward the kittens. Two black shadows pounced.

Talia laughed. The grey one took a step back, but the black one stayed still. Talia gave her another bit of meat. The cat repeated her earlier behavior. Talia reached out to touch her head. The cat moved back, but didn't hiss.

"I'm sorry to invade your home, Little Sister," Talia said, emptying the rest of her rations onto the floor. She stood up. "Looks like we'll have to look elsewhere."

Honor frowned, but said, "Of course, My Lady."

They backed out of the room. The two adults pounced on the food, and the kittens descended in a cloud of fur.

Outside, Talia said, "I had a cat when I was young. Or rather, my father had one. An old grey one. He acted as though he didn't like anyone but my father. He would sit in Father's lap when he read to me. Sit and purr. And when I went to bed, the cat would settle into the window, but I always woke with him on my pillow." Talia stopped and reflected. "The cat disappeared after my father died. Ran away, I guess. Probably scared by all the people suddenly wandering around the castle. Luna told me he went looking for my father. I wonder, though. He probably died, or just wandered off. I wonder if Luna even remembers the kind lie she told me as a grieving child." Talia resumed walking.

"Maybe the Aunts ate him," Honor whispered to Nova.

Nova hit the soldier on the arm for suggesting such a thing. Talia didn't notice.

"Come, My Lady," Nova urged. "We must find another place."

They eventually found another room, further from the Ring, but behind a solid door. "Not the best," Nova commented, "but we can keep the cloth items and other non-food materials here safely."

"I'll set a Ward on the door, and we can head back." Talia looked around the room, but her thoughts were far away. She put her hand on the wall. Her fingers brushed the damp stone.

"My Lady," Honor said, trying to get Talia's attention.

Talia kept staring at the wall.

Nova approached her, and put her hand lightly on the Heir's shoulder.

Talia whirled, startled.

"My Lady. Are you ready to go back?"

Talia shook herself out of her thoughts. "Yes. Let's go." She led them out of the room. She stopped at the closed door, put her hands on it, and projected a Locking Ward into the stone. She set the ability of her Ladies and The Nine to open the door into the Weave. She finished, and turned away from the door.

"Let's go back." She began walking back toward the ruins Ring. Nova and Honor looked at each other.

"She's somewhere else," Nova observed.

"Somewhere we'll have to help her climb out of," Honor confirmed as they followed. "Again."

"That is our duty."

Honor could only nod.

$$\left(\!\!\!\begin{array}{ccc} & \text{\rotatebox{90}{}} & \end{array}\!\!\!\right) \approx \diamond$$

After giving orders to clear the mountain, and urging everyone to help one another, Talia took her Geode satchel into one of the empty rooms off the library. She sat on the floor, and set the Geode in her lap.

"Mother," she Sent into the Geode Web.

Silence.

"My Queen."

The Web vibrated.

"My Heir," came the response.

"It is good to speak with you," Talia said with relief. *"I have news."*

The Queen cut her off. *"You shouldn't contact me. It's not safe."*

"The Geode Web is as secure as a Send over touch," Talia argued, confused, and beginning to feel hurt. *"Miranda assured us."*

"I am no longer so sure. There have been whispers. I no longer know where the loyalty of the Mistress of Shadows lies. She has abilities unknown to us."

"Mother."

"Heir. Do not contact me until the child is born. Goddess guide you." The Queen broke the connection.

Talia put the Geode back in its satchel. She pushed her emotions into their private box in her mind, and took a deep breath. Her hands clenched, then released as she exhaled. When she was calm again, Talia stood, and returned to the library, back to the chaos arising from their party leaving the Exile Queen's mountain.

☾ ∭ ☼

It was late, and the sun was down at the ruins. Shatter had just sent Steel through the Ring to the campsite. Only Talia, Willow, Honor, and Goldberry were left.

Goldberry knelt in the Ring after Steel left. "This needs some time to rest. The Weave is overheating. And being disagreeable," she noted, with a bit of wonder.

Talia sat down on one of the crates. She stared out at nothing. Shatter looked at Willow, who shook her head. Honor stepped up to Shatter, and put her hand on the Captain's arm.

"She had a moment earlier in the day," she Sent, as she Showed Shatter the incident with the sea cats.

Afterward, Shatter thanked her, and went to sit by Talia. "Something about those cats touch something in you?"

"Just another example of how males can foul up our lives," Talia replied matter-of-factly.

"Not all males are that bad," Shatter reminded her. "Only some of them are bastards."

"Just the ones I let into my life, apparently."

Goldberry sat down on Talia's other side. "You're a good judge of character, My Lady. But he lied, and intentionally deceived you. You're not to blame for that."

"My mother thinks I am," Talia replied.

"She does not. She's just protecting you," Shatter disagreed, finally getting an idea about what was bothering Talia.

"Maybe." Talia reached out, and took Goldberry and Shatter's hands.

The sound of scratching drew their attention to the door. A low meow came from underneath it. Honor looked at the door, then back at Shatter. Shatter stood, and gestured for Honor to step closer.

"It's one of the sea cats," Talia said, standing. "Open the door," she ordered Honor. They heard more scratching.

Honor looked at Shatter. Confused, Shatter looked to Talia.

"Goddess bless," Talia said, exasperated. She gestured, and the door opened.

The black sea cat walked into the room. Four kittens clung to her back. She walked as though the room was hers. She drew close to Talia, then sat back on her haunches. The kittens slid off. Two were black, with a little white, and two were red with lighter stripes. They moved to scamper into the room, but their mother gathered them into the circle of her tail and held them there. She looked back at them, and meowed. They settled down, and began to groom each other.

Talia went down on one knee before the cat. "Why are you here, Little Sister?"

The cat reached out with her paw, and brushed her own nose. The dirt rubbed off, revealing a white line across the bridge. She then reached out, and put her paw on Talia's knee.

"Meow," she said, tilting her head.

Talia tilted her own head back at the cat. The others looked at one another in confusion. Honor put a hand on her sword, but Shatter waved her off. Willow got a faraway look in her eyes.

The cat meowed again, prodding Talia with her paw.

"She wants to come with us," Willow finally said.

Talia smiled. "Is that what you want, Little Sister?" She reached out toward the cat's head.

Purring, the cat grabbed Talia's hand, and pressed it to her own head. The kittens looked up, and began to purr, too. Talia's face took on a look of bliss as she scratched the cat's ears. Purring more loudly, the cat leaned into Talia's petting.

Shatter finally found her voice. "My Lady, that is a wild animal. We cannot know what it will do."

"Doesn't look wild to me," Goldberry commented, moving closer. The cat saw her, and stopped purring. She looked at Goldberry with golden eyes. Goldberry held out her hand for the cat to sniff. "Welcome to the family, Little Sister," she said, as the cat licked her fingers. The cat sneezed, then let Goldberry pet her. The two black kittens escaped their mother's tail, and tried to climb Talia's legs. The two red ones looked at Shatter and Honor with suspicion in their tiny eyes.

Willow went to Goldberry's side, and let the cat sniff her. The cat purred, and let Willow scratch her ears.

"Foolish children," Shatter commented to Honor. "My Lady, they'll be more mouths to feed. And they're wild. We can't just let them into our tents."

Talia looked at Shatter. Her emotions were plain. She knew Shatter was right, but she wanted this cat and her kittens. The cat sensed that, and moved to Talia's side. She caught the Heir's hand again, and pressed it to the side of her own head. Talia's eyes grew wide.

"She understands. Not in words, but images. She's showing me that she needs a new hunting ground. A new place for her children to grow up."

"Talia," Shatter began, her tone that of one trying to explain something to a child, "you're just projecting your own emotions. These cats might be a danger to your child."

Talia held out her hand. Shatter stayed where she was. Talia gestured again, impatient. Shatter finally stepped closer, avoiding the kittens. She took Talia's hand.

Her eyes went wide. The cat hissed and growled, then finally meowed. She let go of Talia's hand, and went to sit before Shatter. She sat on her haunches, and looked right up at Shatter. Her tail whipped, and gently wound itself around Shatter's leg. Shatter went down on one knee. The cat put her paw on Shatter's knee.

Wordlessly, the two made a pact.

"All right, Little Sister," Shatter told her. She scratched the cat's head. "If you keep the vermin away, and keep your kittens under control, you can come."

The cat purred, and gathered her kittens into the circle of her tail again. They meowed in protest, and she meowed back at them. Willow and Goldberry both tried to pet the cat. Feeling suddenly closed in, the cat hissed, and they stepped back.

"It's all right," Talia told the cat. "We'll give you your space." She gestured her Ladies back. "We'll all need time to get used to each other." The cat began to purr again. Using her tail, she picked up each kitten, and set it on her back. When all four were situated, she laid her tail down her back, and the kittens wound their own tails around it, securing them to her. She looked at Talia with expectation.

"Now what?" Shatter asked. "Can she travel through a Ring? Or will you have to walk with your new friends?"

"I'll ask," Talia said, and put her hand on the cat's head. She tried to transmit the idea of the Ring into the cat's mind, but the animal pressed back against the idea. Talia then showed her the memory of the cliffs where the camp was being built. The cat reacted by reaching into Talia's mind, and she found something there. The cat communicated a sense of understanding. Talia dropped her hand, and stepped back.

The cat rubbed her head against Talia's leg, then proceeded to do the same thing to Shatter, Willow, and Goldberry. When she tried to rub against Honor, however, the soldier stepped back. The cat gave a meow, and tilted her head in question.

"Not right now," Honor replied. "Maybe later."

The cat meowed in response, and walked out of the room. She gave a single backward glance — and a shake of her tail — before disappearing into the night.

Goldberry looked at Talia. "What passed between you two?"

Talia tore her eyes from the door. She rubbed her hand where the cat had gripped it. "She took the memory of the scent of the cliffs from my mind."

"Makes sense," Honor said, shutting the door. "Sea cats mostly hunt by smell."

"You reacted oddly to them," Willow noted. "Anything you need to share?"

"Another time," was all Honor would say.

"My Lady," Shatter interrupted, trying to get things back on track. "We need to get moving."

"Yes," Talia agreed. "Goldberry, how's the Weave?"

Goldberry knelt back down in the Ring. "It's stable."

"Good. Go through."

Goldberry nodded, and stood on the Ring. She disappeared.

"Willow, take Honor through. We'll be along," Talia ordered.

"Yes, My Lady," Willow agreed, taking Honor's arm. They disappeared.

Talia and Shatter were alone.

"You think I'm a silly child to take in a wild cat," Talia said.

"I think there's more to this than we know. I felt something when I touched the cat. Not unlike a Fairy mind, but simple. I can't explain it. But I do think this sea cat will be useful."

"I think so, too," Talia agreed. "Now, let's join the rest of our family."

Shatter offered Talia her arm, and together, they stepped into the Ring. Talia paused a moment, looking around the room, crowded with crates and chests. "Another part of our journey begins," she said wistfully.

"'Time only goes one way,'" Shatter quoted.

"'And we must follow its flow,'" Talia finished. She closed her eyes, and left that place for another.

Chapter Five
On the Shore of the Sea

The sun had not yet risen when Talia, the Ladies, and The Nine gathered on the shore. The tide was coming in. They stood in a triple circle on the firm sand: seven of The Nine formed the outer circle, the Ladies the middle, and Shatter, Flora, and Shieldbreaker constituted a small circle in the center. Flora had her left hand on the stump of Shatter's right arm. Shield gripped Flora's right hand and Shatter's left, completing the circle. Shatter faced the horizon, where the sun would rise. Talia stood behind her, also facing the sun. She Wove the Circle of her Ladies and The Nine together, and readied to send the Power into Shatter to catalyze the Healing that Flora and Shield were Weaving.

"All must be done as the sun rises," Flora had stressed for the seventh time earlier. "Our Healing, the flow of Power from the Ladies and The Nine: all of it."

"Don't worry, Mum," Talia had reassured her. "I'll be there to grant you Power from all of us. We'll return Shatter to her whole self."

"To worry is my job, Mistress."

Shatter had stripped to the shirt she wore under her mail. Water still showed on her arm and shoulders from the ritual cleansing in the sea.

"Are you ready?" Flora asked.

"I am," Shatter replied.

"Open yourself to the Goddess and her mercy to return what has been lost," Shield chanted in a ritual tone.

Shatter closed her eyes. Flora looked to Talia as the red light that comes before the dawn formed over the water. Talia dropped fully into the Circle. *"We are here to return our Sister to balance,"* she Sent to everyone. She Wove their Power and good will into a silver line, which she presented to Flora.

Flora felt the first rays of the sun on her wings. "Goddess," she called out, "grant your servant your blessing." Flora took the silver line of Power, and pressed it to Shatter's empty shoulder. The golden light of the sun and the silver light of the Circle's Power mixed. Light flared under Flora's hand. She Pushed the Power into the wound, finding the ends of the nerves and blood vessels. The light washed over the clean cut of the bone. Flora formed the image of Shatter's right arm in her mind. She pressed that image into the light. Flora expected it to click into Shatter's arm like a pestle into a mortar, but it didn't. The meeting point became slippery. The image of the arm wouldn't join with Shatter's body.

"More," Flora Sent. Her mental exertion rose. Talia called for more Power, and the Ladies and The Nine answered. More silver light flowed into Flora.

It didn't matter. The potential arm of light wouldn't join with Shatter and grow. Flora began to sweat. She moved her right hand, still linked with Shield, to Shatter's shoulder, pressing harder with the light. The sun was fully risen now, and beat hot on her back. Shatter's calm face began to show strain. Her mouth clenched. Her hand became a fist.

"I can't," Flora gasped. *"It won't join."* She gathered herself and Shield into another Push. Shatter's cry of pain joined a blinding flash. Talia broke the Circle. Shatter moved away from Flora, and bumped into Min, driving them both to their knees.

Flora and Shield collapsed to the sand.

Talia and Nova rushed to their sides. Steel broke through the others to help Shatter up, but the Captain waved her off. Her face was full of pain as she sat down on the sand.

"Flora." Talia pulled her maid to a sitting position. Flora's head lolled; her eyes were closed. "Mum," Talia called again, with more fear in her voice. Nova called to Shield in a similar fashion.

After a moment, Flora muttered, "I hear you. Stop yelling."

Talia embraced her in relief. "What happened?"

"My head hurts," Flora whispered. Her eyes opened. Unfocused, they looked around. "Shield, Shatter?" she asked.

"Shield is by your side. Still unconscious. Shatter is in pain, but awake," Talia informed her.

Min and Goldberry knelt by Shatter, their hands on her, Looking into her. Their Power tamped down the pain Shatter felt.

Talia reached into Flora, and eased her pain as well. Flora took a deep breath. Nova had gotten Shield to sit up, with the help of Helm, and was rubbing the Medic's hands. Nova's Healing Power reached into her.

"It wouldn't join," Flora told Talia. "I've done this before, and it always joins with the Fairy. But the end was slippery, and wouldn't join."

"It's okay," Talia soothed her. "We can try again later."

"No," Shatter pronounced sternly. "No."

Talia turned. Shatter was sitting on the sand, her left arm rubbing the stump of her right. The skin was bright red, like a sunburn. "It hurt too much."

"I've seen this done before," Steel told them. "It always just joins, and the limb begins to grow back. Never have I seen this sort of rejection."

"Could there be some darkness from the wound still present?" Goldberry asked.

"I don't know," Talia said. "I thought it was gone."

Flora struggled to speak. "I'm sorry, Shatter. I failed."

"No, you didn't," Shatter said, sliding in the sand to sit beside Flora. She put her hand on the older Fairy's face. "It just wasn't meant to be."

Flora shook her head. "Goddess. I tried so hard."

"I know," Shatter comforted her. "No one doubts that. It wasn't meant to be." She pressed the words home.

Flora shook, as tears began to flow down her face. Talia gathered her maid into her arms, and she began to sob on Talia's shoulder.

"Captain," Shield said in a low voice, "I'm sorry."

"Nothing to be sorry for," Shatter assured the Medic, putting her hand on Shield's shoulder. "Your skill is not at issue. Fate intervened."

Shield nodded, and laid her hand atop Shatter's.

"Steel," Shatter called out, "bring me my ringmail shirt and glove."

A little confused, Steel passed the bundle of ringmail to her Captain. With her help, Shatter put it on. The right arm hung limp. Shatter held the mail glove in her left hand. She closed her eyes in concentration. Nothing happened for a moment, but then the empty sleeve began to move. It was as though an arm was filling it, putting it on. The arm began to stretch and move around: up and down, the elbow bending, rising, and going down. The empty end went to the left hand and pulled on the glove. The fingers flexed and waved. Shatter held it up in front of her face, amazed as the fingers moved.

Talia broke the stunned silence. "When did you figure that out?"

"It came to me in a dream," Shatter said. She thrust the hand into the sand, and pulled out a handful of grains. She brought it up to her face, and let the sand run through her fingers. She smiled.

"That will take a lot of energy and concentration," Elanor cautioned, throwing a piece of driftwood at the hand.

Shatter, startled, tried to catch it, but the arm disappeared, the mail flopping to her side, and the glove falling to the sand. Steel caught the piece of wood.

Shatter smiled. "Well, you Ladies will have to teach me."

"Maybe we can anchor it to the bone, like we do a Shield to the stone," Min suggested, excitement in her voice.

"Or Weave it into the mail," Goldberry countered, catching the excitement.

"We can discuss this later," Talia said. She still held Flora. Her tears had stopped, but Talia still held her tight. "We have one more thing to do."

The excited hum of conversation settled into silence. Shield set down her water bottle. "It's simple. All you do is hold your charm, and let the Weave release." She stopped.

"And the child will start to grow," Talia finished for her. Shield nodded.

"Mum," Talia gently prodded Flora. "I need my arms."

Flora laughed slightly, and pulled away, wiping her eyes.

Talia, still kneeling in the sand, reached under her shirt. She pulled out the silver charm that had remained around her neck throughout their long journey. She held it before her, letting the still-rising sun shine on its smooth surface. Around her, the Ladies and The Nine dropped to their knees.

"Goddess, grant this child your mercy and strength," Talia intoned. "Grant her your love. Grant her a Realm that will accept her." She grasped the Weave, and with a twist, unknotted it. She felt the Power run down to her middle. She felt the cocoon of Power disappear like mist in the sun. And it was gone. She felt a moment of absence, as the Weave had been part of her for almost a year. Then she felt a little light, a growing potential. Talia relaxed. It was done. Here on the sand of the sea, where the First Fairies had arrived, her child began to grow.

She wanted to cry, but all she could do was laugh. She looked across the sea at the sun. A cheer rose from all sides. Talia felt hope.

$$(\approx \diamond$$

After a day of cutting down trees, stripping the branches, and cutting the trunks to size, the company settled in for a meal prepared by Flora and Talia. Talia had wanted to join the others in the labor, but — to a woman — they had refused her a place working with the trees.

"I'm perfectly capable of working," Talia protested to Flora. "I feel fine. Better than fine, actually — I feel great."

"They're just looking out for you. Don't worry: they'll settle down in a few days. You can join in soon. But remember, your Power will be unreliable, as the child grows and pulls Power from you," Flora reminded her, motioning for her to stir. "There will be changes. I can guide you, but expect the unexpected. And with the child being half Human, there might be some odd effects."

Talia expelled a breath, brushing hair from her face. "It's never easy."

"No, Mistress, it's not," Flora confirmed, while giving her charge a side squeeze as she gathered more herbs. "But we'll get through it together."

Sitting down on the warm ground to eat, with the sea air strong around her, Talia felt a surge of happiness, and a warm sense of family. Everyone was tired, but they still joked and bantered. At one point, flatbread flew, and Flora protested. The kittens played, and got in the way. The mother cat sat by Talia's side, meowing at the kittens when they attacked her tail.

"I must find you a name, Little Sister," Talia commented, petting the cat's head.

"What about Nesa?" Willow suggested. "My brother used to call me that."

"Nesa." Talia tested the sound of the name. She looked down at the cat. "What do you think, Nesa?"

She put her paw on Talia's leg, and rubbed her head on Talia's arm.

"Nesa it is, then," Talia told her. She raised her voice. "Everyone: meet Nesa, the newest member of our family."

A small cheer went up.

"Now, if she could only teach her kittens to behave," Steel said, pushing one of the black ones away from her food.

The two red ones had curled up in the Twins' laps. "May we name them?" Silidin asked, stroking the purring form before her.

"You must ask them," Talia counseled. "See what fits them best." Nidilis nodded, her face rapt at the little form in her lap.

"This one is a scoundrel," Flora said, pushing the second black kitten from her pot. "Nesa," she said, mother to mother, "call your children."

Nesa yawned, stretched, and stood up. She stretched again. Flora cleared her throat. Nesa finally strolled over and picked up the kitten from Flora, then ambled over to the other black one, who was still trying to get at Steel's food. She picked her up by the scruff, and took the two over to where Raven and Min were sitting. She deposited one in each of their laps. Then, she returned to Talia's side. She yawned, and went to sleep, her side against Talia's leg.

"Rogue, you shall be," Raven said, as one of the black kittens scampered up her arm to sit on her shoulder.

Min fed the other a bit of meat. The kitten then settled down in her lap. "We must find your name," Min whispered.

Talia, absently petting Nesa, called to Shatter: "Captain. Would you come here?"

"Yes, My Lady," Shatter responded, standing, and crossing to her.

"I have something for you," Talia said, pulling the silver charm from her pocket. "Since you wouldn't let me help in the work on the camp, I had time to work on this." She put the charm in Shatter's hand.

61

"And what is this, other than your charm? I don't need that kind of Magic." Laughter rippled through the group.

"No, you most certainly do not," Talia agreed, as the laughter died. "This is just a vessel. I've prepared it for you. You can use it for your arm. It will hold the Weave, and allow you to use it without conscious effort. As long as the charm touches your skin, you'll be able to control the arm. It can even come and go, as you wish."

Shatter went to her knees beside Talia. "Thank you, My Lady. It's been taxing. I can hold the arm, but I can't do other things while I do." She kissed the charm. "This is a great gift."

"For a great leader," Talia told her. "You have so much to carry, we must make sure you have enough hands." She pivoted. "Here, sit with me." She took Shatter's hand. "We shall work on it together."

Talia and Shatter Joined. Talia took the cobbled-together Weave Shatter had created, and evened out the edges. She guided Shatter, showing her how the flow could be made smoother.

"*Amazing, My Lady,*" Shatter commented. "*Is this what you learned in the Tower?*"

"*This, and other things. Now, put on the charm, and we'll anchor the Weave to it.*"

Shatter put on the silver charm, feeling it settle on her chest. Talia guided her to take the Weave, and meld it with the metal. With a mental snap, it became part of the charm. Rising out of their Circle, Talia opened her eyes.

"Now, try it," she urged.

Shatter concentrated, and the mail sleeve filled out. She slipped the glove on and flexed her hand.

"Now, forget about it. Grab Steel's drink," Talia commanded.

Shatter's Power pulled the cup from Steel's hand. It floated to her right hand. Shatter smiled as she took a drink. Steel smiled back, and calmly stole Elanor's cup.

"Concentrate. Reach as far as you can," Talia instructed.

Shatter reached out. First, over the sea and past the breakers, she could See the sea birds scooping fish out of the water. Then, inland, the shadows of animals settling in for their slumber, and others getting ready for the night's hunt, were visible. At first, her arm wavered, but then it solidified. Pride bloomed on her face. "Thank you, My Lady."

"I just showed you the path: you walked it," Talia told her. "You'll have to practice. There are things you might have to re-learn." She looked at Steel. "I wouldn't spar with Steel until you have full control, for instance."

"Understood, My Lady." Shatter saluted her with Steel's cup. As it reached her lips, it flew across the circle to Elanor. More laughter erupted.

Talia stood up. "I will bid you all good night." She reached out to Flora. "Would you come with me to my tent, Mum? There are things I've been avoiding that we need to talk about."

"Of course, Mistress." Flora climbed to her feet, with Shatter's help. She and Talia linked arms, and moved off into the night.

(∭ ☼

Days turned to weeks, and weeks to months. The house grew from log walls, to an open space under a roof. Magic, strength, and skill raised the building quickly. Despite Talia's protests, the next task was to section off two rooms for her and her child.

"I will not stay here until there is shelter for everyone," she told Shatter when presented with her room. The walls were hung blankets, but it was enough to give her a place of her own.

"You will. We won't let you sleep on the ground any longer." She pointed to Talia's growing belly. "This child deserves a roof, and a bed."

"So do the rest of you," Talia protested, but she could see that she wouldn't win this argument.

Talia relented. "We'll take turns. It's only big enough now for a few of us at a time. The others will make do with the tents, and the dome over us all."

"That'll change soon," Shatter assured her. "Flora has moved most of the cooking inside already."

Talia smiled. She missed the smell of bread. "I assume you have plans for more houses, or to at least enlarge this one?"

"More," Shatter told her. "At least two more. They should be ready by the turn of the month."

"You're amazing," Talia pronounced, sitting down. The carved chair Steel had made was a welcome relief for her feet. The child wasn't very large yet, but it still sapped her strength. "I wish I could be of more use. I hate being stuck in here."

"Flora likes the company."

"Yes. Your Heir is cooking all day."

"We all understand. The exhaustion will pass in a few weeks. Your body is getting used to the changes. Soon, you'll have more energy than you know what to do with."

Talia grunted. "So Flora says. I'll believe it when I feel it."

"You will, My Lady." Shatter knelt beside Talia. Her tone became serious. "I need to talk to you about something."

Talia sensed the change, and gave the Captain her full attention.

"You remember Canin?" Shatter asked.

"Of course. The Elenite boy we helped."

"Yes. Part of his story involved finding a Fairy hunter in an Elen town."

"And I promised that we would find him when my exile was over. I remember."

"Well." Shatter took a deep breath. "After the other two cabins are raised and sealed, I'd like to take a few soldiers and find him."

Talia looked at her. "I'm sorry. I didn't intend for any of this to happen." She gestured to the log house. "We were supposed to return to Fae-Treval after a year, and now we're on the other side of the Realm, building houses."

"I followed you where your path took you," Shatter said. "But this path still calls to me."

"I understand, but how will you get there, and is it safe? My Aunts are still looking for us."

"I know of a Ring near the Elen town Canin mentioned. It won't be a long journey."

"Who would you take?"

"Raven, for her Shadow ability. Helm, because she has hunted these Humans before."

"A Lady should go with you. Min or Elanor, maybe, for added Power."

"No," Shatter disagreed. "This is a journey for soldiers."

Talia prickled. "My Ladies can't hold their own?"

"Of course they can, but this is personal. Something I must do. Something only soldiers must do."

"We Iridescents don't understand," Talia said, only half jokingly.

"That's not it. It's just that this is something I must do for all my Sisters and Brothers who have fallen to him and all the other hunters like him."

"How do you know he's still there? Canin said he was old, and we don't know how long ago that was."

"He's still alive," Shatter said with confidence. "I've dreamed of the place Canin described. I've walked those streets. He'll be there."

"When you're ready," Talia told her, taking her hand in both of her own, "I'll send you off with my blessing."

"Thank you, My Lady." Shatter stood. "Now, I must go and see how things are going. No telling what mischief Harpoon has led them into." Shatter bowed, and left through the rough door.

Flora brought Talia a cup of tea. "Mistress, this will help you."

"Thank you." Talia sipped the bitter tea. She made a face. "You're sure?"

"Yes, Mistress. Merry-Weather gave me that every day of my first pregnancy. Got me on my feet very quickly."

"To get away from the tea, I bet!" Talia retorted.

(☾ ⌇ ☼

As Shatter promised, by the end of the month, both cabins had been raised and secured. This allowed everyone to pack up their tents, and move under a roof. Elanor, Min, and Goldberry joined Flora and Talia in the main house. The remainder of the Ladies took the first cabin, while The Nine took the second.

"We're used to close spaces," Steel reminded Talia, when she commented on their crowded conditions. "And we don't spend much time inside anyway, between patrol, and guard duty, and training. So there's plenty of room."

"As you say," Talia agreed skeptically.

Chapter Six
Storms

Gil and Willow sat on the edge of the cliff, watching the sea. Their feathers waved in the rising wind. They enjoyed the shade of the single, stubborn oak tree on the edge of the cliff. Willow marveled at how the roots delved deep and held the tree almost leaning over the edge.

"Harpoon says a storm is coming," Gil said.

"I hope those cabins will hold," Willow replied. "I just got used to being dry."

"I'm sure they will," Gil declared. She turned. The Twins were coming toward them. She elbowed Willow, and they stood.

"Gil," Silidin said, her face full of worry. "We need your help."

"Our cats have run away," Nidilis said, her face mirroring her twin's concern.

"I'm sure they're fine," Gil reassured them. "They're wild animals, you know. They're probably just off hunting, or doing other cat things."

The Twins shook their heads. "They weren't with us last night," Silidin complained.

"They always sleep with us," Nidilis explained. "We haven't seen them since dinner."

"What about Nesa and the others?" Willow asked.

"They're with Talia and Flora," Silidin said, concern filling her voice. Gil began to feel the same concern.

"You must help us!" Nidilis pleaded.

Willow looked at Gil. "If this is another of your jokes?"

"No," Silidin said. "We swear by the Goddess, it's not."

"Well," Gil started, looking at Willow. "You know what my father always said."

"'Never trust Iridescents,'" Willow put in.

"No, that was my grandmother," Gil replied.

"'Beware the girl who cries hawk?'" Willow suggested. She was enjoying taunting the Twins, after all they had put her through.

The Twins looked at each other with rising anger. "If you won't help us," Nidilis said, turning away. Silidin grabbed her arm.

"I know we treated you both badly, but I thought we had made up for it." She bowed her head. "If not, what can we do? We need your help. We're scared for them." Silidin looked right at Gil.

Gil held her gaze for a moment. "What he said was, 'Always be the better Fairy, and help your Sisters,'" Gil finished. She took Silidin's hand. "When did you see them last?"

The relief was clear on Silidin's face. "After dinner. I think they went running off. They were chasing something. I don't know." She seemed on the verge of tears.

"We'll find them," Gil promised, glancing at Willow. After a moment, Willow nodded, too.

Gil stretched out her senses. She could See all the little creatures running and flying around the cliff top. The coming storm was driving them to shelter.

"Could they have gone to the beach?" Willow asked.

"They do like to eat the shells that come up at low tide," Nidilis replied.

Gil started in the direction of the trail descending the cliff. She could Feel an echo of the missing kittens' activity in that direction. The others followed.

She reached the head of the trail. It was narrow and rocky. Gil knelt, and saw some faint prints in the earth.

"I think they did come this way," she announced. "Stay up here. I don't like the feel of this trail. The surface seems looser than before."

"I'll keep in Send with you," Willow offered.

The Twins moved to glance over the side of the cliff. The wind had begun to rise.

Gil began moving down the narrow trail. She gripped the stone on her right. Her senses reached out. She was sure the cats had come this way.

A third of the way down, a sudden gust of wind hit her. She grabbed the stone with both her hand and her Power. Her foot slipped, and she was forced to fan her wings to get her feet back.

"*Are you okay?*" Willow Sent.

"*Yes. Just a gust of wind.*" She anchored herself to the wall, and took another step. The wind rose again, and she was forced to fold her wings tight to her back to avoid being picked up and carried away. She took a few more steps. The trail ended.

Gil reached out with her senses, and Felt the sea cats huddled on a ledge a few feet down. Fear filled their feline minds.

"*I can See them,*" Gil Sent. "*The trail must have collapsed. They're on a ledge below me.*"

The responsive cry of fear from the Twins filled Gil's mind. She pressed it back.

"*Can you reach them?*" Willow asked.

"*No,*" Gil replied.

"*Can you use your Power to lift them up?*" Silidin asked.

Gil Reached out. She touched the first red kitten, but a night on the ledge had made the cats jumpy, and the kitten pushed back at Gil. Scrambling, she backed up into a hole the two had dug into the wall. The other panicked, and pushed her way in beside her sister. Loose stones rolled off the ledge.

"*No,*" Gil said. "*They're too skittish. They'll panic, and hurt themselves, or fall.*"

"*Then I'll have to come down,*" Silidin said.

"*No. The winds are too strong. They'll drive you into the wall,*" Gil objected. She had turned and pressed her back to the cliff face.

"*You may be a better flyer,*" Silidin countered, "*but I can hover better. Support me, and I can hover, and reach in and grab them.*"

"*Maybe we should call for help,*" Willow suggested.

"*No time,*" Nidilis said. "*That storm is coming fast. The wind is rising, and I feel rain.*"

At just that moment, Gil felt the first few drops hit her. She Reached out again. The kittens were scared: the slightest thing might drive them to bolt, and fall.

"*Stay away from the wall,*" Gil told Silidin. "*I'll try to calm them.*" Gil anchored herself to the cliff, and Reached out. The minds of the two cats were chaotic, full of confusion and fear. She tried to surround them with calm. Their minds Pushed back. Gil put more energy into her effort. She felt her feet slip. She grabbed at the stone, and stood on the side of the cliff, shaking.

With the help of her sister and Willow, Silidin descended, slowly. She finally came level with the ledge.

"*I can see them,*" she Sent, "*but I can't reach them. Can you get them to come out?*"

"*I'm trying,*" Gil replied. The rain was starting to fall harder, and the wind had picked up. She was buffeted about, and had to let go of her connection to the cats to keep her place on the wall.

"*I can't reach!*" Silidin complained, drifting closer to the wall. Her wings faltered.

"*We're losing her!*" Willow Sent desperately.

Gil watched Silidin drift away from the cliff, and begin to fall. She Reached out with what little Power she could spare.

"*We have her,*" Talia's Send cut in. Silidin bobbed back up to the ledge. Gil could feel Min and Elanor's Power backing her up.

"*Raven,*" Talia called out. "*Your turn.*"

"*Silidin,*" Raven Sent deliberately. "*Do not move.*"

Gil saw an arrow fly right above Silidin and strike, hard, into the stone. A line of Fairy silk rope trailed behind it.

"*Gil,*" Raven Sent. "*Do not move.*"

The second arrow flew over Gil's head, and struck right above her. She was hit by a few stones. Another rope hung right by her hand.

"*Will it hold?*" Talon asked.

Raven responded, "*I used all the Power I could without breaking the arrow. Gil,*" she called, "*test the line.*"

Gil reached out, and pulled on the rope. It held tight.

"*Now,*" Talia ordered, "*Silidin, get the cats. Then you'll both use the ropes to get down.*"

"*I still can't reach them,*" Silidin Sent. "*They're in the back of a hole. Even with the support, I can't reach.*"

"*Gil, can you get them to come out?*" Talia asked.

"*If someone can support me.*" She felt Goldberry and Nova's Power anchor her to the wall. "*Good.*" She Reached out. The cats were still scared. "*I can't. They're too scared.*"

"*Hold a moment,*" Talia commanded. Her presence dropped out of the Send. She reappeared moments later, bringing another mind with her. "*Call to them,*" Talia instructed.

Gil felt a wordless call come through the Send. She could feel the kittens' fear recede a bit, but they still wouldn't move. Gil pulled the feeling of the new mind into herself and Projected it. The kittens calmed. Gil had an idea.

"*I think I can get them out,*" she Sent to everyone. "*But it'll be a leap. Silidin, be prepared to grab them. Hold your arms like you're accepting a hug. When they hit you, wrap your arms around them. They might claw you, but don't let go.*"

"*I won't,*" Silidin swore.

"*Then you'll have to drop,*" Gil continued. "*You can't be in the air too long, or they'll struggle out of your grasp.*"

"*We can Push her down,*" Talia offered. "*Raven, you and Shield will have to catch her. She'll be out of our range.*"

"*We're ready,*" Raven agreed.

"*Gil, we go on your count,*" Talia Sent.

Gil concentrated. She wrapped the kittens with their mother's love. She told them to come to her when she called. The kittens agreed, and tensed to move.

"*Silidin, Talia, Raven: I'm ready.*" She took a deep breath, and centered herself. "*On three. One. Two. Three!*" Gil called the kittens.

They sprang out of the hole, and into Silidin's arms, which she immediately wrapped around the furry, wriggling bundles. Pain in her chest shot through the Send, but she didn't let go. Then, she fell. Gil held her breath.

"*We have her!*" Raven called out.

"*How is she?*" Gil asked in a worried tone.

"*And the cats?*" Nidilis added.

"*She's bleeding, but nothing that can't be Healed,*" Shield answered.

"*I have the cats,*" Raven Sent. "*They're well, too.*"

"*Now,*" Talia Sent, relief in her mind, "*Gil, take the line down.*"

"*Shield your hands,*" Raven advised, "*or you'll rip them apart. Use your wings to slow down as you get to the bottom.*"

Gil grabbed the Fairy silk rope. She felt the hold on her release. With a call to the Goddess, she pushed off, and glided down the rope. Rain began to fall, hard.

"*She's down,*" Raven called out. "*We're setting up a Shield until Silidin is Healed. And the rain lets up. We'll have to go down the beach and find another way up.*"

"*Good work, all,*" Shatter Sent. "*Let me know when you leave, and I'll send Talon and Harpoon to meet you halfway.*"

"*And Ladies,*" Talia Sent, "*come straight to the main house.*"

"*Yes, My Lady,*" Gil confirmed in resignation.

After enjoying a glad reunion, and getting into dry clothes, the Twins, Gil, and Willow stood before Talia and Shatter in the main house. Everyone else was crowded in behind them. Nesa was at Talia's feet, bathing the two red kittens. Gratitude filled her licks, and anger filled her tail, which was wrapped around them both.

"Are you all right?" Talia finally asked.

"Yes, My Lady," Silidin said, adjusting her new shirt. "Shield Healed all the claw marks on my chest."

"That'll teach you to wear your ringmail all the time," Steel said from the side.

A slight chuckle rippled through the group, quickly subdued by the looks on Shatter and Talia's faces.

"Captain," Talia addressed Shatter. "I believe you wanted to speak."

"As this is about the safety of our Ladies," Shatter said, "yes." She fixed each of them with a hard eye.

"I'm proud of all of you for working together to rescue the smallest members of our family. I'm angry that they had to be rescued at all, however." She looked at the Twins. "You should have alerted someone that there was a problem. Your soldiers, at least. Elanor, at best." She stared down at the adventurers. They all lowered their eyes. "You put yourselves in danger. If you had waited a moment, and called for help, we wouldn't have had to scramble to save Silidin. You could have been killed."

She put her hands in her belt. "And don't tell me there wasn't time. 'Make time,' as Flora has told me repeatedly throughout this journey."

Flora wordlessly agreed as she put down a plate of raw meat for the kittens. After a look to their mother for permission, they dove into the plate, and soon devoured most of its contents.

"Am I understood?" Shatter asked.

"Yes, Captain," all four of the Ladies confirmed.

"My duty is to keep all of you safe. I can't do that if I don't even know you're in danger. Now." She fixed them with a hard eye. "Flora needs help in her garden. Willow and Nidilis, you two will be hers until she decides you're free. This is on top of all other duties you've already been assigned."

"Yes, Captain," they replied meekly.

"Helm, Harpoon. You were supposed to be coming off night watch. You will stay on night watch, and you will fulfill your other duties from the new duty rotation as well."

"But they had nothing to do with our actions," Silidin protested.

"Did the Captain ask you a question?" Steel snapped.

Silidin wilted.

"Exactly. They're responsible for you. That's their duty. That was made clear to you in the very beginning." Shatter looked at each of the Ladies. "Am I understood?"

"Yes, Captain," they replied as a unit.

"Gil, Silidin. You will take over one duty from Talon and Honor. They'll be too busy with repairs to the cabins after the storm to see to everything they've been assigned. The two of you will oversee the privies for this moon."

Gil sighed, but looked up with resignation. "I understand, Captain." She looked down at the kittens, who were licking the final bits of blood and juices from Flora's plate. "A little smell is worth their lives."

"And," Steel put in, "any soldier who just happens to stop by to help with any of these tasks will have me to answer to."

"Yes, Lieutenant," everyone confirmed.

The cabins held, as storms swept in from the sea. They brought strong wind and punishing rains. Talia and the Ladies were forced to create a Shield dome to keep out the driving rain. Despite how well the dwellings were built, the wind still drove water through the cracks in the walls and roofs.

"Talon and Helm will have a time resealing everything when this storm passes," Shatter commented. Steel and Raven had joined Shatter for her daily chat with Talia. They were finalizing plans about what would be done next.

"How long will that be?" Talia asked, passing tea around.

"Harpoon says a few days," Steel told her, taking the cup, and holding it tightly in her hands. The wind and rain had made them all cold.

"After, we'll need to replenish supplies," Shatter informed everyone. Flora made a noise of agreement from the other side of the house.

"A quick trip down the coast to Realm's End," Steel suggested. "Just for a few days."

"The last time you took a quick trip . . .," Elanor said, leaving the sentence hanging.

Shatter nodded, rubbing her shoulder. "Steel will lead the excursion. Only for necessities. After they get back, Raven, Helm, and I will depart."

"I don't see why you can't go when the weather clears," Talia countered. "Your journey will take longer. Better to start as soon as possible."

"I don't want to leave too few behind," Shatter advised. "Steel will need to take two or three soldiers, and at least Willow or Gil. That will leave few here to defend you."

"Nesa will defend us." Talia smiled, reaching down to pet the cat, who stretched languidly, and went back to sleep.

"I don't doubt that," Shatter said. "But I won't leave till Steel and the supplies return."

"As you say, then." Talia stood. Her energy was back. The rain kept her inside, but she wanted to run, or fly. She settled for doing

Patterns. She was in the middle of the First when she noticed all of them staring at her.

"Was there anything else, Captain?"

"No, My Lady," Shatter said hurriedly, caught slightly off guard.

"Good. Stay if you wish." She continued the Pattern.

Steel looked at Shatter, then at Flora. Both shrugged.

"I will see to the patrol," Steel said, and left.

Raven got up, and stood before Talia. "That motion must be more fluid," she counseled, demonstrating. Talia repeated the motion. "Better," Raven told her. She began to mirror Talia's motions.

Flora sat down beside Shatter, who was watching Talia.

"Are you sure you have to do this?"

Shatter knew what she meant. "Yes. I must."

"Canin said this hunter hasn't killed in years. He's no threat anymore. Why put yourself and others in danger?"

Shatter tamped down a surge of irritation. "He may not be killing anymore, but he still must be punished for what he did. He may be training others. Canin didn't accept his teachings, but others might. Those Elenites who tracked me, for example."

"It won't bring back your arm," Flora told her. "Or those you lost. They've Returned to the Cycle. They have new lives now."

Shatter became even more angry. "You don't understand. I lost Brothers and Sisters to those like him. I will avenge them."

Raven stopped and turned at Shatter's raised voice. Talia also stopped and looked at Shatter. Her hand went to her belly.

"Vengeance is a sword without a hilt," Flora told her. "Until you understand why you must go, you should stay." She got up, and went back to her bread.

Shatter started to say something, but shut her mouth with a loud click. She took a deep breath, and stood. "I'll be outside." She left.

Talia and Raven exchanged looks, but didn't say anything. They went back to their Pattern.

Talia didn't see Shatter for the rest of the day. The next morning, Steel came alone for the daily chat.

"She took one of the patrols with Helm," she told Talia. "She said she had some thinking to do."

"And you — what do you think?"

"I'm just a soldier. This man killed my Sisters and Brothers, not in war, but for sport, and trophies. For the good of the Realm, he must be stopped." Steel's statement was filled with simple determination.

Talia nodded. "I understand. Tell Shatter I'll see her tomorrow."

"Yes, My Lady," Steel agreed, understanding the order.

The next morning, Shatter was there when Talia stepped out from behind her curtain. The others had left, leaving Shatter and Flora — forehead to forehead — deep in a personal Circle. Talia watched, opening her Sight just a little to take in their emotions. She got resignation from Flora, and steadfastness from Shatter. After a moment, they separated.

"My Lady," Shatter said, standing. "I want to apologize for what I said the other day. Flora caught me off guard."

"She does that," Talia commented, crossing to take her Captain's hands. "What did you decide?"

"I need to find this man, because I must close a circle. I lost a brother to a hunter. By stopping this man, I will close that part of my life." Shatter was no longer filled with anger, but determination.

Flora stood, announcing, "I need some tea."

"I understand," Talia told Shatter. "Go, with my blessing."

"Thank you, My Lady." Shatter touched Talia's hand to her lips. "I will return swiftly."

"You'd better," Flora warned. "Otherwise, I'll have to come and get you."

"Yes, Mum," Shatter agreed.

The rain did eventually stop. Steel, Spear, and Willow left the next day. They planned to use the Ephemeral Ring to get to the ruins Ring, then travel to the Ring Raven and Spear had found further up the coast from Realm's End.

"Make sure the Wards are strong around that Ring," Talia ordered them. She had never visited that Ring, but had worked with Raven to set up the Wards. "That's a weak spot."

"I understand," Spear confirmed. "The Ring is deep in the ruins we found. Its Song was weak, and we only found it because we knew what we were looking for."

"Regardless," Shatter told them, "be careful. Make sure you remember your story, and don't talk too much. Just get the supplies, and return."

"Yes, Captain," Steel assured her. "I'll make sure we aren't followed."

Talia turned to Willow. "Make sure you scan everything you buy for any hidden Wards or crystals. We don't know how far my Aunts have spread their agents."

"I will, My Lady," Willow promised.

Talia hugged her. "Be safe, and let the Goddess guide you."

Goodbyes were said. Goldberry gripped Spear's hand. "I keep sending you off. I must come with you sometime."

"You know why," Spear reminded her. "Goddess keep you safe."

"And you," Goldberry said back.

Steel stepped onto the Ephemeral Ring, and disappeared with a wave. Spear and Willow followed.

Shatter took Raven and Helm away to work on their plans. Talia kept Goldberry and Elanor, to work on strengthening the Wards around their compound, which they were simply calling the cliffs. They were in the middle of a Circle when something startled Talia. A surge of Power rising within her pulled her out of the Circle.

"What was that?" Elanor asked, concern in her eyes as she looked at Talia.

Talia could only shake her head. She closed her eyes, and focused inward. The ball of potential within her shone with a silver light. The light flickered, pulsed, and then settled back down to glow

77

within her. Talia put her hand on her belly. She felt a kick. Smiling, she reached out and grabbed Elanor's hand, pressing it over the spot.

"Do you feel it?" she asked.

Elanor was still, trying to sense any movement. Then came another one. "Ah, I feel it. She wants to be part of our Circle."

Talia let go of Elanor and brought Goldberry in. Gold smiled as the child moved again. "Goddess's greeting, little one," she said. "Well met."

Flora rushed in from outside. "What's happening?" she demanded, running to Talia's side. "I felt a surge."

"She's moving," Talia replied. Goldberry stepped aside, and let Flora in. She put her hands on Talia, and closed her eyes. She concentrated for a moment, then smiled.

"She's awake. Your Circle must have quickened something in her," Flora informed them, letting go, and stepping back.

A sudden surge of anxiety hit Talia. "Is it dangerous? Could this hurt her?"

"No, child," Flora soothed her. "It's perfectly normal. Babies begin to move around this time. They react to all kinds of things. See?" She took Talia's hand and put it back on her belly. "Feel her. She's growing. Her thoughts are simple, but there. Feel her light. This is a strong one."

"Strong like her mother," Elanor commented.

Nesa pawed at her leg from the floor, and Talia looked down. One of the black kittens, the one who hadn't been named yet, was by her side. She meowed for Talia.

"Here," Talia said, reaching down. She picked up the kitten, who settled into her lap, and began to purr against her bump. Talia could feel the light of her child match the rhythm of the purr.

Min walked in. "That's where you went." She approached Talia. "She was by my side, and then gone."

"Nesa brought her to me," Talia said. "I guess she felt I needed a kitten in my lap."

"Getting big," Flora commented, brushing the kitten's ears. She walked away, Nesa at her heels.

Min looked at Talia, sensing the mood of the room. "What happened?"

"The child moved."

Min laughed. "And she was off like lightning to be by your side."

"Lightning," Talia tested, petting the cat. "Is that you?"

Min's face became serious. "We can't call her that, after all lightning has done."

Talia agreed. "Quicksilver then, for how fast she moves."

"That's better." Min stroked the kitten. "Quicksilver." The kitten grabbed her hand, licked it quickly, and then promptly returned to sleeping.

"That's settled, then," Talia said. "I'm glad you came. I felt a weakness in the Ward. The Weave has come loose to the north. Could you take someone and check it out?"

"Raven is with Shatter for their mission. I'll see if Shield is free," Min agreed. "What do you think it is?"

"Maybe nothing. Perhaps just a shift in the ground. I just want to be sure."

"I'll check it, and let you know." Min leaned down and kissed Quicksilver. "Take care of her." Min left.

Flora returned with more tea. Talia saw it, and held up her hands.

"No, Mum — no more of that. I will use my Power as the Heir to command you: no more tea!"

"This is different," Flora assured her. "Now that the child has moved to the next phase, a new tea is needed." She pressed the cup into Talia's hands. "Drink."

Talia sniffed it, and drank. "That's better."

"Now, don't sit with that cat too long," Flora told her, taking back the empty cup. "You need more exercise." She turned to Elanor. "Gather the Ladies. We'll practice the Patterns."

"Yes, Mum."

"Bring them to the cliff," Talia said. "I want to watch the sea as we practice."

"Very good." Elanor bent and kissed Talia. "We'll meet you there." She left.

Around this time, unbeknownst to Talia, Shatter concluded her planning session with Raven and Helm.

Talia sighed. She looked down at Quicksilver. "Sorry, little one. Flora is sending me off." She picked the kitten up as she stood up, then set her back on the chair. Quicksilver grumbled, but settled back into a ball. "Keep Flora company."

Talia took Goldberry's arm and walked out into the sun. The sea air grabbed her hair, whipping it around her face. Talia felt a surge of emotion: the heat of the sun, the feel and smell of the air, the taste of the tea, the potential building within her — they all gathered inside her. Fighting not to run, she and Goldberry hurried to the cliff.

The other Ladies were already there. Harpoon and Helm were there, too, since they were never far from the Twins. Talia settled everyone into a long line, with herself in the center. She faced the sea. The sun was warm, and the sea birds called.

"Ladies," she called, "First Pattern."

☾ ♒ ☼

Two days later, Steel and the others returned. They brought supplies and tools. They replenished Flora's fund of herbs. Everyone gathered around to see what else they'd brought.

"I got some looks when I asked for these herbs," Steel informed Flora, passing her the bundle. "The shopkeeper wanted to ask what I needed with mid- and late-pregnancy herbs, but I just glared at her."

"That's even more suspicious," Flora chastised her. "A grin and a wink would've been better." Steel shrugged. She caught Talia's attention.

"Did you find them?" Talia asked.

"I did." Steel picked up a long, wrapped bundle.

Talia motioned for Shatter to join her. As she did, Steel passed Talia the bundle.

"I asked Steel to see if she could find these for you." She unwrapped three longbows. Shatter took one, marveling at the simple curve. Steel passed her the string. With a practiced motion, Shatter strung it. She tested the pull.

"Thank you, My Lady," Shatter said. "These are well made."

"You only had your short ones," Talia said. "These are better suited for hunting."

When Raven and Helm approached, Shatter passed the other bows to them. Raven strung hers, and tested the pull. "I'll have to practice," she said. "It's been a long time."

"Many thanks, My Lady," Helm said with a bow.

"Any problems?" Talia asked.

"None, other than the shopkeeper flirting with Willow," Steel replied, with a wink at the Lady in question.

She heard, and joined them. "It was just another male asking if I needed a strong Fairy around." Willow smiled. "I turned him down with a smile."

Steel grinned again. "I gave him a glare."

Talia smiled, but was concerned. "Please: we don't need any attention brought to us."

"It was only a foolish male speaking to a pretty girl." Steel shrugged it off. "They don't see many in that town. We were careful, and stuck to the story. We also left in a different direction, and doubled back."

"The Ring?"

"It was secure," Spear assured her. "Nothing had been disturbed since Raven and I were there. I strengthened the Wards, as we discussed."

Talia nodded. Elanor came up behind her. "Everything is secure. I Joined with Spear to check. The Wards are stable."

"Goddess grant us safety," Talia beseeched. Her anxiety lessened. "Now, we just have to prepare for Shatter, Raven, and Helm's departure."

"We must leave in the night," Shatter told her. "The Ring we're going to is near the border. The sun rises earlier there."

"I want you to take the first Ephemeral Ring." Talia prepared to press the matter, as she knew Shatter wouldn't easily agree.

"I would have to destroy it if we had to escape," Shatter objected, while looking at Elanor.

"I would rather you destroy it and escape," Elanor told her, "than be trapped, captured, or killed without it."

"As you wish," Shatter acquiesced. "Now, we must pack." She took her new bow and the quiver of arrows Steel had brought. Raven and Helm joined her.

Talia watched them go. Min and Nidilis came to her side. Talia took their hands. "We must watch them go again," Talia said wistfully.

"That is our path," Min said with resignation.

"Do they feel the same when we leave them?" Nidilis asked.

"No," Talia said firmly. "They feel worse."

Chapter Seven
Elen-Ford

Elen-Ford was a small town. Bisected by the Diamond River, it was the site of the only bridge in either direction for leagues. The town's purpose was to provide for the needs and wants of the merchants traveling across the Realms. Taverns, inns, and drink houses were plentiful. Once, there had been few unfilled rooms, and the tables had always been occupied. Now, with the tensions between Fairies and Humans on the rise again, merchants were visiting less and less. There had never been many Crafthouses, though, as the spinning of Fairy silk was a lesser concern here. Only two houses remained in operation.

The Human side of the river was mostly deserted. Only a few hardy inns and taverns were still in business. The Fairy side was a little better, but there were still more empty buildings than full. The Queen had closed the border, allowing only Fairy travelers to pass.

"If she keeps that border closed," an old man complained to the uninterested barkeep at one of the local Human drink shops, "this town will be gone by next year. Only the bridge will remain."

"Maybe we should burn it down," an Elenite beside him said. "Show those Fairies we control ourselves."

"They would just rebuild it," the barkeep commented with resignation.

"Maybe further up the river," the old man cursed. "Cut us right out."

"If there's going to be another war," the Elenite told him, "they'll need this bridge. We should do something: maybe block it, and demand payment to the town."

"Then the Fairies would burn it down," the barkeep told him with certainty.

"That would only hurt us." The old man thumped his chest. "Prevent Human merchants from crossing. Damn wings." He thumped his cup on the bar.

"That was the last of the red," the barkeep informed him. "I don't expect another shipment for some time."

"Damn wings," he cursed again. "Better get home. Dark coming." The man stumbled off his chair, and out the door.

The barkeep raised his eyes to the back of the tavern. He raised a bottle. The Elenite saw this, and turned. He didn't see anything there.

"If you aren't going to order another drink," the barkeep told him, "pay up and leave."

"I have a right to sit here," the man retorted. He looked around. The tavern was mostly empty. "I don't see anyone looking for a seat."

"You stink. Order, or go." The barkeep turned to another large Elenite at the end of the bar, who was hefting a club menacingly.

"All right. I'll go." The man dug out a coin, and shoved it across the bar. It slipped off the edge, and fell to the floor. The Elenite smiled at his little snub. The bartender frowned, and gestured to the door.

"I'll never be back," the man swore as he exited.

The bartender bent to pick up the coin. "Even your money stinks," he observed, wiping it with his rag.

☾ ∭ ☼

The old man stumbled in the street. A dozen faces stared as he passed, but no one spoke to him. He got lost. Made a wrong turn. Now, it was beginning to rain, and the water was getting inside his ragged boots. He felt foolish. Once, he had been someone, but now, this was his life. Lost in this damned half-breed town. Ah, there was his alley. He turned down the narrow passage, boots clicking on the bricks. The old man made his way up a dark and dingy staircase, eventually reaching his door with a sigh.

"There's a bottle inside, with just a bit left," he muttered to himself. "Then I can sleep."

He opened the door. Did he forget to lock it? He couldn't remember. "Damn kids. If they've been in my chest, I'll cut them," he muttered, as he pushed the door closed behind him, and headed down a narrow hall to his cot. That something was amiss penetrated his wine-soaked mind, and he tried to turn, but hands caught his arms and propelled him forward. A form materialized out of the darkness, sitting on his cot.

"Who are you?" he slurred, trying to break the strong grip immobilizing him. "Get out of my room."

The figure raised its head, and wings spread out, filling the space. Anger turned to fear, and he struggled again to break free. A blow to the back of his legs brought him to his knees. Another form was visible to his right, sitting on his storage chest.

"So, you've finally come home. We've been waiting," the form on the cot said, wings retracting.

"Father-damned Fairies, what are you doing here? Get out!" he yelled.

"Don't waste your breath — this whole room is in a bubble of Silence," the Fairy to his right said. "Scream all you want; your neighbors won't hear you."

"What do you want?" he asked petulantly. "I have nothing."

"Oh, but you have much," the first one said, gesturing to the second. She stood up, and pushed the man's chest closer to him.

They were both female, he realized, as he caught sight of the curve of their breasts in the dim light. He looked at the chest: the lock had been broken. "Damn Fairy bitches. I have nothing. Leave me be." He struggled again, but the one behind him held his arms tight.

"Show him the 'nothing' he has," the first commanded. He could hear the voice of a soldier, a leader.

The second smiled, and opened the chest. She reached in, and pulled out a mass of tangled chains, medals hanging from all of them. They jangled as she shoved them in his face.

"From the Fairies you killed," the first accused.

"I didn't kill them," he denied. "I took those from the dead."

"You killed them," she repeated.

"It was war," he replied. "It was them or me. So, yes, I killed them."

"In war, maybe." The first Fairy took the mass of chains. She looked at them carefully. Her fingers moved over the inscriptions. Only the clinking of metal could be heard as she inspected them. She found the one she'd been looking for.

"But this company wasn't in the war." She pressed the medal into his face. "They were border guards. Children. You killed them with poisoned arrows. Like cowards. Then robbed their dead bodies. Buried them." She spit in his face.

Fury gripped him. "You damn Fairies started it: you burned my home. Burned it, with my family locked inside. You shot my wife as she tried to get my son out, then shot him as he crawled out of the wreckage." Tears of old pain and rage filled his eyes. "Made me watch." His fury gave him strength, and he pulled his arms free. He pushed his sleeves up, to show his burn-scarred arms. "Held me over her burning body. Laughed as the fire burned." The third Fairy took his arms back, wrenching them in the process.

"I didn't do that. We didn't kill your family." The first Fairy set the medals on the cot. She sat, so she could look him in the eye. "We didn't do those things. We were honorable soldiers."

"But other Fairies did. Fairy soldiers watched, and laughed. Fairy officers stood by, and allowed their men to do these things. You may not have been the ones who acted, but you allowed my family to be killed." He took a breath. "How many half-breeds fill this town? How many of them came from rape? All of them!" he yelled. "All of them! Your women can prevent children from being born, but Humans have no such Magic. My sister killed herself rather than birth a filthy half-breed." He spit at her.

"You hunted them," she accused. She gestured to the chest. "Took their medals. Took wing tips, and fingers. I see the fingers of children here." She stood. "You say we started this, but you continued it. We left after the war. We stopped. You did not."

"You're a fool if you think the killing stopped," he spat back. "After the truce, Fairies still killed Humans. You just justified it with laws. They crossed the border illegally, or smuggled. How many did you kill just for the crime of trying to feed their families? Feed them from lands that used to be ours?" He struggled. "Let me stand. I'll face you."

"And give you the honor you didn't give your victims?" she asked him. "Why should I? You killed my brother with poison. Took his medal, and buried him."

He laughed. "I remember when we found out you hated that. We burned the bodies at first, just to get rid of them, but then the King told us, 'That's what the Father-cursed ones want.' 'Return,'" he mocked.

"'Fire Returns them.' So, we started burying them, and concealing the graves." He laughed again. "I overheard one group crying for their lost ones once." He smiled, as he could see the fury rise within her. "I made sure to bury them deep, too."

She stood up, and crossed to him. Her right hand, in a mail glove, clamped tightly on his throat.

"Honorable warrior," he croaked, "do it." He began to gasp, as her hand tightened. But then she released him. He struggled for breath.

"Is this all?" she demanded, kicking the chest.

He just glared.

"Stand him up," she commanded. The one behind him pulled him to his feet, and held him still as he got his feet under him. The first reached under his pillow. She pulled out a knife in a sheath.

"This is good quality," she commented, pulling the blade out. She tested the edge. "Still sharp. Only thing you've kept clean." She held the hilt out to him. "If you want to face me, then face me."

His arms were released. He rubbed his wrists, but didn't reach for the blade. "It's not fair — you bitches are young. I'm old. There's no honor in fighting an old man."

"No honor in killing children," she spat. She poked him in the chest with the hilt. "You're right — it's not fair. There's no way that I can bring all those you killed here to stab you. It's not fair that I can't bring you before a Law Master, and hear you confess all the things you did. Not fair that Sisters and Brothers still wonder where their loved ones are. Not fair that there are still Fairy graves." She shivered, and presented the hilt again. "Not fair, but it's all you deserve."

He looked from one face to the other. He could feel the breath of the third on his neck. "Then that's all I have." He took the offered hilt. "This was my father's. Fairies killed him." He stopped, as he felt a blow from behind. He looked down, and saw a blade coming out of his belly. He gasped as the third Fairy twisted it.

"Foul bastard," she whispered in his ear. "It hurts to be stabbed in the back."

The second's knife entered his chest. "Mother and Father never came home. Her medal is in your box. They're lost," she hissed.

The knife slipped from his hand. The first stood before him. "Not fair," he whispered.

"No, it's not." She eased her knife into his chest. Slowly, it slipped between his ribs. The knife in his belly twisted again. He tried to spit. The first Fairy drove her blade into his heart. A gasp, and he was still. They all stepped back, letting the body fall.

"What now?" Helm asked after a moment.

"I wish I could burn this whole place down," Shatter said, wiping her knife on the body. "But others live here. The whole town might burn."

Raven went to the chest. She pulled out another mass of chains. She found one, and pressed it to her forehead. "I hope the Goddess can grant you mercy," she whispered.

Shatter looked down at the body. She looked at Raven. "Can you carry him and the chest?"

She looked down, considering. After a moment, she nodded.

"Good. We'll take all the medals, and any other," her voice tightened, "'keepsakes' he collected."

"What will we do with him?" Helm asked.

"At dawn, in the center of the market," Shatter began.

☾ ∿ ☼

In Elen-Ford, you had to get to the market early. Let the sun get too far overhead, and the freshest items would be gone. Sometimes, there'd be nothing left.

Mothers, both with children and without, moved through the market, grabbing vegetables, and scrawny chickens and pigs. Arguments had already broken out over the most choice items. At the market's center stood a fountain. It had been dry for a long time.

A flash of silver light brought all eyes to the fountain. There was a shimmer as a Shadow Ward disappeared, revealing an old man tied to the center pillar. He was dead, and dried blood covered his front. His feet rested on a wooden chest. After a moment, a hooded Fairy appeared out of another Shadow. Her wings spread. All eyes fixed on her.

"This is a hunter," she called out, her Power driving the words to all ears. "A Human who killed Fairies for sport. He killed and buried countless victims. He killed children." She stepped back. "Human tradition calls for the dead to return to the dirt. He deserves no such honor. He gave no honor to those he killed."

Two arrows, their tips aflame, hit the body. Their fire spread quickly. A few screams could be heard from the crowd.

"Remember this," the Fairy warned, her wings beginning to beat. "Remember the fate of hunters, and other Humans who trespass against us." She took to the air. She flew over the buildings, and two more rose and followed her. Rising into the sun, they disappeared in the shimmer of a Shadow.

After the Fairies left, all eyes were drawn back to the body burning in the fountain. Smoke rose. No one moved. After a few minutes, when nothing else happened, most returned to their daily shopping. A few stayed, watching the body burn — some with anger, others with satisfaction. In the shadow of an alley, one Elenite watched covertly, his eyes shining in the flames. His fingers worried a bit of black Fairy silk as the chest caught fire, and began to pop. The secret watcher put the silk away, and covered his brown braid with a hood. Bowing, he turned and disappeared into the dark of the alley.

☾ ♒ ☼

The Fairy Embassy between Elen-Ford and Elen-Bend was small. Neither town had a large enough population to merit a full Embassy, but the cliffs of Bend, above the Diamond River, had the proper winds, and Fairies enjoyed gliding and flying from them. A large group of Feather-wings had just returned from the cliffs and hosted a large party at the Embassy. Those who were returning home had gone through the Embassy's Ring. Now, it was quiet.

Two male Leather-wing guards were stationed at the door. The one to the right cocked his head.

"I heard there was still some of that roast left in the kitchens." He turned to the other guard. "Maybe you should go and get us some."

"I'm not really hungry," his companion replied.

89

"You will be when you smell it," the first guard stressed. "Take your time. Cut me some good slices. Not too thin, but not too thick. Take your time," he emphasized again. He touched the medal hanging around his neck. "And bring me back some of the flatbread. Not too burned. Take your time."

His companion finally got the hint. "I am feeling a bit hungry now. Maybe I'll have some in the kitchen."

"No. Bring it back. Just make sure that you get the best pieces."

The second guard nodded, and left.

After a moment, the first guard Sent an all clear.

Shatter, Raven, and Helm appeared at the door. Helm gripped the arm of the guard. "Thank you, Eagle-Claw."

"Least I could do for my sister's Sisters."

"Are you sure you won't be caught?"

"The group was large, and most went through the Ring less than an hour ago. That'll mask your location enough. You should go through all together, though." He unlocked the door, and ushered them in. The Ring was guarded by a golden Ward. Eagle-Claw raised his hand, and the Ward dropped.

"Hurry," he urged. "There's a Paramount staying with the Ambassador, and he has a nose for Wards."

Shatter gripped the guard's arm. "Goddess keep you," she said.

"Goddess protect you," he replied.

Raven stood between the others and put her hands on their shoulders. They disappeared.

The guard restored the Ward, and locked the door. He re-took his position at the door. A little while later, his partner returned with a plate of roast.

As they ate, his partner told him, "The Ambassador's awake. Someone left a package at his door."

"Oh?" Eagle-Claw said, around a mouthful of bread.

"Yes. Brandywine said it was full of the medals of lost Fairies. And a note saying that they were from a Human hunter who'd had a change of heart."

"With a knife, maybe," Eagle-Claw commented.

The second guard laughed in agreement, and took another piece of meat.

(☾ ∿ ☼)

Wingless burst into the meeting room of the Three Sisters.

"This had better be good," Dina told him.

"It is. Three Fairies killed and burned an old Human hunter at the Elen town of Ford."

"Good," Tra said. "One less of those scum."

"Three Female Leather-wings," he stressed. "A bartender described one of them, who'd been asking around about the old man. She matches the Heir's soldier called Raven." He crossed his arms and waited.

Dina lit up. "Where?"

"Elen-Ford," he repeated.

"What Embassy is near there?" Tra asked, reaching for a map.

"There's one north, and another to the south. The town is too small for its own," Wingless told them, smiling.

"Get people to both," Tra commanded. "Maybe it won't be too late to Scan the Rings."

Wingless nodded.

Dina looked at him. "Well, get going. Gren isn't here, and she won't return for days."

"As you wish." Wingless bowed mockingly. "Ladies," he said, turning and leaving.

"After all these months, one of her soldiers pops up." Tra ran her fingers over the map.

"We must find her," Dina demanded. "The child might have been born. It needs to die, or at least be in our hands."

"We will find them, Sister. She made a mistake. Now we'll drive a wedge into it, and break her open."

Chapter Eight
The Waiting

"*We're through the broken tower Ring, My Lady,*" Shatter Sent to Talia through the Geode Web.

"*Thank the Goddess. Elanor is preparing the Ephemeral Ring now.*"

"*No need. We've decided to walk home.*"

Talia's concern radiated through the Web. "*Is there something wrong? Are you being pursued?*"

"*No, My Lady. What we did, took a toll we hadn't expected. We need time to reflect.*"

"*If that is what you need, Captain,*" Talia acquiesced, her disappointment and concern equally bright in her mind.

"*It is. Plus, Helm wants to try fishing with the longbows.*"

Talia laughed. "*Then you must take the time.*"

"*Is there anything we need to pick up at Realm's End?*"

Talia was silent for a moment as she considered. "*No. We have what we need for now.*"

"*Then we should be no longer than two days.*"

"*Goddess guide you,*" Talia beseeched.

"*Goddess keep you,*" Shatter replied, then broke the connection.

$$\left(\approx \dot{\varnothing} \right.$$

Tra was sitting in the dark, her black Geode in her lap. She drifted in meditation. The Geode Web vibrated. She mentally opened her eyes.

"*We have something,*" Wingless Bastard announced. His excitement buzzed over the connection like a second glass of good wine.

"*Be quick: using those knives burns me.*"

"*Pain is meant to be shared,*" he reminded her. She growled, and Sent some of the pain to him.

"*Thank you,*" he said. "*I sent men through the Ring in the north to all the destinations that had been used in the last week. All but one*" *returned.*" His smile, filled with dark glee, transmitted clearly over the Web.

"*What do you mean? They killed him on the other end?*"

"*He never got to the other end. I think he was lost between Rings. The other end was locked.*"

Tra's blood surged. "*Dark Mother,*" she whispered. "*That's it. Where?*"

"*Somewhere on the far coast. On the sea of the First.*"

"*Get people there,*" she commanded.

"*Already moving, My Lady. I'll also send letters with all the ships I can trust. We'll find them.*"

"*We have our wedge,*" she laughed. "*Go.*"

Wingless broke the connection.

☾ ∿ ☼

Honor, on watch, was the first to spot them: three forms walked up the beach. "*Captain!*" she Sent.

"*Honor! We're here,*" came Shatter's reply.

"*I'll alert the others,*" Honor said, as she broke the connection without waiting for a reply. Her glad cry was heard across the cliff settlement.

By the time Shatter, Helm, and Raven had flown up the cliff, everyone was gathered. Talia didn't know what to expect, so she told the others not to rush in with an exuberant homecoming greeting.

Her worry was confirmed when she saw the party's faces as they crested the cliff. All three were worn and tired. Talia put a hand each on Min and Nidilis, to stop them from rushing their soldiers. "Give them a moment," she whispered.

Shatter stopped a few feet from the group. Raven and Helm stood behind her. A rod of driftwood lay over Helm's shoulder. Several fish were stuck to it.

"We're back, My Lady," Shatter announced.

"Welcome back, Captain," Talia said formally. "Did you close the circle?"

Shatter looked at both her soldiers. They nodded. "We did, My Lady."

Min could contain herself no longer, and broke from Talia's grip, flinging herself into Raven's waiting arms. "I missed you," she told her soldier, gripping her tight.

"I missed you, too, My Lady," Raven replied through teary eyes. She stroked Min's hair. "I was worried about you."

Min broke out of her embrace. "Worried about me?" She poked Raven in the chest. "You were the one out hunting. I was worried about you. What did you have to worry about?"

"That you would stay up too late reading, and forget to eat."

Min tried to hit her again, but folded her in another hug at the last moment.

"Nothing for me?" Helm asked plaintively, holding up the fish. "I even brought dinner."

Nidilis embraced her even harder, and took Helm to the sand, sending the fish rolling away. Nesa, Rogue, and the two red kittens pounced on them. Quicksilver stayed on Flora's shoulder until Flora embraced Shatter, then jumped off to join her family with the fish.

"Captain, you mustn't do anything like this again," Flora scolded Shatter from the embrace. She pulled away, and gestured back to Talia. "It isn't good for the child."

"You know I had to go, Mum," Shatter told her, pulling her back into a hug. "But I'm glad I'm back." She looked at Talia over Flora's shoulder. "You've gotten bigger," she observed.

"Is that any way to talk to a lady?" Talia said, moving deliberately across the sand. Her belly was larger. She joined the hug with Flora. "Thank the Goddess you're safe," she told Shatter. A kick from the child signaled her agreement.

"My," Shatter reacted, feeling the kick. "She really is growing."

"And keeping her mother up." Flora pulled away, getting back to business. "We didn't know when to expect you, but there's stew simmering."

"I welcome it," Shatter said. She didn't let go of Talia.

"So, you found him," Talia both asked and stated.

"We did," Shatter confirmed, closing her eyes. "She was right: vengeance is a sword without a hilt. I thought I would feel different, but I don't. My brother's still dead. And I'm still here."

"Right where you should be," Talia reminded her, before wiping her eyes, and pulling away. "Greet the others. We'll talk later."

"Yes, My Lady," Shatter agreed, turning to meet a greeting from Steel, whose hard grip of Shatter's arm turned into a rough embrace.

"Captain," Steel told her with conviction, "next time, you can stay here."

"Agreed," Shatter said, thumping her Lieutenant on the back.

Behind them, Helm freed herself from Nidilis and sat up, but was then tackled by the other Twin. Their struggles stirred up the dust. Min wouldn't let Raven go. She only allowed her other arm to embrace the others.

Harpoon and Talon descended on the Twins, pulling them off, and playfully tossing them aside. Helm got to her knees before Goldberry and Nova took her down again in a tumble of arms and wings.

Steel and Shatter watched for a while, the other soldiers brushing by their commander to grip her arm. Shatter nodded to each. She finally looked at Steel, who took the hint.

"Enough, Ladies," she commanded. "Back to work. I want those walls done today."

Shatter looked at Talia with one eyebrow raised.

"Steel put up some walls for me, and a door," Talia said with pride. "Cut my area in half for the nursery."

"Good. You didn't just sit around while I was gone."

"No, Steel worked us hard." Talia took Shatter's arm. "Let me show you." She took her Captain toward the house, while Steel herded the others toward the Ladies' cabin.

"Mine!" Silidin called toward the cats. "Get away from those fish!"

A few weeks later, Talia stumbled out of her room to rouse Flora before sunrise.

"Something's wrong," she said, panic in her voice, and etched on her face. She clutched her belly. "She won't stop moving."

"Mistress, back to bed." Flora led her back, outwardly projecting calm, while desperately Sending to Shield as she did so. Stumbling out of her bed, Shield was at Flora's side in a few moments.

"Lie down," Flora guided Talia, then pressed her charge to the bed. Shield appeared, and put her hands on Talia's belly. Behind her, Shatter appeared at the door. Flora looked up at her.

"Start water, and brew the tea from the red bottle," Flora instructed. Shatter nodded, and pulled the door closed.

"What's wrong?" Talia asked. She grabbed at Flora's hand. "Tell me."

"She's upset," Shield replied. "She's twisting in the womb. We must calm her, or she'll hurt herself."

"Did you have a dream?" Flora asked. She joined hands with Shield. Together they Looked into Talia's womb. The child's distress was evident. She twisted and shook. Flora reached into her forming mind.

"I dreamed of the plantation, and the Blood Ring," Talia told them, her voice low with fear. "It was calling to me, pulling at me."

"Shatter! Tea!" Flora called.

"You must be calm," Shield soothed Talia. "Breathe." She pulled her hand away from Flora, and laid it on Talia's chest. "With me: breathe in." Talia did as instructed. "Breathe out." Talia obeyed.

"We need to wrap her in calm," Flora told Shield. "Good, Mistress. Calm."

Shatter came running through the door, and pressed a steaming cup into Talia's hand. "Drink."

Talia did.

Flora and Shield began to wrap a calming cloud around the child. She settled down, and stopped twisting, but she didn't quiet completely.

Flora and Shield looked at each other. *"Something's wrong. Talia's dreams shouldn't affect the child that way,"* Flora commented with concern.

"Outside influence?" Shield asked.

"I don't know." Flora looked to Shatter. "Gather the Ladies. We need a Ward over this house."

Shatter took one quick look at Talia and disappeared out the door.

"We need something stronger," Flora said. "I don't have it."

"What do you need?"

"Ground silverweed. Hopefully, the trading post has it."

Steel appeared at the door. "Can I help?"

"Get Willow and Honor. I need them to fly to Realm's End," Flora responded.

"She's not the fastest flyer," Steel reminded Flora.

"But she's good at finding things. If the trading post doesn't have what I need, she'll have to find it wild," Flora explained. "Go."

Steel turned and bolted.

Flora looked down at Talia. The tea had taken effect, and her eyelids drooped.

"Mistress, everything will be fine," Flora comforted her charge. Talia smiled dimly.

☾ ∭ ☼

Outside, Elanor led the Ladies in a Circle to raise a Ward over the house. She gestured, raising her arms from the north to the south, then turning and gesturing from east to west. Elanor anchored the Ward to the ground and then, with the aid of the Circle, poured energy into it. It flared with Silverfire, then settled into a shimmer. Elanor took a deep breath.

"Min, stay here. Make sure the Ward stays powered. I'll go inside." She turned, and almost ran into Steel.

"Willow, Honor," Steel called, "Flora needs you inside."

They followed Elanor and Steel in. Flora and Shield both had their hands on Talia's belly. Willow felt her heart fall. Talia was pale, and her eyes were moving rapidly under her lids.

Flora turned. "I need you and Honor to fly to Realm's End. I need ground silverweed. Do you know it?"

Willow nodded. "What about the Ephemeral Rings?" she asked.

"I already tried," Shield replied. "Something's interfering with them."

Shatter frowned at the implication, but Flora continued.

"Good. If they don't have it, you must find it wild. Fly swiftly. Send to me when you find it." Flora turned back to Talia. Willow stared at the Heir.

"Let's go," Shatter urged, chivvying them out the door. "Keep to the coast. Use the wind." She passed each a vial. "Use this if you need to."

Honor nodded.

"Stay safe, and fly with the Goddess," Shatter beseeched. Steel handed them their sword belts. Willow and Honor ran to the cliff edge, where they launched themselves, and took to the air.

☾ ∿ ☼

"I said, I need ground silverweed. Do you have it?" Willow demanded.

"Strong stuff. Especially for a little thing like you. What do you need it for?" the Feather-wing shopkeeper asked.

"I don't have time to flirt," Willow informed him. "Do you have it?" she asked again, with dark intensity.

His eyes narrowed. He put his hand on hers. "You don't have a Leather-wing at your shoulder this time, so you can't make demands of me. But," a leering smile cut his face, "if you. . . ."

He didn't get a chance to finish. Willow jerked her right hand from under his as she used her left to slam down her forked knife, trapping him at the wrist. He tried to pull away, but she twisted the knife, so the blades threatened to cut his skin.

"She may not be here today, but I remember what she taught me." She stared into his eyes: a mixture of anger and fear stared back. "Help me, or don't. Choose swiftly," she told him simply. She put her other hand on the hilt, and pressed the knife further into the wood.

"All right. I have it." He gave up. "It's in a locked chest. It's used to calm blackflower addicts." He wiggled his hand. "Let me go, and I'll

98

get it." The unspoken curse was visible in his eyes, but not on his lips, as he (wisely) wished to avoid losing a hand.

Willow waited a breath, then pulled the knife out. The shopkeeper rubbed his hand, and ducked through the door behind him. Willow looked around. Honor was leaning against the outside door, holding it closed. She smiled, and tapped her own knife. Willow thrust hers back into its sheath with a snap.

The shopkeeper returned. He held up a vial. "This is all I can sell." He held it out for Willow to examine. "It'll cost you twenty."

"You'll take ten," Willow countered, holding out the coins. "Fee for your disregard."

"Yes, My Lady," he agreed, putting the vial in her hand, and taking the coins. He closed his fist over them with a contemptuous motion.

"Thank you," she said primly, and left. Honor gave the shopkeeper a look, then followed Willow out.

The shopkeeper moved to throw the coins after them, but thought better of it, and slipped them into his pocket instead. Then he pulled a folded piece of paper out from under the counter. He hesitated, but then his hurt pride got the better of him, and he opened the paper and began to write.

☾ ∿ ☼

They flew through the night, with the moon and their Sight leading the way. Willow focused on 'forward.' She ignored the aches in her wings and arms, the pain in her head, and her labored breathing. Her vision narrowed till all she was following was the glow of Honor's aura ahead of her. Each stroke of her wings brought more pain. Her Healing couldn't keep up. The world winked out.

She came to, wet, and covered in sand. Honor was collapsed beside her, also covered in sand. Her breathing was hard, but steady. Willow began to cough, spitting up some saltwater. She reached into her small pack, and pulled out her water bottle. A few swallows brought the coughing under control.

"You fell into the sea," Honor said faintly beside her. "I heard the splash, but couldn't find you. Then I saw your wings. Pulled you up the beach." Willow passed her the water. Honor took a few sips.

"Thank you," Willow told her earnestly. She pushed back the wet hair that had come free from her braid. "I need to rest."

"Only for a short time," Honor said, flopping back on the sand. "Moon is getting low. Sunrise will be in a few hours. We need to get this back to Talia."

Willow nodded, too tired to speak. She tried not to close her eyes.

"Wake up!" Honor was yelling at her, pulling her into a sitting position.

"I. . . ." She shook her wings. They were wet, and full of sand, and felt like rocks on her back. "I'm trying."

"Try harder." Honor jerked Willow to her feet. "Shake your wings." Willow tried, but more coughing doubled her over.

"Here," Honor said, kneeling before her charge. She held the vial Shatter had given her. She uncapped it. "Just two drops on your tongue."

Wake hit her like the sun suddenly rising directly in front of her. Willow stood straight, and shook out her wings, flinging sand and water all over, but mostly on Honor. Honor brushed the water off her face and took two drops of Wake for herself. Her wings unfurled.

"This energy won't last. Use all of it that you can to Heal and keep your wings going."

Willow's head buzzed, and all she could do was nod.

Honor saw the danger, but they had no choice. "Stay right behind me. I can keep you in my thoughts. Focus on flying."

Willow managed to speak around a tongue that was suddenly too big: "And not falling into the sea again."

"Just so." Honor clapped her on the shoulder. "Now, let's fly, Sister." They took off running, wings grasping at the air. They flew on, under the setting moon.

Chapter Nine
The Conflict

Spear was on the sunrise watch. She scanned the beach below, and the sky in front of her. Behind her, the Ward over Talia's house shimmered. Spear couldn't bear being inside, and had volunteered for watch. The tension and fear that gripped the cliffs were like a bad mushroom in her mouth.

Talia was in and out of consciousness. Flora and Shield fought to keep the child calm. What was disturbing her, neither had the energy to speculate. Shatter sent groups to patrol the woods to allow them a wide berth around Talia's troubles. Besides, she rationalized, it was possible that maybe something or someone was nearby, and attacking the child. Elanor, Min, and Goldberry threw all their knowledge into the Ward. They tried every frequency and nuance of the Weave. Nothing seemed to help.

"Maybe we should take her back to the Exile Queen's mountain," Steel suggested.

"She cannot be moved," Flora declared. "It might make it worse."

"But what's causing this?"

"I don't know," Flora snapped. "And if you have nothing better to offer, go."

Steel swallowed a retort, and left.

Spear picked through the pile of stones she had gathered around herself as she sat and found a smooth one. She threw it — with all her strength — off the cliff, and toward the sea.

"Goddess," she pleaded, "help us."

"*I'm not the Goddess, but I can help,*" Honor Sent.

"*Honor!*" Spear called out, standing. "*I can't see you.*"

"*I'm at the base of the cliff. We can't fly up. Willow has passed out. We have the silverweed.*"

Spear Sent back to the camp. She didn't wait for a reply, but stepped to the edge of the drop-off and plummeted down the cliff face. She knew just how long she had, and opened her wings to hit the ground softly. Spear opened her Sight, and could See Honor sitting on a sand dune further up the beach, with Willow lying at her feet. Spear ran through the sand, slipping and sliding.

Honor held out the vial as Spear got close. Spear was torn: she wanted to take the vial back, but didn't want to leave her Sister.

Harpoon, dropping like a stone, hit the sand and rolled, not far from them. "Go!" she shouted. "I'll tend to them."

Spear took the vial. Honor smiled, then passed out. Spear turned, and used her Power to push herself off the ground and up the cliff. Goldberry and Nova met her at the top.

"Flora says just a few grains in hot water," Goldberry relayed, running beside Spear back to the main house. Spear yanked the door open. The Twins greeted her. Silidin held a steaming cup. Nidilis took the vial from Spear's hands before she could drop it. She poured a few grains into the cup, and the Twins headed to Talia's bedroom together.

Flora met them, holding out her hands for both the cup and the vial. She smelled both, then nodded in approval and went to Talia.

"Drink this, Mistress," she urged, as Shield raised Talia up. Talia did as directed, then collapsed back on the bed. Flora turned to Goldberry: "A few grains in your ointment." Goldberry took the vial, and left.

Flora and Shield put their hands on Talia's belly, and plunged back into a Circle. The Twins and Spear moved out of the bedroom, and toward the door. Shatter was waiting there.

"How are Willow and Honor?" Flora asked Shatter.

"Harpoon and Gil are setting up a tent for them. They should be fine. Just exhausted," Shatter reported.

Spear returned to her spot on the cliff. She watched the sun rise, and thanked the Goddess.

☾ ⌇ ☼

"Are you ready?" Wingless Bastard asked. "The sun will set soon. The last bloodletting is needed to activate the Blood Ring."

"I am," Bastile said, rubbing his bandaged wrists. "Which do you need?"

Wingless smiled, but it was both cruel and apologetic. "No. From your manhood."

Bastile narrowed his eyes at the Fairy. "What do you mean?"

"Just the tip, and just a drop. You'll hardly feel it."

Bastile looked long and hard at Wingless. "Why do you do this? You're a Fairy. Why do you hate them so?"

"You delay," Wingless snarled. "If we miss this sunset, it'll be months before the right conditions come again. You cannot wait for the Power of this Ring. It will allow my people to make more blacksilk blades. Arrow tips. Everything you need to win the coming conflict."

"A conflict you started," Bastile commented.

"You wouldn't be where you are without me," Wingless reminded him. "I can withdraw my support. I can leave. But what would happen to you then? If you don't have the stomach for all that must be done, there are others who do. I can support them. They would be glad for all that I bring."

"They would put their prick on the table for you?"

"In a heartbeat. Or the prick of their brother." Wingless stopped. "But I prefer working with you. You understand. But if you've lost your nerve. . . ."

"I haven't," Bastile declared with conviction. "Just answer my questions."

"This is a conversation we should have had when we started this partnership." Wingless smiled cruelly. "This is like asking the whore if she's clean after you pull out." He looked into Bastile's eyes, and saw the anger filling them. "But I will answer one question."

Bastile wanted to stab the bastard. But Wingless was right: he was in too deep. He had given too much. Sacrificed too much. "You choose."

"You give me that power, hmmm?" Wingless smiled. "Well, they cut off my wings. They didn't know that what they gave me by doing so was more than they took away, of course." He folded his arms over his chest. "There. Now, the sun is near. Will you piss on this, or will you become a King?"

Bastile looked at him with new understanding. "They only do that to those who commit crimes. Crimes not punishable by death." He tilted his head. "What was it?"

"I answered a question. For more, you'll need to give more of yourself." He looked the Human up and down. "Are you prepared for that?"

Bastile couldn't help but shiver at the cold, unfeeling look in Wingless Bastard's eyes. He found the Fairy's adopted name to be supremely fitting. "Let's get it over with."

Wingless smiled, showing his rotting teeth. "This way, My King." He led Bastile through a door, and down, down to where the corrupted Song echoed.

(∭ ☼

Goldberry sat up in bed with determination on her face. The sun was high in the sky. She walked with purpose to Talia's room, where she found Flora and Shield asleep on the floor. Min and Elanor sat on either side of Talia, their hands on her belly. Nesa sat purring at the Heir's feet.

"We've been thinking of this all wrong," Goldberry announced.

"What do you mean?" Elanor asked.

"We've been trying to put more Power, more strength, into the Ward over us. And that hasn't helped." She gestured to the fitfully sleeping Talia. "The child is still in peril."

"What do you suggest?" Min asked, raising her head. She had dark circles under her eyes, and fatigue colored her face.

"What if this is an attack that's focused on the child? On her aura?"

"Talia's personal Wards would keep it out," Elanor argued. "And the child's aura is in harmony with the mother. It stays that way until right before birth. It protects the child."

"For Fairy children," Goldberry stressed. "But this child is half Human. What if she's out of harmony with Talia's aura? That would allow an attack in."

"It would have to be very focused," Min pondered. "They would have to have something of the child. But that's impossible. She's still inside Talia."

Elanor sat up straighter. "But they do have something of her: her father's blood."

"Goddess curse that bastard," Min swore. "His blood might allow an attack that no Ward can deflect."

"Unless we know the exact harmony of her aura. Then we could keep them out," Goldberry said, hoping.

"That's a large leap," Flora commented from the floor.

"Mum," Goldberry said, embarrassed. "I didn't mean to wake you."

"Well, you did." She sat up. Quicksilver jumped away. "I don't know everything that you Ladies do, but this fits with what's been baffling me."

"What's that, Mum?" Elanor asked.

"The child was in distress after Talia's dream. At night," she stressed. "Then again, the next night, around sunset. If we hadn't all been here, keeping the child calm with all our strength, we might have lost her. And she settled down with the sun." She looked to the sky. "And the sun will be setting soon. If this is Blood Magic, it will come with the dark." She stood up.

"So, we need the child's aura?" Min said. "We can just Look into her, then." She gestured at Talia. "Simple."

"No," Elanor contradicted. "Talia's out, but her defenses are strong. As strong as she could make them. We'll have to get around them to See the child."

Flora moved to Talia's head and put her hand on Talia's forehead. "Mistress," she whispered, "we need you to drop your Wards. Just for a moment."

"No," Talia muttered. "No. Danger. Must keep her safe."

"Mistress," Flora stressed, and stretched out her Power. "It's Flora. I need you to let me in."

"No!" Talia Pushed back. She was still unconscious, but her mind reacted strongly. Flora was pushed away, both mentally and physically. Flora shook her head.

"I was afraid of that. The silverweed keeps her calm, but disconnected. She won't be able to drop her Wards." Flora folded her hands together. "I have an herb that will drop her Wards, but only for a short time." She left the room.

"So, I'll have to work fast: get in, find the child's aura, and get out," Goldberry planned.

"If you're still in her mind when the Wards snap back . . .," Elanor warned.

"I'll be mindlost. I know," Goldberry finished. "The Keepers care for the mindlost. I know what can happen."

"I'll do it," Min offered.

"No. It should fall to me: this is my idea," Goldberry protested.

Flora returned, a bottle in her hand. "Goldberry's right: it should be her."

Goldberry nodded.

"And we don't have time to fight over it," Flora finished. "Once I give her the herb, you'll have to hurry."

Goldberry sat down, and put her hands on Talia's belly. Flora opened the bottle, and put a flake of its contents on Talia's tongue. Goldberry opened her Sight, and waited. She Watched the Wards fall away, and she plunged in, like a diver entering rough water. There was only darkness: she summoned a Light, but the darkness snuffed it out.

"Goddess guide me." Goldberry reached within herself. "Mother of Waves, I need your light." A blue-green light appeared in her hand, then darted off. Goldberry followed it. Darting around mountains, and pits of dark water, the light led her on. Finally, between the peaks of two sharp mountains, she approached another light. The closer Goldberry got, the brighter it became, till she could only walk forward blindly. She felt a small hand in hers.

"Aunt," a voice addressed her, "why are you here? It's not time yet."

"I need to see your aura," Goldberry replied.

"Aunt, you know it."

"I don't. You're only potential. I can't see it."

"You can. Now go — Mother is coming."

Goldberry felt a Push, and the light vanished. She felt the Wards close, and she felt her mental hem catch in the door. Goldberry opened her eyes.

"Well?" Elanor asked.

"I. . . ." Goldberry stopped. She felt only confusion. How could she already know the child's aura? "Goddess, I cannot see." She fell to her knees. "Mother, help me see." The blue-green light danced in her Goddess Sight. It zipped around the point of a thorn, then struck the point and flared.

Goldberry sat up. She grabbed Elanor's hand. "I know."

"Do we need to alter the Ward over the house?" Elanor asked.

"No, it must be on her skin," Goldberry told her. She took the blue-green light in her hands and expanded it out till a globe of shimmering light enclosed Talia. Goldberry felt the dark fingers of a hand jerk back. A cry of frustration and anger smote her mind's ears. Goldberry held on, Weaving the Ward. She desperately searched for something to anchor the Weave into. The only thing she could find was the single remaining silver button on Talia's shirt. With her last ounce of strength, she anchored the Ward into the metal, and the cry faded away.

☾ ∭ ☼

Goldberry woke to pale sunlight and the calls of the sea birds. She was in her bed, with a blanket over her. Her head pounded with a dull ache. She felt someone's hand on her left arm. She turned in that direction.

"Good morning, hero of my child," Talia greeted her. She was in a chair, with blankets over her legs and across her shoulders. Despite her bright greeting, there was a deep tiredness in her still-slightly-glassy eyes. Talia passed Goldberry a cup of water, and helped her sit up to drink it.

Afterward, Goldberry collapsed back onto the bed. Her head began to pound.

"Here," Talia said, putting both her hands on Goldberry's arm. "I can't do much yet, but I can Heal."

107

Warmth spread throughout Goldberry's body. She sighed as the pain went away and turned her head back to Talia.

"How is she?" Goldberry asked.

Talia tightened her blankets over herself before responding. "She's fine, according to Flora. Once your Ward was up, she settled down. I think she's still asleep." She touched her belly. "I cannot thank you enough."

"It was my duty, My Lady, and my responsibility," Goldberry replied humbly.

"It was more than that," Talia replied. "You saved both of us. I will not forget this."

Goldberry could only bow her head.

Talia fingered a bundle in her lap. "The one bad thing is that now I must keep this shirt." She held it up: the color was gone, and the fabric was worn from too many washes on the rocks. Goldberry could see the shine of her Ward on the last button. "Goddess shows her sense of humor in the fact that this was the only thing I had with me that he made. Everything else, I left behind."

"We only need the button," Goldberry put in. "We can craft it into something she can wear."

"Yes. That's a good idea." She folded the shirt back into her lap. Her voice became dark. "Again, I have misjudged him. To strike at his own child." Her fist clenched. "This will not be forgotten."

Goldberry quickly tried to divert Talia's anger. "He might not have been a willing participant. Only his blood would have been needed."

"I do not see Prince Bastard giving up this blood involuntarily."

"Unless he was dead," Goldberry suggested.

Talia only shrugged.

"Where are the others?" Goldberry asked, looking around.

"Sleeping, or outside." Talia gestured to the corner. "Flora and Shield practically collapsed after the child was out of danger. Elanor was sitting with you when I woke. I sent her off to sleep." She patted Goldberry's arm. "You should sleep, too."

"Yes, My Lady, but first, what do you remember?"

Talia considered. "Not much. I was in the dark, running. Hiding. Then a blue-green light appeared, and the darkness went away. And

I could finally stop running." She made the Sign of the Three. "Now, sleep. I'll sit beside you."

Goldberry wanted to say more, but sleep called to her, and she could not resist.

Chapter Ten
A Family by the Sea

Things settled back down to a simple rhythm: mornings were for practicing the Patterns, led by Shatter or Steel, then weapons training; afterward, the designated hunting, foraging, and fishing parties set out, while others worked on building, or repairs to the house and cabins; after a mid-day meal, Talia, Min, or Elanor led exercises with their Power, or, if more hands were needed for work on the buildings, they moved there; then, as the hunting, fishing, and foraging groups returned, a sunset meal was made and served.

As the child grew, Talia became unable to participate as much as she wanted in the work of the compound. Steel was able to pull from her huge store of martial knowledge to show Talia specific Patterns for pregnant Fairies, though.

"We mustn't lose our edge, even when we're having children. These motions adapt as your body changes," Steel explained to Talia. "My wives did them up until they gave birth."

Talia wasn't sure she could do them, as her belly grew, but Steel and Flora wouldn't be denied, so she did them every morning, always under the watchful eyes of at least one of the two.

Her Magic was undampened, and became even stronger as her pregnancy advanced.

"It's like I can pull from her potential," Talia mused to Elanor one afternoon.

"Will that hurt the child, or limit her, steal her Magic?" Elanor worried.

"No. I had the same question, and Flora and Goldberry reassured me that it won't hurt her. It's her potential, not what she will have. Right now, she has almost limitless potential, and I can borrow that." Talia smiled. "But not too much."

Together, the Ladies worked to strengthen the armor and ringmail of The Nine. Then, they turned their attention to their own mail. Min became obsessed with defenses against the black blades of the Blood Cult. She used all the information she had taken from the destruction of the knives to create countermeasures. Though she was unable to test what she did, Min still had faith that what she Wove into the ringmail would protect them from the black blades.

"They were full of darkness, fear, and despair. I've incorporated light and hope into the Weave to counteract them," Min explained.

Goldberry poured her own link to the hope of the Goddess into each suit as well. Each time she sat, as the sun rose, a suit in her lap, she felt her link to this odd band of exiled Fairies become stronger. Tears came every time she worked with a suit.

Nesa and her kittens, who were almost fully grown, were always around. The two reds followed the Twins everywhere. Rogue and Quicksilver hunted alongside Harpoon, and fished with Talon. Rogue curled up with Min as she Wove Protection Spells, and batted at the dangling ringmail arms. Flora shooed Quicksilver away from her food all the time, but couldn't go to sleep if Quicksilver weren't curled up at her feet. During the day, Nesa was Talia's shadow, unless she was sitting guard with Shatter, or hunting with Raven. At night, she moved from bed to bed, in her own pattern, dividing the darkest hours between the eight Ladies. She always seemed to be in Goldberry's bed during the new and full moons.

$$\left(\text{☽} \text{⋙} \text{☼} \right)$$

Talia woke to the sound of wooden swords hitting ringmail and other makeshift swords. She rolled over, and saw that the sun was up.

Swinging herself out of bed with effort, she called out, "Flora, I've missed the morning training. Why'd you let me sleep?"

Silence.

Talia could hear voices, but not in the house. "Did you forget about me?" she asked the emptiness. Not even the cats were about.

The outer room was empty, too. The oven was banked, and cool. Shaking her head, she headed for the door.

Outside, she followed the sound of voices and sparring. Between the cabins and the cliff edge, the Ladies and The Nine stood in a circle around the combatants. Talia had to get closer before she could determine who was fighting. As she stepped up behind Flora, Elanor, and Min, she figured out it was the Twins, sparring with Harpoon and

Helm. All four were dressed — from shoulders to ankles — in ringmail, and wore helms. The Twins each wielded two wooden shortswords, and the soldiers each had a long sword and a dagger. Talia watched the Twins whirl and dodge around the slower soldiers. They moved as one, striking both high and low on Harpoon. She fell, but Helm moved in, pushing the Twins away with a flurry of blows to give Harpoon time to rise.

"Hold!" Steel called. The four fighters stopped. "Silidin's blades are beginning to crack. Five minutes."

Talia stepped up behind Flora. "Why didn't you wake me?" she asked.

Flora turned, and laughed the most honest laugh Talia had heard from her since they'd left the palace. Elanor turned, grinning.

"I told you," she said to Min. "Pay up." She held out her hand.

With a sigh, Min unclipped a throwing knife from her belt and slapped it into Elanor's hand. Drawn by the sound, Raven turned.

"Hey," she said. "I gave that to you."

"Well, you'll have to give me another one," Min pouted. "You have so many."

"You'll have to earn this one, Sister," Raven retorted.

Min smiled. "That's how I get all my gifts."

Talia looked at Elanor, the question clear in her expression.

"I said you would forget that this is the full moon of your birth moon," she explained, clipping the knife to her belt.

Flora burst out laughing at the look on Talia's face. "I'm sorry, Mistress," she said after a moment. "They made me promise not to remind you."

Talia put her hands on her hips and glared at them. "I didn't forget," she said. "I just didn't know it was tonight."

"You forgot," Elanor countered with a smile, and kissed her cheek. "We were in the wilderness last year. You made me promise. We couldn't make your spice cake."

"And I don't smell it," Talia said, with a pointed look at Flora.

"I went back to the ruins Ring," she said with a smile. "Min made me. She didn't want you to be reminded by the smell."

"You're a sneaky court cat," Talia hissed at Min.

Min gave a cheeky bow.

"Hush," Raven interjected, "they're starting again."

Talia shouldered her way into the circle, pushing Min into Raven. Raven responded by stepping back and putting her arms on the shorter Min's shoulders. "Now stay still, loser," she whispered.

Min responded by elbowing her in the stomach.

Willow glared at them both.

"Children," Flora said. "Our Sisters are fighting. Pay attention."

Silidin's weapons had been replaced. Steel stepped back. The two pairs of combatants bowed to each other.

"Fight!" Steel called, as she quickly scrambled back from the fighting area.

The Twins exploded into motion. Talia opened her Sight. She could See that they were using their Power to accelerate their speed and reaction times. This was a dangerous thing to do when fighting with a partner, but since the Twins were linked in a way that only they understood, they fought as one Fairy.

Harpoon and Helm moved back to back and did their best to defend themselves. Talia could only See where the Twins were based on where the soldiers' blades went, and how they were hit.

There was a clang as the soldiers took simultaneous blows to the head, knocking their helms together. Then something passed between them, and they were moving too fast to be seen. The center of the ring became a blur of motion and silver.

Talia felt Shatter and Steel's anxiety rise, and she was a moment from calling a halt when the Twins materialized on the ground with the clatter of wood on ringmail. Helm and Harpoon stood over them, wooden blades held to their chests. Holding up their broken swords, the Twins called out, "Yield!" together.

Helm and Harpoon were smiling, and about to help the Twins up, when a streak of red struck the two soldiers in the chest. Seizing the advantage, the Twins knocked their legs out from underneath them, and were up and on top of them in an instant. Helm and Harpoon looked up into the smiling faces of the Twins and the growling jaws of the red sea cats.

"Unfair," Helm called out.

"Yield," Harpoon laughed.

"What did you teach us . . .," Silidin began, climbing off Harpoon and grabbing her cat.

"About not fighting fair?" Nidilis finished, pushing her cat off, and helping Helm up.

"You learn too well," Harpoon laughed, rubbing the ears of the cat on Silidin's shoulder. "But you yielded first, and they cheated."

"Who was on their back last?" the Twins taunted, as they took off running toward the cliff. They shed their ringmail, and glided out into the air. Helm and Harpoon followed, skimming the water with them.

"I guess we're flying today," Elanor said with resignation, joining them.

Talia watched as the others took to the air. She and Flora walked to the edge of the cliff. The two red sea cats were tussling around in the Twin's ringmail, sniffing at it, and batting it around. Talia smiled as she watched her family dive and glide through the sea air. She wanted to join them, but the child put too much weight in the wrong place for her wings to carry her safely.

Flora jingled the ringmail, urging the cats to keep playing. Out of nowhere, Rogue and Quicksilver appeared, and a sea cat wrestling match started over and around the ringmail. Flora stepped back, avoiding the whipping tails. She laughed.

Talia looked down, and Nesa was sitting on her foot. "Little Sister," she said, "our children are having fun."

"Meow," Nesa replied, and flopped over to allow Talia to pet her belly.

With the help of her wings, her Power, determination, and Flora, Talia was able to sit down. Nesa jumped into her lap, and began to groom. Talia petted her absently, listening to her purr, and the sounds of Fairy wings and crashing waves. The day progressed, and Talia began to doze in the sun. The wind in the tree whispered soothing sounds. Flora was fully asleep beside her, her wings spread out and serving as kitten beds.

Elanor flew up, and landed on the edge of the cliff. She shook herself, spraying the resting members of the party with water. Talia started, dislodging Nesa. Flora sat up, sending the kittens skittering.

"Elanor," she scolded. "I was having such a nice dream. You were babies again, and you were nestled in my arms."

"Sorry, Mum," Elanor apologized. "I didn't mean to wake you. I was trying to wake the sleepy mother here."

"I was dreaming, too," Talia said. She brushed at the kittens, who — now that nap time was over — were attacking her feet and wings. "I was in the Garden. No one was around. I was at peace."

Elanor flicked drops from her wet hair at Talia. "Come join us."

"You look like one of the First," Flora observed. "Hey, give me that!" she yelled, realizing Quicksilver had managed to free a pouch of herbs from her belt, and was now carrying it off. She scrambled up and gave chase. The reds and Rogue soon followed.

Talia looked back at Elanor. She did look like one of the First Fairies: her red hair hung wet and loose around her. Her clothes were almost sheer from the water. Her wings waved languidly.

Elanor saw the look in her eyes, and raised her eyebrows. "Come swim with me?" she asked seductively.

"No," Talia laughed. "It took too much effort to sit down." She gestured to her belly. "I can't do the swimming we used to do, anyway."

Elanor settled to the ground, and folded her arms over her chest. She suggested a compromise. "Then we can float. You used to love that, too."

"I did," Talia agreed. She pushed down her own surge of passion. "I'd like that. You'll have to help me up, though." She held out her arms.

Elanor smiled, and stood. She grabbed Talia's hands, and levered her up. Talia laughed, and stumbled into her arms. Elanor joined in Talia's laughter, and gripped her tightly until she was stable.

"I deserve a kiss for that," Elanor whispered.

"You do," Talia agreed, and kissed her. They held the kiss for a long time. The kicking of her child finally made Talia pull away.

Elanor pushed her hair back to cover her desire to kiss Talia again.

"Now, you promised floating," Talia reminded her, covering her own emotions with humor. "I'll need more than you to get down the cliff."

"Yes, My Lady," Elanor said, turning and Sending for aid.

With Willow and Gil's help, Talia half flew and half floated down to the beach. Soon, she was bobbing out beyond the breakers. With Elanor at her side, she spread her arms and legs out, and floated on the water. The motion of the waves soothed her. She felt all her worries drift away.

Elanor was floating at her side, arms over her belly. "Talia," she said after a while.

"Yes?" Talia replied, breaking out of her meditation.

"I love you."

"I love you, too."

"Talia."

"Yes."

"It's getting cold."

"I want to see the moon rise."

"We can do that from the cliff. Wrapped in blankets."

"It's my full moon. I'm the Heir." She glanced at Elanor. "Here, snuggle close." She pulled Elanor closer, and warmed them both with her Power. They bobbed in the water for a while.

Soon, the moon rose over the sea. Talia watched its reflection, shining like a silver line in the water. She kissed Elanor on the side of her head.

Elanor squeezed her in response.

"Talia, this is really nice and peaceful," Elanor commented soon after, "but I'm getting tired." She stopped for a moment. "And there should be spice cake back at the house," she offered enticingly.

Talia let go of Elanor, and began swimming back to the shore. Elanor dipped under the water, unready for Talia to let her go, despite her words. Spluttering, she reached the surface, and followed Talia toward the beach. Flora appeared there, and began calling to them. Above, on the cliff, the Ladies and The Nine were gathering for the song to the rising moon.

Chapter Eleven
On the Full Moon

Shatter crouched in the underbrush. She held her short bow in her hand, strung, with an arrow at the string. Gil crouched beside her. She held a long spear with a cross piece not far down the haft from the head.

"*Where is he?*" Shatter Sent.

"*In that direction,*" Gil indicated.

Shatter strained her hearing and her Sight.

"*I don't sense anything.*"

"*He's there,*" Gil assured her. "*I can feel him in the underbrush. Maybe a couple hundred yards out.*" She paused. "*This isn't the best use of my gift. Might even be counter to why the Goddess gave it to me.*"

"*He's been digging up Flora's garden,*" Shatter Sent. "*The Goddess will forgive us. She might not.*"

Gil's Send was full of 'that isn't funny.'

Shatter sighed. "*I understand, but he's dangerous. We need to get him away from this area. If you can convince him to move on, I won't have to kill him.*"

"*I'll try.*" Something brushed by Gil's leg. She looked down to see Nesa crouched at her side. "*Do you see him, Little Sister?*" she Sent. She still wasn't sure the cats understood her Sends, but she didn't want to speak out loud.

Nesa whipped her tail once, and then curled it tight. She was preparing to pounce, Gil knew. She Sent to Shatter. "*She senses him, too. There's a clearing close by. Let's move up to the edge. I'll see if I can lure him into it.*"

Shatter Sent agreement.

Slowly, they began to move. Even without the benefit of Shadow or Silence Wards, Shatter moved easily through the underbrush. Nesa followed just as easily. Gil followed in Shatter's footsteps, as she'd been taught. Her sense reached out into the woods. They were beyond the perimeter of the compound's Ward. A part of Gil's mind marveled at where she was now, compared to where she'd been just two years before.

They reached the edge of the clearing. *"Stop!"* Gil Sent with more force than intended.

Shatter stopped, and crouched. *"He's there,"* she guessed.

"Yes," Gil confirmed. *"He's rooting in the dirt."*

"If you can get him to move, do so," Shatter ordered. *"If not, then."* She let the thought end, incomplete.

Gil reached out with her senses. She felt the presence of the boar. He was huge. Young, but scarred from many breeding combats. She could feel the power radiating from him. His tusks were long, clean, and sharp. He sniffed the air, then went back to rooting in the dirt. She felt his elation as he found a bunch of tasty roots. His head dipped lower as he gobbled them up.

"I have a good shot," Shatter said, pulling back on her bow.

"Wait," Gil begged. She stretched out, trying to reach the mind of the huge boar. *"The food isn't good here,"* she tried to persuade him. *"Over the ridge, there's much better ground."*

The boar stopped eating, and his head came up. The images of these roots and Flora's garden came to Gil. Then the image of another boar — female — and her piglets. Something she might call pride was strong in the great boar's thoughts.

"Please," she Sent, *"you must find another place."*

The boar shook his head, sending dirt and grass flying. His feet pawed the ground, and he turned and looked right in their direction. He bellowed, then charged.

Shatter stood, firing. Her arrow bounced off the boar's tough hide. She pulled another, and drew the bow string back. The boar saw her, but ignored her, and continued heading right for Gil. Shatter fired again. The arrow hit the boar in the side. Gil stood, but was frozen. Her spear was loose in her hand.

"Set the spear!" Shatter yelled, pulling another arrow. Gil didn't move. The sight of the huge animal bearing down on her had banished all other thoughts from her mind.

Shatter pulled back, but her bow string snapped. Cursing, she tried to Push Gil out of the way with her Power. At the same moment, a black blur struck the head of the boar, pushing him aside just enough to miss Gil.

The boar skidded to a halt, shaking his head. Nesa went flying off into the brush.

"Run!" Shatter yelled, waving her arms to get the boar's attention. She pulled her long knife. Its reach was insufficient, but she would make the best of it.

"Here, you bastard!" she yelled. The boar saw her, and charged. Shatter tensed, ready to leap and strike when the boar was on her. She could see the clods of fresh dirt on his tusks. She was gathering herself to leap over those sharp weapons when the boar was suddenly shoved to the left. It slid into the underbrush, and lay still.

Shatter took a breath, then looked. A spear was sticking out the side of the now-dead animal. The shaft was still quivering with the impact. Shatter turned to see Gil standing in the clearing, lowering her arm. She took a long breath, then dropped to one knee.

"Did I get it?" she asked.

"Yes," Shatter said with amazement and pride, "you did."

"I'm sorry," Gil said.

Shatter didn't know who she was speaking to. 'Probably both of us,' she thought.

A rustle in the brush turned Shatter's head. She looked down to see Nesa walking up to her. The cat stopped at her feet, and looked up at her.

"Are you hurt?" Shatter asked.

Nesa shook herself. Her tail whipped around. She licked at her right leg, then looked up at Shatter.

"Good," Shatter said. "You were very brave." Nesa winked at her, and went back to bathing.

Gil was walking across the clearing. Shatter could see the waver in her step, and the glassiness in her eyes. These were things she had seen many times after a first kill. She started to remind Gil that what she had done had been necessary. That the boar would have killed her otherwise. But Gil already knew.

So Shatter praised her instead. "That was a good throw. Raven would be proud. Talon, too."

"I froze. They'll only remember that," Gil said woodenly, as she stopped and looked down at the body.

"I won't tell them, if you don't," Shatter promised. "You recovered well. That's all I know."

Gil smiled around her sorrow. She pulled her dagger. "You'll have to show me where the heart is."

"I can do that," Shatter offered.

Gil shook her head. "He was my kill. He's my responsibility."

Shatter considered for a moment, then offered Gil her blade. "Use this. Yours won't reach." She set her foot on the side of the boar and pulled the spear out. "Just follow the wound. You hit the heart."

☾ ♒ ☼

Talia sat in a chair near the edge of the cliff and watched the full moon rise. Further down the cliff, Goldberry and the Twins led the group in a song to the Goddess on the rising of the moon.

She heard footsteps behind her. She reached up, and took Elanor's hands as she laid them on her shoulders.

"Why aren't you with them?" Elanor asked.

"Nova's voice was irritating her," Talia replied, nodding to her belly. "For a Fairy, she has a horrible voice."

Elanor chuckled, and sat down on the ground at Talia's side. They held hands, and watched the moon rise, rippling silver on the sea.

"Next full moon," Talia pronounced, after a peaceful period of silence. Down the cliff, the others had moved on to another song, and were whirling through an accompanying dance.

Elanor cocked her head in question, not understanding.

"She'll be born next moon," Talia clarified.

"How can you know?" Elanor asked.

"I just do," she replied, her voice low and far away. She watched the moon.

Elanor was also quiet. This place had become a home. Despite the hardships and difficulties, she was happy here. Now things were about to change again.

"Will we return to the palace?" Elanor finally asked.

"I can't see that part of my path yet. I've concentrated so hard on getting to her birth, I haven't given much thought to what happens after."

"What does your mother say?"

Talia's hand tightened on Elanor's. "I haven't spoken to her since we left the Exile Queen's mountain. 'Security,' she said. 'No contact.'" Talia stopped. Elanor wanted to rise and hug her, but held back.

"I understand, but part of me wants her. Part of me wants to take a Ring back, and be in my chambers. Hear Flora and Luna fussing over everything. Hear the cacophony of the training grounds, the singing from the Keep of the Goddess. Everything. I miss it."

"So do I," Elanor admitted.

"But here, we can hear the waves. Feel the sun and wind. I don't want to leave here, either."

"We can decide later," Elanor comforted her. "Flora won't let the child travel by Ring for a while, anyway. The path isn't decided yet."

"No, it's not," Talia agreed. She turned to Elanor. "My dreams are strange. Full of dark and light. Something's coming."

"She's coming." Elanor pointed to Talia's belly, trying to bring some levity to what had become a rather serious discussion.

Talia smiled. "Maybe it's just a new mother's fear."

"I'm sure it is." Elanor put both of her hands on Talia's arm. "Would you like to stay here tonight, like we did when we were young? Under the full moon?"

"I can't do that; she'd kick up a storm."

"I don't mean that," Elanor clarified quickly. "Though I do want you — that's not what I was talking about. I want to spend a night under the stars and moon with you. Like we did when we were children."

Talia smiled wickedly. "Before we discovered the pleasure we could give to each other."

"You started it," Elanor reminded her, looking innocent. "I was just a pure, young Fairy. You corrupted me."

"You didn't resist very much."

"I did not," Elanor admitted.

Talia sighed. She wanted to say yes, but she didn't want to put herself in a position where she would have to say no to Elanor again.

Her body and mind were so focused on the child that she had no room for anything else.

"You promise that there are no ulterior motives? Truly, this belly gets in the way. And she'll protest."

"You're the one who brought up pleasure. My intentions are pure," Elanor assured her. "I wouldn't do anything to disturb my niece. Goddess knows I speak the truth."

"Your intentions are never pure, but I understand. Flora wouldn't let me sleep out here, though."

"I brought a tent, and your blankets." Elanor gestured behind her. "And several bedrolls, for the comfort of your Highness."

"Ah, comfort. I miss that," Talia mused. "Well, put up the tent," she relented. "We'll sit under the moon, like we did when we were children."

Elanor jumped to work before Talia could change her mind.

☾ ⌇ ☼

True to her intuition, the child began her journey on the morning of the next full moon. Talia woke to the twin sensations of her water breaking and Nesa leaping out of the bed to avoid the liquid.

"Flora," Talia called, but her maid was already starting to move. Flora had maneuvered her cot into Talia's little room a week before. The room was small, so Flora had to sleep half in the small nursery, with her bed in the doorway.

"Is it time?" Flora asked, knowing. She pushed Quicksilver off her and got up. Quicksilver ambled over and sat beside her mother, who was cleaning herself beside the door.

"Well, go," Flora ordered, gesturing the door open. "Get Shield." Nesa stopped her bathing and looked at Quicksilver. She started to bathe, but a head bump from her mother sent her out the door. Nesa resumed her bath.

Flora got Talia up, and began pulling off the wet bedding. Min poked her head in. "Tell Shatter to get the pavilion set up," Talia ordered, taking off her wet gown. Min darted off.

"You aren't having this child outside," Flora decreed, throwing the bedsheets at the door. "We've talked about this."

"Mum, you've talked," Talia countered, putting on a robe. "I will have this child under the sky, and on the shore of the sea. I agreed that it would be too difficult to get to the beach. So, it will be on the cliff. I want to hear the sea."

"Foolish child." Flora set her fists on her hips. Her wings quivered so much Talia expected feathers to start falling out. "I've lived this way for months. Slept on hard ground, wet ground. Now we finally have a decent shelter, and you want to go and have your child on the grass." Exasperated beyond words, she blew out a great breath. "The breeze will be bad for the newborn."

"We'll set up a Shield that will keep out the wind," Elanor put in from the door.

Flora whirled, and threw a pillow at the interloper. "Keep out of this. You're a foolish child, too."

Elanor ducked away.

Talia struggled to tie the robe that was too small for her belly. She gave up. "This is what I want, Mum." She put both her hands on Flora's shoulders. "This is what she wants."

"How can you know what the child wants?" Flora asked with exasperation, looking away from Talia. "We've grown as a people. We have buildings now; we no longer have to live off the land. Yet you want to go backward."

"Yes, I do. It's important that this child be born under the sky, and with the sea within her hearing."

"You've been reading too much of the Exile Queen's ramblings," Flora protested. "But you must have it, I see."

Shield finally arrived, with Quicksilver at her heels.

Flora looked at her. "I doubt it's possible, but please try to talk some sense into her," she begged Shield. "I guess I'll make sure Shatter and the others are creating something that won't fall on us." With that final pronouncement, Flora left. She called for Goldberry to start breakfast as she exited the house.

"I won't even try," Shield said. She crossed to Talia and put her hand on the Heir's belly. "She seems fine. Ready to join us."

123

"I know," Talia said, leaning against the bed. "Could you hand me that satchel?" Talia pointed under the bed.

Shield picked the bag up and passed it to Talia.

"Thank you. Now I need a few minutes of privacy," she announced.

Shield looked worried.

"She's not coming right now. We have hours. I need a few moments," Talia stressed, in her Heir voice.

"Yes, My Lady." Shield bowed out of the room, grabbing Elanor as she tried to enter.

"I'll call for you in a moment," Talia promised Elanor, as Shield shut the door.

Talia then sat down on the bed and took the Geode out of the satchel. Closing her eyes, she called to her mother over the Web.

She floated in the nothingness for a long time. A contraction almost broke her concentration. Talia was about to give up when her mother's presence finally came to her.

"*Daughter.*"

"*Mother — it's time.*"

Talia was hit with so many unshielded emotions from her mother: pride, fear, annoyance, and frustration, among others.

"*I'm sorry, Talia,*" her mother finally said. "*This couldn't come at a worse time. There's been a major attack at the border. The Human King is dead, and Bastile seeks to show everyone that he's powerful. It's all I can do to keep my sisters from calling Air and Grass to muster, and attack the Humans ourselves. 'Burn them all,' Dina screams.*"

"*I understand, Mother,*" Talia said dutifully, but it was an obvious lie. She wanted to scream, 'I need you — forget the Queen, be my mother!'

"*I would if I could,*" the Queen responded to her unspoken demand. "*It breaks my heart that this child will be born without me by your side. Goddess curse them. I swore I wouldn't miss this. Goddess's mercy.*" Talia could feel the tears behind her mother's words.

"*You must do what a Queen must. Don't let either of our enemies win. Strike at the Humans, and take charge of the Aunts. Send Air.*

Strike the Humans hard and fast. Reinforce the border. Show him we won't allow this to happen. He stuck his hand in: chop it off. Then let him pull back and decide if he wants to risk the other one." Talia clutched her belly as the child reacted to her emotions.

A wave of pride washed over Talia. *"I will do as you say, My Heir. I will chop his hand off, but it's more like he's waving his manhood at us."*

"An even better thing to chop off."

"Goddess protect you," the Queen beseeched. Talia felt a hand on her head, and a kiss on her cheek. *"I love you, Talia. Tell Flora I expect a healthy grandchild."* Then her mother was gone.

Talia felt tears of both sorrow and pride forming in her eyes. She almost broke down, but she took a hard rein on her emotions, and pushed them all down. "I will deal with Bastile soon enough," she swore to herself. She took a deep breath. Talia felt a small hand in hers. "Thank you," she whispered. She got to her feet, and moved carefully to the door.

☾ 〰 ☼

It was a long day. Talia's mental discipline and control over her body kept the pain away, for the most part. Flora's sturdy presence and competence gave her confidence. Elanor was at her right hand, Goldberry on her left. The pavilion that Shatter and the rest of The Nine had constructed had an almost-transparent cloth roof, so Talia could watch the clouds, and see the birds flying overhead. Elanor was even better than her word: the Ward around the pavilion was perfect. It kept out the worst of the wind, but allowed in the sweet smell of the sea, and just a hint of breeze. The Nine formed a circle around the pavilion. Flora kept the other Ladies busy running errands and performing small tasks.

Despite what Talia had felt earlier, now the child seemed to be in no hurry to enter the Realm. Though she had turned, and was pointed in the right direction, she didn't move any further. As the sun climbed, Flora kept checking her, and shaking her head.

"She doesn't want to come," Flora said, after Talia asked again. "Children can be stubborn. She'll come when she's ready."

Talia concentrated on keeping herself calm, and her body prepared. Fear and anxiety grew as the day got longer. Hunger gnawed at her, but she couldn't eat.

She pushed Elanor away. "No more water. I can't. I need something else."

Flora and Shield looked at each other. "Captain," Flora called out, "please fetch your gift. It's time." Talia watched Shatter, who had been pacing the perimeter of the pavilion all day, dart off to The Nine's cabin. She returned carrying something covered in a cloth in both hands.

"My Lady," she said formally, presenting the object to Talia. "Talon and Helm found this on a patrol." She pulled off the cloth. Underneath was a glass globe, half-filled with a golden substance.

"Honey!" Talia reached out for the globe. "This is a true gift. Thank you." She tried to take the globe, but Shatter held it back. Talia narrowed her eyes at her. "Isn't that for me?"

"Yes, but you might drop it," Flora said, stepping up. She reached into the globe with one of her spoons. "And Talon took a great many stings to get this for you."

Talia felt the fool, eating from a spoon in Flora's hand, but once the honey hit her tongue, and the sweet, wild flavor went down her throat, she forgot about her embarrassment, and reached for more.

"Only another mouthful," Flora told her. "I think she's moving."

Talia took another spoonful, and as she swallowed, a contraction moved through her body. Caught off-guard, she cried out, squeezing Goldberry and Elanor's hands.

"She's opening up more," Shield informed Flora.

"We'll need the heated water now," Flora advised Shatter, who left without comment, setting the globe down carefully first. Talia breathed, and concentrated.

More hours passed. Min took Goldberry's place. Willow offered to give Elanor a break, but she wouldn't leave.

"You should go — stretch your legs and wings for both of us," Talia told her.

"I will not leave you," Elanor replied. "I will always be by your side. No matter what."

"Stubborn," Talia commented.

"I am," Elanor agreed.

"Why is it taking so long?" Talia demanded of Flora. "She should be born. I want her to be born."

"These things happen as they happen," Flora comforted her. She put her hand on Talia's belly. "She's quiet now. Her mind is preparing for the rough journey. She's in no danger. If that should change, we'll take action. Right now, it's best to let things go as they will."

"Just like her father," Talia cursed.

"Don't say such things," Flora said, swatting Talia's hand. "She'll be nothing like him. All he did was help create her. We shall raise her; we shall guide her on the path of a Servant of the Moon and Sun."

"I'm sorry," Talia said, both to Flora and to her child. Flora smiled, and kissed Talia's forehead.

"Mistress, I love you, but you must control this anger toward him. It could lead you down a very bad path."

"He deserves my anger," Talia reminded her. "He betrayed me. Used me. I will love this child, but I cannot find any room in my heart for him."

Flora patted Talia's hand. "Goddess guide you."

"I must get something," she said to Shield. "I'll be right back." Flora got up and left.

"She's right," Min started.

"I will not hear any more talk of forgiving him," Talia stated. "I need more honey." She pointed at the globe. Shield wiped her hands on a towel, and picked up the honey globe.

With the setting of the sun, the contractions began in earnest. The Ladies conjured Fairy Lights around the pavilion, then formed their own circle by the entrance. Nesa and her children prowled the perimeter. Talia had wanted them with her, but Flora had put her foot down, and Talia was too tried to argue.

Talia's concentration wavered as the contractions moved through her. She could only maintain her breathing. Elanor took over keeping her pain down, and regulating her heartbeat.

"She's getting close," Flora consoled Talia. "Soon."

Talia could only stare up into the sky. Stars were starting to come out. "Where's the moon?" she asked.

"It will rise soon," Goldberry assured her.

"She shall see it," Talia said, her voice far away.

"Concentrate, Mistress. Concentrate," Flora urged. "She's coming."

Time began to dilate for Talia. Her body was slow, and wallowing in the pain. Her mind was racing: everything that had happened to her, from the moment Bastile had brought her his dresses to now, swirled and mixed through her head, along with a whirlpool of emotions. The pain and horror of the plantation, mixed with the elation of finding the Exile Queen's mountain. The pain of losing Silvermane rested alongside the joy of the Sisterhood of The Nine. The ecstasy of being with Elanor, and the shame of betraying her, only to be betrayed herself by Bastile. Joy and wonder at the personality of the ruins Ring, with the horror and disgust she had felt when she was faced with the Blood Ring.

Her vision blurred.

"I can see her head."

"Push, Talia."

"Just breathe. Breathe."

"Her shoulders are caught."

"Goldberry, the child — keep her calm. Keep her breathing."

"Elanor, keep her still — keep her pain down."

"Nova, bring me my bag."

"One comes out, and the other gets stuck."

"Nova!"

"She can't take much more."

"Cut her out."

"No. A little of this. Keep her calm. Now, ease her."

Talia felt the potential she'd been living with for nine months disappear. Fear sliced through her. Her heart stopped.

A cry restarted it. She opened her eyes to a weight on her chest. A small, pale, golden-haired form rested in her arms. The light of the moon shone in the child's eyes. She cried again. Talia reached out, and took her damp hand.

Elanor eased back on the control of her emotions. Joy burst into her heart. Love filled Talia as the warmth of the baby settled into her breast.

"She has wings," an amazed Flora said.

"Goddess bless, she is beautiful," Goldberry uttered.

Talia could feel the Ladies surround her. The circle of their arms and wings cradled around her. They began to sing, softly, the Song of Greeting a New Life to This Realm, Returned from the Cycle. The Nine began to beat a slow rhythm on their chests, then started to chant.

"A servant is arrived. Servant of the Moon and Sun. She is here."

It all washed over Talia. The joy and love pushed aside the fear. Her daughter was here. The child breathed slowly and steadily. Her mind found Talia's.

"Hello," Talia greeted her. Joy and recognition answered.

Talia opened her eyes, and looked around. All her exile family was there: Elanor at her right; Min, weeping and clutching her left arm; Flora, still standing at her side, her hands under the baby; Shield, sitting back on her knees and breathing deeply, calming herself; Shatter, standing in front of her, her hands on the shoulders of Nova and Willow, joining the Ladies' Circle.

"My Lady," Shatter requested, "introduce me to my new charge?"

Talia looked into her child's eyes.

"She is Sunrise Moonrise. A new day, and a new hope for the Realms."

129

Chapter Twelve
Sunrise

Talia was dreaming. She was moving through the corridors of the palace. She looked down. She wore sturdy pants for flying. Her favorite boots clicked on the stones. She fingered her braid, which hung down over her right shoulder. The grey was beginning to overwhelm the black. 'You should do something about that,' she thought. Her hand ached in the morning chill. She rubbed at the missing fingers. 'A willing sacrifice,' she thought, as she had for Goddess-only-knew-how-many times.

"Mother," a voice called from behind.

Talia turned. The sun was in the window, so she could only see the silhouette of the person who had called, but she knew those wings as well as she knew her own.

"Don't you want to meet with the Queen? She's come all this way to celebrate the anniversary."

"She comes to see the one who made all this possible. That's you. I was just there."

"No, Mother; you're just being modest. She's come to honor both of us."

"I must fly for a time," Talia announced, turning. "I'll return for the feast. Goddess keep you, Daughter."

The dream dissolved with the low cry of a baby.

☾ ♒ ☼

Talia awoke from of a light sleep with the rising of the sun. She should have been tired, but she felt a new sense of life within herself. Somehow, she knew this was the right path.

She had sat with her daughter for a while, as each of her Ladies and The Nine had filed by and met the new member of their family. Nesa had finally been allowed in, and had merely sniffed at the child. She gave an approving look at Talia, then hopped down from the bed.

Sunrise began to fuss, and Talia let her nurse for the first time. A cascade of new emotions hit her. She had created life. And was now feeding a new Fairy. She felt pride, and a sense of responsibility. She had always been responsible for her Ladies, but this went well beyond anything she had felt before. It left her feeling drained.

A rustle at her side made her open her eyes. Spear stood before her. She hadn't come with the others to greet little Sunrise. Her expression was full of so many emotions, Talia's mind couldn't pick any specific one out.

Talia simply held out one hand, while the other held the child. Spear hesitated, then took Talia's hand.

"I wanted to tell you something," she started.

Talia waited. Behind Spear, Flora ushered Shield out.

"I had a son. He was beautiful. But I couldn't. . . ." She stopped again, her emotions overwhelming her ability to talk.

"Take your time. I'm not going anywhere," Talia reassured her.

Spear tried to smile. "I couldn't nurse him. It was like this thing that came out of me was a stranger. His father was gone. I was alone. There was only the midwife, and she was busy. She sat the child on my chest, and left. She had others to tend to."

Fear filled Talia as she imagined what Spear might reveal next. Sunrise whimpered. Spear tried to pull away, but Talia held her in place.

"Speak if you wish, or stay silent. But stay," Talia urged her.

A tear ran down Spear's face. "I left him. I staggered out, and left my son. I dimly remember voices calling after me, but I ignored them. I went back to my barracks. My Lieutenant looked at me strangely. He put me in a bed, and called our Medic. I don't remember anything else."

Talia paused. "The child?" she asked with hesitation.

"He died. Separation trauma, the midwife said. She said she didn't blame me, but I knew she did. I blamed myself." She stood up straighter. "I pledge my life to you and your child. I will not fail again."

"I have accepted your pledge, and renew it now," Talia said formally. "I'm sorry you had to go through that." Flora had returned, a soft blanket in her hands. She took Sunrise and wrapped her. The look in Spear's eyes was heartbreaking.

"Would you like to hold her for a moment? Flora needs to take her for a bath, but a moment won't hurt," Talia offered, letting go of Spear's hand, and pulling a blanket over herself.

"I can't," Spear replied.

"Of course you can, child," Flora countered. "You're a brave and powerful warrior. She's but a small thing. She needs a protector. She needs Aunts." Flora offered her the wrapped baby. "She can't replace your lost one, but she can help heal you."

Spear hesitated another moment, then opened her arms, and took Sunrise. Her face filled with awe as she looked at the sleeping child. "Greetings, Sunrise, my new charge. I will protect you."

Talia smiled, and wondered at the ability of the Goddess to lead us down the paths we need to tread.

(﷼ ☼

Talia still ached all over, but she got up, and pulled on a robe. Flora was asleep on her cot in the doorway. Sunrise was nestled at her side, Flora's wings forming a perfect cup for her. Talia started to reach for the baby, but stopped. Instead, she removed the Geode from its satchel, and set it on the bed. Then, she went to Flora and gently removed Sunrise from the nest of her feathers. Flora muttered, but didn't wake.

Talia marveled at the sleeping child. "So much weaves around you, little one. I hope the Goddess is ready for you." Talia returned to her bed. She climbed back in, and sat, with the baby in her arms, and the Geode at her knees.

She reached into the Web.

An answer came quickly. "Talia," her mother called out. "I was worried."

"We're fine. I wanted you to meet Sunrise." She opened herself, and Showed her mother everything from the last day. The emotions blanketed her. Talia could feel her mother reaching out to Luna and Merry-Weather. Their familiar presences joined the Web, and Talia felt them begin to cry.

"She's beautiful! A marvel!" Luna gushed.

"A worthy child," Merry-Weather commented, hiding her emotions behind a gruff shield.

The Queen was silent. She took in everything that had happened, from the prior morning up till that point. Talia could sense her taking each moment, and feeling it like fine cloth. Running it through her mind.

"She's a mirror, through which I can see the past," she finally said. *"She looks like you did when I first held you. She will be a great Fairy."*

"She's part Human, too," Talia reminded her.

"She has wings — little ones, but she does have them," Luna put in. *"She'll be able to pass."*

Talia didn't know how to react. She started to speak, but stopped as Merry-Weather stepped in. *"I think we should leave them."* And Talia felt Luna being Pushed out of the Web.

"She will be of both worlds," Talia stressed. *"I will not hide her true nature."*

The Queen was silent.

"Mother, you must see that she could be a bridge between us. She's his Heir, too, after all. You must see that."

"We will discuss this when you return," the Queen said simply. *"When do you expect that to be?"*

Talia took a mental breath. *"She can't travel for several weeks yet. The Ring would be too hard on her young mind. And I need to recover. It was a difficult birth."*

"I understand. We will not speak of this child, this Sunrise, until you return. Then we can decide, and present her to the court." Talia felt the anxiety behind the words, but she was still hurt by her mother's hesitation.

"I will contact you when we're ready to return."

"Goddess guide you, and protect the little one," her mother said. Talia felt a brush on her head, and another on Sunrise's. Then the Queen was gone.

Talia opened her eyes to see Flora sitting on the bed in front of her.

"Your mother," she said simply.

"And Luna and Merry-Weather," Talia added. Flora's face split in a smile.

"My sister gushed, and my mother held back," Flora guessed.

Talia smiled, too. "As if you were there." She readjusted Sunrise and accidentally woke her. She began to fuss. Talia opened her robe, and let her nurse.

Flora stood up, a look of pride on her face. "I'll bring you something to eat."

"Good. I'm hungry. Honey is good, but it doesn't fill me up."

"Then, we must make plans," Flora said, crossing to the door.

"Yes, we must," Talia agreed, looking down at her daughter.

☽ ⌇ ☼

Tra burst into the room. Wingless Bastard and Gren were entangled on the couch.

"Get off her, Bastard," Tra commanded. Wingless looked up and slowly got up, smoothing his clothes. Gren smiled, and left her dress open.

"I have news," Tra informed them. "The child has been born."

Gren clapped. "Oh, good. Another morsel."

Wingless smiled. "That fits with what I know."

"And you're just telling me now?" Tra looked at him with disgust.

"I was on the way, but she diverted me." He smiled at Gren. "I've found a town on the sea that some of the Ladies and The Nine have been seen in. I'm working on a way to bend that to our advantage."

"What's your plan?" Tra demanded.

"I keep my own counsel. But if this works, it will benefit us both."

Tra clenched her fists in anger and raised one. "I could kill you for that. Tell me what you're doing."

"Then who would speak with your voice to the Human King?" Wingless returned fearlessly. "Who would create the blacksilk blades? Who would blame the Fairies who need to be blamed? Who would supply you with the blood you need?" His voice dropped. "You need me, and I need you. I'll get the child for you. You needn't worry."

"I want her dead. And Talia along with her," Tra ordered. "Simple enough."

"Yes, My Lady." He bowed mockingly. "I will bring you their heads."

Tra glared again. "Well — get moving!"

Gren grabbed his arm. "He isn't done yet." She pouted. "I will set him on his way — after I get what I want."

Tra took in his smile with disgust, and left.

Wingless turned to Gren, unbuttoning his shirt again. She reached out for his pants. "But first," she said, hooking her fingers over his belt. "I'll make a deal with you."

"Yes?" he asked, looking down at her exposed body.

"I want the child." She licked her lips again.

"Done."

☾ ♒ ☼

Shatter, Steel, Elanor, Min, and Goldberry gathered in the main house. Talia and Flora came out of the nursery, with Flora toting the bundled Sunrise. Talia sat down, and took the baby.

"Has everyone eaten?" Talia asked. They nodded.

"Good. We started out on this path with the intention of keeping me safe until this child could be born. Now she has been. So, what's our next move?" Talia looked at the others expectantly.

"I thought we would be returning to the palace," Goldberry offered when no one else spoke.

"I talked to the Queen both this morning and last night. She told me there's been a sizeable attack by the Humans at the border," Talia informed them with some reluctance.

Shatter and Steel looked at each other. Min looked very worried.

"The timing of that is curious," Shatter commented.

"That was my thought, too," Talia agreed. "My advice to the Queen was to strike back enough to bloody them, then hold. She said Bastile is King now." Everyone looked shocked. This was only the second time Talia had said his name during their exile.

"We're still in danger, then?" Min asked. "There are too many variables. Who's supporting who? Where does the Blood Cult fit in? Who are they supporting? Are they playing all sides? To what purpose?" As she folded her hands, her many questions filled all their minds.

"All of these are good questions, and we need the answers." Talia shifted Sunrise. "But first, we must have a celebration, and formally Present my daughter to all of our exile family and the Goddess."

"Shouldn't that be done at the Shrine of the Goddess, or the Great Hall, before the whole court?" Goldberry asked.

"Yes, but she can't travel for a few weeks, and I don't want to wait," Talia explained, as Flora nodded in agreement. "We'll do it on the shore of the sea," Talia proclaimed.

Flora pulled out a piece of paper. "I made a list. Send Willow, Honor, Gil, and Talon," she started.

Steel took the list. "Use the Ephemeral Ring?"

"Yes," Talia confirmed. "To the broken tower Ring."

Steel nodded, and left.

Shatter sat back in her chair. "We must know more about what's going on. We should send a group back to gather information."

"There's danger in that," Elanor cautioned.

"There's danger in not knowing what's happening, and who our enemies are," Shatter returned.

"I agree," Talia told them both. "We'll decide who and where after the Presentation. We have a day or two to come up with a plan."

"I will, My Lady," Shatter volunteered.

$$\left(\rightwave \mathbin{\Large\approx} \mathbin{\Large\leftcircle} \right.$$

"So. Looks like you're having a celebration of some kind," the Feather-wing shopkeeper remarked to Willow as he looked over her shopping list.

She nodded.

"Celebration of a birth?" he asked.

Willow glared at him. He threw up his hands. "You've been buying pregnancy herbs for the past six months. Doesn't take an Iridescent to figure that out."

"Yes. One of my Sisters," Willow admitted.

"Good. Goddess's good wishes to her." He stopped. "I wanted to apologize to you. What I said to you on your last visit here was wrong, and what I wanted to do was even more wrong." He smiled. "I want to make it up to you." He gestured to a door in the back of the shop. "I have something for you and your Sisters."

"Bring it out, and we can decide," Willow replied.

"It's too large, and I would have to take it back apart. It would be simpler for you to come and see it."

Willow narrowed her eyes, and her hand went to her knife.

"I have no ill wishes for you. I know what you and your Sisters," he gestured to Honor and Talon, who were looking for other items, and Gil, who was haggling with another shopkeeper over the cost of a handcart, "are capable of. On my honor, I only wish to show you this gift."

Willow looked to Honor. She looked the man up and down, then nodded.

"Lead the way," Willow said.

☾ ≋ ☼

Honor was beginning to get nervous: Willow had been gone too long. Honor could still sense her, beyond the door to the back of the shop, and she was calm. Honor looked over at Talon, then gripped the hilt of her knife, and moved toward the door.

Willow opened it.

"That took a while; I was worried," Honor informed her charge with relief. "Are you all right?"

"It was nothing. He made a crib, but it's too large," Willow told her. "Then he tried to sell us other pieces of furniture. I had to pull my knife on him to get him to stop."

Honor clapped her on the back. "Good. Talon has all the items Flora wanted. It will be a long walk with all of this. Even with the handcart Gil bought."

"I thought you were strong and brave," Willow teased her, following her out of the shop. "That nothing was too much?"

Honor laughed again.

☾ 〰 ☼

The group sent for supplies didn't return until late in the day.

"I can't be ready for this Presentation in the morning," Flora protested. "I won't stay up all night baking and cooking. Even with all of you lot to help."

"Tomorrow will be fine," Talia assured her, as she returned Sunrise to her bundle after changing her. "We can cook and bake throughout the day. We'll all work on the food. By midday, it'll be ready. Then, we can go down to the beach and do the ceremony, then return here."

"I thought you would want it at dawn," Flora said, calming down a bit, "what with her name and all."

"It doesn't matter. Most Presentation ceremonies are at the end of the day. Whenever we're ready will be fine," Talia said easily, making sure Sunrise was tucked in securely.

"Good. But keep Shatter away from the food. It will be enough for her to stir the soup," Flora advised, taking Sunrise from her. Talia sat back, and watched Flora and her daughter. 'Is this how she was with me?' she wondered. 'If so, it's no surprise that I see her as my second mother.' Talia rose, and went and hugged the two of them.

"What was that for?" Flora asked, accepting the embrace.

"Just that I love you, Mum, and I hope she will, too." Talia stroked Sunrise's thin, golden hair.

"Only good thing he gave her," Flora commented. Talia shook her head, and sat down.

"What will you do, Mistress?" Flora pressed. "You can't avoid this forever. We must have a plan when we return. Do we hide the child's parentage? Openly announce it? Do a little of both? We must be ready."

"I don't know. That's been the only thing on my mind since this morning." Talia sank into her chair. "All of the options are dangerous. Each puts her in opposition to some part of the Fairy court."

"Then you should give her up," Flora said flatly. "If you know she'll come to danger, then you should send her someplace like that young man Canin came from. And return to the court as if nothing happened. I've seen it done before." Her hand absently rubbed her leg.

Talia was shocked. "I could never do that to her! Canin was so broken, because he was abandoned by his mother. I would never do that! How can you even suggest that?"

"To get you to think, Mistress," Flora said, leaning over to put a hand on Talia's arm. Her smile took the sting from her harsh words. "Then you must find a way around, or through. We'll support you. Your mother will as well. I know Lady Titania and Lord Oberon will, too. Paramount Miranda will bring the Tower of Learning to your side. You have more allies than you think. Your Aunts are just loud. No decent Fairy will follow those cruel women."

"I hope you're right, Mum. I hope you're right."

☽ ♒ ☼

The morning was clear and warm. From the first rays of the sun, Flora took command: everyone was roused from their beds, and given a task. Since they wouldn't be staying at the compound much longer, no thought was given to moderation: all the supplies they had brought or scavenged over the prior months were fair game. Flora directed teams to dig cooking pits, so Shatter took Talon down to the beach to clear a perfect spot.

Flora declared Talia still recovering, so she sat in front of the main house, directing those coming and going from the crude oven inside. Talia's memory was triggered by all the smells emanating from behind her. The Twins, Harpoon, and Helm were the primary assistants, running back and forth at Flora's command to find ingredients and perform other necessary tasks.

Soon, the cooking pits smoked, and sent even more aromas into the air. Willow and Gil were tasked with keeping the kittens from burning their feet looking for treats. Nesa spent most of the day under Talia's chair, watching the commotion from a safe distance.

Min and Elanor kept the Fire Spells on the cooking stones supplied with Power.

Everyone was happy, and full of energy.

Periodically, Talia would stop, and call one of them to sit with her and hold Sunrise. The child slept through most of the day, waking only to nurse and be changed.

Talia watched each of the Fairies with whom she had lived for so many months hold her child in turn. She watched them each progress from fear of dropping her, to comfortably nestling the baby in their arms.

Steel took her for just a few moments, and quickly gave her back. "It's a baby. My wives' are cuter," she teased with a wink, and went back to work.

When everything was ready, Shatter took everyone but Talia and Flora down to the beach. Talia stood close to the edge of the cliff, but was unable to see what was going on below.

"Are you sure you can make the flight with the child?" Flora worried for the third time.

"Yes, Mum, I am. My strength is back. I tested my wings earlier, and they're strong. It will be a slow descent. I'll hold her to me with my Power. Everything will be fine."

"I'll go down first," Flora stated. "I'll be there if anything goes wrong."

"That's where I want you to be," Talia agreed, as she kissed her on the cheek.

"*We're ready,*" Shatter Sent.

Flora kissed Sunrise, and walked to the cliff's edge. She unfurled her wings, and floated down out of sight.

Talia waited a few breaths, then she stepped to the edge as well. Holding her child close with her Power, she unfurled her wings, and caught the wind down the cliff. She floated down like a leaf on the wind. Sunrise woke, and cried with joy as the wind hit her face. Talia cried, too. She touched down softly.

Before her lay a path of stones. Above each was a glittering Fairy Light. They gave an otherworldly look to the sand. Talia followed the path. It wove around the dunes, and emerged onto a clean stretch of smooth white sand.

The Ladies and The Nine were there, in two lines, on either side of the path. The Ladies were dressed in their simple, silver, belted tabards bearing the silver symbol of the Heir on their chests. At their throats and sleeves, their ringmail shone in the setting sun. The Nine were similarly dressed, in the purple and green tabards of the Heir's Guard.

Shatter stood at the head of the line. She bowed to Talia, and offered her arm. Together, they walked between the lines of the Fairies who had shared their lives for so long a time, through so much pain and sorrow. Talia met each pair of eyes as they passed.

Goldberry waited at the end of the line, the cloak of a Keeper on her shoulders.

"Why do you come here?" she asked. "Under the eyes of your Sisters? Under the sun, and the watch of the Goddess?"

"I come to present my child," Talia replied. Shatter helped her unwrap Sunrise.

"Is she a Servant of the Moon and Sun?" Goldberry asked.

Talia turned, and held up her child. Shocked by the sudden breeze, Sunrise tried to curl up. Talia Sent her an encouragement. Sunrise took a breath, and began to cry, her small iridescent wings extending out.

"She is a Servant of the Moon and Sun," the Ladies and The Nine proclaimed together.

Talia lowered her squalling daughter, and wrapped her back up. Flora stepped forward, and took the child. Flora sang softly to her, and she stopped crying.

Talia took a deep breath. "She is my daughter; I am the Heir to the Fairy Realm. She is my Heir," she pronounced, both to the group and to the greater Realm.

"We will defend her," Shatter declared.

"We will defend the Heir," the others echoed.

"It might be a hard path ahead," Talia warned them, "but together, we can walk it."

A cheer went up. Talia took her daughter back, and walked back up the path, as the others fell into line behind her.

☾ 〰 ☼

Talia led them back to the main house, where they set about enjoying a meal of celebration. Everyone took turns serving, and being served. They talked, and joked, and speculated about the future, and what their families back home were doing. A sweet wine from Realm's End filled all their cups. The Twins fed the red cats from their plates. Quicksilver and Rogue chased each other around crazily, until finally settling down on the still-warm stove.

After the main meal, Flora brought out what she had been baking all day.

"Now," she warned them, setting out the trays, "I did my best, but without the oven of the palace, this might not be what all of you remember." She pulled the cloth off, and revealed the traditional spice cake. "Remember, there's a white stone somewhere inside: watch your teeth."

As the mother, Talia cut and served the cake. She was filled with so many good memories of other Presentations. As a child, she had been so eager for the stone to be in her piece, until Flora told her it meant she would be the next to have a child. From then on, she actively poked at her piece after each Presentation to make sure the stone wasn't there.

"You ruined a whole tray one year, looking for the stone to avoid it," Flora remembered as everyone was served.

"And Merry-Weather was beside herself," Talia finished. She looked back at the small crib Steel had made. Sunrise slept within it. "Everything happens when it should," she said, gripping Flora's arm. "For all the sorrow he's caused, he gave me this child."

"That is the way of things," Flora agreed with a yawn.

"Why don't you go to bed?" Talia suggested. "It's been a long day."

"It's been a long several days. I'll see if the stone showed up, and then I'll go to bed."

Turning from Flora, Talia looked out over the seventeen other faces before her: women who had followed her into this exile. Who had left their own lives behind. Who had sacrificed, and fought on her behalf. Who had learned new things, and found new talents they had never known they possessed.

Her Ladies and The Nine.

"Before we eat this wonderful cake Flora has made, I just wanted to say: thank you. I wanted to take this journey alone." She reached down and took Elanor's hand. "I'm glad I didn't. I'm grateful for your dedication to me, and to each other. I'm humbled. Thank you.

"Now, eat!" she commanded.

The sound of forks on plates filled the evening air. Talia waited. Flora watched with concern as the company tried what she had made.

"It's good, Mum — better than the palace kitchen," Elanor complimented her. Others echoed the sentiment. Then Min stood up. She held aloft a white stone. Cries of congratulations filled the air. Min smiled, but then the expression on her face changed. She sat back down, and tucked the stone away. She took another sip of wine, and got a faraway look in her eye. Raven leaned in, and whispered in her ear. Min smiled, and whispered back. Both laughed.

Talia looked over her people. 'This is a night I shall always remember,' she promised herself.

Chapter Thirteen
Before

"Strike hard. Focus on the soldiers: they're the most dangerous. But don't ignore the Ladies, either — they're almost as deadly as the soldiers. All of them have been trained by the absolute best in the Fairy Realm. Ignore that to your peril."

"The Father will guide our hands."

"And take no time for any fun with them. There'll be plenty of fun to be had after. There are several playmates waiting here for each of you. They're part of your reward."

Laughter.

"The crossbows should punch through any armor they're wearing, but they should all be asleep. The herbs in the wine will have seen to that. But don't take any chances: the blacksilk blades kill swiftly, but sometimes not quite as fast as you might hope."

"We know our duty to the Father, and to you. We will not fail."

"Good. I'm counting on that. Bring me the child, and kill the rest."

Chapter Fourteen
Fire and Shears

Talia woke to a psychic scream.

She opened her eyes to chaos. Smoke filled her room. The open door to the nursery was a sheet of flame.

"Sunrise!" she screamed, leaping out of bed, and running at the door. The heat forced her back. She tried to conjure a Shield, but her Power was weak. The main door of the house crashed in behind her. She turned to see Shatter charge into the room, blood running down her face. Her sword was gone. She held a blood-stained knife in her hand.

"We've been attacked!" she yelled over the roar of the flames. "We must leave."

"Sunrise!" Talia called again.

Behind Shatter, more flames roared to life in the doorway.

Shatter grabbed Talia. "We must leave now." Talia tried to twist away. "She's gone. We must leave!"

Talia screamed. It was the most heart-wrenching thing Shatter had ever heard. It cut through the crackle and roar of the flames. Talia screamed again, and with it came her Power, smashing through the wall. Shatter dragged Talia through the opening, and into the smoky air of the compound.

Talia looked back, and saw the house collapse in flames.

"*To the cliff! Three running!*" came a Send from Talon.

"*Wait!*" Shatter Sent. "*Wait for us!*"

"*No! They killed her!*"

Shatter turned in that direction, but Talia was already in the air. Shatter followed.

Three Human men were running away from the compound, away from the flaming cabins. Talon was in the air above them. With a scream, she dove. The last man turned, drawing a weapon, and was hit full on by Talon. Talia increased her speed as both the Fairy and the man tumbled, and they rolled off the edge of the cliff together. Behind her, a bow twanged.

The other two men went down.

Talia landed, and grabbed the nearest man. She flung him over onto his back, snapping the arrow in his shoulder. He screamed. Behind her, Shatter landed, and grabbed the other attacker.

"No!" she cried, but it was too late. Steel had landed, and driven her sword into the man's chest.

"She's dead!" she screamed, hacking at the dead man again.

Shatter dropped to her knees. Blood was running down her wings.

Talia grabbed the man again, lifting him up, and slamming him into the tree on the cliff's edge. An arrow appeared in her hand, and she drove it through his shoulder, pinning him to the wood. Another arrow went into his other shoulder.

Talia grabbed his face. He was Elenite.

"You killed my daughter!" she screamed. "Why?"

"We must purify. She was a stain. A half-breed." Despite the pain, his voice was calm.

"You're a half-breed!"

"It was the only way I could get into the Father's House."

"Who sent you?" Steel asked, twisting one of the arrows. He screamed. Talia twisted the other arrow.

"The King. The King serves the Father. He will purify all!" he screamed.

"The King," Talia repeated woodenly, and drove her knife up under his chin, pinning his head to the tree.

"The King," Steel echoed with defeat, falling to her knees.

Shatter went to the edge of the cliff, and looked down. Talon lay at the bottom, twisted around the man she had hit. Their blood spattered the rocks. She watched as the last of Talon's aura dissipated as she died. Shatter screamed to the rising sun.

Talia turned around. The flames from the three buildings matched the red in the sky. Her emotions had spilled out of her in a flood, and she was left cold. Her hands were covered in blood. She wiped them on the dead man.

"Shatter, Steel," she commanded, "back." She turned, without a backward glance, certain that the soldiers would follow, even if only because of their training.

Flora was crying, and her arm was burned, but she was trying to stop the bleeding from Elanor's severed left wing. Shield knelt beside an unconscious Min. Her Healing flowed into the Lady, trying to stop the swelling in her head.

Spearhead and Raven ran up as Talia, Steel, and Shatter returned to the compound. "The attackers are all dead. Most didn't even try to run," Raven reported. She looked to Shatter for orders. Shatter was staring down at Flora working on Elanor.

Steel stepped in to fill the momentary void in leadership among the soldiers. "Who's left?"

"Goldberry and Nova are over there," Raven gestured toward the remains of the Ladies' cabin. "Willow." She stopped and pointed.

Willow was farther away. She knelt in the grass. Steel approached her. Honor lay dead beside her, her body riddled with crossbow bolts.

"She Sent a warning," Willow sobbed. "It woke me. I ran out through the fire. She. . . ." Her tears took over.

Steel put her hand on Willow's shoulder. "Come," she urged, "the living need us."

Willow wrenched away from her touch. "My fault." She sobbed.

"Willow." Steel grabbed her shoulders and pulled her up. "She's dead. Others might still die. We need you." Willow nodded, and let Steel lead her back to the group.

"Help Flora," Talia commanded. Willow knelt beside Flora, and put her hands on Elanor's back. Healing poured into Elanor. The bleeding stopped. Her heart settled back into a regular rhythm.

"She's out of danger," Flora informed Talia. Flora sat back, tears still filling her eyes. Her right hand moved to her burnt arm. Talia ripped her own nightgown, and used the torn fabric to bind Flora's arm. She sent Healing and Painkilling into her maid. Flora sighed, and settled to the ground. Talia began stroking her hair.

Willow settled back on her heels, her shock and guilt paralyzing her again. Shield looked up, and motioned for Willow to join her at Min's side. Willow stood woodenly and stumbled over. She knelt, her hands waving ineffectively. Shield grabbed her hands, and pressed them to Min's head, beside her own.

147

"Healing," Shield commanded.

The pitiful cry of a sea cat cut through Talia's shock. She got up, and went over to where Shield and Willow were kneeling beside Min. Spear was to her right, also on her knees. Before her lay Rogue. Her body was twisted. She meowed quietly. Nesa was licking at her head, crying. Talia knelt. Nesa put her paw on Talia's leg, and looked into her eyes, asking for help.

Talia looked at Spear.

"Her back is broken," Spear said. Her voice became reverent. "I saw her defending Min. Min fell, and he was about to kill her, but Rogue attacked him. He shook Rogue off, and crushed her. I killed him." She reached down and touched Rogue's fur. "A brave warrior." Rogue turned her head a little, and licked Spear's hand.

"Can't you do something?" Willow asked. She had turned from Min. Shield was rising, a look of relief on her face.

"You have to do something," Willow pleaded.

"There's nothing to do," Spear told her. "There's too much damage. The only thing we can do is give her mercy."

"No," Willow cried. "You have to! She can't die, too. Talia," she turned, pleading, "you must."

Talia was petting Nesa. Her face was still.

"I can stop her heart," Spear said quietly.

"No!" Willow sobbed, dropping to her knees.

"Take her," Talia told Spear. "I'll do it."

Spear pulled the crying Willow to her feet, and took her away. Talia looked at Nesa. The cat's golden eyes met hers. "I'm sorry." Talia Reached out. She found Rogue's tiny beating heart, and stopped it.

Nesa meowed. She bumped the now-still body with her head. She looked up at Talia, and put her paw on Talia's arm.

"I'm sorry, Little Sister. You've lost your family, too. It's my fault." Nesa growled, scratching four bloody lines on Talia's arm. Talia didn't react. Nesa picked up the body of her kitten in her mouth, and walked off into the woods.

Talia stared at the blood on her arm. She ran a finger over the wounds, and held it up. The blood glittered in the red light of the dawn.

☾ ∭ ☼

Steel went to find Goldberry and Nova. They were sitting on the ground outside the Ladies' cabin. Goldberry was bandaging cuts on Nova's arms. The fire was dying.

"They were from a blackblade, but I think I got to them in time. I pushed the darkness out," she told Steel.

Steel couldn't reply. She was staring at the carnage. The door was riddled with crossbow bolts, as were the walls. Helm's body, hit with at least seven bolts, had fallen just outside the door. Harpoon was further outside. She had fallen among five Elenite crossbowmen. Her sword was broken, the hilt buried in the last attacker's body. She had taken even more bolts than Helm.

"She rushed them," Steel commented to no one. "I was too far away to help. I saw her get hit, but she just kept going. She killed them all." She bowed her head in sorrow.

Goldberry came up behind her. "The Twins are inside. They were still asleep. There are two dead men with crossbows in there." Goldberry broke, and Steel pulled her close. "They shot them. Helm must have killed them, then gone to the door."

"She was brave," Steel confirmed. "Don't talk." She hugged Goldberry tighter, as the Lady sobbed into her side.

☾ ∭ ☼

"Where's Gil?" Willow asked, pulling away from Spear. She darted back to the ruins of the Ladies' cabin. Spear was right behind her.

"She must have burned," Spear tried to tell her.

"No!" Willow said. She reached back, and yanked a feather out of her wing. The pain watered her eyes, but it also drove the crushing guilt out of her mind for a moment. She spied a blood trail leading out the door and followed it. Spear looked around for help, but everyone else was lost in their own torment. She gripped her sword, and followed Willow.

149

The blood trail didn't go far. They found her, face down in the grass. One of her wings had been hacked off. Two Elenite bodies lay beside her. One was headless. The other had been hacked apart. An axe was still standing upright in his split skull.

Willow stood, looking down at the body of her wing Sister. She gripped the self-plucked feather in her hand so hard that the barbs cut into her fingers and palm. She wanted to cry, but she couldn't. All she could feel was sorrow.

"Talon must have caught them," Spear was saying. "She didn't die here. She was being dragged. One died quick, the other. . . ." Spear trailed off. She planted her sword in the ground, and went to one knee.

"Goddess have mercy," she asked.

"There is no Goddess here," Willow stated with certainty. Her eyes spied something. She walked toward the woods. Bending down, she picked up the head of the first killer. It had rolled some distance. "All there is, is death," she added, holding up the head by its filthy hair. She walked back to the bodies. "All that remains for us now is sorrow."

Whatever she had been using to hold herself up suddenly left her, and she fell to her knees before Gil's body. The head of her Sister's first attacker fell from her hands and rolled away. Willow pulled Gil's body into her arms. She held her like Gil had held her, a year ago, on the first night of their exile, when the crushing weight of what was happening had settled upon her. Willow wanted to cry, but nothing came. She was empty.

Spear just watched her. She tried to call to the Goddess again, but the words got stuck in her throat.

☾ ∿ ☼

"Look what I've got," Gren said, dropping an unconscious baby wrapped in a blanket before her sisters.

"Is that?" Dina asked.

"It is," Gren sang. "I popped in right before the attack, grabbed the baby, put another half-breed in its place, and left." A pair of shears appeared in her hand. "Shall we take its wings first?"

150

"The child was supposed to die," Tra reminded her. Dina stood, and waved her hand over the baby.

"Feel the Power, and the potential, of this child," she said in awe. "We could create a Blood Ring that reaches across the Realms with her blood." She licked her lips.

Tra stood as well, and waved her own hands over the baby. After a moment's consideration, she said, "I have another idea. King Bastile's wife is pregnant. We can make sure the baby is stillborn. If we cut off this child's wings, and cloak her so she appears Human, then we can take her to the grieving Bastile, and present her as a replacement. We have enough leverage to get him to agree. He'll have to make her his Heir."

"Humans will never accept a female Heir," Dina said, still eyeing the child as a roast.

"Just so," Tra said. "It'll force him to name her as his successor, as Queen of the Human Realm, which will enrage the Humans, and cause more blood to spill. And if he won't name her as Heir, he'll be forced to sell his own daughter to some Lord whose money or influence he needs to keep his throne. His reign will end, either way. He'll be in our debt, and we can use that as a lever to destroy our sister, and become Queens of the Fairy Realm."

"But I want her blood," Gren whined, waving the shears.

"I can see potential in this," Dina admitted.

"It will be glorious. Whatever he does, we'll win." Tra smiled her coldly evil smile.

"I agree," Dina said, grabbing a bowl.

"If we must," Gren sighed, relenting. "I want to take her wings, though."

"You may. They'll make powerful Ephemeral Rings."

The survivors gathered in the area where they had enjoyed their meal of celebration just the night before. The table had been turned over. Raven, Steel, and Shatter brought their fallen Sisters and laid them out, covered by whatever cloth had survived the fire.

Shatter stood before them. "Silidin, Nidilis, Gil-Galin, Harpoon, Helm, Talon, Honor." She said their names over and over to herself. Steel, Raven, and Spearhead joined her. They joined hands, and silently repeated the names together. After a while, they moved off toward the bodies of the men.

Min was still unconscious, and Shield stayed by her side. The Medic needed to give Min more Healing periodically. "The blow cracked her skull," Shield informed Talia. "I can't Heal the bone until she's stabilized. She'll need more time to recuperate." Talia only nodded.

Elanor slept, her back bandaged. Shield worried about blackblade infection, but she seemed to be Healing. Nova was another matter, though. She slept, but was wracked by fever. "I'm watching her wings for black. She might lose her arms," Shield warned.

Talia didn't respond. She sat on the ground, a bundle at her feet. She had gone back into the house. Flora had tried to stop her, but she had given her maid a dark look, and Flora had let her go. She had found bones in the burnt and shattered crib. She had wrapped them in the ruins of her nightgown. There had also been a blade in the crib. A steel, Human-forged blade. She turned it over and over in her hands now. Flora had made her put on a dress that was too big for her, but was one of the few things to survive the fires. Talia stared out over the sea.

Beside Min, Willow slept. She had started crying again, and wouldn't stop. Talia had finally had to cast a Sleep Spell on her. Now, she shuddered and twitched uneasily in a dream.

Flora sat, with Goldberry at her side. Quicksilver's body lay in her lap. She stroked the cat's fur, and talked.

"She woke me, scratching and yowling. I opened my eyes to fire, and a man with a crossbow standing over me. I moved, and Quicksilver attacked him. I heard her scream. Elanor killed him. Then I saw another man strike Elanor. Her wing fell to the ground. I just stared. She killed him, too. We staggered out. I saw Min fall, and then the man who had been attacking her fell, too." She stopped, and gripped Goldberry's hand. "Goddess's mercy. What has happened?" She kept stroking Quicksilver's still form.

Goldberry, in a soft voice, said, "The red ones died with the Twins." She pulled a smile. "They never even named them. Only called them 'Mine' and 'Yours,' and they all knew who was who." She looked to where the Twins' bodies lay. A small lump rested on each of their chests.

Flora wiped her eyes. "Nesa took Rogue away."

Talia answered the unasked question. "She won't be back. She won't return to this place. The kittens will join our Sisters in the Pyre."

Goldberry expected Talia to say more, but she didn't. She just kept turning the steel blade over and over in her hands.

"You're bleeding," Goldberry noticed, pointing to her arm. "Let me bandage it."

"No. Nesa gave me these. I deserve them," Talia shot back. "I brought her here, and she lost everything. I deserve the scars."

Flora wanted to speak, but did not. She bowed her head, and called to the Goddess for strength.

Shatter and the others returned. Spear went to Goldberry's side.

"Not a scratch," she assured her, but Goldberry forced her to remove her mail to make sure. "I was hit, but the ringmail turned it." She gestured to a bruise on her side. "Goddess thank the maker." Goldberry hugged her intensely.

Raven went to Min's side. She Joined with Shield, and plunged into a Healing Circle.

Steel collapsed on the ground beside Elanor. Finally allowing herself to feel, she curled into a ball, laid her head on Elanor's lap, and cried tears of grief. And ashamed tears of joy that Elanor was still alive.

Shatter sat in front of Talia. "My Lady, we must leave. They might come back."

"They wouldn't dare," Talia told her. Her anger burned. "If they do, they'll face my wrath."

"Talia," Shatter started, but Talia interrupted.

"The Ephemeral Rings have been destroyed. We'll have to walk." She gestured to the bodies. "We can't carry them. No. We'll stay. Sit the Vigil for them. Then we'll Return them to the Cycle in the morning. Then we'll leave."

"My Lady," Shatter began again.

"How did this happen, Captain?" she cut in. "How did all these men get into our compound? We had both Wards and guards. How?!" she shouted. She pointed the blade at her Captain. "How did this happen?" She pointed to the bundle at her feet.

Silence enveloped them all. Talia resumed turning the blade over in her hands.

"There was the mark of a destroyed Ephemeral Ring by the house," Goldberry finally said. "I could feel Blood Magic on the remains."

"How did it get here?" Shatter asked.

"Who betrayed us?" Talia added, not raising her head.

"The wine," Flora announced. She pointed at a shattered bottle lying on the ground beside Spear, who picked it up and passed it over. Flora sniffed the remains, then tasted them. "There was something in the wine that made us sleep."

"Then that will be next," Talia decreed. "Realm's End. Some will go to the Exile Queen's mountain." She looked up at Shatter. "Captain, you will make up for this failure."

"Mistress," Flora admonished her.

"Silence!" Talia snapped. "All of you failed." She stood up, brushing away Shatter's hand. "All of you must make up for this. We will start with the shopkeeper." She picked up her bundle, and turned toward the cliff, and the sea beyond.

Shatter snapped to her feet. "Soldiers," she commanded, "up."

Spearhead leaped to her feet. Steel was slower to respond, but rose as well, after a moment's hesitation. Raven was still in the Circle with Shield.

"Burn the bodies now," Talia commanded, her back to the others. "Bring me any blackblades they had. Keep several crossbows. Burn the rest with the bodies." She considered for a moment. "But first, cut off their heads. Leave them unburned, and put them on stakes. We'll leave them as a warning to any who might come back." She walked off toward the cliff, not looking back.

Talia sat cross-legged on the edge of the cliff, the bundle of bones in her lap. Part of her knew she should cry, or scream to the sky. But she couldn't. A coldness filled her. She turned it over and over in her mind; a wall of ice formed. Behind it was everything but her rage. She took all her memories of Sunrise; all the times Gil had helped her ride. All the times the Twins had finished each other's thoughts; her times in the Garden with them; how happy they had been when Harpoon had shown them the first Pattern, and they had done it correctly. Tears started. She pushed them away, behind the wall. She tapped the pommel of the knife blade into her palm. The blade's tip was gone.

'The point broke off in her chest,' a voice in her mind commented, 'so savage was the killing thrust.'

'You failed your daughter,' another voice said. 'You were asleep.'

'She died while you slept,' a third voice giggled.

'Silence,' she ordered the voices. 'I will destroy you. All of you.' Bastile's face appeared before her. "I will do more than destroy you," she said out loud. "I will make you suffer." She thrust the blade through her hand. She looked at it, and felt the pain. "On my blood, I will." She pulled the knife out, and wiped the blade on the bundle. "I swear to you, I will."

Talia set the blade down at her side. She gripped her wounded hand with her right. She began to Heal it, but stopped just as the wound closed. She held her hand up to the sun, looking at the new scar. "Goddess, witness this pledge. I will destroy every Human, Elenite, or Fairy who acted to kill my child. I will curse them. Burn and bury every last one. Nothing will stop me."

The crash of the waves below was her only answer.

The sun was going down when Talia heard footsteps behind her. "What do you have for me, Captain?" she asked, not turning.

The sound of a bag hitting the ground beside her gave rise to no reaction. "I brought you what you wanted," Shatter replied. "It was done as you asked. The bodies have been burned, and the heads are ready."

"Good. Set a guard for tonight. Make sure there are no sleepy eyes."

"We will not fail," Shatter promised.

"Good." Talia reached for the bag. "You may go." Shatter turned, and walked back to the compound.

Talia opened the bag, and saw all the blackblades. She felt the darkness around them. Felt the corruption of the silksteel. Talia wrapped her hand in cloth and picked one up. She held it before her eyes. The darkness filled her vision.

Talia opened her Sight. She Looked into the darkness, and something Looked back.

"*I will find you,*" she promised the presence. "*You cannot hide.*"

"*Neither can you,*" a mocking voice — a familiar voice — said in response. "*I've been over your shoulder all this time. Find me, and you find your doom.*"

"*We shall see,*" Talia said, and sent a beam of Silverfire into the blade. A scream came through in response.

The blade burst into light. She pressed more Silverfire into it. It began to melt in her hand. She threw it, and it exploded in a rain of sparks over the beach.

"*Are there any chests still intact?*" she Sent back to the camp.

"*One,*" Goldberry responded.

"*Bring it to me,*" Talia commanded.

"*Yes, My Lady,*" Goldberry replied.

Talia tied the bag closed, and began to Weave a Ward around it. The darkness Pushed out, seeking to break the Weave. Talia's fury rose. She pulled all her grief from behind the ice wall, and added it to the Weave. Red light bathed her hands. "Curse you, curse you," she chanted, Pushing the Weave around the blades. "Curse you." The Weave finally snapped into place. The darkness was contained. Talia took a deep breath, and pushed her emotions back behind the wall.

More footsteps approached.

"Mistress, I have what you wanted." Flora set a chest on the ground. She knelt beside Talia.

"Mistress, we're about the start the Vigil. Won't you come back?"

"I'll stay here. I'll sit my own Vigil with her."

"Mistress."

"Go, Flora. The others need you. I would be alone."

Flora put her hand on Talia's arm. She flinched. "What about your mother?"

"The Queen will be told when I tell her." Talia jerked her arm out of Flora's grip. "I said, go."

Flora stood up. "Yes, My Lady," Flora said formally, and left.

At the compound, Fairy Lights shone above the survivors of their troop. The seven bodies were laid out under the Lights. Shatter and the soldiers, with nothing to change into, stood in their blood-, dirt-, and soot-covered clothes. Their swords were in their hands, points grounded. They stood in a line behind the dead, facing the sea and the rising moon.

Goldberry walked among the bodies. She chanted between tears. She forgot most of the words, so she simply called on the Mother of Waves to guide her Sisters' Return. Flora and Elanor sat side by side behind Gil and the Twins. Elanor's pain was kept in check by her Power, but her grief flowed freely. She kept looking out toward Talia. She wanted to go to her, but Flora held her in place.

Willow sat numbly at Honor's head, all her tears gone. She stroked her soldier's face, and whispered words too low for anyone else to hear.

Min was awake, but her eyes were glassy, and she was propped up by a broken chair. Shield, Flora, and Goldberry had repaired the physical damage, but only time would tell if she would ever recover her mind. Flora didn't think she even realized what had happened.

Nova was still unconscious. Her fever was back. Flora kept a hand on her, monitoring her breathing and her heart. She feared the girl would lose her arms, or possibly even die. 'Maybe the sun will bring good news,' she thought hopefully.

The moon rose, and for a moment, Talia was silhouetted on its white disc. Flora needed to call out to her, but the wall between them was too high.

Goldberry finally sat down at Min's side. Min put her head on Goldberry's shoulder, radiating a child-like call for comfort. Goldberry pulled her close. "It's all right, Sister. It's all right. The Mother will get us through this." Min began to cry, sensing the grief of the moment. Goldberry just held her closer.

"We should say something," Elanor finally said. "We should tell stories. This is their Vigil."

Flora shook her head. "I can't. I'll fall apart. They know. The Goddess knows. Right now, all I can do is ask Her mercy for them."

Elanor tried. She put her hands on the Twins. "I remember when they first came to court." Then the emotions hit her, and she had to stop. She felt a hand on her shoulder.

"They will be missed," Steel pronounced.

The other soldiers moved closer, each touching one of the Ladies. Together, they formed a Circle, and together they Shared their grief and pain. Shared it at a deep level. Pain bound them, and each tried to find the light in the darkness.

The night passed.

☾ ∿ ☼

When the sun rose, Talia returned to the compound, carrying the small chest. It glowed red with a Ward. She set it down, and looked at the seven bodies. Her gaze then went over the remaining Ladies and soldiers, who all stood up straighter.

"Bring them closer to the edge," she commanded. "I want them to be by the sea for their last part of this Cycle."

Shatter snapped to, and gestured for Steel to take Honor's head, while she took her feet. Flora and Goldberry moved to help.

"No. The soldiers can do it," Talia informed them. "Can Nova be awakened?"

"No," Flora answered. "Her fever is worse."

Talia considered. "Carry her, and after the Pyre, we'll see what can be done. If not, we'll have to take her arms."

Talia turned to Elanor, who was beside Min. "How is she?"

"Still in a daze. I can't sense anything other than basic thoughts," Elanor said, an edge to her voice. "You could have helped."

"Then guide her," Talia responded, either ignoring or not hearing the scold her Second offered. She moved on to Willow, who was still sitting on the ground, despite Honor having been carried off.

"Get up," Talia ordered her. Willow didn't move. "I said, get up! Honor your Sister!" Talia grabbed Willow's arm, and jerked her up. Willow came to her feet, and stood unsteadily.

"I'll guide her," Goldberry offered, stepping to her side. She took Willow's arm, and led her away.

Talia turned to see Flora staring at her. Talia returned a blank look. Flora stopped, and began to pick up Nova. She struggled, until Shield stepped in and helped her. Talia never moved.

She watched the bodies being moved to the cliff edge. When they were all there, she walked to the edge. She stopped behind the line of Ladies and soldiers. She gestured, and the bundle of bones floated from the edge to settle on Gil-Galin's body.

She raised her arms. "Goddess!" she shouted, making all of them jump.

"Return our Sisters to your Cycle. With your mercy, honor them with a better next life."

She closed her fists, and jerked them down. Red-gold fire erupted from the bodies, so hot that everyone had to step back. Talia moved closer. The smokeless fire turned her face red. She raised her arms again. The fire grew into a pillar that reached up into the sky. The others all shielded their eyes.

"Mother of Waves! Take our Sisters!" Talia cried out. The fire grew higher. The oak tree caught, and disappeared into the flames.

There was a crack, followed by the rumble of falling stones. Flora opened her eyes, and saw that the portion of the cliff where the bodies had lain was gone, collapsed. Talia floated in the air, her wings still, her clothes smoking.

"Mistress!" Flora yelled.

Talia turned. The fire in her eyes made everyone step back. Talia walked to them, as if the ground were still there.

"We have work to do," she informed Flora. "Bring Nova." She brushed through the group. After a moment, Shatter and Shield picked Nova up, and followed.

Chapter Fifteen
Grief, Fire, and Sand

Nova screamed.

Talia concentrated harder. The darkness in the wounds was growing. She pushed it back with Silverfire, but it was still there, waiting. She tried again.

Another scream.

"Stop," Elanor begged.

"You're killing her," Shield added, from where she knelt at Nova's head.

"This won't work," Flora said, reaching out to touch Talia's shoulder. She jerked her hand back, as sparks burned her.

"Don't touch me," Talia snarled. "The Weave is delicate."

"Min tried that with Shatter," Elanor reminded her. "It didn't work. The darkness lies deep within the wound."

"I'm stronger," Talia snapped. She sat back, flicking her hands. "This will work."

"And kill Nova," Shield stated, putting her hands on Nova's wound. "I won't let you do any more."

Talia curled her lip, and prepared to strike the Medic with words.

Shatter stepped in. "Lady Talia, this has been tried. Silverfire cannot defeat this darkness. It can only drive it back." She knelt down, and looked the Heir in the eyes. "I want it to be different, but it isn't. She'll die if we don't take her arms."

"Then do it," Talia ordered briskly, standing. "And be quick." She strode away.

The wounds were on Nova's forearms. Shield tied a cord tight right below the elbows.

"Should we wake her?" Elanor asked.

"No," Shield decided. "She's too far gone. I hope the shock doesn't kill her." She stood up. "Put her on the table."

Shield directed the group. "Flora, Goldberry, be ready to stop the bleeding and stabilize her. Elanor, can you cauterize both wounds?"

"I can," she agreed, moving closer.

Shatter handed Shield her sword. "Are you sure you want to do this?"

"I must," Shield said, testing the edge. "Will you remove the other arm?"

Shatter nodded. Raven and Steel moved to pin Nova's arms to the table.

"We must strike together," Shield instructed, raising her blade. "She cannot take two shocks." Shatter nodded and raised her sword.

Flora put her hands on Nova's head, as Goldberry held her feet.

"On three!" Shield called out. "One, Two, Three!"

The sound of metal striking flesh, bone, and wood was horrible. Silverfire shot from Elanor's hands to the wounds. Flora gagged at the smell. Nova screamed again, despite Goldberry's hold on her, but then she mercifully fell into unconsciousness, and began to twitch.

Shield dropped her sword, and grabbed what was left of her Lady's arm. "Fight!" she ordered her charge's unconscious mind. "Nova, I cannot lose you, too." Shield poured Healing energy into the younger Fairy.

Elanor put her hands on Flora, adding her own Power to the Healing. Flora fought to stabilize Nova's traumatized body. The remaining soldiers Joined with Goldberry. Together, they all poured Healing into Nova.

"Her heart has stopped!" Flora called out.

Shield Pulled all the energy available to her from everyone remaining, and struck a sharp blow at Nova's heart.

Nothing happened. Shield struck again. Flora Pushed air into Nova's lungs.

"Please," Shield begged, "Goddess, help me."

Nova began to breathe again, and her heart resumed beating. Shield held the energy for a moment, until she was sure Nova's heart was beating on its own. Then she withdrew, and almost collapsed. Shatter helped her sit down.

"She'll live," Flora proclaimed, breaking down in relief.

Elanor found Talia in the burned shell of the main house. Talia was holding the satchel she had kept the Geode in. She shook it, and heard the crunch and jingle of the Geode's broken crystals.

"The heat shattered it," Talia explained as Elanor entered. She slung it over her shoulder.

"She lived," Elanor announced. "In case you were wondering."

"Good," Talia said. She looked around the room. "There's nothing left."

Talia moved to leave, but Elanor stepped in her way. "Nova is alive."

"I heard you."

"You did not. All of us saved her. You weren't there."

"That was your duty. She should have been wearing her ringmail," Talia reminded her. "You didn't fail this time."

Elanor stepped back in shock, as Talia pushed her way out the door.

☾ ⌇⌇⌇ ☼

"Captain Shatter!" Talia called.

"My Lady?" Shatter turned from where she was putting together litters to carry Nova and Min.

"Do you have the crossbows?"

"Yes, My Lady." She pointed to three crossbows on the ground.

"And bolts?"

"Of course."

"Good," Talia said. She turned, and looked at the burnt shells of the cabins. "Have we salvaged everything we can?"

"Yes, we have," Elanor advised her, coming out of the house. "Some clothes. Some gear." She gestured to a small pile by the bows.

"Most of our weapons survived," Steel added. "Only a few bows. But enough for everyone."

"Good," Talia repeated. Redfire sprang from her hands to strike the vestiges of the house. Elanor had to run to get clear of the flames. The wood caught, and began to burn. Talia moved the fire to the Ladies' cabin, then that of The Nine. She watched the flames eat what remained of the wood. She raised her hands and gestured, and the scattered chairs and tables from around the central clearing rose up and flew into the flames as well. Sparks rose as they hit the fires.

"We put so much time into all of this," Spearhead lamented in a whisper to Goldberry. "And now it's gone." Goldberry could only squeeze her hand, and try to wipe away the tears that still streamed down her own face.

Talia stood still, and watched the licks of fire. They tried to expand onto the grass, but every time they did so, Talia gestured, and they were pushed back.

Flora started to go to her, but Elanor stopped her, shaking her head. Flora clung to Elanor instead, their tears reflecting the flames.

The fires began to die, as most of the wood was devoured into ash. Talia raised an open hand, and brought the flames down, until the last one was snuffed out. Only smoke, slowly spiraling upward into the sky, remained.

She turned to the survivors. "Time to go." She looked at Shatter. "Lead us back to the Ruins."

"We'll have to walk along the cliffs for a while, until we can find a place to descend to the beach," Shatter advised.

"Lead the way, Captain," Talia said impatiently. "You have a route. Show us." She went over and picked up one of the crossbows, along with a quiver of bolts.

Shatter gestured for Spear and Shield to take Nova, while Steel and Raven took Min. The others picked up what they could. Elanor leaned on Flora, her Power stretched thin to tamp down the pain of her missing wing. Willow hadn't moved. Goldberry gave her a hand up, and helped her strap on her gear and weapons. She began to cry again when she touched the hilt of the knife Honor had given her. Goldberry saw Talia glaring at them.

"Come, Sister — we must go," Goldberry urged. "Take my arm, and follow me." Willow did so, moving in a daze.

Talia watched them walk slowly away, then turned back toward the compound. She walked to the circle of heads Shatter and Steel had made. Talia looked at each face.

"You were the lucky ones. Goddess curse the others. Your Father cannot hide them from me." She looked one more time at the collapsed part of the cliff. Tears formed, but she pushed them violently back. Her hand clenched on the blade she had thrust into her belt, its broken tip catching the sun.

$$\left(\!\!\!\!\! \textrm{☽} \textrm{〰} \textrm{☼} \right.$$

The survivors made their way across the cliff. Shatter finally found a gentle slope, and, with some effort, everyone reached the beach.

Talia drove Shatter hard, commanding the Captain to keep pace with her. She strode across the sand, her head held high.

As Shatter walked, with every step, she said a name. She started with those she had been bound to protect: "Silvermane, Silidin, Nidilis, Gil-Galin," then those she had commanded and led to their deaths: "Macemother, Eagle, Harpoon, Helm, Talon, Honor." Then she started again.

Steel, carrying Min with Raven, felt the thump of Harpoon's medal against her chest with every step. She replayed Harpoon's rush of the crossbowmen — killing them, and then falling herself, her body full of bolts — in her mind. Steel was always too far away to help. She swore that Harpoon's sacrifice would not be in vain.

Raven talked to the sleeping Min. She told her stories, and jokes, and tales — anything to keep her voice in Min's head. Anything to keep the pain and fear away.

Spear could only see the small bundle that had rested at Talia's feet. She had to stop and let Shield take the lead, because her eyes were too blinded by the sight.

Shieldbreaker could think of nothing but how she might help Nova and Min. How could she Heal them? How could she put their broken selves back together? "I will not lose any more," she swore. "Goddess, witness this vow."

Flora took Goldberry's place, and walked beside Willow. Goldberry went to help Elanor stay on the path.

"My fault," Willow kept saying.

"It was not," Flora told her firmly.

"It was. I heard her, but I wasn't fast enough. I could've saved her." Her stricken face turned to Flora. "The flames, and the screams."

"It wasn't your fault," Flora stressed again. "It was the wine. It was drugged. You couldn't have acted faster."

Willow shook her head. "My fault."

"It is not." Flora stopped, grabbing her. "Honor wouldn't want you to torture yourself like this."

"She doesn't want anything anymore," Willow said, her voice full of despair. "She's dead. I wish I were, too."

Flora, shocked, was unable to reply, and Willow continued walking.

"Fall behind, and you'll be left," Talia called back.

Flora caught up to Willow.

"Go away, Flora," Willow said without emotion. "There's nothing you can say." She quickened her pace to walk beside Min's stretcher.

Talia, meanwhile, was planning for justice.

☾ ≈ ☼

"My Lady," Shatter called out, "we need to stop."

Talia was still ahead of the others. She stopped, and looked back. The soldiers carrying the stretchers were pale, and sweating under the mid-day sun. Elanor was grey, and leaning heavily on Flora and Goldberry. Willow had simply sat down in the sand.

"If we must," she replied. She sat down on a fallen log, and set the crossbow in her lap. Her fingers traced each part.

Shatter and Steel passed out water and what little food they had scavenged. Willow refused both, and sat with her head between her knees. Goldberry sat beside her, putting her arm around her, but she wouldn't raise her head.

"How is she?" Flora asked Shield, who was rising from Min's side.

"She's still unconscious. I can't get much from her," Shield replied, taking a sip of water. "I don't know. Maybe when we return to the mountain, I can spend more time Healing her. Till then, we can only hope."

"You must take care of yourself, too," Flora reminded her. "You've been pushing yourself too hard."

"When they're Healed, I'll rest," Shield assured her. She got up, and went to Elanor.

Shatter sat down beside Flora. "How are you, Mum?"

"It's all too much," she replied. "We've had no time to think, or even deal with what's happened." She looked at Talia, sitting apart from the others. "I don't know what she needs, but it's certainly not this. Not pushing us across this beach, back to the mountain."

"She won't talk to me," Shatter admitted, concern filling her words. "She looks at me with such. . . ." Shatter stopped, looking for the right word. "Contempt. I failed her. I see it in everything she's done since."

"You didn't fail us," Flora countered, taking her hand. "You saved those you could."

"It wasn't enough," Shatter said, looking at Talia, who was now staring at them. "I'd better go." She stood, and went to Talia.

"Captain," Talia addressed her. "Are they ready to move?"

"We need rest, but if we must, we can move."

"Good." She stood up, and slung the crossbow over her shoulder. She started down the beach without a backward glance.

Shatter got everyone moving. Willow stood without prompting, and went to walk beside Nova's stretcher.

Elanor was helped to her feet by Raven and Steel. "If you need, we can make you a stretcher, too," Steel offered.

"No. I can walk. I just have to keep the pain away." She frowned with determination, and began using her father's spear as a walking staff.

"You'll pay at the end of the journey," Raven warned her.

"We all will," Elanor replied ominously.

(⁓⁓ ☼

They reached the ruins after the sun went down. Talia wouldn't stop, just conjured Lights for them to see by. Steel went first into the Ring room. She called out an all clear and the others filed in, utterly

167

exhausted. They sat on chests, or on the floor. Talia brightened the Lights.

"Raven, Spearhead," she commanded, "go through the Ring, and make sure the library is safe. I'll give you a 100-count to return."

"Yes, My Lady," Raven agreed, drawing her sword, and standing back to back with Spear in the Ring. They disappeared.

The count was only fifty when Raven returned. "It's safe. No one has been there."

"Below?" Talia asked.

"Still locked up tight. Spear stayed, to make sure the Illusion is still strong at the front door."

"Good." Talia gestured to Steel. "Go through. I want to stay in the library. I'll send the others through in a moment. Raven, find some of the preserved food we left."

Steel did as she was asked.

"Flora, Shield — take Min through. Goldberry and Willow, you're next with Nova."

"We'll need bedding," Flora told her.

"Then find some," Talia ordered. "Captain Shatter can help." Talia went off to help Raven.

Flora looked at Shatter, who pointed toward some of the crates. Flora went in that direction.

The others disappeared through the Ring. "We'll take the whole chest," Flora decided, as they carried one to the Ring.

Talia only nodded. Raven gestured to a second chest that held some preserved food.

"Good." Talia looked at Shatter and Flora. "Go on. We'll be along in a moment."

Flora took Shatter's hand, and they disappeared.

Talia turned to Raven, as she was moving the food chest to the Ring. "In the morning, I want you to leave early. I'll be taking Shatter and Steel to Realm's End. Tell the others that you're going hunting, but I have another job for you." She handed her the crossbow. "Can you use one of these?"

Raven took it. "I've used them a few times. They're mostly used by Humans. But I can hit anything with anything."

"Good." She smiled, coldly. "Very good."

Talia and Raven arrived in the library Ring. Talia gestured Raven out, then knelt in the Ring. After a period of concentration, she stood up.

"Gather around," she ordered everyone. "Join hands. I only want to do this once."

Everyone but Spear's unconscious patients joined in a Circle.

"*I have put new Wards on both this Ring, and the one at the ruins. This is the key.*" She Shared it with everyone. "*Make sure that when Nova and Min wake up, this is Shared with them. These locks aren't lethal, but they will hold anyone but us who tries to go through the Ring. So we can deal with them.*"

Talia broke the Circle. "I will be taking Captain Shatter and Lieutenant Steel to Realm's End in the morning." She looked at the two soldiers.

"We'll need our armor and helms," Shatter said.

Talia nodded approvingly. "The rest of you will stay here."

She picked up her satchel, and headed toward one of the smaller rooms. "I am not to be disturbed," she decreed over her shoulder. She entered the room, and shut the door. The glow of Wards soon shone underneath it.

Flora moved to the chest Raven had brought. "I think there's a pot in here. I'll start some food."

Talia sat on the floor, her legs crossed. The satchel gaped open in her lap. She pushed her hands into the shards of the Geode, wondering if it would still work. It did. She reached out for her mother in the Web.

The Queen answered quickly. *"Talia, I'm glad you contacted me."* She stopped, caught off guard by the flat affect of her daughter. *"What's wrong?"*

"They killed her," Talia stated.

The Queen knew instantly who she was referring to. *"Talia, Goddess's mercy. What happened? Are you all right? The others?"*

"Elenites sent by the King." Talia held herself in iron control, not wanting to break. *"Seven died, besides Sun . . . her."*

"Goddess's mercy, who? We'll send help. Where are you? I can't See."

"Silidin, Nidilis, Gil-Galin, Harpoon, Helm, Talon, and Honor."

"Talia." The Queen's voice became harder. *"Where are you? Lower your Ward. I must send help to get you and your people home. And the Fallen."*

"They've already been Returned, My Queen," Talia informed her. *"I will not be returning to the palace. There are those here who need to be questioned and punished."*

The Queen was shocked. *"How could you do that? Without contacting me, without giving their families a chance to sit Vigil and say goodbye?"* The Queen broke. *"You didn't even give me a chance to say goodbye to Sunrise."*

"Don't say her name," Talia snapped. *"I made a decision. We couldn't carry bodies: we had wounded. I was afraid they would come back."*

"Talia," her mother pleaded. *"Come home. We can get through this together."*

"Get through!" Talia cried in anger. *"I will show you what I had to 'get through.'"* Without warning, she poured all that she had experienced and felt into the Geode Web. Her mother cried out, but Talia didn't relent — every smell, every emotion, the feel of the bundle of bones — was forced on her mother.

"They killed my daughter, and I will have justice," Talia proclaimed, finally ending the flow of pain.

It took the Queen a few moments to recover. Tears filled her eyes at the memory of the fire, and her anger rose as she saw the running

Elenites in Talia's mind. She felt great fear as Talia stabbed her own hand, and swore to the Goddess.

"Talia. You must come home. We'll find those who are responsible. We can Heal the wounded. We can help."

Talia refused. Her mind radiated only steel determination.

"Heir," the Queen commanded, *"you will drop your Wards, and allow me access to the Ring. You and your people will return to the palace."*

"I will find all those responsible for her death, and I will punish them. They knew. Somehow, they knew she had been born. I don't trust anyone in your court," Talia stated. *"Anyone who hinders me, I will consider an enemy."*

"You call your Queen an enemy?" Zellandine replied, in a cold voice. Her voice softened. *"Your mother?"*

"Don't try to use the Ring," Talia warned. *"I've added more Wards."*

"You go too far, Heir."

"Goodbye, My Queen." Talia broke the connection. She put the Geode satchel inside a steel chest, and sealed it with a Ward. Talia then dropped into a deep meditation. It was the only thing that kept her from screaming.

☾ ♒ ☀

The Queen put the Geode back in its case and wiped her eyes.

"Luna," she called.

"Yes, Mistress?" Luna inquired, entering the Queen's chambers. She knew something was wrong the moment she saw the Queen's face. "What's wrong?

"Get Lady Titania and Lord Oberon." Luna hesitated. "I will explain, after you bring them here."

"I'll Send," Luna started.

"No," the Queen snapped. "Go to them. Pull them out of bed, or wherever they are. Speak to them with a Send through touch only." The Queen raised her hand. "Go!" Luna went.

Merry-Weather was at the door. "My Queen?"

171

"Find Paramount Miranda. Bring her here," the Queen commanded.

"What has happened, My Queen?"

"Something horrible," the Queen replied. "Something that might destroy us all."

Chapter Sixteen
Realm's End

Talia emerged from her room with the sunrise.

Steel and Shatter were ready to go. They had donned their full plate armor, and held their dragon helms in their hands. Shatter had replaced her sword with a hand-and-a-half one from the armory.

"A bastard sword, for killing bastards," Shatter informed Talia.

Talia nodded with approval. She had changed into a black dress. Her only weapon was the bare knife in her belt. She looked around. Everyone but Spearhead, who sat beside the Ring, was asleep.

"Raven left earlier. Hunting, she said," Spear reported as the group's leaders approached.

"Yes. I ordered her to see what she could find," Talia replied, picking up one of the crossbows and a quiver of bolts. "Let's go." She stepped into the Ring with Shatter and Steel, and disappeared.

☾ ∿ ☼

They arrived at the ruins Rings a moment later.

"Do you want to go to the broken tower Ring?" Shatter asked Talia.

"What's the travel distance?" Talia replied.

"About the same," Steel advised. "A few hours at a good pace."

"Then we shall set a good pace," Talia announced, exiting the room.

Once outside, she turned to Shatter.

"Captain," she asked, "how do I use this?" She gestured to the crossbow.

Shatter took the weapon. She investigated the magazine, and loaded four bolts. She cocked the string back, and loaded another bolt. "This is the trigger." She raised the bow to her shoulder, aimed at a tree, and pulled the trigger. The arms snapped, and the bolt flew, striking the tree.

"You pull this lever forward, and it cocks the string, and loads another bolt." She demonstrated. "Very deadly at short range." She stopped.

Talia nodded, pushing out of her mind the image of the Twins in their blood-soaked beds. Steel covered her own rage by walking to the tree and pulling the bolt out of the wood. She snapped the bolt in her fist, and threw it into the sea.

Shatter, remaining focused on her duty, removed the loaded bolt, and un-cocked the bow. She presented it back to Talia.

"I don't expect to use it, but I need to know how."

"My Lady." Shatter bowed.

☾ ∭ ☼

"You're the Fairy who's been selling my Sisters goods for the past few months, aren't you?" Talia asked the Feather-wing shopkeeper.

He looked at her. He was in the middle of a transaction with another Fairy. "I'm sorry, My Lady. I must finish with these good Fairies, and then I can answer your questions."

"You're done." Talia turned and addressed the two Feather-wings who were buying supplies, saying, "Take your goods and go. I'll take care of it." Steel appeared at their shoulders, and helped them gather their goods and exit the shop.

The shopkeeper looked annoyed at first, but then he looked around, and realized that his shop was empty. Shatter had already cleared everyone else out, and was standing at the door. Her sword was out, held loosely in her hands.

The shopkeeper sighed; he was dealing with one of those Iridescents. He put on a smile. "What can I do for you, Lady?"

Talia thumped the crossbow onto the counter between them. "Can you sell me more of these? And the bolts?"

He looked at the weapon on the counter. A bead of sweat appeared on his brow. His hand shook a bit as he touched the crossbow. "I don't sell these. They're mostly used by Humans and Elenites. Not many of them around here. I have some fine longbows, though. I believe I sold some to another of your company. She wanted to try fishing with them. How'd she do?"

"She's dead," Steel growled. She had come around the counter, and was now behind him, blocking his escape.

"I know they're used by Elenites," Talia informed him. She picked up the crossbow. "They came to our compound and killed half my Sisters with them." She cocked the bow and pointed it at him. He tried to move, but Steel held him in place. "I know you sold us drugged wine. It made us sleepy, and slow to act." Fury took her eyes. "Who provided the wine and herbs?"

"I don't know," he started, but then his eyes glazed for a moment. He took a deep breath. "It was a wingless Fairy. He paid me to furnish the wine."

"How much did you get to betray us?" Steel asked, as she grabbed the front of his tunic. "Why would you do it? Betray one of your own to Elenites and wingless scum?"

He shook off Steel's hand. "Because you're arrogant, and haughty. You take what you want, and leave us with nothing. You sit in your palaces, and get fat off our labor."

Steel moved to strike him, but Talia held up her hand. "Wingless, you said. Who was he? How did he get an Ephemeral Ring into our compound?"

"I don't know." He pulled up his sleeve, showing a fresh cut. "He made me forget. I just remembered now."

"And he left you with only the knowledge of the wine. The block was triggered to fall when I asked the question." Talia waved the crossbow back and forth in front of him.

"Any Iridescent asking about your group. He also left a message," the shopkeeper said dully.

"What is it?" Talia demanded.

"Tell Elanor, if she survived, that I look forward to seeing her again."

Steel smashed his head into the counter. "How dare you speak her name?" She pulled him up.

"He said he only wanted the child, that was all," he told Talia, panicked, blood running down his face. "No one was supposed to get hurt. They were only going to take the child."

Talia put down the crossbow. She pulled the blade from her belt, and grabbed his collar. "Does this look like he didn't want to hurt us?" She held the broken blade in front of his face. "This was in my daughter's body." He tried to pull away, but Steel held him in place. "In the burnt wreckage of our home. You chose to believe his lies." She gripped his face. "I should rip into your mind, and find out what else has been hidden in there." Her eyes narrowed, as his grew.

"My Lady," Shatter called out from the door.

Talia whirled, fury lighting her eyes. The sound of a fist hitting the door filled the room.

"Whoever is in there, release the shopkeeper and come out," a voice called from outside.

"This is none of your concern," Shatter called out, checking the door bar.

"It is. I am the Law Steward for this town. If you have a disagreement with this man, bring him out, and we can discuss it."

"He is accused of a crime," Shatter replied through the door, after a look from Talia. "We seek justice."

There was a pause. "Bring him out, and we will discuss this accusation," the Law Steward said. "Fail to do so, and we will use force."

Talia curled her lip, but motioned for Steel to bring the shopkeeper out from behind the counter. She made a motion in front of her face. Shatter and Steel closed their face guards.

"Step back, into the street," Shatter commanded. "Lower your bows."

They heard whispers and shuffling outside. Shatter peered through a crack in the door. She turned to Talia, and nodded.

"He goes first," Talia commanded. She put the blade back in her belt.

Steel moved the shopkeeper to the door. Shatter pulled the bar back, and opened the door. Steel stepped through it, pushing the shopkeeper in front of her. Shatter stepped out to the left, and Talia to the right. In front of them, a group of Feather- and Leather-wings stood facing the storefront. All of them were dressed in blue uniforms, with swords and knives at their belts. Three had longbows, each with an arrow on the string, but not pulled back. An older, scarred Leather-wing stood in front of the uniformed group. His hands were tucked into his belt. Behind them, a crowd of townspeople had gathered. A gasp arose from them at the sight of Shatter and Steel in their armor and dragon helms.

"Put away your sword, soldier," the Law Steward commanded. Shatter didn't move.

"I am the Heir of the Fairy Queen," Talia announced to the crowd. "This Fairy caused the deaths of seven of my Sisters. I demand justice."

More muttering rose. The Law Steward bowed his head, stopping himself from bowing lower.

"That's a serious charge, My Lady," he finally said. "This is something for the Law Master."

"Then bring her," Talia commanded. "I will not leave with this man free."

"He isn't here. He's away, and will not return for some time," the Law Steward advised her.

"Then, as the Heir, I will dispense justice in his stead." Steel pushed the shopkeeper to his knees and took hold of his left wing. She stretched it out. Shatter raised her sword.

"Hold!" the Law Steward yelled, both to his soldiers, who were raising their bows, and to Talia.

"I demand a trial!" the shopkeeper yelled. Steel cuffed him.

"Those longbows could punch through our armor," Shatter Sent. Talia acknowledged the warning with a thought.

"Yes, Law Steward?" Talia addressed him with contempt.

"My Lady," the Law Steward began, speaking slowly in an attempt to keep things from escalating, "with all due respect, we don't know you. You're obviously a Noble, with your wings, and soldiers, and fancy armor, but the Heir? In this little town? You must give me more. I will not allow you to do this to a citizen of this town. That is the law your mother serves." He pointed at her. "If you are who you say you are, you must respect the law."

Talia gestured for Shatter to stand back. Steel released the shopkeeper's wing, but kept her hands on his shoulders. "And you must respect my duty as a mother hunting the murderers of my child." Gasps and muttering filled the crowd.

The Law Steward motioned for his soldiers to lower their bows. "I'm deeply sorry. That's a tragic loss, and a strong accusation. What proof do you have?"

"He confessed to me," Talia stated. "He sold us drugged wine. It put us to sleep, allowing our enemies to enter our compound and kill my Sisters."

The Steward looked to the shopkeeper. "What do you have to say for yourself?"

"I invoke my right not to betray myself," he said. Looking up at Talia, he added, "A law your mother created."

"Cheeky bastard," Steel rumbled from under her helm.

"That is his right," the Steward pronounced. "He will be taken into custody. I swear to the Mother, he will be held, and your accusations shall be investigated."

Talia's hands clenched. "I will not be denied justice."

"You're not seeking justice — you want vengeance," the Steward returned.

"And you're a fool if you believe that he acted alone in this town. He allowed enemies of the Fairies inside our Realm. Gave them Goddess knows what else," Talia fumed. "The Governor of this area will hear of this."

"Yes, she will," the Steward promised. "Now, I will take him into custody." Talia didn't move. "My Lady, you and your soldiers can accompany me and my soldiers. You will be free to inspect our cells, and assure yourself that he will not escape. My clerk will take all the information you have."

"I should kill him now, and save the bother," Talia said.

"That would be murder, and Heir or not, you will be held," the Steward advised her. His voice took on steel and command. "Now, stand aside."

Talia considered for a moment. Her eyes swept the crowd and the armed Fairies before her. She saw resentment in many of their eyes.

"Very well, Law Steward," she relented, her contempt abundantly clear, "you may take him." Steel allowed the shopkeeper to stand. He walked, shakily, across the ground to the Steward and his soldiers.

"Remember this day when your contracts with the palace are canceled," Talia promised him. "When your children go hungry for lack of work."

The Steward's eyes narrowed. "That's cruel. I'm only doing my duty."

Talia's words were lost in the twang of a crossbow, and the impact of a bolt on flesh. The shopkeeper fell to his knees, a bolt in the middle of his back. Another twang, and his head burst, as a bolt passed through it and stuck in the ground at the Steward's feet.

Screams rang out as the crowd ran for cover. The Law Steward yelled, and pointed to the roof of the shop. The archers took aim, but couldn't find anything to fire at. When no more bolts flew, Talia walked across to the body. She looked down at it, then at the Steward.

"Crossbow bolts. Looks like someone didn't want him to talk. I'll search this shop and his home." She stared right into the Steward's eyes. "If you object, you can tell the Law Master when he returns." The Steward couldn't hold her gaze. He dropped his head.

"As you wish, My Lady."

Talia turned on her heel, and returned to the shop. Shatter made a point of shutting the door and throwing the bar.

☾ ⌇ ☀

Later, as the sun was going down, Talia, Shatter, and Steel were walking toward the broken tower Ring. They had decided to go that way to throw off anyone who was following them.

"We found nothing but a mix of coins from all over the two Realms and various Elen towns," Steel was saying. "And a single bolt of Fairy silk. Should we be offended that our lives were so cheap?" Her attempt at a joke fell flat, and Shatter glared at her. Talia remained

179

silent. She hadn't spoken since they were at the shopkeeper's house, which had been a small thing, containing little of note beyond the coins.

Talia had taken the coins, and glared at the town soldier who had shown them where the shopkeeper had lived, daring him to say something. He did not, and only shuffled his feet, and petted the two sea birds the shopkeeper had kept as pets. They were the only thing that kept Talia from burning the house down in her rage.

Steel wanted to say more, but Shatter gestured for her to stay quiet. The rest of their walk passed in silence.

Talia turned everything over in her head. They had also found a burned spot behind the shop where an Ephemeral Ring had been destroyed. Talia had spent a long time probing that spot with her Power. Everything she had tried had turned up nothing other than the taint of Blood Magic, though.

When they reached the concealed entrance to the broken tower Ring, Talia turned to Steel and Shatter.

"I pulled something from him. It was only a flash, before that fool interrupted. But I saw that wingless Fairy mention returning to Elen-Flax. And he said he would send more silk."

"That silk bolt bore the mark of an Elen-Flax Crafthouse, and it is the closest Elen town to the Human castle and palace," Shatter remembered.

"And it has a large Embassy and garrison," Steel added. "I was stationed there before the War."

"We have a place to start, then," Talia decided, opening the Ward. They began to descend to the Ring.

"I'm surprised you didn't try to hunt down whoever killed the shopkeeper," Shatter commented as they walked.

Talia gave her a look of contempt, then pity, and finally smiled. "She was gone before I spoke with the Steward," she responded, reaching the bottom of the stairs. She stepped into the Ring chamber.

Steel gave Shatter a look. "She?" she mouthed. Shatter's hands clenched.

Talia knelt in the Ring. "It's weak. We must go through one at a time. Steel, you go first, and then Shatter. I'll be last, so I can add to the Wards."

"Yes, My Lady," Steel agreed, stepping up and vanishing.

Shatter looked at Talia. She looked back, daring Shatter to ask the question Talia could see in her Captain's face.

"Yes, My Lady," Shatter finally said, and entered the Ring.

After she was gone, Talia smiled. She knelt in the Ring, added new Wards, and then disappeared.

((☽ ∭ ☼))

Raven was waiting in the ruins Ring chamber. She was cleaning the game she had killed. "Flora wouldn't want the smell in the library," she reminded her leaders.

Steel greeted her warmly. Shatter only gave her a look. Talia took her arm. "You did well," she told her. "Now, back to the mountain."

((☽ ∭ ☼))

They returned to a muted welcome. Min was sitting up and eating. Talia could sense that she had returned to her normal mental state. Talia began to smile, but the expression quickly turned to a frown.

"Where's Willow?"

181

Chapter Seventeen
Repercussions

Shield woke early. She heard Talia and the others leave. She lay there, trying to organize the thoughts her dream had brought. When she felt she understood the message, she sat up. Upon rising, she went to Flora's side. Flora looked old, older than she had ever seen her. She was sleeping fitfully, her eyes moving wildly under her lids. Shield put her hand on Flora's shoulder, and Sent a request for her to wake.

Flora's eyes flew open. She struggled out of sleep and kicked off her blanket. "What's wrong?" she said, too loud.

"I have an idea," Shield said. She Shared it with Flora.

After a moment, Flora sat up and announced, "I'll make some tea."

A short time later, with a cup in her hands, Shield explained to a sleepy Goldberry and Elanor what she wanted to do. "This will take all of us," she said. "I want to enter Min's mind, and sweep it out."

"Sweep it?" Elanor asked, taking a large drink of her tea.

"Yes. There was so much damage. While we were able to Heal most of it, bits of flotsam," Shield said, lacking a better word, "were left behind. We'll go in and sweep them all out. Flush them from her mind. And then — I hope — she'll wake up, and be back to herself."

"We could also damage her beyond repair," Elanor cautioned.

"That's the risk, but the longer she's like this, the greater the chance she'll never recover," Flora explained. "This is the best plan we have."

"It will take all of us." Shield motioned to Spear, who joined them.

"What about Willow?" Goldberry asked, gesturing to where the youngest member of their family was sleeping beside the still-unconscious Nova.

"She's too fragile for this work," Flora said. "Let her sleep."

They settled into a Circle around Min. Shield sat at her head. She put both hands on Min's head, pushing through her thick white hair to touch her scalp. With Flora on her right, and Elanor on her left, she formed the Circle.

"Follow my lead," she directed. "Lend me Power." She plunged into Min's mind. She could feel bits of bone and scar tissue all throughout Min's head. She began to gently break them up and flush them out. Min's blood carried the small bits away. Soon, they had swept out all the flotsam. Shield was about to leave, when she saw a large scar on the brain, right under where Min's skull had been broken.

"*We must Heal that.*" Shield pointed. "*But be careful: we don't want to damage her mind.*"

Shield gathered Healing Power from the others. She cast its silver light on the damage. She gently massaged the scar, returning the area to health. Shield could feel Min returning, feel her mind coming back into alignment. She watched the last of the scar disappear under her Healing. Shield smiled, and withdrew from Min's mind. She dismissed the Circle.

Shield looked down, and found that Min's eyes were open. They were clear.

"What happened?" Min asked, turning toward Flora. "I remember feeling sleepy, then nothing. Just heat, and pain, and then I woke up here." She looked around. "Why are we back at the Exile Queen's mountain?" She stopped, registering the looks in the eyes of those around her. "What's wrong? Where's Talia? Mum?" She gripped Flora's hands. "What happened?"

Willow was dreaming.

She was back at the shop in Realm's End.

There was a wingless Fairy with her in the storeroom. Willow turned, but the shopkeeper was blocking the door.

"Scream or Send, and your Sisters will be dead," the wingless one warned her. "Plus, the room is Warded."

"What do you want?" she asked. The scent of blood was strong in the air.

"I want you to help me."

"Never."

"I wasn't finished. I want you to help me, or I will kill your whole family, Willow." He pulled out a chain and tossed it to her. Willow caught it. There were two rings on the chain.

"This is my mother's," she accused.

"And this is your father's." He held up another chain, with a white stone. "I wanted you to have proof that I have your family. Your parents, your sisters and brothers. I also have your aunts and their children. I might even kill the birds that your mother feeds." He stopped. His eyes bored into hers. "I won't simply kill them, though. I'll bleed them for days. Cut off their wings. Use them in any manner I and my people see fit." He looked up, thinking, considering, smiling. "We'll have so much fun. And when I finally allow them to die, they'll all know it was because of you. They'll curse you into their next lives."

Willow began to tremble. Her fist clenched on the chain. "My Sisters will never let you leave here."

"If you refuse me, I'll kill those outside." He drew a blackblade. "You know what these can do?" Willow nodded.

"I'll have to kill the soldiers outright, but the other Feather — I'll have so much fun with her." He smiled cruelly. "I'll show her all the best torture. My men will exhaust themselves raping her. And it will all be your fault. Again!" He laughed. "I'll even make an Illusion of you watching and laughing. It will be horrific."

Willow decided. She bowed her head. "What must I do?"

He held out a rolled piece of cloth. "Take this, and put it inside your Wards, close to where Talia and the baby sleep."

"What will you do with them?"

"I only want to capture them. Her Aunts want them alive." He held up his hands. "No harm will come to them. But if you don't do this, death will follow you." He gestured at her with the roll. "Choose. I have little time."

Willow looked up. "Make me forget. You have the Power. Make me forget all of this. Plant a suggestion, so I'll hide this without my conscious self even knowing. Then, I will do this thing for you."

He laughed. "I misjudged you. I agree."

He came closer. "Drop your Wards," he commanded.

"Curse you," Willow said, taking the roll, and dropping her Wards. She closed her eyes.

"Oh, I am, little sister. I am."

Willow rolled over, whimpering.

Min had exhausted herself crying. She refused to believe that Raven was safe. Elanor and Goldberry had to hold her down. They pressed her into a Circle, and Showed her everything that she had missed: from the aftermath, to the Vigil and the Return, to the trip across the sand. The only thing that made her smile was hearing Raven talk to her unconscious form almost nonstop.

"Mum." Min held onto Flora. "What will become of us?"

"I do not know," Flora told her honestly. "We must trust in the Goddess."

Min could only weep a little more before she fell back asleep.

Another dream: After the Presentation of Sunrise, Willow stole away from the group. She went to the side of the house, just under the window Shatter had cut into the logs so Talia and the baby could see the rising sun. Willow unrolled the cloth the wingless fairy had given her. She turned, hearing footsteps.

"There you are," Honor said. "I was looking for you." She held out a bottle. "I got this for you."

"Thank you," Willow said, moving quickly to her soldier's side. She grabbed the bottle, and took a long drink.

Honor laughed. "Save some for me." They walked off into the night.

Flora softly stroked Min's hair as the still-recovering Lady lay asleep in her lap.

Shield sat beside her. "Thank the Goddess that worked."

"Yes, thank her," Flora agreed.

A scream came from the other side of the room. Min sat up, as Flora started.

"Nova!" Shield shouted, getting up. "Goddess, no." She ran to Nova's side.

The young Fairy was sitting up, her stumps held out in front of her.

"What did you do!" she screamed.

Shield got to her side first, and gripped her shoulders. "I saved your life." She tried to Send calming into her patient, but Nova's panic Pushed it away.

"You cut off my arms!"

"You would have died," Shield pleaded. "Blackblades. The infection was spreading. There was nothing we could do."

Nova moaned, tears falling all down her front. "How will I Weave? How will I feel the stone?"

"We'll help you. They can be regrown," Shield comforted her. Flora sat down beside her. Nova flinched away.

"It didn't work for Shatter," she reminded Shield. "It didn't work."

"It will this time, I promise," Shield pledged. "I did what I thought was right. I couldn't lose you after losing so many others."

"You should have let me die," Nova said, broken. She pulled away, and tried to roll herself back into her blanket. Shield tried to help, but Nova's Power Pushed her away.

"Go away. I hate you. Go away," she sobbed.

Shield could only look at Flora with despair. Flora shook her head and put a hand on Nova's back.

"Go away," she sobbed again.

Flora could only settle back. Elanor and Min clung to each other. Goldberry and Spear took Shield away to sit in a corner.

The scream woke Willow from her nightmares. She stuffed the blanket into her mouth to stop herself from screaming, too.

'How could you?' she asked herself. 'How could you?' All the crippling guilt she had been feeling for the last few days suddenly came into focus. Her unconscious mind had known what she had done. She cast a Silence Spell around herself while everyone was occupied with Nova. Willow screamed into her blanket, "It was me; it was me, it was my fault, my fault." Her hand went to her chest. She felt two chains around her neck: one with two rings, and the other with a stone.

Her heart stopped. "No, no, no," she moaned into the silence. "Mother, Father." Willow sat up. Everyone was looking at Nova, or at themselves. Spear, who had been guarding the Ring, was turned away, talking to Shield. Willow cast a Shadow over herself, and crept to the Ring.

She said a heartfelt "I'm sorry" to the silence, and disappeared.

Willow appeared in the library Ring.

Talia and the other survivors were there, encircling her.

"Where did you go?" Shatter demanded.

Willow stepped out of the Ring. Her hands shook. Her face was white.

"I went home," she started. Her legs collapsed underneath her, and she fell to her knees.

"Why?" Steel demanded.

"I had to know."

"Know what?" Elanor asked.

"If. . . ." Willow stopped, shaking her head.

"If they kept their promise," Talia finished. Her face was still.

"Willow," Flora's heartbroken voice asked, "what did you do?"

"They caught me, at Realm's End," Willow sobbed. "A wingless Fairy. He said if I didn't do as he asked, they would kill my parents."

"And," Talia prompted.

"And my sisters and brothers, and my aunts. Everyone." She raised her eyes. They pleaded with Talia. "I had no choice."

"And what did you find at home?" Elanor asked, her voice cold, her hands shaking.

Goldberry tried to go to Willow, but Steel stopped her.

"They were all dead," Willow told them, her voice flat. "All. Had been. Before," she broke. "Before the wingless Fairy found me. I betrayed you all for nothing. He killed them anyway."

"What did you expect!" Steel screamed. She pushed Goldberry aside and strode to Willow, her knife in her hand. "How could you!" She grabbed Willow's hair and pulled it back, exposing the younger Fairy's neck to the blade.

"I was trying to save them," Willow pleaded. "He said they only wanted to capture you. Not kill. Only capture." She looked into Steel's eyes. "I was lied to."

"You fool," Steel snarled. "Betrayer. The Three Sisters lie. Their agents lie. You were a fool to believe them." She looked at Talia for direction.

Talia only stared at first, but eventually, she gestured for Steel to let Willow go. Steel did, pushing Willow's head forward as she did so. Steel stepped back. Her hands clenched with frustration and fury.

Talia took a step forward. Willow looked up.

"I'm sorry." Willow's voice was quiet. Resigned.

"I'm sorry, too," Talia said, also resigned. Her hand went up.

"Talia! No!" Goldberry yelled.

Talia's hand twisted. The sound of Willow's neck breaking stabbed through the room. Her body fell to the floor. Flora's scream filled the silence.

$$(\;\approx\; \text{☼}$$

The door opened into the Queen's chambers.

"I'm sorry to disturb you," Lord Oberon said to the Queen.

She looked up from her desk. Oberon could see her red, tired eyes. Her face was pale and drawn.

"What is it?" she asked, looking up from a pile of maps and dispatches.

"I just received a message from one of the Law Stewards in town. The bodies of an entire family have been found. The whole extended family." Oberon struggled with the news. The Queen waved him to a chair. "Wife, husband, her sisters and their children. Even the pets."

"How did they die?" the Queen asked, fearing the answer.

"Bled. All of them. Tortured. Raped. It was horrible." He shook his head, and his wings shivered with his distress. "I don't know if the Law Steward will return to her position. She's seen some awful things over the years, but this was beyond imagining."

"Who were they?" the Queen asked, making the Sign of the Three.

"The family of one of your Heir's Ladies. Willow."

The Queen felt her whole body go cold. She took a deep breath. "I want every family member of my Heir's Ladies found and brought here. Send my personal guard to fetch and protect them. This may be retaliation, or something else. I want that house closed off. No one is to disturb anything. I will contact Paramount Miranda, and have her send her people to search for anything the murderers may have left."

"The Mistress of Shadows?" Oberon asked.

"Cannot be trusted," the Queen cut him off. "We will keep this as contained as we can. Hurry. I fear finding other families slaughtered in a similar fashion."

Oberon bowed, and hurried out of the room.

The Queen took a moment. "Goddess, please watch over my daughter and her Ladies. They need your guidance and mercy." She reached for her Geode.

$$\left(\!\!\text{︵}\!\!\text{︾}\!\!\text{☼}\right)$$

Goldberry knelt, resting Willow's lifeless head in her lap. Flora was at her side, holding Willow's cooling hand. Elanor and Min clung to each other, still in shock. Raven went to stand with Spear and Shield. She reached for Shield's arm, but was brushed away. Shield strode to the far side of the room, turning her back on the others.

189

Shatter, paralyzed, could only collapse into a chair. Steel went to stand beside Talia, who was radiating iciness.

Her hands now still, Talia stood looking down at Willow.

Goldberry looked up, tears in her eyes. "How could you do this? She was manipulated. She needed our help. Not this."

"She betrayed me. She gave them access to my child. She deserved worse," Talia replied. Her emotions were tightly controlled.

"She followed you. We gave up everything for you," Goldberry accused Talia. Her hands stayed on Willow's head. "We sacrificed, and suffered. For you. And you killed her. You killed her!"

"She killed my child," Talia returned. "She didn't hold the knife, but she allowed her to die."

"She had no choice," Goldberry whispered. "Goddess forgive her."

"She might, but I never will." Talia turned to Steel. "Get rid of the body."

Shock finally penetrated Steel's frigid fury. Her eyes grew. Elanor and Min, momentarily yanked out of their grief, turned toward Talia in disbelief. Even Shatter raised her head.

"No. You will not." Goldberry stood. Her wings flared out to their full width behind her. "She will go home. She will be given a proper Return." Her aura flared. Silver light grew around her head and hands.

"She doesn't deserve that honor," Talia said angrily. Her own aura appeared, dark and red. She gestured Steel forward. Shatter finally stood up.

"Will you kill me, too?" Goldberry challenged. "Will you cast me aside, like you did Willow?"

Talia's eyes narrowed. Red light began to play around her hands. "Do not defy me. Stand aside."

"Mistress," Flora begged. "This is too far. Willow deserves to Return."

Talia turned to her maid. "I did not ask for your counsel. Stand aside, or both of you will feel my wrath."

Steel froze, not knowing what to do. Elanor and Min both reached out to Talia. Fear was evident on Elanor's face.

"Mistress," Flora said, her voice going cold. She had stood, after gently folding Willow's hands. "We will not stand aside. We will not let you defile one of your Ladies." Goldberry moved to stand alongside Flora. They joined hands over Willow's body. Their auras joined, forming a silver barrier to Talia's growing red.

"Mistress." Flora's voice turned pleading. "Let go of your anger. You aren't thinking clearly."

"Talia," Elanor said, stepping up and putting her hand on Talia's arm. "Please."

Shatter took a step toward Talia, and Steel moved to intercept her. Shatter put a hand on her sword hilt.

Min looked across the room at Raven. Raven gripped Spear's arm, preventing her from going to Goldberry. Shield was turning, her hands moving. Min saw something in the corner of her eye. She turned, and saw Nova standing in the Ring.

"Nova!" Min yelled. Everyone turned toward the Ring.

"Goodbye," Nova said, and disappeared.

Shield was the only one moving. She reached the Ring, falling to her knees.

"Where did she go?!" Talia demanded. Her aura began to fade.

Shield put her hand on the Ring. She looked up at everyone. The look on her face made Goldberry's defensive aura wink out. She fell to her knees, sobbing.

"She went nowhere," Shield finally said. "She's gone. Gone." She looked straight at Talia. "What have you done to us?" Her tears came. She slumped over, her sobs filling the room.

Min collapsed. Elanor grabbed her, just barely keeping her head from hitting the floor and easing her down at the last moment. Flora, moving slowly, went to Shield, and gathered the sobbing woman to her. Raven darted across the room to Min's side. Spear went to sit beside Goldberry, while still keeping her eye on Talia.

Talia's aura faded even further. Emotions warred on her face. She looked at Elanor, but Elanor refused to look back. She was helping Raven lay Min more comfortably on the floor. Talia looked around the room. All she saw was pain reflected back at her from the remaining members of her company.

Steel moved toward Goldberry and Spear. Shatter let go of her hilt, and hit Steel in the face so hard that her head snapped back. When she recovered, she just stared at Shatter.

"I wasn't going to do it," she finally told Shatter. "I wasn't." Steel turned, and went to sit away from the others.

Talia looked at Shatter, who wouldn't meet her eyes. Shatter went to join Flora and Shield. Talia turned, and left the library.

She descended to the second level. The door to the mushroom-overrun garden was closed. Talia wrenched it open with her Power and strode into the chamber. The smell was even worse than she remembered. She shut the door behind her, and cast a Ward on it.

She released her anger. She screamed. Redfire, brighter than anything she had ever cast, filled the room. The fungus caught fire and burned. It wasn't enough. Talia continued to scream. Rocks were wrenched from the floor and the walls. They flew across the chamber, smashing into the stone. Soon, the large space was filled with smoke, fire, and dust. Talia's voice started to get hoarse. She stopped screaming, but continued to burn things, and throw stones. Her mind continued to scream. In the smoke and dust, faces appeared: her Aunts, Bastile, Wingless, the Elenite she had killed on the cliff. At every face, she cast fire, and threw stones. The faces would wink out, then reappear, smiling, and mocking her. She began to scream again. Though her throat was raw, her voice needed to be used.

Eventually, the whole chamber began to rumble. Talia stepped back, as the one pinpoint of clarity in her mind alerted her to the danger. She cast a Shield in front of herself, and watched the stones fall. When a significant portion of the walls and ceiling had finished falling, Talia sat down on the floor. Her anger and grief had been blunted, but still remained inside her. She began to meditate. She looked for silence to hold her.

Sometime later, a voice interrupted her meditation.
"Talia."

"Paramount Miranda?" Talia answered. *"How are you contacting me?"* she asked with suspicion and fear. *"I don't have my Geode."*

"You forget: I am a Paramount, and your teacher. I have secrets."

"If you've contacted me, in the name of the Queen, to get me to come home, you can leave now. I will not."

"I do speak to you at the urging of your mother, but," Miranda cut off Talia's anger, *"I do not seek to bring you home. I seek to help you."*

Talia could feel no deception in her teacher's thoughts. *"Go on,"* she prompted.

"I understand your emotions. Your mother shared with me all that you have experienced. If I were you, I would want justice, too."

Talia relaxed slightly.

Miranda continued, *"My students are working to find all the information they can on your Aunts and the Blood Cult."*

"Where are my Aunts?" Talia demanded.

"They disappeared, along with their families, two nights ago."

"The night of the attack."

"Just so. I haven't been able to find them. Yet. Rumors come of them being seen in the Elen towns, and even in the Human Realm."

"That make no sense. My Aunts hate Humans."

"That was my thought, too, but eyes have seen them. Rumors also say King Bastile's Queen is with child."

Talia's anger rose. *"He will pay. One of the Elenites said the King sent him."*

"If he did, he will pay. I promise you that. I am at your disposal, as is everything that the Towers of Learning have." Miranda stopped. She considered her next words. *"There is a Paramount I think you should speak with."* An image leaped into Talia's mind.

"Paramount Holly," Talia said. *"I met her in my travels to find the Exile Queen. She told me of a rising of the Blood Cult in her youth."*

Miranda's surprise was striking. *"Your mother didn't tell me that. There is more to Holly than you know. What did she tell you?"*

"That she was part of a Blood Cult led by another, and he was killed, and she escaped because of her mother."

"Partially true. I suspect that the leader was her brother, and he didn't die, but escaped. Where he is, we don't know. It is suspected

that he is also the leader of the new Blood Cult that is stirring up all the problems on both sides of the border."

Talia felt a cold anger fill her. *"The only face I know is a wingless Fairy. He manipulated one of my Ladies into betraying me. He taunts me. I think we've crossed paths before. Once at the Prince's Crafthouse, and again at Riverbend plantation."*

Miranda went still in the Web. *"Share everything you know, and everything you saw or felt around him. Everything. Hold nothing back."*

Talia did. All the scenes and emotions flashed through her mind. The last image was the shopkeeper's message.

"He seems to know Elanor, or maybe he was just taunting me," Talia commented into the silence.

"There is more here," Miranda finally said. *"I must think on this. I see you have a possible location. An Elen town. What do you intend to do?"*

"I intend to go there, and find him, or at least his hiding place. I'll let you know what I find."

Silent encouragement emanated from Miranda. *"I wish I could do more than give you information, but my ability to act is hampered by your mother. She wants you to return home. I will tell her you refused me, as you feel you need to act on your own."*

"Thank you, Paramount. Any aid will be welcome."

"You need to speak with Paramount Holly first. She can give you important information about the Blood Cult, and how to fight them. Do you have her Ring's Frequency?"

"I do."

"Good. I will contact you when I have more news. If you need to contact me, use this Geode Frequency."

"It's different from before."

"Yes, it is," was all Miranda would say.

"I will do as you suggest."

"Good hunting, my student." And Miranda was gone.

194

Back in her Tower, Miranda went over and over the information Talia had given her on this wingless Fairy who was destroying all he touched.

"It cannot be," she muttered to herself. "Goddess's mercy, it cannot be." She called to one of her Seconds. "I need to speak to Law Master Darkwood. She retired a few years ago, but still lives in the castle. Bring her to me as soon as you can. And ask her to bring anything she still has on Lady Elanor's attacker."

Chapter Eighteen
Farewell

Talia walked up the stairs to the library. With each step, she became more sure of her path. Sure, both of what she was doing now, and what she had already done. This was the path. Anyone who would hinder her was her enemy, and deserved both her wrath and her contempt. By the time she reached the library door, all doubt and hesitation had disappeared.

"You can't leave," Steel was saying. "You'll violate your Oath."

"She's violated her Oath to us," Goldberry replied, the anger of a long argument apparent in her voice. "She swore she would defend us from harm, not kill us!"

Steel started to reply, but saw Talia enter, and went silent instead. Everyone else fell silent as well. All but Goldberry and Steel dropped their heads. Those two looked right at Talia: Steel with hope for support, Goldberry with defiance. Shield was by Goldberry's side. Spear was farther away, sitting by herself. Min and Elanor were closer to Goldberry, their positions showing that they were trying to persuade her to stay. Shatter had returned to the chair she had collapsed into after Nova's suicide in the Ring. Steel was closer, standing strong. Raven and Flora stood in the middle, torn between the two sides.

Talia held the women's gaze for a long beat.

"Anyone who wishes to leave may do so," she said with a contemptuous gesture. "I release you from your Oath to me or The N. . . ." She stopped. "The Heir's Guard." Steel tried to speak, but Talia made a flinging motion with her hand. "I have somewhere to go. When I return, I expect those who remain to be committed to my cause. Those who leave will not be allowed back into this company. If you take any action to hinder me in any way, I will consider you an enemy, and a betrayer." She looked down at the wrapped body of Willow. "And you know how I deal with betrayers." She looked at Steel. "Search any who leave. They will take nothing they have been granted or gained in my service."

Shatter shook herself out of her paralysis. "Where are you going, My Lady?"

196

"I have someone I need to talk to."

"Do you need an escort?"

"No. Stay here. Prepare yourselves for an assault on our enemies." She turned to Elanor. "We need to replace the Ephemeral Rings. See to it." Talia stepped into the Ring, and disappeared.

Goldberry looked at Min and Elanor. "You should come, too; you owe her nothing. Not after what she did to Willow."

"I can't," Elanor told her. "She needs us more than ever now."

Min could only shake her head, and embrace Goldberry. Concealed by the embrace, Min slipped her shard of the Geode into Goldberry's hand. *"In case you need us,"* she Sent.

"I will miss you, Sisters," Goldberry told the others, pulling away. "Goddess watch over you." Elanor joined Goldberry and Min. The three put their heads together, saying goodbye.

Shatter walked toward Shield, who was removing her sword belt, which she handed to Steel as Shatter reached them.

"Why now?" Shatter asked, pointedly staring at Steel with an implied order for her to leave. Steel sniffed, and walked away. "You've lost Sisters and Brothers before. Why now?"

"This is different," Shield admitted. She touched Shatter's arm. "I can't explain it, but it is. Nova was my fault."

"It wasn't," Shatter disagreed. "She made the choice to end her life."

Shield shook her head. "I should have stopped her. I've seen that despair before. I should have stayed by her side. I failed. I can't live with that. I must go somewhere else to find myself again." She took a long, emotional breath. "Poor, lost Nova. She'll haunt me. I can't be what you need right now." She looked around. Her eyes focused on Nova's bedroll. "I can't be here."

Shatter gripped her arm. "I understand. Go with the Goddess."

Shield put her other hand on Shatter's enchanted arm. "Is there anything you want me to tell your family?"

Shatter pulled a disc on a chain from her pocket. She pressed it into Shield's hand. "Take this to my wife and husband. They'll understand." Shatter pulled away. "It was an honor to serve with you."

"The honor was mine," Shield replied.

197

Spearhead approached Goldberry.

"Please come with us," Goldberry pleaded. "She'll sell your life cheap to get her vengeance."

"I can't," Spear said simply. She embraced Goldberry. "We were told not to leave our Lady's side. Now I must. Forgive me."

"This will not bring back your son," Goldberry told her.

"I know. I thought the Goddess had given me another chance with Sunrise. Now, all I know is that I must stay. Justice must be found for her life."

Goldberry started to argue, but stopped. "Goddess keep you. Her mercy and strength be with you." She kissed her soldier on the cheek. "Do you want me to take a message?"

"No. I have no one. My family is here now," Spear said, looking down. Tears began flowing, and she walked away.

Goldberry moved to embrace Raven. "Take care of them," she requested.

"I will, Sister. Goddess guide you."

Raven moved to Shield, and gripped her arms. They looked at each other in silence. Raven then moved to stand behind Min.

Shatter hugged Goldberry. "I'll miss your songs," she told her. Goldberry began to cry.

"Keep them safe, Captain," she begged. "I see nothing but pain in the future."

"I will, Sister. I will." Shatter broke away, and went to Steel. She took Shield's sword from her. She turned, and presented it back to Shield. "I give this to you as a token of all the lives you have defended with it. Goddess guide your hand." Shield took the sword, and bowed.

Goldberry wiped her eyes, and looked at Flora. She had been quiet throughout the debate with Steel. Her eyes were red, but her face was resolute.

"Mum," Goldberry asked her, "please come home. I fear for your spirit, if you stay."

"I will be where I always intended to be. At her side. You're right — she needs us. This is my path, and I will walk it with my head held high." She gripped Goldberry's shoulders. "I have no fear. The Goddess will protect us all."

"She helps those who help themselves," Goldberry reminded her.

"She will. This is where I need to be. Fear not." She handed Goldberry a scroll. "This is for my sister and my mother. Tell them I'll be home when this is done."

Goldberry had no more tears within her. "I will, Mum." She pulled away. She walked to the Ring, where Shield was standing ready, Willow's body at her feet. She looked at those remaining with Talia.

"Goddess keep you safe, Sisters," she beseeched. "It was an honor."

"The honor was ours," Elanor answered for them all.

"Soldiers," Shatter snapped.

They drew their swords, and saluted Goldberry and Shield with them. Shield returned the salute. Then Goldberry took Shield's hand. She started to say goodbye, but the words stuck. "I'll miss you," she said instead, and disappeared.

☾ ♒ ☼

Goldberry took them through the ruins Ring, then the broken tower Ring, and then through a Ring in an abandoned town to the north of the palace, where Goldberry had played as a child. Eventually, they arrived in the Ring in the Shrine of the Goddess in the palace, surprising a clerk on his way to deliver messages.

"Please tell the Keeper that Lady Goldberry and soldier Shieldbreaker are back, and wish to see her. We have returned a Fallen Sister to her home." All the emotions of the past year collapsed onto her at once, and Goldberry sat down heavily on the floor as Shield pulled Willow's body out of the Ring.

She gestured to the clerk, who was staring wide-eyed at them. "Go! We have news for the Keeper and the Queen."

☾ ♒ ☼

They were taken to a room, and given food and drink. Willow's body was taken away to be prepared for her Return. The Keeper arrived quickly. She embraced Goldberry, and gripped arms with Shield. When Goldberry started to talk, the Keeper held up her hand. "The Queen is on her way." Clean clothes were brought, but Goldberry and Shield politely refused them. The Keeper sat with them in serene silence as they waited.

Shortly, the Queen arrived, bringing with her a golden-haired Iridescent. Goldberry and Shield stood, but the Queen waved them back to their seats.

She nodded to the Keeper. "I see you have been given refreshment."

"Yes, My Queen," Goldberry confirmed.

The Keeper stood. "There are many things in motion," she told them. "I must see to them, and the honor of our Fallen Sister. When you need me, please call. There will be a Shrinekeeper outside the door, if you need anything." She touched hands with the Queen, and swept out of the room.

"With all respect, My Queen," Goldberry started, "our families — I fear for them."

"It has already been taken care of. Your parents, and the families of all the Ladies, have been brought to the palace." Goldberry sat back, relieved. The Queen looked to Shield. "We have brought those we could find of The Nine's family and partners here as well. Captain Shattersteel is working to make sure that those who are still missing are found."

"Thank you," Shield said.

"The Sister you brought?"

"Is Willow, My Queen."

The Queen's face fell. "We've found her family. They were all brutally murdered." She noticed Goldberry's expression. "As you apparently know."

"Yes, My Queen." She stopped, not knowing how to proceed.

"Go on. What you say here is only for us." She gestured to the Fairy with her. "Goldenmane has my complete trust and faith."

"Talia murdered her, after it was revealed that Willow had been forced to betray our location and smuggle in an Ephemeral Ring so

Elenites could attack our compound." Goldberry spoke quickly, hoping to get the information out before she lost her nerve.

The Queen lost all expression. "I have a hard time accepting that."

"It's true, My Queen," Shield confirmed. "We saw it, and those who are still with Talia did as well. Willow returned from finding her family and confessed to Talia, then Talia broke her neck." Somehow Shield's matter-of-fact restatement struck Goldberry harder than her own telling of the events had.

"Why did she come back?" Goldberry lamented, starting to break. "She was free. She didn't have to return. She knew." Shield put her arm around the younger Fairy.

After a look from the Queen, Goldenmane offered Goldberry a cup of water. Goldberry took it with a nod of thanks, and drank.

"We found the bodies of the family," the Queen said, as Goldberry composed herself. "That's what prompted all the other families being brought here."

"She's lost," Goldberry finally said. "She's mad with grief, and desire for vengeance. Anyone who stands in her way, she calls an enemy. She says she wants justice, but how is this justice? Willow was manipulated, forced by evil people to do a bad thing. She made a horrible choice."

"Willow did what she thought was right," Shield added.

"And died for it," Goldberry returned, bitterly.

The Queen sighed, crossing her arms. "Goddess's mercy. I need to know as much as you're willing to tell me. Talia Shared with me what she saw happen. Please tell me your stories, both of you."

Goldberry began her story, telling as much as she could, from the birth of Sunrise, to the events of the following night, and the aftermath. Shield filled in details where she could. Goldenmane listened with wide eyes, and had to cover her mouth several times. The story of the sea cats hit her hard, and she had to step out for a moment after Goldberry told them about Rogue's death.

The Queen stopped Goldberry's recitation, and focused on the image of Talia sitting alone on the cliff as the others all sat Vigil for the Fallen. She asked Goldberry to Share the moment with her. Goldberry took the Queen's hand, and Gave her the memory of Talia just sitting there, the bundle of bones in her lap.

Goldberry broke, and they stopped for a bit as she huddled into Shield's embrace. The Queen sat back, her emotions guarded, but strong.

"We can continue later," the Queen finally offered.

"No." Goldberry sat up, wiping her eyes. "There isn't much else. Talia became a stone after that. Albeit a stone that would unexpectedly explode with bursts of anger. She was cold and unfeeling, where she had been empathetic before. She drove us harder than she ever had. Her focus was on justice for her daughter, and nothing else."

Shield took over, and told the Queen of the return to the mountain, and the deaths of Willow and Nova. Shield's recitation of the story came in a flat tone. She kept a steel grip on her emotions, as she knew it was the only way she could get through the tale.

The Queen showed visible shock when hearing of Nova's actions, and Goldenmane made the Sign of the Three. Then the Queen reached out, and took Shield's hand.

"It wasn't your fault. You did the best you could."

"I should have done more," Shield disagreed flatly.

The Queen could only look at her, seeing the heartbreak in Shield's eyes. "The Goddess gives us all a path to walk. Sometimes it is dark. We must bring our own light."

Shield nodded.

The Queen sat back. "She and the others are at what you call the Exile Queen's mountain?"

"Yes, My Queen," Goldberry confirmed. "But the Ring has been Warded very strongly. Maybe not to the level of killing, but I wouldn't risk it."

"I understand," the Queen said. "I think that's enough for now. There will be more questions in the future, but for now, I will let you see your families and partners."

"We have messages to deliver to the families of the others," Goldberry informed her.

"Goldenmane can arrange that." The Queen gestured to the Fairy. "She will be my voice in all things for the two of you. Anything you need, she will provide."

"Thank you, My Queen," Goldberry said, bowing her head. Shield did the same.

The Queen looked at Goldenmane. She pulled out a pouch, and handed it to the Queen, who removed two silver discs. She pressed one into Goldberry's hand, and the other in Shield's.

"These are my tokens. Use them as you will. They will grant you anything that you need, within reason." She looked into Shield's eyes. "There is a place on my Guard for one as loyal as you."

Shield lowered her eyes in embarrassment. "Thank you, My Queen, but I don't know if I can remain a soldier." She looked at Goldberry. "I don't know what I'll do, but I'll keep that in mind."

"Good," the Queen said. "Whatever you decide, you have my full faith." Her voice grew even more serious. "There will be talk of how you abandoned my Heir. That you're cowards, and betrayers of your Oaths." Goldberry looked at Shield. "Don't listen to them. You have both made a difficult choice. You followed your path, and We praise you for doing so. We need to know of any Fairy who speaks to you with such dishonor. I will always be available to you. Lady Titania and Lord Oberon can also be of help. Luna and Merry-Weather, as you know," she smiled, "will always be there for the Ladies of the court."

"Thank you," Goldberry said simply.

"I must go, but Goldenmane will remain, to see to your reunion with your families." The Queen rose. The others followed suit. "Goddess bless you in your path."

"My Queen," Shield said as the Queen was moving to the door, "I wish to speak with Nova's family as soon as possible."

The Queen looked at Goldenmane, who nodded. "It will be done."

The Queen left. Goldberry and Shield sat back down. Goldenmane looked at them.

"Shall I bring each of you to a private room for your reunion?" she asked.

Shield looked at Goldberry. Shield's anxiety rose at the thought of facing Nova's parents. She summoned all her courage and resolve.

Goldberry squeezed her hand. Shield nodded. "No. They can come here. I left one Sister before; I will not leave another."

Talia arrived in Paramount Holly's Ring. She tried to walk out, but ran into the shimmer of a Ward. She put her hands on the surface, feeling the Weave. She was in a small room, and Talia could see Holly collapsed in a chair on the other side. Her head was on the wing of the chair, and she was asleep. Talia could tell by the Weave that sound was blocked, but not — for some reason — smell. She took in the sharp tang of powerful sleeping herbs. A lot of them, used over the course of years. The room stank of them. If Talia's rage hadn't been so focused, she would have smiled, even laughed.

Her hands traced over the surface of the Ward. Her mind followed the lines of the Weave — every line of Power, every anchor to the floor. Until she found a flaw.

"Ah," she said, smiling. Her Power wiggled into the flaw, and she brought the Ward down. She walked around the room, taking in all the disorganized books and scrolls lying around. The old food, and the stale wine. The only things that were fresh were the bundle of sleeping herbs in a chest beside Holly's chair, and a teapot on a cold warming stone.

Talia stood before Holly, her contempt hard in her eyes. She reached into the Paramount's mind, easily piercing her ineffective Wards. She moved through the fog of herbs and sleep, until she found the Paramount's consciousness. Grabbing it like a stone under water, she pulled.

Holly sat straight up in the chair, her arm knocking her cup to the floor. Her red eyes took a moment to focus, then saw Talia. The Paramount tried to move further back in her chair.

"How did you get in here?" She gestured to the Ring. "My Wards?"

"Are useless," Talia told her. She gestured, and a chair pulled itself through the mess to stop behind her. She reached back, and brushed off the seat. Talia settled into the chair, crossing her legs. "I've come for information."

Holly looked around, slight panic in her eyes. She fumbled at the table.

"Need this?" Talia held up a vial. "'Wake,' I think the soldiers call it." She tossed the vial at her. Holly missed it, and it rolled under the table.

"Goddess Mother," Talia swore. She motioned, and the vial floated up and settled into Holly's hand. She pulled the stopper, and took several drops.

Talia took note of this, but didn't react.

Holly's eyes became clearer, and she sat up straighter. "Where are the rest of your people? Not going through my Tower, are they?"

"No. I'm here alone." Talia moved forward in her seat. "What we have to talk about is private."

"What's that?" Holly asked, trying to sound calm, but with obvious nervousness.

"About the Blood Cult, and its leader." Talia leaned forward; her hands clenched. "You knew."

"I told you everything before," Holly answered. "I have no new information for you."

"You told me lies." Talia grabbed the woman's hands, and pinned them to the arms of the chair. "Now you will tell me the truth." The menace in her eyes made Holly go pale.

"I didn't lie to you," Holly started. Talia tightened her grip. "I just didn't tell you everything," she quickly finished.

Talia waited.

"If you can let go of me," she pleaded.

Talia released her with a contemptuous breath.

"I didn't tell you who the leader was. He was my brother. We shared a father, but not a mother. When they were caught, my mother made sure he would be punished to the full extent of the law. She shielded me. But she didn't do the same for him." Holly looked down. "My brother and I were close. Maybe too close." Shame colored her face. "Our father and his mother came to me, begging me to help them free their son, or at least help him avoid death. He pleaded, and made promises, and, finally, threatened to reveal everything he knew about my activities with the Blood Cult. Even my mother wouldn't have been able to save me if he'd done that, so I finally agreed to help him fake his suicide. That was after his wings were cut off." Holly stopped.

"So, you let that monster back out into the world."

"He disappeared. I forgot about him. I went on with my life. Tried to forget the past." Holly tried to conjure a Ward to keep Talia out of her mind.

"You know more than you're saying." Talia's Power brushed aside Holly's attempt to fortify her Wards. She formed all the images she had of the wingless Fairy into a bundle in her mind, then forced it into Holly's. "Look. See what he did. I saw seven of my Sisters slaughtered. I killed one of my own Sisters, because he made her betray me. His corruption forced another of my Ladies to kill herself. Look!" she shouted. "I will rip the information out of your mind if I have to." She grabbed Holly's arms again. "You will tell me of the wingless one, or I will destroy you."

"It's not him," she whined, her mind shrinking away from all the brutal images Talia had transmitted. "It's not him."

"Goddess curse you! Stop lying, and tell me where he is!" Talia's Power became a spear of light. She pressed it into the Paramount's mind. "Tell me!"

"He's dead!" she screamed. Talia sat back, the light disappearing. "He's dead," she said more quietly. "I killed him."

Talia pulled fully back out of Holly's mind. Her assumptions had been shaken.

"When?" she finally asked.

"Years ago," Holly said, her eyes focusing on a point on the wall behind Talia. "It was the first time I'd heard from him. He must have found another patron." Her hands shook, and she reached for a cup. "Water, please," she begged.

Talia floated a pitcher to her. She drank.

"When was this?"

"Years," she said again, wiping her mouth. "You would have been just into your womanhood, just out of childhood, but not yet an adult. His son had done something horrible, and he wanted my help for him to escape. 'Just like before,' he told me. He was just like before, too: calm and smooth. Seductive." Holly's voice became lost in memory.

"Son?" Talia asked, confused.

"He had done something to several girls and boys at the palace. He was going to lose his wings. My brother pleaded." Holly looked up at Talia. Her eyes became stronger. "I refused him. I remembered all that he had done to my friends, all the children who had fallen under his sway. How he abused and manipulated my best friends. He broke them, but they were dependent on him. They couldn't get away on their own. I saw it again in this son of his, and I refused him. Told him to go, and never return."

Holly stopped. Her eyes returned to the spot behind Talia. "He became angry. And I remembered that, too." Her voice became stronger. "I stood up to him, for the first time in my life. I told him no." She smiled, almost laughed, at the memory. "He couldn't believe that I would deny him anything. He threatened to expose me. To expose everything. My mother. The lies. The deception. The Blood. That I was a willing participant. So, I killed him." She pointed. "You can still see the blood on the wall."

Talia turned, and saw a brown splotch on the wall.

"I killed him with a knife. You should have seen the surprise in his eyes." She did laugh this time. "All that blood, running through his fingers, and he couldn't use any of it." She settled back into her chair.

Talia turned back to the Paramount, a Shield rising in her mind. Fear crept into her body for the first time during this encounter.

Then Holly collapsed into herself. "But now he was dead. And I couldn't touch him. Didn't dare touch his blood — it was too much temptation. The room reeked of it. But I couldn't call anyone — what could I say?" She began to pick at the hem of her dirty dress.

"What did you do with him?" Talia breathed, the horror of it all crossing over her emotional wall. "Bury him?"

"I couldn't do that. But I couldn't leave him lying around, either. I wanted him gone. So, using just my Power, I chopped him up, and burned him in that oven." She pointed. "A bit at a time. The place stank. Still stinks. I can still smell it." She reached for a pack of herbs.

Joel C. Flanagan-Grannemann

Talia stopped her. Something in her memory worried at her. "When was this?" She gripped Holly's hand. "When exactly was this, you old woman?"

"I don't remember, it was so long ago. So long." Her eyes drifted to the celling. "The smoke stained."

Talia grabbed Holly's head, both with her hands and with her Power. "I'll pull it out of you!" she swore. "I might kill you, but I need to know. When!"

"I don't know," Holly blubbered. "I don't know!" Talia began to apply pressure to her mind. "I can't." Tears came. "Please — I've been so alone, so alone, for so long. Please!"

Talia let go of her in disgust, and sat back in her chair, watching the sobbing, broken woman.

"It was," she began, her face brightening, "it was when the Diamond River overflowed its banks, and destroyed the bridge at Elen-Ford. That's when it was. I remember," she crowed.

Talia went cold. She threw up her strongest Ward, as her self-deception began to evaporate. Holly didn't seem to notice. She kept smiling, and repeating what she had said.

'I was young, just out of childhood,' Talia thought. Elanor and I were playing, flirting, flying, with the other boys and girls of the court. Elanor and I. A memory hit her so hard, so brutally, that she almost lost all her Wards, and her wall. 'No,' she wished. 'It can't be.'

Talia grabbed Holly with her Power, forcing her mind to clear. "The son." She asked, clear and slow, "What happened to him?"

"I don't know. He was a rapist, so he would have lost his wings," Holly said simply. She smiled. "I hope they cut his manhood off, too."

"She wanted to," Talia said quietly.

Holly stared at her, not understanding.

Talia released her. The wall in her own mind had been restored, strong. She had knowledge now, but what would she do with it? How would this help her? She needed more.

"Can I make you some tea?" Talia asked. "Not this, but something else? Maybe some food?"

"That would be fine, child," Holly said, falling back into her own self-made deception.

"Then we can talk," Talia said, standing.

"If you remember," Holly was lecturing, her hand waving a piece of bread, "we gain our Power from the sun and moon. It enters our body through our wings, and lives in our blood until we need it."

Talia sat back, trying to be patient. She wanted to just grab the old fool, and shake the knowledge out of her. But after some tea, and some food Talia had been able to find, Holly appeared to be a model Paramount again.

"So, we take that Power into our blood and use it, but we must Join with others to do greater things. We're limited."

"But with the use of blood?" Talia prompted.

"Yes. The Blood Cult discovered that they could increase their Power by taking blood from others. It must have first happened on a battlefield: the blood of a Sister splashed on you, and you struck out and killed the enemy. I can just imagine that rush, that burst of Power." Holly's eyes became dreamy.

"So, you drink it?" Talia hurried her.

"No! Never do that," Holly admonished her. "That will hasten the corruption. That's why those Elenites stink. Drinking blood. Horrible." She shivered at the mere thought.

"Then how?" Talia demanded.

"Just a drop on your skin, or better, your wings." She looked at her hand, made a decision, and thrust it out at Talia. "Here — see for yourself."

Talia looked at the hand, with its dirty fingernails and flaking skin, with revulsion.

"If you're going to walk this path," Holly said with a clarity Talia hadn't heard from her before on this visit, "you must get past this." She took out a small knife, and made a cut in her finger. She offered it to Talia, the blood forming a dome.

Talia didn't move.

With an exasperated breath, Holly smeared the blood on the back of Talia's hand. Then she shrank back into her chair, her old fear returning.

Talia started backwards, watching as the blood disappeared into her skin. A warmth filled her hand, then spread down her arm, tingling, and pleasant. It reached her chest, and she felt as though she had just downed a goblet of the strongest wine, or gone flying with the west wind. Talia's most-prominent emotion went from anxiety to wonder. She felt her Power pulse, almost leaping out of her skin.

"That." Holly pointed to a steel-bound oak chest in a corner.

Talia knew what Holly intended. She gestured, and the chest collapsed inward with a horrible noise, grinding and shrieking. In a moment, it was only a ball of wood and steel.

Awe filled Talia's face and mind. She felt the warmth spread.

"We used to smear each other with our blood and pleasure each other, like beasts in heat," Holly said dreamily.

The sound of her voice struck Talia like cold water. She pushed the warmth away. She was left feeling empty and cold.

Talia opened her eyes to find Holly staring at her.

"Now you understand. It's like nothing else. Blood, freely given. I dream of it." She gestured to the herbs. "That's why I use these."

Talia got up and paced the room. Holly watched her.

"With this, I could do things that I could never do alone before."

"Yes, but you'll pay the price. You'll always want more. You'll do anything for more." Holly's voice turned dark. "It will bring out the worst in you. You've seen the horrible things they've done. You can't fight evil with more evil."

"I will fight with everything I have," Talia snapped at her. "This will give me the power I need. To destroy them."

"It won't end there," Holly warned, trying to get her to understand. "It never does. You'll wind up like my brother."

"I will not," Talia contradicted. "I'm stronger. Stronger than any of you." She stopped. "You can teach me."

Holly sighed. "There isn't much to teach. All you need is blood, and that will give you Power. How you use it is up to you. The Weaves are the same, just stronger. You must be careful, though: more Power means more chance of feedback and backlash."

Talia nodded, not really hearing her.

"You said you never had any contact with this wingless Fairy?"

"No, just your Aunts. They held my brother and nephew over my head like my brother himself did."

Talia descended on her, grabbing the front of her dress. "What did you tell them?"

"Nothing," she whined. "They contacted me after you were here, but I didn't know much, so I just told them you were going south. They seemed happy with that. 'She'll be out of the way,' they said."

"Anything after?" Talia asked, sitting back down.

"No. I've had no contact with you since, so I had nothing to tell," Holly said simply. "What do you want me to tell them?"

"Remember," Talia started.

"You will kill me horribly if I betray you," Holly finished, the beginnings of a real smile on her face. "So will they. I'm caught in the middle." She spread her hands wide.

Talia considered. "Tell them I'm heading north with my people. That should get them worried."

"Yes, My Lady. Is there anything else I can do for you?"

"I need to replace my Ephemeral Rings. Do you have anything I can use to build more?"

Holly stood. "I have better." She went to a cabinet on the side of the room, pushing aside books, scrolls, and bones to get there. Finally, she came up with two rolls as long as her arm. They were each tied with a white and silver cord. She returned to Talia, and presented them to her with a flourish.

Talia took them. At her touch, she felt the Rings begin to sing. It was the strangest — though still harmonious — Song that Talia had ever heard from an Ephemeral Ring.

"I can see you find the Song strange," Holly remarked at Talia's expression. "It's like hearing colors. They're old. My father's ancestors made them long ago. They're prickly — only worked for me a few times. Now, it looks like they want to go with you, though."

Talia held them, opening her Sight. She Saw lines in the Ring she had never Seen before, ways of Weaving alien to her.

"Thank you, Paramount," Talia said sincerely. "These will help."

Paramount Holly bowed. "I serve you, My Lady."

"You serve me because I'm standing here." Talia turned cold. "Remember my promise."

"I will," Holly said, going pale. "The Aunts will only know what you want them to."

Talia looked at her. She wasn't fully satisfied that Holly could be trusted, but she had little choice but to take the chance. She nodded, and returned to the Ring. She disappeared without another word.

Holly waited a beat. Then, when Talia didn't return, she went back to her chair, and collapsed. She put her head in her hands, and alternated between crying, screaming, and laughing. After a few minutes, she recovered, and sat up. She looked at the warming stone under the kettle. The stone began to glow. She reached for her chest of herbs. Then, with a deliberate motion, she shut it.

"What did she make earlier?" she asked the silence. "I must be prepared to speak with the Three Sisters. What did you think of her, brother?" With a wave, a shimmer appeared in the air, uncovering a skull pinned to the wall with a long spike. She smiled. "I did lie to her. It was a spike, not a knife, that I killed you with." She laughed, and went to find the tea Talia had made.

Chapter Nineteen
You Don't Knock

"What are you doing here? Get out!"

"I just hoped to offer my condolences on your loss."

"You're doing no such thing."

"True, but one must be polite."

"You've said it. Now go."

"My King, we have many things to talk about." Wingless eyed the two guards at the door. He was cloaked in Magic, and appeared as a Human. Another disguised wingless Fairy stood at his shoulder, with a basket in his hands.

Bastile sighed at the implied threat. He waved the guards out.

"Now," he said, sitting down. "I have preparations to make. This is a hard time for my beloved wife."

"Don't be a fool: she's not your 'beloved' anything," Wingless sneered, sitting down. "She was just a means to an end. Access to power and allies. Men who allowed you to keep your crown."

Bastile almost attacked the two Fairies. His fingers itched on his knife. Wingless smiled, an invitation in his eyes. Bastile slouched back, his grief returning like a blow. "What do you want?" he asked sullenly, while fingering a piece of fabric in his pocket.

Wingless smiled more widely. "I've come with an answer to your child problem."

"My son was born dead; how can you solve that?" Bastile shot back, anger overriding his grief for a moment.

"I have a child for you." Wingless gestured to the basket in the hands of the other Fairy. He opened it, and showed it to Bastile. A golden-haired baby was sleeping within.

Bastile leaned closer. His heart leapt a little. "He isn't moving," Bastile said, puzzled.

"She," Wingless corrected, "is under a Ward. She's held still in time until I release her."

"Who is she, and how did you get her?" Bastile looked up at Wingless, suspicion in his eyes.

"You're learning," Wingless complimented Bastile. "She's a foundling; her parents and family were slaughtered. She's the only survivor." Wingless sat back, folding his arms over his chest.

"Did you kill them?" Bastile asked, reaching out to touch the baby. A shimmer stopped his hand.

"No, I did not," Wingless answered truthfully. "She was born only a few days ago, to her. Once I remove the Ward, she'll begin to grow as any normal Human would."

"What's that?" Bastile pointed to a silver cord, with a worn silver button, tied around the baby's wrist.

"Something from her family. Only thing she has left."

Bastile sat back. "And if I refuse?"

Wingless looked hard at him. "If you deny this child, you will never have another."

Bastile shrugged. "My wife is young and healthy. Once she gets over this, she'll have other children."

"You mistake me. If you do not take this child, you will never have any other children. None. Not by any other woman, whether wife, mistress, or whore." Wingless brought his fist into his open hand with a thump. "None."

Bastile narrowed his eyes, but inside, his heart stopped. Fear built up: fear of this bargain, and its as-yet-unforeseen consequences.

"You bastard," he snarled. "You did this. You killed my child." He stood up. The other wingless also stood, his right hand pulling a curved knife. "You did this," Bastile accused again.

Wingless just stared at the enraged King, still keeping his seat. He waved for his guard to sit down as well. "You know who I am, and what I can do. You have an opportunity here. This baby will be your Heir, or you will have none." He opened his hands. "You can choose to give this poor orphaned girl a home, or you can doom your wife to more grief. You can doom all the other women you will ever touch to grief." He leaned forward. "And I will make them grieve."

Bastile sat down. Again, he was trapped. "How will this work?" he finally asked.

Wingless smirked in triumph. "Who knows of the baby's death?"

"Just my wife and the midwife."

"Good. And I assume she was kept in isolation after the baby was confirmed, and that she's still in that isolation?"

"Yes," Bastile confirmed numbly.

"Good." He gestured to the basket. "Take this baby to her. Tell her whatever you want. That you found her, that this is your bastard, born on the same day she lost your son. That a bolt of lightning from the Father hit your lap, and the baby just appeared. I don't care. Just make sure that she accepts the child."

"She won't believe any of that."

"She'll believe what you tell her to believe," Wingless said. "Isn't that the way of Humans?"

Bastile could only nod.

"And make sure you pay off the midwife, to make sure she confirms that this is a child of your body. If not," he gestured to his guard, "I can have her taken care of."

The other Fairy grinned.

"That won't be necessary," Bastile said quickly. "I'll make sure she falls into line."

"Good." Wingless stood, and passed the basket to Bastile. He waved his hand over the baby. Bastile heard her take a breath, and begin to cry.

"She'll be hungry," Wingless said as he left. He stopped at the door. Bastile was staring down into the basket. "Just to be sure," he muttered. He cast a Weave over Bastile, to erase the memory of Wingless bringing him the child. All he would remember was that an agent of the Three Sisters had made a bargain with him.

Bastile sat with the basket holding the crying baby in his lap. When the cries softened, Bastile finally took the child out and held her. Her bright green eyes stabbed into his heart. He stroked her soft hair. His grief fell away. He smiled. The baby smiled, too.

"I have a daughter," he said to her with reverence. "Welcome to my home. It's a new day. I will call you Aurora, after the rising sun." He rose, and went to present this miracle to his wife. He tried to set aside all thought of the cruelty of the Three Sisters who were his allies, hoping the Father would show him mercy for his many trespasses.

☽ ∭ ☼

When Talia returned to the library, Spear was standing guard beside the Ring. Talia surveyed the room to see who had stayed. Shatter and Steel were sitting close, talking over some maps. Min and Elanor sat under the dome, meditating. Flora and Raven were asleep. All eyes turned to Talia as she stepped out of the Ring.

Elanor walked to her. "Did you find what you were looking for?"

"I did." She handed her Second the rolled Ephemeral Rings. "These are from Paramount Holly. Make sure they're not trapped, or otherwise altered." Elanor took them, her eyes going wide at their odd Song.

"That's good, because we don't have anything left to make more," Elanor informed her, taking the rolled Rings to Min.

Talia sat down with Shatter and Steel. Steel turned the map so she could see. "This is what I remember. There's a Ring at the Embassy."

Talia looked over the map. "Our use of the Embassy will be limited. How big is the town?"

"Fairly good size," Steel told her. "They produce much of the silk we sell to the Humans. How things are now, though, I don't know."

"Are there any Rings we can use besides the Embassy's?"

"I might know of one," Steel replied. "There used to be one at the garrison that we would use to return home. That was a long time ago, though."

"It's a risk," Shatter warned Talia, "if it's Warded or guarded."

"We must take risks," Talia stated firmly. She turned to Steel. "When would be the best time to go through?"

"Early morning," Steel responded. "Before the sun rises."

"Take Spear, and scout both the Ring and the town. We need updated maps, and information. Regardless of what you find, return at mid-day."

Steel nodded. "We must get some rest then." She stood up, and went to Spear. After a quick conversation, Steel woke Raven, then rolled herself into her bed. Raven took Spear's place at the Ring.

"I will speak to you before you leave," Shatter ordered. Spear nodded, and went to find a place to sleep.

Shatter turned back to Talia. "We all need rest."

"Sleep, then," she replied, standing. "I have many things to plan. Be ready when Steel returns. We must strike at them quickly." She walked over to Min and Elanor. Shatter watched her go, then took her bedroll and laid down close to where Flora was sleeping.

Min and Elanor had the Ephemeral Rings rolled out on the floor. Talia came up behind them. She put her hand on Elanor's back, close to her wound.

"We must treat this," she said.

"Flora thinks that sunrise would be the best time to start the re-growing," Elanor told her. She gestured to the Rings on the floor. "These are wonderful. Strange, but wonderful. And they're strong. We could move many through them at one time, and they wouldn't overheat."

"Holly said they were well made. It's good that she didn't lie." Talia took one of the Ephemeral Rings. "Before dawn, the three of us will go up on the mountain and do the Healing ceremony."

"You don't want Flora?" Min asked.

"She needs her sleep," Talia said. "I want her to rest and recover." She stood.

Elanor caught her hand. "You need to rest and recover, too."

Talia looked at Elanor's hand on hers. She didn't move or speak. Elanor finally let go. "I will rest," Talia finally said. "Just in private." She retreated to one of the small rooms and shut and Warded the door.

Min looked at Elanor, who could only shake her head. They stood together, and went to make up beds near Flora.

An odd sound brought Talia out of her meditation. She sat cross-legged on the floor. In front of her lay the Ephemeral Ring. Talia frowned. She had left it behind her, and rolled up. Now it was unrolled, and in front of her. She opened her Sight, and her senses were filled with a calling Song from the Ring. Before she realized it, she was standing in the Ring, and traveling through it to another.

It was dark. Talia conjured a Light. She was standing in a Ring in the middle of a small room. The walls were lined with books and scrolls. A simple table and chair stood in front of her. Talia could feel the powerful Preservation and Shadow Wards on the room. She looked around, and the shelves continued, unbroken, around her. There was no door. She looked up. Above her was a narrow shaft cut into the stone. She could see the glint of stars far above. She tested to make sure there wasn't a Ward around the Ring.

When her hand crossed the Ring's boundary, there was a flash, as a Ward recognized her and fell away. Talia stepped out of the Ring. There was a scroll lying on the table. Talia gestured, and it rose and unrolled before her.

"The knowledge you seek is here," read the words in Old Fairy. "Beware, my descendent, for the path forks, and how you walk it shall determine your destination."

Talia gestured the scroll back to the table. Only days ago, she would have felt amazement at the Exile Queen reaching out from the past to give her a message, but now it only annoyed her. She was filled with anger. Talia conjured a spark of Redfire and burned the scroll.

"I will follow any path I need to in order to get justice for my child," she told the spirit of the Exile Queen. "I do not need your warnings: I need your help."

She closed her eyes, then put a mental hand on the ice wall within her mind. She felt the cold, and the pain behind it. Then she felt the ice begin to melt under her fingers. Felt compassion reaching through — calling her to let go, and allow the wall to melt completely. Water began to run down her arm. Pain and grief followed. Talia jerked her hand away. The pain was too much. Her desire to see those responsible punished froze the wall solid again.

"I will not let them escape me," she swore, opening her eyes. She turned, and went to the shelves. She bent down, and pulled out a book, which she took to the table. Talia ran her hand over the cover as she sat down. In poison green letters, in Old Fairy, it said 'On Curses.'

☾ 〽 ☼

A wave of Power washed through the library, startling Flora out of her sleep. She sat up, looking around. Shatter was closest, stirring a pot on some warming stones. She moved to sit beside the confused and worried Flora.

"It's all right, Mum," the soldier soothed the older woman. "That felt like Talia."

Flora looked around again. Besides the Captain, only Raven was visible, sitting by the Ring.

"You're safe," Shatter assured her. "Talia, Min, and Elanor went up the mountain to greet the sun and start Elanor's wing re-growing."

"They can't do that by themselves," Flora chastised. She threw off her blankets, and tried to rise, but Shatter held her back.

"Talia said she would take care of it." She met Flora's eyes. "She told me to keep you here. She wanted you to sleep."

Flora harrumphed, but sat back down. "The others?" she asked.

"Steel and Spear went to scout Elen-Flax. Raven, you see," she spread her arms, "and me."

"So, it wasn't a bad dream," Flora whispered, lowering her head. Her hands gripped the blankets. "Poor Willow and Nova. Goldberry and Shield are gone." She stopped.

"They have their own paths to walk," Shatter said, taking her hand, pulling it out of the knot Flora was making of the blanket.

"And leave us to walk ours," Flora said in a strange voice. Shatter couldn't decide if it was bitter or wistful.

"Mum," Shatter said. "We must be strong, and loyal to our Lady now."

"You're afraid of her now," Flora said, raising her head. "Afraid."

"No. I'm just making peace with the truth of the situation. She'll take no resistance to what she wants in her quest for justice," Shatter told Flora sternly. "Make sure you understand that."

"Is that a threat?" Flora asked, shocked.

"No. Never. I just don't want you to wind up. . . ." Shatter stopped, her head dropping.

"Like Willow," Flora whispered. "She would never."

"I think there's very little she won't do at this point," Shatter informed the motherly Fairy.

Flora took a deep breath. "I understand. I was young, but I remember her grandmother. She was a cruel Fairy. But she did keep everything running."

Shatter could only nod. She then motioned to the pot. "Would you like some porridge? It's about all we have."

"I thought Raven brought back game."

"She did, but not for breakfast."

Flora could only smile. She reached for a bowl.

$$\left(\text{\fontsize{1em}{1em}\selectfont ☾ 〰 ☼}\right)$$

After they ate, Flora tried to take stock of what they had. Shatter rose, and was going to relieve Raven when Min appeared in the Ring. She stepped off, and greeted Raven. Three breaths later, Talia and Elanor appeared. Elanor stepped off the Ring and spread her wings: both of them. They were intact again, as they had been only days before. The left wing was slightly different, however. The Iridescent colors were darker. There was more red, making the wing darker and brighter overall.

Raven and Shatter were stunned silent. Flora hurried forward.

"That shouldn't be possible," she said. She looked at Elanor. "How did this happen?"

Elanor looked, with some embarrassment, at Talia. She was still standing in the Ring, a look of triumph on her face.

Flora looked from Min to Elanor. Both hung their heads, their hands clenched at their sides. She looked to Talia.

"Well, Mistress," she asked again, "how did you do this? Even if the three of you had the Power, the wing shouldn't be fully grown already. This is impossible."

Talia looked at Flora for a long moment before responding. "I've found ways to make the impossible, possible."

220

"What ways?" Flora demanded. She looked at Min, who was still looking down at her hands. Flora marched over to her, and grabbed one of them. She forced it open, exposing a cut across the palm. Flora grabbed the other one, and found a similar wound. She turned, and looked at Elanor in disbelief.

Elanor folded her arms across her chest. Her look was defiant.

"It this what you wanted to talk to that Paramount about?" Flora accused, turning to Talia. "That woman who was part of the Blood Cult as a child? Has she infected you?"

"That's enough," Talia snapped, her voice even. "I will use any power at my disposal to get justice for my child."

"But Mistress, this? This corruption?" Flora started.

"I said, enough." Talia's voice rose. "If you find this distasteful, you can go. I won't stop you." She walked off the Ring. "I have studying to do." She looked at Shatter. "Send for me when Steel and Spear return." She walked by Flora without further comment.

Flora watched her go. When Talia entered her little room and shut the door, Flora turned to Elanor.

"You should know better. You saw what these Cultists can do. You saw the Blood Ring," Flora accused.

"What I saw was a Power we can't match," Elanor returned. "This gives us an edge."

"Only Talia took the blood," Min defended. "And then, only on her wings. She didn't drink it."

Flora's withering look caused her to shrink away. "It was only a little," was Min's whispered, childlike, defense.

"We have studying to do, too," Elanor said, rescuing Min from Flora's anger. She took Min to the back corner of the library. They sat on the floor, and sank into a Circle.

Flora looked at Shatter. She was pale, but there was no reproach on her face. Flora turned to Raven.

"I need to feel the sun on my face. Can you come with me outside?" She turned to Shatter. "With your permission, Captain?"

Shatter nodded, without saying anything.

They settled on the mountain top, in a little bowl, on soft moss. It was the very place where Talia and Elanor had made love less than a year before, where the two had decided what their relationship would be. They didn't know this, though. Flora sat, her eyes closed, her face to the sun, her wings spread. Raven sat at her side, facing away from the sun, sharpening knives.

Flora listened to the grinding of the whetstone on the metal. It was a rhythmic sound, back and forth. Stop, examine, start again. Set one down and pick another up. Flora heard Raven mutter as she worked out a notch in one blade. Heard her swear when she dropped another. The skitter of the metal on stone. Finally, she heard Raven set the stone down without reaching for another blade.

"What would she say if she could see us now?" Flora asked, her eyes still closed.

Raven didn't respond, but Flora heard her turn slightly to look at her.

"What would she think of this family that's now broken? This company of Fairies which would have once done anything for each other, but is now fractured and splintered?"

"She betrayed us," Raven said, finally. "She didn't deserve to die, but she betrayed us."

"Willow," Flora stressed the name, "made a decision she thought would save the ones she loved. She couldn't see the lies. She still did what she thought was right."

"I wouldn't have made that decision."

"Maybe, maybe not," Flora said. "I don't know. I thank the Goddess that I didn't have to make that horrible choice."

"But she did." Raven was angry now. She stood. Flora kept her eyes closed, and remained seated. "She let those monsters into our home. Let them kill our Sisters. Forced Nova to kill herself. Led us to this."

Flora finally opened her eyes. Raven was standing with her back to her. Her wings were tightly folded.

"That's why I'm glad I didn't have to make that decision."

Raven turned. "What would you have done? Would you have chosen your sister and your mother, or your Lady?"

Flora looked up. Tears glistened in Raven's eyes. Just one hovered in the corner of each eye.

"I don't know," Flora answered, with all the compassion and wisdom of her long life.

"I can't make that choice, either. I might have tried to save my family. I might have betrayed us, too." With that admission, Raven finally broke, and sat down heavily. She saw again Willow's last moments, the resignation in her eyes.

Flora remained seated.

Raven turned her eyes to the sun. "Curse you!" she screamed to the sky. "Curse your path. Curse me for not defending her. Curse me for not saving her." Her voice almost disappeared. "Curse me."

Flora finally went to the soldier, and wrapped her in her arms and wings. Raven didn't cry again. Her tears had been boiled away by all the Pyres she had witnessed. Burned away by the pain of the life she had chosen. The path she had walked. She just clung to Flora, and hoped: hoped she would never have to make such a choice herself.

$$\left(\text{∭} \; \text{☼} \right.$$

Raven and Flora appeared together in the Ring. Steel and Spear had returned. Everyone was huddled over a table, where Steel was sitting, drawing. Shatter looked up, and nodded understanding at Raven.

"There are many Crafthouses," Steel was saying. "I figure one of them is where that wingless Fairy and his foul people live." She pointed to one, close to the edge of town. "This one used to make silk for all the merchants, but in the last year, its production has dropped precipitously. Now, they sell very little." She looked to Talia.

"Might be," was all Talia said. "When we get there, I'll be able to sense if they're there. Did you make arrangements?"

"Yes, My Lady," Steel replied. "A Fairy I know will be on duty at mid-morning. She'll let us through."

Talia looked around the circle. "In the morning, then. Ringmail for stealth. We'll be a hunting party, returning to town."

"Do you intend to just walk up and knock on the door?" Flora asked.

"We're not going to knock," Talia said, darkness and fury in her eyes. "We'll walk right in."

Chapter Twenty
Bloody Reunion

"They're here," Talia confirmed, opening her eyes. "I can feel the corruption."

Shatter smiled coldly.

Across the street stood a Crafthouse. Its overgrown yard showed that it didn't do much business, but the strong gate and the contingent of guards proved something else was going on there. There were two guards at the gate, and two more at the only door into the house.

Raven had already flown to the roof of a building across from the Crafthouse to serve as lookout.

"Will the Ephemeral Ring be in range?" Talia asked Elanor.

"Yes. It's strong. Unless there's interference inside, we'll be able to escape with Torcs." She touched her throat.

"All right," Shatter said, reaching out. They Joined into a Circle.

"*We'll go in. Raven will cover, and take out the guards at the door. Steel and Spear, the ones at the gate are yours.*"

"*I'll distract them,*" Min offered, smiling. "*They'll only have eyes for me.*"

"*Once we're inside, we're looking for information. Maps, notes, anything,*" Shatter reminded them. "*Don't take risks. Kill only in defense.*"

"*The wingless one is mine,*" Talia announced.

"*Spear, hold the door. If we can't use the Ring, we'll need an escape route. We'll split up. I'll stay with Talia. Steel, don't leave Min and Elanor. We don't know what the inside looks like. Ten minutes. That's all. In and out.*" She looked around the Circle. "*Understand?*"

Everyone acknowledged her instructions.

The Circle broke. Talia began to pull fist-sized stones from a bag. She passed two to each of them. "These contain Silverfire. All you do is twist the Weave, and after a three count," she spread her arms, "this place will burn as we leave." Steel took hers with a smile.

"Goddess keep us," Shatter beseeched. Steel and Spear disappeared into a Shadow. Min smiled, and conjured an Illusion. Her hair expanded out into sensual waves, and her simple black clothes

225

became a sheer, low-cut dress. She spun, looking to Elanor for confirmation of her transformation. Once she received it, she glided out into the street, and headed toward the guards at the gate.

The guards' eyes turned to her. "I was looking to buy some silk," she purred softly, as she got close. "I heard this is a good place."

The closer guard looked her up and down. "Maybe," he replied. "What do you have to trade?"

"Go away, whore," the other said, raising his spear. He turned to his companion. "She'll lead you astray."

"But it will be fun," the first said, reaching out as Min got closer. He put his spear in the crook of his arm, so he could take Min's offered hand.

"I said, go away." The second guard started forward, but stopped with a muted snap. Spear appeared behind him, holding his twisted head. She lowered his body to the ground.

The first guard turned at the unusual sound, but Steel was already at his side, driving a knife under his ribs.

"Not for you," she whispered as he died.

Raven's bow twanged twice, and the guards at the door fell. Min dismissed her Illusion and conjured another one — of the two guards, still standing — to cover the bodies. Steel opened the gate. Shatter, Talia, and Elanor crossed the street, and entered the yard. They hurried across the overgrown grass, and stopped at the door. Spear checked the dead guards, then pulled them aside. Shatter and Steel took aim at the door. Elanor gestured, and the door flew open. The group stormed into a large room.

They surprised several Humans and Elenites sitting at a table. They scrambled, grabbing at weapons, but Shatter and Steel's arrows took them down before they could do anything with them. Talia's Power grabbed one, and threw him against a wall. When he was the only one left, she went up to him.

"Where's the wingless one?" she demanded.

He shook his head, fear in his eyes.

Talia got closer. "I know he's here. Where is he?"

"I'll never tell you," the man spat, but his eyes glanced in the direction of a door in the corner.

"You just did," she said, and struck him in the chest, her Power crushing his heart. He slid to the floor as she released him. Talia gestured to the door, and Shatter followed her toward it. Spear closed the entrance door, and disappeared into a Shadow.

Steel led Min and Elanor toward a door in the opposite direction. *"Eight,"* Shatter Sent.

Beyond the door, Min saw two hallways. She felt something down the left-hand one. She gestured Steel in that direction, then led the way.

Halfway down the hall was a door. Min stopped. Further down the hall, another door opened, and Humans poured out. Steel dropped to one knee, and started firing. Elanor conjured a Shield as the Humans began to return fire with crossbows, the bolts sparking on the Shield. Elanor winced.

"Blackblade tips," she said, increasing her concentration. Steel took careful aim, and took down one of the bowmen.

"Min!" Steel yelled, notching another arrow. "We don't have much time."

Min opened the door. Inside, two men were sitting at a table, across from one another. Thick spools of thread sat between them. One man, his hands occupied with knitting needles and thread, had a half-finished rug in front of him. The other, pushing a completed rug away, turned as the door opened. He grabbed a small crossbow, and aimed it at the door.

Their eyes met.

"Min," he said.

"Canin," Min replied.

The other man fumbled, trying to free his hands. Canin paused a breath, and heard the cries from the hall. Min raised her hand, Silverfire shining. The second man drew in breath to yell. Canin adjusted his aim and shot the man before he could.

Min looked at him. His hair was still in a messy braid, but his eyes were harder, and older.

"What are you doing here?" she asked, lowering her hand.

"Waiting for you," Canin said, putting down the crossbow. "We'd better hurry." He pulled out a satchel, and started to push thread into it. He folded up the finished rug and stuffed it in as well. He walked around the table. "I had a dream," he said.

"Min," Elanor yelled. "They're coming! We can't hold them. There are too many."

Min couldn't respond. She was pushed into the room by Elanor and Steel. Steel shut the door, and turned. She took in the room, raising her bow at Canin.

"Canin!" Elanor cried, unbelieving.

"What are you doing here?" Steel demanded.

"Waiting for me," Min answered in his stead. She went over to him, and took his hand. "He killed that man." She gestured to the floor.

Elanor looked confused. Behind her, the door thumped, and a bolt crashed through it, just missing her shoulder.

"Get out," Shatter Sent, shouting to them all. *"Too many. Get out."*

"He's coming," Min announced, raising Canin's hand.

"Go!" Steel commanded, pulling a stone from her pouch. Elanor pulled one out, too.

"Concentrate on me," Min told Canin, touching her Torc.

"Always," he said, as they disappeared.

Steel shook her head, and took Elanor's hand.

"Only Min," Elanor said, dropping the stone at the same time as Steel dropped hers. The door opened. The men stormed into a blast of Silverfire, and a room devoid of Fairies.

$$(\approx \varnothing$$

Talia and Shatter followed a twisting hallway. Humans and Elenites kept appearing in doorways, and around corners. Some had weapons, while others just rushed at them empty-handed. Shatter shot them all down. Talia, following in her wake, made sure they were all dead.

At the last bend in the hallway, they reached a closed door. Solid. Underneath it, a dark light glowed. Talia stepped up to the doorway. She could hear the corrupted Song behind it.

Shatter went back to the bend, her last arrow on the string. She glanced around the corner. A bolt skipped off the wall by her head.

"They're gathering," Shatter announced, firing her last arrow.

Talia gestured back, and a Shield appeared. More bolts hit, sending sparks flying.

"Blackblade tips," Shatter informed her.

"He's here," Talia declared. More bolts hit the Shield.

"We must leave," Shatter urged, dropping her bow, and pulling her sword.

"I need more Power," Talia said, concentrating on the door. Her Weave was building.

Shatter sliced into her left hand, and smeared the blood on Talia's wing.

Her aura exploded into light. Shatter had to step back. The sound of bolts hitting the Shield stopped.

"Now!" Talia shouted, pushing the Weave into the door. The door exploded inward. She stepped over the threshold.

The room within was lit by the dark light of a Blood Ring. Three men turned. One raised a crossbow. Talia gestured, and he fell dead. The second turned to the third, who slowly turned and smiled at Talia.

"Ah — you found me," he smirked. The knife in his hand plunged into the neck of the man beside him. He thrust his hand into the blood flow. As blood coated his arm, he stepped backward into the Ring.

"You will pay," Talia promised, conjuring Silverfire at him. His blood-soaked arm went up, and the fire stopped, splashing at the border of the Ring.

"You've learned. Good." His face began to shift. It became younger. More recognizable.

"I know who you are. You'll pay for that, too," Talia swore, pouring more energy into the fire. Wingless Bastard smiled, and raised his other hand.

"Talia!" Shatter yelled in warning, pulling the Heir out of the way. A crossbow bolt passed through the space where she'd been standing.

"Not today," he taunted, and disappeared. The light of the Blood Ring began to throb, and lightning danced around the room.

"Curse you!" Talia said. "Get out," she ordered Shatter.

"*Get out,*" Shatter Sent, shouting to everyone. "*Too many. Get out.*"

Talia took another look at the Blood Ring, and saw it start to collapse. She grabbed Shatter's arm, and touched her Torc. They disappeared, as the Ring exploded in a shower of lightning and flame.

(☾ ⌇⌇⌇ ☼)

Spear was the last one out. Talia stood at the edge of the roof, watching the Crafthouse burn. She saw the people gathering to watch.

"Doesn't look like anyone is rushing to fight the fire," Elanor observed, coming to her side.

Talia didn't answer. Her hands were clenched in anger. She turned.

"I almost had him," she accused Shatter. "You broke my concentration."

"I saved your life," Shatter retorted. "He triggered that crossbow. It would have gone through your chest."

Talia turned, redirecting her anger elsewhere. "Who's that?" She pointed to Canin, standing with Min.

Min turned. "You remember Canin. The man we met in Bell-Oak? He saved me."

"Why was he there?" Talia demanded, fire dancing on her fingers. Min stepped in front of him.

"I will tell you everything," Canin promised. "But I think we should leave now." He motioned to the ground. The Fire Brigade was coming. Survivors were stumbling out of the burning building. They were yelling, and gesturing around.

"You will," Talia confirmed. She turned to Raven. "Can we reach the garrison Ring from here?"

"No," she replied. "But it won't be far until we can."

Shatter looked over the edge again. "I think we should all Shadow, and move out. It's a short walk to the garrison. It'll be a buzzing nest by the time we get there. It might be better to hide, and wait for things to die down a bit."

"We can see when we get there," Steel agreed.

"Lead the way." Talia gestured, anger still blazing in her eyes.

"Can you cover him, too?" Elanor asked Min.

"With Raven's help," Min replied, looking to the soldier. Raven narrowed her eyes at Canin. She held out her hand. Canin pulled his wooden knife from his belt and handed it to her.

"That's all I carry." He gestured to the satchel he had brought out, now in the hands of Spear.

Raven tucked the knife away. She put her hand on Canin's shoulder and, working together with Min, covered them both in a Shadow.

The others disappeared into their own Shadows, and together they moved off through the busy streets.

$$\left(\text{☾}\,\text{〰}\,\text{☼}\right)$$

They stopped at an abandoned building across from the Fairy garrison. Steel had gone on alone to make sure the way was clear. Everyone but Talia collapsed to the floor. Min and Canin sat, holding hands, but not speaking.

After a few moments, Talia gestured Spear to replace her at the window, where she'd been standing lookout. She then crossed the room, and knelt in front of Min and Canin.

"Now. The story," she demanded.

"After I left you," Canin started, "I left the Fairy Realm. I didn't know where to go. I wandered for a while. I couldn't go back to the Exile Forest, not yet. I found work where I could, helped where I could." He looked at Shatter. "Then I decided to go to Elen-Ford and see if you had kept your promise. It was a long wait. I was ready to kill him myself, when I saw Raven talking to the barkeep of the bar he was always drinking at. I waited, and saw him leave. I followed. Saw him wander through the streets, though for years he had been able to find his way back blind drunk. Eventually, I saw him go into his home, and not come out. In the morning, I watched your public burning." He gave a nod to Raven. "Then I watched the aftermath. I saw some come and spit on the man, and others bow to him. I watched, and I began to think. I had heard rumors of what was going on between the Humans and the Fairies. I knew you had to be involved." He gripped Min's hand. "I decided that I would do what I could. So, I found a cell of these people, and offered my services. They were quick to take me in."

"So, you served him," Talia began to rage. She grabbed him by the shirtfront, and hauled him to his feet. "What did you do?!"

Canin didn't struggle. He stood still, and looked her in the eye. He recognized a change in her, the change in all of them. He didn't understand why, but he knew his life depended on answering her questions to her satisfaction. "I did what I needed to do to blend in. They needed hands, and I gave them mine. I discovered I had a knack for weaving Ephemeral Rings."

Min stood up, but didn't move to block Talia. Elanor stood at Canin's other side.

"I thought you didn't have the knack for spinning?" Elanor asked pointedly.

"I don't, but this has nothing to do with making silk." He gestured at the satchel on the floor with his chin. "I take the threads, and make the pattern. Others give the Ephemeral Ring Power. He said my patterns take less work to accept the Weave."

"He!" Talia said, shaking him. Shatter moved to the window to make sure no one could overhear them. "You know this wingless Fairy?"

"Only to fear him and his people," Canin admitted. "He calls himself Wingless Bastard. I was just a weaver. That man I killed was my watcher. He made sure I did what I was supposed to do, and never escaped."

"He's telling the truth," Min said. She put her hand on Talia's arm. "Let him go."

"I sense no deception," Elanor echoed.

Talia took one more look, then let go of Canin. "If you betray me, I will kill you," she promised.

"I won't," Canin swore with a bow. "As I said, I dreamed of this day. The Mother sent me here. This is my path: to help you."

232

Min embraced him, and kissed him. Talia returned to the window. Elanor followed her.

"Only Min," she said, "could find a lost love in the middle of a battle."

Talia didn't reply.

"This could help us," Elanor continued. "We need to build more Ephemeral Rings."

Talia turned. "Steel is returning."

"The Ring will be clear in about an hour," she reported when she arrived. "The fire at the Crafthouse has stirred everyone up. The Captain is pulling everyone in. I was able to get a way in from an old flame, but he can only promise us a few minutes. We'll have to hurry."

"Good," Talia said. She turned back to the window.

"There's something else," Steel started hesitantly. She looked to Shatter.

"Go ahead. What is it?"

"The Human King has had a child." There was a sharp intake of breath. Everyone turned to look at Talia. She didn't respond. Elanor saw her hands clench, though.

"He will present the child to the court in a week's time at the Human castle," Steel continued. "He has invited the Fairy Queen to attend." Talia's hands turned white. "She's sending the Herald and Lord Oberon as a hand for peace."

Canin looked at Min, a question in his eyes.

"I'll tell you later," she whispered.

Talia turned away. "Then we shall go, too."

"And we will give him justice," Steel promised, putting a hand on her sword.

"Worse," Talia said, smiling without joy. "I will make him suffer as I have suffered."

Chapter Twenty-One
Fairies Prepare

"So, you woke up and didn't remember anything? Flora had to tell you what had happened?"

Min nodded.

"That sounds horrible," Canin said, squeezing her shoulder.

"She Shared her view of it all," Min corrected. "And the others did, too. That was almost worse: I got to see it from all of their points of view."

"Did you Share with Willow?" he asked carefully.

"No. She was already gone, and then, after. . . ." She stopped. She buried her face in his chest and began to cry again. Canin just held her.

"I'm sorry," he said later. "I'm making you relive this."

"No," she said, sitting up. "I need to tell it. You need to understand what we've been through, and who Talia is now. You need to know what she's capable of."

They were alone in one of the small rooms off the library. They had shoved the table against the wall, laid down blankets, and made love until Canin thought his heart would burst. All the past longing had been resolved, and all his wishes that they could be together again had been granted. Then she'd told him everything: from when they'd parted outside Bell-Oak, till now.

She moved to sit across from him, pulling a blanket over her legs. Canin stared at her, watching her hair move and flow around her shoulders and body, watching her move her wings and rub the healing wounds on her hands.

Min marveled at him, too. She had pulled his hair out of its braid, and now it hung around his face. He brushed it back, unused to having it hang free. She watched the scars on his chest move with him. Watched him watch her.

"I'm sorry," he finally said.

"For what?" she asked.

"I should have had the courage to stay with you."

234

Min smiled. "You had your path. I have mine. It's good that they've come together again. You needed to discover yourself."

"I did. But in doing so, I aided your Lady's greatest enemy."

"You did, but you're making up for that now," she said, moving back to him. She took his hands, and put his fingers on her palms, on the wounds. "I am not the woman you met. I've changed, too."

He ran his fingers over the healing wounds. Then he entwined his fingers with hers. "I will not leave you again."

"We can't make that vow," she rebuked him earnestly. "Only the Goddess knows our path."

"I," Canin started, but she stopped him with a deep kiss.

"No more talk," she whispered, pushing him back. "I want you." She settled on top of him with a little gasp. "More of this." She put his hands on her breasts. Canin complied.

☾ ♒ ☼

"*Paramount.*"

"*Talia. I'm glad you've contacted me. I have news.*"

"*News that the Human King is presenting his child to the Realm? Or news that the Fairies are sending an emissary to be part of it?*"

"*I'm sorry I didn't contact you sooner, but the Queen has tasked me with many duties.*"

"*You said you would help me. That you would feed me information. Yet I had to learn this from soldier gossip.*"

"*The details have just been worked out.*" Miranda's tone became more stern. "*I needed to know everything before I could contact you.*"

Talia was silent.

"*I need you to explain what you and your people just did in Elen-Flax.*"

"*We struck against the Blood Cult. The one known as Wingless Bastard was there, and he escaped.*"

"*I know. We've been watching that Crafthouse. We were close to being able to go in and capture the whole lot. Now, you've destroyed everything.*"

"*I told you I wouldn't be denied justice.*"

"*The Queen has called for your surrender or capture. The Fairies at each of our Embassies have been alerted about you and your people. Those who helped you have been detained, and await the Queen's Justice. You won't be able to use those Rings again.*"

Talia's anger filled the Web. "*You say you want to help me, but you're denying me access to the Rings.*"

"*The Queen is denying you access. I can only do so much,*" Miranda countered, waffling. "*The Blood Cult must be stopped, but what you've done was too. . . .*"

"*Violent? Bloody?*" Talia suggested. "*They're a vile and bloody group. They must be struck hard. I did that.*"

"*That is not your Queen's way, and if you continue, she will be forced to do more than try to capture you.*"

"*I told her,*" Talia growled. "*Anyone who hinders me, I will consider my enemy. Do you intend to hinder me?*"

Miranda didn't respond for a long time. Talia still felt her in the Web, but she couldn't get any feeling from her old teacher.

"*I will help you as much as I can,*" Miranda finally said. "*I will Share all the details I know.*" A rush of information hit Talia. She absorbed it, then set it aside.

"*I need a way into the Human Realm, and the ceremony.*"

"*What do you intend to do?*"

"*I intend to make him suffer as he made me suffer.*"

"*The child.*" Miranda Saw some of Talia's plan, and guessed more. "*I will not be a party to murder.*"

"*He was a party to my child's murder!*" Talia's anger struck across the Web. Sparks flew from Miranda's Geode. She blocked the pain, and held on to the link.

"*Child, you are losing control. You must calm yourself. I can help you, but you must be calm.*"

"*I am not your child, and I am not your student anymore,*" Talia said, cold settling in her mind. "*You have given me what you can. I will not be contacting you again.*" Talia broke the connection.

Miranda opened her eyes. Lady Titania was batting out the sparks that had caught on the silk cloth under the Geode.

"That did not go well," she understated.

"No, it did not," Miranda agreed. She flowed Healing into her burned hands. "You must warn Oberon. She's planning something. Something terrible, I think."

"Has she fallen to the temptation of Blood?"

"Maybe, but her anger and pain are so deep, I can't tell for sure."

"The Queen must know."

"I will tell her. You must prepare your husband to defend the King's child."

Titania sat back. "What a strange situation. We must defend a Human against one of our own."

"She calls anyone who hinders her an enemy. She could destroy both Realms in her quest for justice."

"'Justice,' she calls it," Titania remarked. "What she wants is pure vengeance."

$$☾ \approx ☼$$

Talia's anger wanted to bust out. She wanted to burn and destroy.

"But you don't have time for that," she reminded herself. She pushed the anger away, and marked it for future use. Taking a few deep breaths, she plunged back into the Geode Web. Talia felt the broken crystal cutting her hands. Fitting, considering who she was contacting.

"*Paramount Holly*," she called.

$$☾ \approx ☼$$

Hours later, there was a knock at the door.

"That's enough," Elanor called through the door. "We need you out here."

Min woke, stretched, and stood. Canin was watching her. Suddenly, she became conscious of her nakedness, and gestured her shirt to herself.

"How long have you been awake?" she asked, pulling on the shirt.

"A few minutes. Every day I woke up alone, I would remember feeling you sleeping on me back at the inn. I wanted to memorize every moment." He stood, and began to dress.

Min smiled, but when he turned to find his own shirt, her expression changed. Fear and concern warred on her face. When he turned back, she had taken on a more businesslike demeanor.

"Now you can show me your new talent," she announced, moving to the door.

"Yes, Beautiful," he agreed placidly, following her out, and bumping into Raven, who was standing outside the door. She let Min pass, but blocked him.

"Greetings, Raven," he started.

Raven passed him back his knife. "Hurt her," she said low, as she passed him a cup of tea, leaving the rest of the threat unspoken, but understood by both.

"Raven," Min commented, pulling the soldier away. "I can take care of myself. He can be trusted."

"Yes, Sister," Raven acquiesced, allowing herself to be led away. Canin took a deep breath, and then came face to face with Flora. Smiling, she handed him a bowl.

"Hurt her, young man," she warned him.

Juggling bowl, cup, and knife, Canin almost dropped all three. "Yes, Mum — I won't."

"Good," she said, taking his arm and stabilizing his meal. "Now, Mistress Talia has been chewing the floor waiting for you two to be properly reunited." She led him across the room, to a table in the middle of the library. His satchel was open, and its contents spread out.

"That one is almost ready," he said, pointing to the rug Elanor was handling. "The others, I've been working on in secret. They're about half done."

"I can feel it," Elanor said, almost grudgingly, to Talia, who was at the head of the table, rolling a spool under her hand. "It will be ready for the Weave."

Talia looked up. "I'm glad you're here," she said to Canin. "We can use your skill." She threw him the spool.

Canin put down the bowl and caught the thread. "I'm here to serve you, My Lady."

"Remember that," she told him. "Shatter, I have more information on the group going to the King's castle. They'll be arriving at the Embassy at Elen-Gold in two days, and riding into the Human Realm. They've been given a compound outside the Human castle walls as a place to stay. A full company of Air and Grass are going with them, along with part of the Queen's Guard, as protection for Oberon and the Herald."

"How do you know this?" Steel asked.

"I have my ways," was all Talia would say. "They'll have Ephemeral Rings with them, of course. I have the Frequency for one an aide of Oberon's will be carrying. She'll make sure to place it in a room we can use. I'll be getting more information when they get there."

"What do you intend to do?" Flora asked.

"I intend to make him suffer as he made me," Talia informed her.

"Mistress," Flora began.

"Flora, I respect everything we've been through together, and everything you've done for me." She stopped, and her voice turned cold. "But I will not have you speak to me this way anymore. You will help, and stay silent, or you will leave."

Silence descended on the room. Canin looked from face to face. He watched the expressions change from shock to resignation.

Flora stayed still. Her face betrayed no emotion. Finally, she said, "I will need more herbs from the ruins." She turned to Canin. "Will you come with me, young man?"

"No," Talia said. "I need him. Take Steel."

Flora nodded, and went to the Ring. Steel joined her, and they disappeared.

Talia turned back to the group, the outburst forgotten. "Canin, I need you to finish these. How long?"

"Only a few hours for both," he said. "I have everything I need in my satchel."

"Good. Find a place to work, and finish them." Talia dismissed him from her thoughts, and turned to Shatter. "We'll need a plan."

"That will depend on where we enter the castle," she answered.

"We'll know that soon." She looked at Canin, who hadn't moved. "I need those ready," she prodded him. "The Weave takes time. The sooner you start, the sooner they can be completed."

Canin could tell she was on the edge of another outburst. He gathered up his gear, and moved to a table away from the others. He shot a look at Min.

"You'll have time for that later," Talia assured her, annoyance beginning to creep back into her voice. "Now, we need to work on our Weaves."

"Yes, My Lady," Min said quietly.

"Shatter, you'll need your full armor. I need him to understand your Power."

"My pleasure." Shatter grinned. "We'll be the most powerful Fairies he's ever seen."

☾ ♒ ☼

With Canin's superior weaving of the silk, Steel, Elanor, and Min were able to create the Ephemeral Weave and merge it with the cloth much more quickly and easily than before.

"Where have you been all this time?" Steel asked, clapping Canin on the shoulder. "Brother, you are Goddess-sent."

"I'm glad to help," Canin replied, a bit uncomfortable, but still happy at the praise. "The Mother guides my hand."

"She does at that." Steel laughed a bit too loud.

He produced two more Rings in as many days. He had never worked so fast, or so precisely. 'The Mother of Exiles is truly with me,' he thought. Though his fingers, arms, and eyes burned from the strain, he was happy: he was where he belonged.

When they weren't working on the Weaves for Ephemeral Rings, Min and Elanor were behind closed doors with Talia. Min returned to the room they had taken as their own, tired and drained. In his arms, she fell into short, fitful bursts of sleep, waking often to alternately push him away, then snuggle closer. Canin got little sleep with all the interruptions. Min would wake with the sun, full of passion, and pull him out of sleep for a short, but passionate, romp, and then she was gone.

Canin was busy, too. When he wasn't weaving, Shatter or Spear were working him through training exercises and sparring. Raven trained him on the bow and crossbow. Canin had rarely used the longbow before, but he had a good eye. She was a talented, but cold, teacher, offering only criticism, without praise.

"Is she jealous, or afraid I'll hurt Min?" he asked Flora during a rare rest.

"It's not that," she replied. "She knows you won't, at least not intentionally. Remember, we've been together for a long time. The soldiers were each tasked with defending their Lady. We've become closer than most. We've all been part of each other's minds in many a Circle. Closer than any lover or partner. Raven and Min are closer than any two people can be."

Canin looked down.

"You cannot be that close to her," Flora told him with sympathy.

"We can get close, for a moment," Canin said slowly.

"All men feel that way, for a moment," Flora replied, with a smile of understanding. "Now, take that feeling, and extend it for days. We know each other. I can't explain it any further." Flora stopped. She took his hands.

"I understand."

"They're being tough on you because they know you're a weak link in this company."

"I have experience."

"Not like these soldiers have," Flora reminded him. She went back to stirring the stew. "They're trained to work together. To support each other. They're killers."

"I would die for her," Canin proclaimed.

"That's easy," Flora stated. "But would you kill for her?"

Canin looked up, and started to speak, but stopped.

"Are you prepared to kill for her?" Flora asked him with a seriousness she hadn't had before. "Are you ready to kill me, or one of them, to protect her?"

Canin stuttered, "How could they? Why would they?"

"Not long ago, I would have said that it was impossible, but now," she drew a deep breath, "I don't know. Talia has changed. I never thought the girl I helped raise would kill one of her Ladies, but she did. She's planning the murder of another child. I still see the old Talia in her at times, but she's fading."

"Do you think she would?" Canin stopped.

"She sees anyone who gets in her way as an enemy. She will strike. You must be ready to defend her, even from herself." Flora looked up. Steel and Spear were returning from below.

"Take this to them," she ordered him, passing him two bowls.

Canin nodded, and took the food to the soldiers.

"Again!" Steel yelled from behind him.

Canin felt the sting of the wooden sword across his back. He stayed on one knee. "I need a break," he pleaded.

"You can have a break when you hit me," Steel responded, prodding him in the back.

"If I don't get a break, I'll never hit you," Canin returned.

"He's right," Shatter said from the other side of the cavern. She was running the Patterns with Raven and Spear. She stopped, and gave Steel a look.

"He isn't a soldier," Shatter reminded her. "He doesn't have the abilities we have."

"He needs to get them," Steel said.

"He will," Shatter predicted. "He just needs time, and instruction."

"I've been giving him that. And he doesn't have the time. Maybe he should train with the Ladies," Steel said with disgust, as she threw down her sword. "Five minutes," she said. "And then you will hit me, or I will start breaking bones. Willow was better than you."

Raven's head came up. She took a step forward, but Shatter blocked her. She started to say something, but Canin stepped in.

"I'll hit you," he promised Steel, "or I will sleep alone tonight."

Raven's anger dissolved into a laugh. "Incentive," she commented, and turned back to her Pattern.

Steel just folded her arms and stared at Canin.

"Here," Shatter said, tossing him a water bottle.

Canin caught it, and took a long drink. The water here was some of the best he had ever tasted. Almost better than the spring in the center of the Forest. He settled back on his heels, and watched Shatter, Raven, and Spear. They moved into the Third Pattern. Canin tilted his head. Something was familiar about the motions. He turned to Steel.

"What are they doing?"

"The Third Pattern," Steel replied reluctantly. "It's part of our training and exercise tradition." She pointed at the sweeping motions of their arms. Her voice softened as she dropped into martial teaching mode. "Those are blocks and feints. And now, those are strikes, for when the opponent is out of position from the feint."

"I know these movements," Canin announced, standing.

"That's impossible," Steel commented, turning to look at Canin directly. "These have been passed down for centuries from soldier to soldier. We don't teach them to non-Fairies."

"Yet I know them," Canin insisted.

Shatter and the others heard the tone in Steel's voice and stopped. They turned to watch.

"We call them something else," Canin told Steel. "And there are only four, but they're taught to all the people who live in the Exile Forest. The Thorn Brothers practice them every day." He took a stance. "We start with Water, flowing into the day, stretching and waking the muscles." He moved into another beginning pose. "Then Earth, as the base for all that comes next. Then Air, as defense and evasion, and finally, Fire, to strike." Then, moving more swiftly than Steel was ready for, Canin struck her twice in the chest. He then dodged her startled return strike, and hit her again in the side. He quickly jumped back out of range.

Steel, shock evident on her face, put her hand over where he had struck her. Behind her, Shatter and Spear were silent. Raven was laughing openly. Steel moved closer to Canin. He raised his hands in defense.

Steel raised her own hands, and both her sword and the one Canin had dropped leapt into them. She pointed both swords at Canin. He tensed. Then, with a smile, she reversed Canin's, and offered him the hilt.

"Good," she commended him. "More of that."

Canin took the hilt, and began to smile. Steel struck him on the shoulder, but Canin brought up his blade and blocked the next blow.

"If you can hit me again," Steel offered, "I'll show you the First Pattern."

"And you can show us yours," Shatter called over the clacking of wooden swords. Canin smiled, but quickly settled into a determined stance as he beat off another flurry of blows.

Shatter turned back. She raised her eyes at the strange look on Spear's face.

"I must have spent too much time with Goldberry," Spear said, "but that sounded a lot like the wisdom of the First Fairies."

Shatter shrugged. "It's also a very basic understanding of the world." She settled into the beginning of the Fourth Pattern. "Now, let's keep working. Who knows what the Humans will have in store for us?"

Behind them came the sound of a curse by Canin, followed by a louder curse from Steel. Then, Canin gave a glad cry that quickly turned into a yelp at the sound of breaking wood.

☾ ∿ ☼

Later that night, when Min returned to their room, Canin was stretching, moving through the soreness of his sparring with Steel.

"You're pretty bruised," Min noted, looking at his back and arms.

"Steel's working me pretty hard," Canin admitted, turning.

"Let me Heal you," Min offered, motioning for him to sit down. He sat across from her, and she took his hands. Her Power flowed into him, bringing warmth, and respite from the pain.

He watched her as she worked, with her eyes closed. After a moment, the warmth dissipated, and his pain was gone.

"Thank you," he said, leaning in to kiss her. Her eyes opened, and she pulled back.

"I have something for you," she said, covering her surprise.

Canin put his hands in his lap as Min pulled something from her pocket. She held it out in the palm of her right hand. It was a silver bracelet. Canin could see faint writing on the silver. Min reached for his right hand with her left. She then took the bracelet, and pressed it to his skin. It passed through his arm, and settled on his wrist.

Canin stared, marveling at the fact that there were no seams or clasps. He looked at her for an explanation.

"It's a Fairy bracelet. Raven and Elanor helped me create it. It will allow you to use the Rings."

Canin covered his surprise by running his fingers over the metal. It was smooth. He couldn't feel the words inscribed on it. He looked up at her, and smiled. "Thank you. How does it work?"

Min yawned.

"I'm sorry: you're tired," Canin apologized, making room for her on the bed. "You haven't been sleeping well."

Min settled in beside him. "No, I haven't."

Canin took a risk and asked, "Because of what you're planning with Talia?"

Min turned in his arms, looking at him with a mix of shock, fear, and a little shame. "No. It's just that the Weave we're working on is complex. Takes a lot of energy."

"What are you planning? What will this Weave do?" Canin asked.

Min was silent. She turned her head away from him.

"I don't know if I can be a part of murdering a child," Canin stated.

Min sat up, and looked at him. She was angry, and scared. "She isn't planning to murder the child."

"What will she do, then?" Canin pressed. "She said she wanted him to suffer like she's suffered. That can only mean the death of the child."

"I'm surprised at you," she retorted. "Your whole being is about protecting the wronged." She gestured to the wooden knife on his belt.

"You've killed to defend those who've been wronged. Talia has been wronged."

"Yes, I have," Canin admitted, "but those were men who had hurt and killed women and children. I've never struck out against an innocent. The Mother of Exiles would strike me down if I did." He looked at her, and took her hand. "I couldn't be with someone who acted to harm an innocent. Bastile is the guilty one. She should strike at him."

"She intends to," Min assured him. "I promise you, she isn't intending to kill the child at the ceremony."

Canin held her gaze for a while, weighing the truth in her eyes and her movements. She kept her eyes locked with his, while still holding tightly to his hands.

"I believe you," he finally decided. "What does she intend to do?"

"I can't tell you," Min replied. At his reaction, she quickly added, "I've made an Oath to her. I'm sorry, but I can't betray it."

"I understand," Canin said. He let go of her hands. "I have something for you, too." He picked up his satchel. "I wanted to give you this when I returned, but they took my satchel, and then we were busy." He blushed a little, and Min laughed. He dug to the bottom of his bag. "Then we were busy with other things. Ah." He finally found what he was looking for, and pulled a scroll from the satchel. He handed it to her.

"What is this?" she asked, handling it.

"It's my letter to you. I wrote every day after we parted." He smiled ruefully. "Well, most days. Sometimes I just told you that I rode for hours. Other times, I explained how much I missed you. And then it was tales of being harassed by Fairies on the road, or being harassed by Humans on the road. Then, about being denied entrance to a town, or being told that I was free to come in, but I had to be back on the road by sunset."

Min looked up, questioning.

"Or I would regret it," Canin clarified. "Rotting corpses in the trees made the point."

Min gasped a little. "I had no idea," she said. She began to unroll the scroll. And continued unrolling it.

"I had to keep adding paper. It was a good thing I took a lot from the Quartermaster. I hope you understand it: I wasn't clear sometimes, and it was dark."

Min stopped his explanation with a kiss. "I'm sure I'll be able to understand what you meant to say." She began to run her hands over his chest. She moved closer, putting the scroll down, and kissing his neck.

"Should we practice with the Ring?" he asked, slightly surprised.

"In the morning," she murmured in his ear.

"I thought you were tired," he said, sliding his hands over her side, and up her back.

"I was, but not anymore," she whispered in his ear, biting.

'She's trying to distract me,' Canin thought. She bit his ear again, harder. 'And it's working,' he decided, as he freed the lacing on her dress.

$$\left(\, \approx\, \right)$$

"I'm putting my trust in you," Talia said to Steel. "I need you to make sure that nothing goes wrong. That no one falters, or backs out."

"I will fulfill my Oath to you and to Sun. . . ." She stopped at Talia's look. "To justice for her," she finished.

"Good. Some might falter. You need to make sure they follow through."

"I will, My Lady."

Talia gestured her out. "Go. I need to meditate."

Steel bowed, and exited the room. She saw Shatter watching her as she closed the door. She smiled, and went to join her.

"What was that about?" Shatter asked, as Steel sat down and took a bowl of stew.

"Just a few details," Steel said between mouthfuls. "I hate to say it, but I'm getting a bit sick of stew."

Shatter looked up, and saw that Flora had heard. Initially, it looked like she was going to say something, but she didn't. Flora had been noticeably quiet since the day Talia had snapped at her. She only spoke when spoken to, and even then, only in short sentences.

Shatter was worried. Flora moved off to deliver a bowl of the stew to Spear.

"We'll make the bastard pay," Steel promised, breaking Shatter out of her thoughts.

"Yes, we will," Shatter agreed. She patted her hilt. "I have the perfect sword."

Steel laughed, too loud.

☾ ∾ ☼

"Thank you, Mum," Spear said, as Flora brought her dinner.

"No thanks needed," Flora replied, putting her hand on Spear's arm.

"*I'm worried. I fear for us all,*" she Sent.

"*We're acting to bring justice for Sunrise. He killed her, and he must pay.*"

"*But is this what the Goddess would wish us to do?*"

"*I don't know. All I know is that I must follow her.*"

Flora broke the connection, and moved off toward Elanor.

☾ ∾ ☼

A knock at the door brought Talia out of her meditation.

"*What is it?*" she Sent, irritated that her rest was being disturbed.

"My Lady," Shatter Sent in response, "I need to speak with you."

Talia pushed down her anger. She gestured the door open. Shatter entered, bowed, then waited for her.

Talia let her wait as she swept the remains of her meditation out of her mind. Shatter was patient, her hands resting on the hilt of her new sword. Her feet and wings were still.

Finally, Talia asked, "What is it, Captain?"

"My Lady, with all due respect, what did you discuss with my Lieutenant?"

Talia's voice became cold. "She is in charge of training, and executing our plans, is she not?"

"She is," Shatter confirmed, still calm and still.

Talia fixed her with a hard stare. "I want to be sure everyone will do their part."

Shatter nodded. "My Lady, it would be more proper for you to ask me to do that." She frowned slightly. "The soldiers are my responsibility; you shouldn't be giving them orders behind my back."

'I will give them any orders I choose,' Talia thought with anger, but her face remained calm. "Then see to it, Captain." Her voice rose slightly. "There will be no failure. You know the price of failure."

Shatter bowed. "I do, My Lady. We will not fail you."

Talia gestured her dismissal. Shatter backed out of the room, bowing, but Talia had already closed her eyes.

Shatter stood outside the door for a long time. She reviewed the conversation repeatedly in her mind. Her soldier's nerves grated at both Talia's tone and her body language. She would have to be prepared for anything. She went to find Raven.

☾ ♒ ☼

Elanor sat under the dome, looking up at the sky, and — in particular — the stars. She sought the peace she had previously always found in the night sky, but it eluded her. She was tired. The Weave Talia was working on was the most complex thing she had ever done. So many lines of Power and contingencies. They moved as if they had lives of their own. Her part was separate from Min's and Talia's, but they would all meld in the end. She couldn't help wondering about the other parts. Hers would sustain the energy of the Weave for an extended period of time.

"For how long?" she had asked.

"That's my part," Talia had replied. "All I need from you is the energy to power the Weave."

"Where do I get that Power?" she had asked.

"Her potential," was all Talia had told her.

Flora sat down beside her. "You need to eat."

"I'm not hungry," Elanor told her, not taking her eyes from the stars.

"You will eat, child," Flora ordered sternly.

"I am not a child," Elanor replied.

"She can speak to me that way, but you cannot," Flora decreed, grabbing Elanor's chin and forcing her head around to look at her.

Elanor started to snap at her, but stopped at the look on Flora's face. What was she doing, treating this woman so? She had been a second mother to them all. Flora was more her mother than Celia had ever been. Her quiet strength had brought Elanor through her darkest time. She would have fallen to the despair if Flora hadn't been there. It hit her then: Flora had lost her daughters. Five young Fairies whom she had raised to be powerful Ladies. And two had died right in front of her. Killed by the woman she had raised from a baby.

"Goddess, Mum, I." She embraced Flora. Tears began forming at the corners of her eyes.

"Be strong," Flora snapped. "Don't cry. We're being watched. Be strong."

Elanor gathered up all her strength and discipline, and managed to hold back the tears.

"Cry inside, child. I know I do. I've lost many, and I fear I'll lose even more."

Together, in the privacy of their Circle, Mother and Daughter cried, and mourned their lost Sisters, as outwardly, Flora sat down, and joined Elanor in looking at the stars.

Chapter Twenty-Two
Before

In the morning, Min and Canin worked with his new bracelet. He stood in the library Ring while an Ephemeral Ring was placed at the other end of the library, far enough away that there was no interference. An amused Raven looked on.

"I can't hear the Frequency, no matter how hard I concentrate," Canin complained to Min. "Are you sure this will work?"

"Do you doubt my skill?" Raven asked, only half jokingly.

"No," Canin stated absolutely.

"Do you doubt mine, Love?" Min inquired with a smile.

"No, Beautiful, I don't," Canin replied with even more confidence.

"Then just follow my instructions," Min said, with the patience of affection. "You don't have to hear the Frequency of the Ring, as we do. The bracelet will do it for you."

Canin began to understand. "I think I'm getting it."

"Good," Min said. "Just concentrate on the bracelet. You'll have to find a way to name the Rings. Color, number, letter — something. But you must be consistent in your mind. The bracelet will learn what you call each Ring, and then it'll be able to take you to the one you require."

"What about the Wards on the Rings?" Shatter asked. "How will he get around those?"

"We've worked on that," Min informed her. "Canin's mind is Fairy enough that he can manipulate the Locking Wards, with help. The bracelet will help with that as well."

"What if he gets captured?" Shatter asked. "Someone could take the bracelet from him, and then access all of our Rings."

"No," Raven corrected her, "they couldn't. The bracelet is keyed to him, and him alone. It can't be removed. An enemy would have to cut his arm off to get it." Canin winced. "And even then, it would be worthless to them." Raven smiled. "More than worthless, actually: anyone, other than Canin, who tries to use it, will be lost in the nothingness between the Rings."

'Like Nova,' Min thought.

Shatter nodded in approval.

"Now," Min urged him, pulling out of her dark thoughts, "just think of the Ephemeral Ring, and go there."

Canin took a deep breath. He trusted Min. He trusted that Raven wouldn't do anything irreparable to him, because it would hurt Min. He gripped the bracelet. "To Min," he said. And disappeared.

One breath, two breaths. Min began to worry. Three breaths. Fear gripped her, and she started toward the library Ring Canin had been standing on. Four breaths. Even Raven looked worried.

Five breaths, and they heard a thump as Canin re-appeared, and fell over.

"Cold," he said, rubbing at the bracelet. "Cold," he said again, pushing the bracelet up his arm. The skin underneath it was white.

Min ran to him. Raven looked relieved. Shatter let out her pent-up breath.

"What happened?" Min asked, rubbing at his wrist.

"I was. . . ." He struggled for words. "Nowhere. It felt like years. Then I was pulled," he made a vague gesture, "that way, and I was here."

"You lost concentration," Shatter told him. "It was like that my first time. You could've been lost. Keep your head. Remember what I taught you: focus on what's in front of you. Let nothing else intrude."

"Just think of Min," Raven added, helping him up. "You're always intent on her."

Min smiled, and sent Healing into his arm.

"If you're done playing," Talia interrupted, coming in from the side, "we all have work to do."

☾ 〰 ☼

Talia took Elanor and Min into her room. They sat in a triangle, with a knife on a silk wrapping lying between them. Each of them conjured her part of the Weave. Talia's was red, and reflected in her eyes. Min's and Elanor's were both white. With a gesture from Talia, the three Weaves drifted together and, in a burst of Power, joined. A black ball of Power floated between them.

252

Talia smiled, the light disappearing from her eyes. "Perfect. The Power will sustain the Weave, and anchor it into her blood and bone. Very well done, my Sisters."

"What will your part do?" Min asked, Canin's question echoing in her mind.

Talia didn't answer at first, but only looked at the Weave, floating there before them. "Make him suffer," she finally replied.

"It won't last," Elanor warned. "The energy will dissipate. It's another day until the ceremony."

"I'll anchor the Weave into the knife," Talia informed her. "And a Ward will keep it there for as long as we need."

"Shall we start, then?" Elanor asked, adjusting her legs.

"I'll do it alone," Talia pronounced. "The two of you may go. Practice your Shadow Wards. We don't know if Wingless Bastard will have agents in the crowd, but if so, they might be able to see through the Wards. Make them perfect."

"Yes, My Lady," Elanor agreed, standing. She moved to the door. Min hadn't stood up yet. She Looked into the Weave. She could See Talia's part. Just a Peek, and she could see what it was designed to do.

"Min," Talia said sternly. She waved her hand, and a Blocking Cloak fell over the Weave. "If your Shadow is ready, you can work with Raven to perfect your part of the plan."

"Yes, My Lady," Min assented, standing. She let her Sight slip away.

"And Min," Talia added as she reached the door, "Canin can stop his work on the Ephemeral Rings. I need him practicing with Shatter and Spear. Tell him to come see me at mid-day."

"I will tell him, My Lady," Min agreed, exiting the room with Elanor.

Talia took a moment to look at her handiwork. It all meshed perfectly. She wished she had Goldberry's touch with Power, but Min and Elanor had made up for it. Though she still missed the Twins' light touch. She shook those thoughts away. This Weave would be the next step in her quest for justice.

She brought her hands together, cupping them in front of her. The Weave collapsed, growing smaller and smaller. When it was just a dot of darkness, she pushed her hands down, and the dot dropped, touching the metal of the knife. Talia closed her fist. Another burst of Power, and the Weave was gone. She opened her Sight, and Saw the knife, shining with a dark brilliance.

A great heaviness descended upon her. She closed her eyes, and sank into a deep meditation.

(☽ ∭ ☼)

At a knock on the door, she struggled out of her meditation like a swimmer emerging from deep water. She still felt tired, but her mind was clear. Talia wrapped the knife in its silk covering, and tucked it behind her.

"Enter," she called.

Canin entered. "You wanted to see me?"

Talia cocked her head.

"My Lady," Canin finished.

"Yes. Sit down." She motioned him to the spot in front of her.

As he sat, she could smell the outside on him. The scents of action and sweat lay atop the smells of sunshine, water, and grass. She smiled.

"I can see Shatter and Spear have been working you hard," she commented. "Would you like some water?"

"Thank you, My Lady," Canin replied, and a bottle floated to him. He took a long drink.

"Shatter tells me you're improving."

"She's a good teacher," Canin praised, putting the bottle down.

"You know your part for tomorrow?"

"Yes, My Lady, I do. I'll guard the Ephemeral Ring with Spear. Keep it hidden, and ready for everyone's escape." His hand touched his knife.

"Good. Min is a good judge. I knew we would see you again. You've made her incredibly happy."

"That's all I want to do," Canin swore. He was nervous and off balance, not knowing what this was all about.

254

"Remember what our purpose is. Remember that the others are all Oath-bound to me and my cause. They will not fail. They will give up their lives if necessary. Are you prepared to do the same?"

Canin felt a cold sweat on his chest. "I will do my best to fulfill my duty to you. And protect your Ladies. The Mother knows, I will do what needs to be done."

Talia narrowed her eyes. "I guess that is all I can expect from you. You're an outsider. The rest of us have been together for a long time. Don't fail me." Her eyes bored into his head.

"I will not fail you," Canin promised, holding her gaze for a long moment before dropping his eyes.

"Good," Talia said, suddenly smiling. She reached out, and took his hands. She pulled him closer. "You've made Min very happy. I can see it on her face. Share that with me." She moved her hands up his arms, slowly. "It's been a long time." She cupped his face, and moved to kiss him.

He tried to move back, but she held him. "My Lady," he said, turning from the kiss. "I love Min."

She settled for kissing his neck. "I know," she murmured. "We're Sisters — we share. She won't mind." Her breath was hot on his face.

"I can't," he protested again, trying to pull away. This time, she let him.

"Too tired?" she pouted. "I can help with that." She took his arm. He snatched it away. She frowned.

"I know you aren't used to how we Fairies conduct our relationships, but I would think a man would welcome the attention of a beautiful woman. A woman who wants him." She played with the knots of her shirt, beginning to undo them. "Or do you need her to be here? I can call her."

Canin tried to get up, but her Power held him. "It isn't that I don't find you beautiful, but I can't." He stuttered. "I just can't. I can't betray Min."

"This isn't a betrayal," Talia contradicted, leaning back. "She and I have shared before. It's pleasure. Just that. I want you to give me some. And you will have some in return." Her eyes narrowed. "Or is there something else? Do you fear me? Do you find something about me repugnant?"

"No, My Lady," Canin said quickly, trying to find a way out of this trap. He couldn't see a way, but he knew that if he gave in to her, he would hurt Min. "It's just that I only want Min. Only her. I've dreamed about her for so many nights. So many days, the only thing that kept me going was her. I'm not used to Fairy relationships. I only know that I must stay true to her."

"Pity, but maybe she'll find that cute," Talia commented, sitting up. "Well, you can go. Go to your true love. Tell her, and see how she responds. Maybe you'll be surprised." She gestured, and he scrambled up, and rushed toward the exit.

"My Lady." He bowed, and fled quickly out the door.

☾ ♒ ☼

Entering the hallway, he ran into Raven and Steel. They smiled at his guilty look.

"She's somewhere," Raven answered his unasked question.

"In a Shadow," Steel clarified. "See if you can find her."

They laughed as Canin fled in search of Min. Steel opened the door to Talia's room, and gestured Raven in.

☾ ♒ ☼

Talia gathered everyone in the library. She stood tall before them, with no indication of hesitation or exhaustion. Her aura shone. Above them, stars were beginning to flicker in the dome.

"All of you know your roles. I trust each of you to do your best to honor the memories of our fallen Sisters, and bring justice to those who killed them. I expect nothing less." She moved her gaze around the circle. Everyone met her eyes and nodded.

"Now, we must get some rest. Dawn comes early." She moved through the group to her door. She looked back just once, as she opened it.

256

"My Lady," Shatter addressed her, raising her sword. Spear, Raven, and Steel followed suit. Talia smiled, and raised her hand in reply as she disappeared into her room.

☾ 〰 ☼

"She was seducing me," Canin confessed to Min, as they got ready for bed.

"And you rejected her," Min said, offhandedly. "Don't worry — she wasn't offended. She found it funny."

Canin stared at her. "I don't think she was amused. She seemed more contemptuous of my desire to avoid betraying you."

Min sighed, and took his hand. "That's just a Human thing. I love you for it, but these things are different with Fairies. We're more fluid about pleasure. You should've let it happen."

Canin couldn't speak. His shock was clear on his face.

Min laughed, and cupped his cheeks. "You'll get used to it. After this is over, we can explore. Maybe not with her, but others." She kissed him. "I do think it's cute."

"Min, I." Canin was at a loss for words. "I love you. I want to be with you."

"I know. I want to be with you, too. That just means slightly different things for you and for me." She patted his arm. "There can be commitments, and relationships. You'll understand, in time."

Canin shook his head. "I don't know. This seemed more predatory."

She shook her head. "I'll teach you," Min promised, "but not now. I need to sleep. After tomorrow, we'll have all the time we need to explore this new world you've found yourself in."

Canin could only kiss her, and lie down at her side.

"Mother keep you safe," he murmured.

"Goddess keep you safe," she returned.

Chapter Twenty-Three
Morning

Spear pointed. "That's the entrance to the Great Hall of the Human King," she said with a sneer. "That's where he'll present his child to the Realm."

"Everyone will go through there: first, the Human Nobles, then the Fairy company, and then everyone else." Shatter was crouched by the window. She was in full armor, her helm on the floor at her feet.

They were in a small room near the top of a tower close to the Great Hall. On the opposite wall was a door, strongly barred, bearing the shimmer of a Ward. Min had also cast a 'You-Need-to-be-Somewhere-Else' Ward on the outside of the door. In the middle of the room, an Ephemeral Ring sat quiet. A closed trapdoor in the low ceiling led to the top of the tower.

When Shatter and Steel had first traveled to this Ring, they'd been ready for a trap, but Talia's information had been good: there'd been no one there, and the door had already been locked. Steel had pulled the trapdoor, and gone up to the top. She was still there, cloaked in a Shadow.

Quickly, Shatter had left, bringing back Spear and Min. Spear had taken a place at the window, crossbow ready. After casting the Wards, Min had gone up the trapdoor, too, because the room was too small for them all. Next came Elanor and Raven, who went to the roof.

The plan was for Elanor, Min, and Raven, under Shadow, to slip into the Hall with the other guests. Talia, with Shatter and Steel, would appear openly at the doors. Spear and Canin would hold the tower room, so they could all escape.

Relying on stealth, Elanor, Min, and Raven wore their ringmail, and carried their swords. Raven, of course, also had her knives. Elanor carried one of Canin's Ephemeral Rings, as a contingency, strapped to her back beside her sword.

Canin came through next. He pressed himself against the wall by the door. His hand rested nervously on the hilt of his new sword. He wore ringmail under his clothes. "Those were Gil-Galin's," Shatter had told him. "Make her proud."

258

"You know what you have to do?" Shatter asked.

"I do," Canin confirmed. "Hold this room." He fingered one of the Silverfire stones in his pocket.

"This is our escape. If you fail, we all die."

"I understand, Captain."

Shatter smiled, and gripped his arm. "I know you won't fail." She went to the Ring, and disappeared.

"Goddess keep us safe," Spear entreated from the window.

"Mother aid us," Canin echoed.

They waited, and watched. Once, Canin heard footsteps on the stairs below. They got close enough that he turned to Spear, who turned her crossbow on the door, but then they stopped, and the person approaching turned around.

After the interloper was gone, Spear let out her held breath. "Min did well with the Wards," she commented, and turned back to the window.

Crowds were starting to gather all around the Great Hall. Lines of Human guards stood on the steps, creating a corridor for the invited luminaries, and keeping the crowd away for now. The smell of cooking, and the cries of vendors, started to fill the air. Canin's stomach began to flip. He hadn't been able to eat, though both Min and Flora had urged him to.

"They're gathering," Steel Sent from above.

"Talia has been told, and she's coming," Elanor Sent a moment later.

"Talia's coming," Spear said, for Canin's benefit. "The Humans are gathering."

Canin wanted to move to the window, but he didn't dare pass over the Ring.

Two breaths later, Talia and Shatter appeared there. Talia wore the bespelled knife on a simple belt around her waist. Shatter's armor gleamed, and she held her helm under her arm.

"I can feel Blood Cultists," Elanor Sent to the others. "Not close, but here."

"Keep the Wards tight," Talia ordered everyone.

"There are Blood Cultists about," Spear said out loud.

Canin nodded. His hand tightened on his sword.

Talia stood in the center of the room. She was the eye of a storm. Canin could almost see all the lines of fate swirling around her. He sent up a silent plea for the Mother to get him through this day.

"The Humans are beginning to enter," Min Sent.

"Where are the Fairies?" Talia asked.

"They're still outside the gate, but close," Steel replied.

"Let the first lines in, then make your way inside," Talia ordered them. "We don't want a sharp-eyed Paramount seeing the three of you."

"Yes, My Lady," Raven acknowledged, and Elanor confirmed her understanding as well.

"Let's go up," Talia suggested to Shatter. She turned to Spear. "Be ready for anything. When the Shield goes up, you'll be blind. Keep an eye on the Humans' auras. We'll have to escape swiftly. Be ready."

"Yes, My Lady," Spear agreed. "Goddess guide you."

Talia turned to Canin, and winked. "Don't step on the Ring."

Shatter pulled down the trapdoor, and jumped to grab the ledge. She pulled herself up, then reached down and helped Talia climb up behind her.

Spear and Canin were left alone again.

"Mother help us," Canin asked again. He drew his sword. Spear smiled, and cocked her crossbow. She began to tap the stock of the bow. Three times with one finger, then with two fingers, then three fingers. She stopped, clenched her fist, and started over again.

Canin watched. Something about the rhythm nagged at his mind. He continued to stare.

Spear eventually felt his staring, and turned her eyes on him. "What is it?" she asked, annoyed.

"What you're doing with your hand, tapping the rhythm." Canin stopped. Spear was glaring at him. Her hand stilled.

"Just a nervous habit," she told him. She gestured behind him. "Watch the door."

"Yes, Ma'am," Canin said, focusing back on the door. Spear turned back to the window. Her hand started tapping again, but she stopped it via force of will.

Talia stood shoulder-to-shoulder with Shatter and Steel. She opened her Sight, and examined the Ward around the top of the tower. She found it perfect. She watched the Human Nobility move slowly up the steps, and into the Great Hall.

"There's Lord Phillip," Steel commented.

"And that horrible Lord Bath. Too bad he didn't make more of a nuisance of himself back in Fae-Treval. I would have been glad to beat him senseless," Shatter offered.

"Keep your focus, Sister," Talia admonished. "We'll get justice with one Human at a time."

Steel grunted, and Shatter smiled.

Talia watched the long line of Humans with disgust. She saw the knot of Priests of the Father — wearing black robes adorned with a white lightning bolt — move through the crowd. She observed how everyone stepped out of the way of the hard-faced men. She smiled to think of how they would react to a woman striking them here, in the heart of their power.

When the last of the stragglers was finally inside, a horn sounded three times from the steps. It was answered from the direction of the gate.

"That means the Fairies are coming," Steel said. She moved to duck down, but Talia held her steady.

"Nothing can see through this Ward," she assured her. "Hold steady."

They watched as a column of Leather-wing soldiers in the green armor of Grass moved toward the Great Hall. They were followed by a smaller group of soldiers in the silver armor of the Queen's Guard. Behind them, the Herald of the Fairies walked, her head held high. She held the flag of the Queen of the Fairies. As the Herald passed, Shatter felt herself stand up straighter.

"It's been so long," she muttered.

Behind the Herald walked Lord Oberon and his aides. Another group of Queen's Guard soldiers followed. Finally, serving as rearguard, a small group of soldiers in blue armor came into sight.

"Air," Steel breathed. "Rearguard. Disgraceful."

"Quiet," Talia ordered her.

The Humans around the Great Hall had fallen silent. This many Fairies had never been seen inside the Human castle before. This spoke to King Bastile's desire for peace.

The soldiers of Grass moved up the stairs, and fell in beside the Human soldiers. Much muttering was heard, and many nervous movements were seen on the Human side, till one sharp-voiced Sergeant called for order from his troops. The Herald and Lord Oberon moved up the stairs, flanked by the Queen's Guard. The soldiers of Air stayed at the base of the stairs, arrayed in a loose square.

"The outer doors will be open," Talia informed Shatter and Steel, "but the inner ones will be closed. We'll Shadow, and fly down. We'll land by the inner doors. I don't trust their soldiers not to hinder us, and we can't afford a delay."

Steel and Shatter nodded.

They watched the Fairies enter the Great Hall. Talia began to feel anxious. Her hands clenched, and she shuffled her feet. Realizing what she was doing, she stopped herself, and stood still. Her hand went to the knife at her belt. She could feel the Weave it held.

Once the Fairies were all inside, the Human soldiers allowed the rest of the people of the castle to enter. Many of them skirted the Fairy soldiers and took the long away around to the entrance.

"Not much longer," Steel said, her soldier nerves kicking in.

Then they heard the clang of the inner doors, and a Human Captain called out, "No more!"

Talia raised her hands, and spread her wings. Steel and Shatter mirrored her, and they each disappeared into the shimmer of a Shadow.

$$☽ \approx ☼$$

King Bastile stood on the second-level balcony, overlooking the Great Hall of the Human Realm. He smiled at all the people who had come to see his new daughter. The initial worry that his Queen wouldn't accept Aurora had proven unfounded. The midwife must have given her something strong, because when he laid Aurora in her arms, she took her as the child of her own body, with no reluctance.

He let it go: after all, the best lie is one you never have to speak. His wife and Queen stood, glowing, in the mid-morning sun. He decided that he loved her. She would never be the woman Talia was, but she would always be at his side. She would never betray him.

She had insisted on holding the baby, so she stood at his shoulder. He glanced at her, and saw her smile back. He even thought he saw Aurora smile.

Bastile felt a surge of pride when the Fairies entered and took their place. It had taken many hours of debate and negotiations to get the other Nobles to agree that the Queen of the Fairies should be invited. Bastile had stood firm, despite pressure from all sides.

"I am the King, and I will invite our neighboring Realm to see my new child. Despite our recent conflicts, we will be honorable Men and allow them to come in peace. I was part of the Presentation of the Queen's niece and nephew to the Fairy court, and it was a grand experience. We shall show the Fairies that we can be grand, too."

Eventually, with the aid of Lord Phillip, he was able to bend enough of the court to his will. Despite the many things he had been required to give up, Bastile was happy.

The Priests of the Father were assembling below him. Bastile stepped to the edge of the balcony, and raised his arms. A hush fell over the crowd.

"Fellow Men of the Realm," he announced. "Welcome. Welcome to the flower of our Nobility," he gestured to the Nobles and their families to his left. To a man, they bowed their heads. "Welcome to our neighbors." He gestured to Lord Oberon and his Fairies, to his right. The Herald and Oberon nodded in return.

"And to the beautiful People of our city." He gestured to those who filled the back of the Hall. A cheer rose. This owed more to the feast that would be held afterwards than to any joy at this simple ceremony, but still, they loved their King.

Bastile turned, taking Aurora from his wife, and holding her up for all to see. "I present to you my daughter, Princess Aurora. Child of my body, and your future Queen."

The cheers and applause were drowned out by the thunderclap of the inner doors bursting open and then — almost immediately —

slamming shut again. Bastile looked with annoyance to the back of the Hall. Cold sweat broke out as he saw Talia — tall and proud in black, with her wings spread wide — standing at the door with two Fairy soldiers.

Chapter Twenty-Four
The Curse

"You're a great leader, King Bastile." Talia was addressing him from the back of the Hall. Her voice was somehow amplified, and easily reached all ears. "To show your new child to your Realm is admirable."

A gasp went up throughout the court. The Humans moved aside as Talia — Shatter and Steel at her back — moved to the center of the room. She looked up at King Bastile and his Queen on the balcony above her. Guards began to move, but Bastile waved them back. The Priests retreated quickly through a side door.

"You were not invited, Heir of the Fairies," Bastile reminded her.

"I decided that I must see you, on your great day," Talia replied. She spread her wings. Her dress — black, with a green slash running down the center — pooled around her feet. A simple silver belt circled her waist. A small knife sat on her hip, the bare blade reflecting light. Shatter and Steel were in full armor, shining green and purple. Their helms were snarling dragons.

Lord Oberon ran over to the interlopers. "My Lady, you mustn't be here. I understand your grief, but this will not help."

"Silence, Uncle. I will speak." Talia raised her hand, Redfire dancing on her fingers. Oberon swiftly stepped back.

"You may speak, but be quick," Bastile told her. He adjusted his grip on his new daughter, her golden hair spilling out of the wrappings surrounding her.

"I thank you, King," Talia sneered. "I have come to give your new daughter a gift."

"A gift?" Bastile was surprised.

"Yes. A gift." She raised her hands. An iridescent Shield formed around her and her guards. "The same gift you gave my daughter." She held up the knife. A black Weave of Power formed in front of her. "Death."

Shatter and Steel drew their swords as the Human guards began hammering on the Shield. Crossbowmen rose from the upper level and took aim. Elanor materialized out of her Shadow and gestured at them. Their bows snapped, and wood rained down on those below. Min and Raven also appeared, hand in hand, and gestured with their free hands. All the Human guards were thrown back. Shatter and Steel drew the blades of their swords across the palms of their hands. Together, they pressed their hands to Talia's wings, leaving bloody handprints. Outside the Shield, Oberon's face went white. He put his hand on the Herald's arm.

"But I will not make it quick, as you did for mine," Talia informed Bastile, her voice cold. "I will not stab her as she sleeps. You will have to wait, and know that you can do nothing." The black Weave grew, both in size and in darkness. Bastile and his Queen were held in place. Steel smiled cruelly.

"You will see her grow, and become a woman, and on her sixteenth birthday, she will die." Talia gathered all her grief, anger, and betrayal, and flung them at the child.

"I curse you!" The black globe flew like a well-aimed arrow, and struck the child lying peacefully in Bastile's arms.

But Talia didn't know. She didn't know that this was her child, stolen from her. The curse struck, and Ancient Powers responded. The Ancients had wanted to protect their children, so they had woven into all Fairies that no parent may curse their child, and no child may curse its parents.

There was a deafening backlash. White Power struck Talia, cutting through her Shield, and driving her to her knees. Her wings went up in Whitefire, leaving them black and twisted. But the child wasn't a full Fairy. Her Fairy blood protected her to a degree, but her Human half was still vulnerable. So the curse changed: it pulled a proficiency with Sleep Spells from Talia's mind, and death became sleep. The Weave of the Curse found another Weave already active in Aurora: the Wards of the Three Sisters, hiding her true self. These two Weaves, each created in anger and hate, became entangled — inexorably linked, one to the other. Talia screamed as the fire drove into her mind. The curse settled into the blood and the bones of baby Aurora.

The backlash threw everyone — Human and Fairy — from their feet. The Queen grabbed Aurora from Bastile and held her close, as they both cried.

The Herald of the Fairies was the first to rise. She pulled a cloth from her belt, and spread it out on the floor. She lifted the silver disc around her neck and Called.

Fairy soldiers appeared, two by two. The first two pulled Shatter and Steel to their feet, and bound their hands behind them. Another set grabbed Raven and Min. Elanor was crawling to Talia's side. Four soldiers surrounded them, but didn't touch them.

Humans were starting to stand up as well. Guards moved toward the Fairies.

King Bastile called, "Hold them!"

"Stay where you are!" The crystal-clear voice of the Queen of the Fairies cut through the rising clamor. Her Power surrounded all the Fairies, and kept the Humans away.

"Queen," Bastile called. "Have you come to attack us?"

"No. I have come to take my Heir home."

"She has struck at my Heir. I demand justice."

The Queen opened her Sight. She Looked at the King's daughter. She could See the curse wrapped around the child. Her Power skittered off the Weave, and wouldn't tell her anything. "I See the curse, but it has changed. I do not See death."

"You lie! Your Heir cast a curse on my child. She promised her death." Bastile grabbed at where his sword should have been. Finding nothing, he stabbed his hand at Zellandine.

"Believe what you will, King. I do not lie. I do not See death. Something changed the curse." The Queen delved deeper, and found more Wards and cloaks on the child. She stored this information away.

The King took a deep breath. "I will allow you and your soldiers to depart. You will leave Talia and her people here to face our justice."

The Queen looked at Talia, who was now standing. Elanor held her tight. "Daughter. You will answer for this."

Talia nodded.

"I will take them with me. She will face our justice," the Queen informed the King.

267

"Not good enough. You have invaded my castle, and the holy ceremony for my daughter." He pointed both hands at the Queen. "If you don't leave her, I will kill all of you."

"No, you will not," the Queen disagreed, gesturing at Oberon. He nodded, and called out a command.

Fairies touched their wrists or necks and disappeared, in ones and twos, until the only ones remaining were Zellandine, Oberon, Talia and her people, and their guards. The King yelled, and his guards ran at the Shield. The Queen gestured, and fire boiled around the Shield. The Human guards backed up.

"You will not touch Us or Our Heir," the Queen pronounced. She looked at Talia, and gestured at the Ephemeral Ring at her feet. "Come, Heir. We will leave."

"Yes, Mother, we shall." Talia and Elanor disappeared. A flare of fire made the soldiers jump back as the Ephemeral Ring they had just left from was destroyed.

"Take them through," the Queen commanded, waving for the remainder of the prisoners to enter her Ephemeral Ring.

"I will not forget this! Father curse you!" Bastile yelled, as he threw cups at the Shield. They hit, and bounced away, rolling around on the floor.

"We won't either," the Queen promised, as the last of her people disappeared through the Ring. She stood there, locking eyes with the King. "Goddess have mercy on you for your hate." She disappeared, and her Shield fell, as the Ring flared in a blinding white flash of self-destruction.

When they could see again, only Humans stood before the King.

(☾ ⌇⌇⌇ ☼)

Spear watched the commotion at the door, and knew that Talia had entered the Great Hall. The Humans moved forward, and the Fairies pulled back. They settled into a double circle, with Grass as the outer ring and Air in the center. She could see officers on both sides running about, looking for orders. The people of the castle, wisely deciding that they didn't want to be in the middle of any conflict, fled.

"What's going on?" Canin asked.

"I wish you were more Fairy," Spear announced, not turning from the window. "Then I could Send to you."

"Maybe Min can make me something," Canin suggested, trying to keep his nerves in check.

"The Humans are moving in, and the Fairies have pulled back. Much confusion." She stopped. "The Shield has gone up in the Hall. I can't See their auras now."

Canin bit the inside of his lip. He knew Min and the others were capable, but he was still anxious.

A sudden shock wave of Power and sound rippled out from the Hall. Spear was pushed back. Canin moved to help her up.

"What was that?" he asked, worried.

Spear was dazed, and couldn't answer. She grabbed the windowsill, and hoisted herself up from the floor.

"Was that Talia?" Canin asked.

"I don't know," Spear admitted. "Back to the door," she commanded.

Canin looked out the window. All the Fairy soldiers were rising to their feet.

"All Fairies," Lord Oberon's Send boomed through, "flee by any available method. Re-group at the compound."

"I heard that," Canin said with awe. Spear shook her head. The Fairy soldiers in the courtyard were rising into the air. The Human soldiers, slow to react at first, were starting to raise their crossbows. The Fairies, who were faster, were firing their own bows, and knocked most of the Humans' crossbow bolts to the ground. They flew off in good formation, with only a few bolts following them.

A sudden burst of light flashed through the windows of the Hall.

"They're all gone," Spear announced.

"How?" Canin asked. "Dead? What?"

"I don't know — they were there, then they weren't. Probably Rings."

"Oberon and his people?"

"All gone. Every Fairy. Gone."

Canin was speechless. He moved back to the door. He didn't know what else to do.

"They know we're here," Spear called out. Below them, Humans were running out of the Hall. Several were pointing in the direction of the tower.

"Cultists," Spear snarled, as she began firing at them.

Canin could hear many footsteps on the stairs below. There was also yelling, and the clanging of weapons. Spear dodged back, as several bolts hit the window and the wall behind her. She began to reload.

"We must go!" Canin yelled. He could hear movement outside the door.

Spear didn't respond, and moved back to the window.

Canin started to speak, but a bolt of light and sparks cut through the door. The bolt hit Spear, driving her into the wall. She slumped to the floor, her body and both wings smoking. Canin was thrown back. The Silverfire stone in his hand hit the floor, and rolled out into the hall.

Luckily, Min had changed the Wards on his stones. Activating them only required that they hit the ground. Three smiling Cultists — who had been charging through the doorway — disappeared in a sudden burst of Silverfire. The other Humans moved back down the stairs to re-group.

Canin pulled himself up, and went to Spear. Her eyes were open, but her arms and legs were jerking in spasms.

"Can you stand?" Canin asked. He realized he no longer carried his sword. It lay on the floor where he'd fallen.

"No," Spear responded, her voice slurred. "Help me up."

He pulled her up, and staggered to the Ring in the center of the room.

"You'll have to do it," Spear muttered.

"I don't know if I can."

"You have to," Spear returned. "Or we're dead."

Canin looked out the door. He could see more Humans gathering, and heard the cocking of crossbows. He gripped Spear close to him. He thought about Min, and how he needed to see her again. He activated the bracelet, and told it where he wanted to go.

"Now!" Spear yelled. She pulled a stone from her pouch, and threw it through the doorway. "Now!"

Canin closed his eyes, and hoped he knew where he was going. He saw a burst of light, and then he was somewhere else.

$$\left(\!\!\!\left(\; \text{\smaller{mm}} \; \text{\Large ☼}\right.\right.$$

"Where's Wingless?" Bastile asked the wingless Fairy pushing him down the stairs. He struggled to hold on to Aurora. Her bindings were coming undone, and she was wriggling in his grasp.

"He's coming," he was told. "I need to get you out."

"Where's my wife?" Bastile demanded, stopping at the bottom of the stairway. He turned to the Fairy. "I will not go any further."

"She's safe," came the reply. "You and the child are more important. Wingless wants you out of the castle. Who knows what Talia will do?"

"All right," Bastile agreed. "Where are we going?" He let the Fairy past him to open the door. The red glow of the Blood Ring entered the stairs. Aurora began to cry.

"Silence that thing," the wingless ordered him, turning. "Or I will."

Bastile didn't have time to reply. The wingless Fairy was pulled into the room by unseen hands. There was a cry, and the sound of a blade cleaving flesh. Bastile moved slowly into the room. The wingless lay, unmoving, on the floor, a sword through his chest. A Leather-wing Fairy with singed wings was standing over him. She twisted her sword in his body, and pulled it out.

"Don't speak to my baby that way," she said.

Bastile looked around. In the evil red light of the Blood Ring, he could see the bodies of the other Cultists. All were twisted and dead. Blood was splashed on the walls and floor. An Elenite stood in the center of the Blood Ring, frozen in place.

Aurora cried out again. The Fairy soldier turned. She strode over to Bastile. With her free hand, she gestured at the baby Bastile held.

"She's mine. Give her back."

271

Bastile couldn't speak — his shock was too great. The Fairy sheathed her sword, and pulled Aurora from his arms.

"There, there," she cooed. "You're hungry, and scared. Soon, but sleep now," she soothed. The baby stopped crying, and sighed as she went to sleep.

"Spear," the Elenite in the Ring yelled, "we're in the wrong place. How do we get out?"

Spear turned, and walked back to the Ring. "You brought us here," she said serenely. "Get us out." She went back to gazing at the baby.

"I don't know if I can," Canin admitted.

Bastile finally fought past his shock. "That's my child!" he yelled.

"No," Spear replied, in a faraway voice. "She's mine. I lost him, and now she is returned."

Bastile, both confused and angry, began moving forward again.

"Stop!" a voice yelled from the stairs. Wingless Bastard came running into the room, and slipped on a puddle of blood. He slammed into Bastile, pushing them both away from the Ring.

"Now would be a good time," Spear addressed Canin calmly.

Canin gripped Spear's arm hard. "Mother help me!" he cried.

"Stop!" Wingless yelled from the floor. He thrust a hand out at Canin and Spear. A lightning bolt shot across the room, striking the wall. Too late: the three were gone.

Bastile climbed to his feet. He stared down at Wingless, who was sitting on the floor, a look of utter confusion on his face.

"What happened?!" Bastile yelled, grabbing his shoulders. "Where is my child?"

"I don't know," Wingless admitted, not even bothering to fight Bastile's shaking. "I don't know."

Bastile let him go, and collapsed to the floor. He stared at the empty Blood Ring, and wondered how everything had gone so wrong.

Chapter Twenty-Five
Lying to Loved Ones

It was dark where Elanor and Talia arrived. Talia screamed as her damaged wings hit the floor. She rolled over onto her belly, and clawed at the floor.

Elanor, in a panic, fell back to sit on the floor. By instinct, she conjured a Light. A small room, without windows or doors, came into view. Books and scrolls lined the walls.

Elanor stared in horror at Talia. Her iridescent wings were now black and twisted. The Whitefire had burned away her dress, leaving her back red, and spotted with blisters. Elanor could only stare.

"Curse them," Talia spit around the pain. "Curse them."

"What happened?" Elanor finally asked.

Talia hammered the floor with her fists. "I don't know. Goddess, it burns. Help me." She tried to move, but one of her wings hit something, and she screamed in pain again.

Elanor crawled over to her. She carefully put her hands on the raw skin of Talia's back. She reached out with her Power. A snap, and sparks, Pushed her back.

"Fool," Talia snarled. She beat the floor again. "Pain blocker root." She struggled to catch her breath. "On the table."

Elanor climbed to her feet. She moved the Light, and saw a table covered in jars, vials, and books.

"Hurry," Talia called.

Elanor finally saw a jar containing blue-green roots. She opened it, and pulled one out. She knelt before Talia, and broke off a piece. Talia grabbed it, and thrust it into her mouth. She chewed. After a moment, she began to relax. Her hands unclenched, and she was able to sit up, with Elanor's help. Careful of her wings, she leaned forward, hands on the floor, as Elanor stood over her.

"What happened?" Elanor asked again. She looked around. "Where are we?"

"Backlash, maybe," Talia answered the first question, her voice slightly off.

"From what? Wingless?" Elanor asked. "Were he and his Blood Cult protecting the child?"

"He wasn't there," Talia said simply, the painkiller making her speak plainly. "You would have recognized him."

"What do you mean?" Elanor asked. She stared at Talia. "I would recognize him?"

"We called him Puck," Talia said. "After the old tale."

Elanor's legs went out from under her. She sat down heavily in the only chair. She stared at Talia. "That can't be. He should be dead. He promised me he would take care of him."

"Looks like he didn't," Talia said lightly. "Another lie from your father."

"Wingless is. . . ." She stopped, the shock of the knowledge driving the words out of her head.

"Is Puck. Yes. That bastard."

Elanor's anger lit up her eyes. "How long have you known?"

Talia looked up. "It was confirmed when I was face to face with him at the Crafthouse. He was happy to finally show himself. I had suspected for a while, though. He's Paramount Holly's nephew."

"And you didn't tell me?" Elanor's hands clenched. She began to shake. "You know what he did to me. How could you not tell me?" Her voice was rising. "How could you?!" She was on the verge of hysterics.

"Because I knew you would react this way," Talia explained, raising her head higher. She tried to straighten, fighting through the pain to do so. "I needed you strong, and I knew this knowledge might break you."

Elanor hugged herself tightly, and said nothing.

Talia spit out the root. She bent forward, hands on the floor, and waited for the pain to flare up again. The Light winked out, as Elanor's mind folded in on itself to protect her. Talia clenched her teeth as the pain returned.

"What did she mean?"
"I don't understand."

"What did she mean? That horrible Fairy. She said you killed her daughter. She was going to kill mine in vengeance. What did she mean, husband?"

"Silence, woman!" Simon snapped.

The Queen of the Human Realm looked up. Her eyes were red, but dry. She pinned Bastile's aide to the wall with her gaze. He stepped back, in unexpected shock. "I am your Queen. You will not speak to me so." She turned to Bastile, who sat in the chair beside her. "I need you to answer me. What did you do to make that Fairy attack our child, and then kidnap her?"

Simon drew breath to speak again.

Bastile raised his head. "Silence," he ordered Simon. "You will not speak."

"But, My King," Simon started.

Bastile threw his cup of wine at his Second. It hit the wall, showering Simon with red mist. He cowered. Bastile looked around the room. Everyone else was looking down.

"I don't know," Bastile finally said, turning to his wife. "I don't know. But I swear to you, I didn't do anything to that woman. I haven't seen her since I left the Fairy Realm."

"She thinks you did," the Queen accused him. "Is she mad, or are you lying?"

Bastile put his head in his hands. "I swear, I did nothing."

"You didn't, but orders were given in your name."

Bastile's head shot up. He turned to the voice. Wingless Bastard stood in the door. He was leaning on one of his Cultists.

"Explain yourself," Bastile demanded.

Wingless shrugged. "Things have been done in your name. And they might have resulted in the death of the Heir's child." He shrugged again. "That is the way of things."

"Everyone out!" Bastile commanded. "You stay." He pointed at Wingless.

The Fairy shrugged again. "Can I sit down? I seem to have twisted my leg."

Bastile waved him to a chair.

"My Lady," Lord Phillip said, offering the Queen his hand.

"I will stay," she stated.

Phillip looked to Bastile, who nodded. Phillip bowed, and left. When the room was clear, Bastile turned on Wingless.

"Explain yourself."

"When you entered into this arrangement with me and my people, you gave me certain 'liberties,' we shall call them." Wingless folded his hands in his lap. "I took some of your Lions of the Sword, and trained them. Gave them access to all the Power we could give them. All the weapons, and," he grinned, "blood. I found some Elenites who hated themselves, and wanted to be part of something. We brought them in, promising them anything they wanted. Promised them a place in your afterlife, if they killed enough Fairies." He smiled again. "And it worked. They wanted a home, and I gave them one." He looked at Bastile. "Are you sure you want me to answer your question with her in the room?" He gestured to the Queen.

"You will answer my questions," the Queen cut in.

Bastile didn't respond; he only raised his hand for Wingless to go on.

Wingless shrugged. "As you wish. Talia's Aunts wanted her child eliminated. She was a problem for them. They want the Fairy throne. This child put all their plans in jeopardy." He smiled with glee. "This child would have been not only the Heir to the Fairy Realm, but the Human Realm, too." He watched for Bastile's reaction.

Bastile rushed over to Wingless, grabbing him out of the chair. "You lie. I never."

"Oh, but you did, and she had the child." Wingless didn't struggle in Bastile's grasp. "Thanks to Fairy Magic, at about the same time your child was born, if I understand correctly."

Bastile let go of him. Wingless slumped back into his chair. Bastile began to pace.

"So, I sent some of these Elenite Lions to attack where Talia and her people were hiding. None returned. I guess they were successful." He gestured. "It appears Talia got some of them to talk, though. I underestimated her."

"I didn't send them," Bastile said, more to himself than to his wife.

"Your word — through me — did, however," Wingless told him.

"You caused this!" The Queen stood up. "You!" She grabbed Bastile by the front of his coat. She was short, only coming up to his chest, but her rage made her seem much taller. "You made the deal with this foul thing. Your people killed her child. You drove her into a rage. She cursed our child with death. And now she's missing. Stolen by Fairies." She turned, and spat at Wingless. "Foul creature. You're cursed."

"You are very observant, My Lady," Wingless said calmly. "I may have underestimated you, too."

The Queen screamed incoherently, and would have attacked Wingless, but Bastile held her back.

Wingless stood, and moved behind his chair. The banter was over; all levity had disappeared from his demeanor. He raised both hands in front of him. "I can kill her," he threatened Bastile. "I will, if you don't contain her."

The Queen thrashed again, and Bastile held her more tightly.

"Damn you!" she raved. "Father damn you."

"Bastile," Wingless warned. His eyes narrowed.

Bastile turned, so that his back was to Wingless. "Wife," he pleaded. "There's nothing you can do. Calm yourself."

"I will not be calm, as long as that thing is in our castle," she spat. "You will decide: him, or me." She pulled herself from his grip. "I must mourn. I've lost my child." She looked into his eyes. "Maybe I will seek that Fairy out. She and I have much in common now. You've killed both our children." She turned, and pulled open a door. She went through it, slamming it behind her.

Into the silence, Wingless mused, "Women. Good thing she doesn't know that wasn't her child."

Bastile turned, grabbing Wingless, and slamming him into the wall. He hit him twice, breaking his nose.

Wingless only smiled. He stared at Bastile, blood running down his face.

"Does that make you feel better?" he taunted. His nose began to re-form, and snapped back into place. "You can break it again if you like."

Bastile let go of him.

"If you want," Wingless offered, "I can leave. I can remove all my support for you and your reign. I'm sure others would welcome my support — especially my weapons."

"You're foul," Bastile told him.

"You say that as if I should be ashamed." Wingless smiled with dark humor. "I am foul. I was born of foul. I grew up in foul. I must be foul for these Powers to work." A spark shot from his hand, pushing Bastile back. "I revel in it." He straightened his shirt. "You've been swimming in the same foul water I have. Decide what you will do." He raised his hand again. Bastile took another step back. "Remember, if she speaks to me again, I will kill her. Consequences be cursed."

Bastile took yet another step back. He found a chair with his hand, and sat down. A bottle lay on the floor. He picked it up. With a deliberate motion, he opened it, and took a sip.

Wingless just watched him.

"Where did the Fairy and the Elenite go? The one who took my," he stressed that word, "child?"

Wingless smiled. "I don't know. Whatever Weave that traitor used disrupted the Blood Ring. I can't sense where he went, or where he came from."

"Traitor?" Bastile asked, taking another sip.

"The Elenite. He was one of mine. I thought he'd been lost at the Crafthouse Talia attacked. Looks like he joined her instead. He made great Ephemeral Rings."

"Find them," Bastile commanded through a mouthful of wine. "And send a message through Simon as to who your Second will be. I will no longer deal directly with you." He set down the bottle. "If I see you again, I'll kill you. Consequences be damned."

"You'll try," Wingless corrected.

"Even you cannot repel a thousand crossbow bolts. Now go." Bastile picked up the wine bottle again.

"Yes, My King," Wingless said, mockingly.

Outside, Simon was waiting. He fell into step with Wingless. "He's getting dangerous," Simon commented.

"He is what he was raised to be: a cruel fool." Wingless brushed away the concern. "Just make sure you keep him supplied with wine. He'll drown himself."

Simon nodded.

"I'll be sending another to be my mouth here. Bastile doesn't like me anymore." Wingless laughed. "But first, I must go to the Blood Ring. It may take a great deal to get it functioning again."

"How many?" Simon asked, offhandedly, knowing his leader's need.

"At least ten. Make sure they're young and pretty."

"I'll bring them with the sunset."

"I think they should all be women, and I would prefer blondes, like the Queen."

Simon nodded, grinning. "I'll do my best. Might not be able to find that many for tonight."

"No matter. I need at least two to start. Take your time with the rest. I certainly intend to."

Chapter Twenty-Six
Consequences

"I demand to speak to Lord Oberon."

"He isn't available right now."

"Then I would speak to Captain Shattersteel of the Queen's Guard."

"He isn't available either."

"Who can I speak to?"

"Someone will be down to speak with you in good time."

"Listen, I have been a soldier since before you were born. I am the Captain of the Heir's Guard. I demand to speak to someone of rank."

The young Lieutenant winced, and looked toward the Sergeant posted at the door. She shrugged her shoulders.

"With all due respect, Ma'am, you aren't a Captain anymore. You have no rank."

"At least remove these bonds." Shatter held up her hands, which were bound with silksteel shackles, connected by a chain.

"I'm sorry. I can't."

"This cell is Warded. You took our Torcs. We can't do anything."

"Lord Oberon's orders. He's taking no chances. You may have unknown abilities."

"At least allow us to wash, and don fresh clothes," Min bargained, coming to the bars. She smiled broadly. Behind him, the Sergeant made a noise somewhere between a laugh and a sigh.

"I think I can arrange that."

"We would be very grateful." Min smiled again, and reached through the bars toward the Lieutenant.

"Save your flirting," the Sergeant spoke up. "You aren't his type."

Min lost a bit of her smile, but the Lieutenant smiled, and shrugged back.

"I'll bring you food, and fresh clothes. Anything else will have to wait for Lord Oberon." He gave them a short bow, and left. The Sergeant smiled, and closed the door. The sound of the bolt being shot echoed loudly through the cell.

Min sighed, and went back to sit beside Raven.

"Good try," Steel offered from her corner.

"You're out of practice," Raven commented.

"My heart wasn't in it," Min confessed, pulling her legs up to her chest.

"Too much Canin," Raven teased.

Min shook her head, then buried it in her arms and knees. Soon, the others heard soft sobs. Raven put her hand on Min's shoulder.

"We don't know that he's dead," Shatter comforted from the cell door.

"We don't know he's alive, either," Min whined through her arms. "He could have been captured. Those Cultists might have both him and Spear."

"There's nothing we can do until we speak to Lord Oberon or the Queen." Shatter turned back to them. "We must be strong. We are soldiers, and Ladies of the court. That must stand for something."

"Maybe we'll keep our wings," Steel said hopefully from the corner.

Shatter wanted to raise her Lieutenant's spirits by agreeing, but she couldn't. Min continued to cry. Raven held her, unable to comfort her. Steel just made patterns in the dust on the stone floor.

☾ ⌇⌇⌇ ☼

After what felt like days, but was maybe only hours, Talia was able to take control of her body again. She forced the pain back. Like an incoming tide, it rolled in, breaking down her walls, but she built more and more, till she could contain it. When it was finally held back, she reached into her Power. It fizzled like wet tinder. She couldn't even make Light. Her Sight was dim, but she could See Elanor, still huddled in the chair. She hadn't moved.

Talia tried to sit up, but the pain broke through again, and she huddled back on the floor. Darkness filled her vision, and she fought hard to stay conscious. The fear of falling on her wings sparked something deep inside. She grabbed on, and held. She pulled that spark into the center of her being, and fed it slowly with anger. It began

281

to burn, and a red light filled her. Talia pressed the light to the onslaught of pain, and pushed it back. Finally, she sat upright, her hands pressed to the floor. Her head came up.

"Elanor," she croaked. Her Second didn't respond.

"Elanor," Talia said again. She could see the Lady's aura flicker.

"Elanor!" Talia shouted.

"What?" came a dim response. She sounded Realms away, but was just beside Talia.

"Light. We need Light."

"Why? All is darkness. Darkness and lies. Why would you lie to me?" Elanor sounded like a child, her voice soft, and full of fear.

"I tried to protect you," Talia said, but even she heard the lie in her words.

"You were there. You found me. You helped me. You knew," Elanor snapped. "You were with me every day. That horrible trial. His face. His laughter. You stopped me from killing him. You said, 'The Goddess will punish him.' You promised me." Elanor moved out of the darkness, grabbing Talia's shoulders. "You lied."

The pain grabbed at her again, but this time, Talia used it. She slapped Elanor.

"I lied to you. Accept it. He's alive. Accept it. We will see him again." Elanor didn't let go. Talia hit her again. "We will see him again, and we will kill him."

"We'll kill him," Elanor muttered.

"We'll kill him," Talia said louder.

"We'll kill him," Elanor echoed, her voice getting louder.

"We'll kill him," Talia said with finality. "We will kill him."

"We will kill him," Elanor agreed, finally believing it. A Light bloomed over her head. Her face was haggard, but it held a new determination as well.

Talia smiled for the first time. "Yes, we will."

Elanor looked around, truly seeing the space for the first time. "Where are we?"

The prisoners were brought food, and a change of clothes. Two soldiers led each of them, separately, to a small room where they could wash and change. When they were all refreshed, the Lieutenant brought a tray of food and drink.

"I can't leave you any knives, but I'm sure you can manage."

"Thank you," Shatter told him earnestly.

"I do my duty," he replied, leaving them.

"At least they had the decency to turn their backs when I was washing," Min remarked, as she dipped some bread into an herbed spread. She sat back, a look of ecstasy on her face. "I've missed this."

The others ate heartily. Raven tried to make small talk, but it fell flat, and they settled into a silence as they ate.

Not long after they finished, they heard voices at the door.

"Now see here, young woman. I will be allowed to see the prisoners. I am the Mistress of the Court. These ladies are part of the court, and I will attend to them."

"I'm sorry, Ma'am, but Lord Oberon has ordered that no one is to see them."

"I wiped Lord Oberon's bottom when he was a child. And if you don't want to be doing similar things for the remainder of your service, you will open this door."

Shatter swore she heard the tapping of Merry-Weather's foot as the Sergeant considered her threat.

"Yes, Ma'am," the Sergeant said with resignation, as she opened the door.

"Thank you, soldier," Merry-Weather said graciously, as she swept into the room. She took a quick look at the prisoners, and the remains of their meal.

"Sergeant," she commanded, "take these dishes up to the kitchen, and bring down more water and tea. They look like they need it." She watched, impatiently, as the soldier gathered the dishes, with Steel and Raven's help. When the Sergeant reached the door, she looked back at Merry-Weather.

"Go. I'll be fine. There are strong bars between me and them. And the Wards are curling my hair. Go on: I need privacy." Merry-Weather waved the Sergeant away.

Shatter could see the guard about to protest that Lord Oberon had ordered that they not be left alone. She felt pity for the Sergeant as Merry-Weather's gaze froze that protest before it was even spoken.

Bowing to a stronger nature, the guard said, "Yes, Ma'am," and left quietly.

Merry-Weather turned to the prisoners. "Where is my daughter?" she demanded.

"She stayed behind," Shatter replied simply.

"Where?" Merry-Weather asked. "And don't play word games with me, Captain. I can make things difficult for you. Or, I can make sure only good words flow to the right ears."

"I'll tell you, if you'll do something for me," Shatter bargained.

"Go on."

"There were two more of our party at the Human castle. Tell me what you know of them, and I'll tell you where Flora is."

"I don't know. You lot were the only ones seen and brought in. The Fairies evacuated pretty quickly."

"They weren't in the Hall; they were in a tower outside. I could Show you, but." She held up her Power-nullifying bonds.

"I'll speak to the officers who were outside. They'll know the place of which you speak. I swear by the Goddess that I will return with any information I find." She began to tap her foot again.

"She was at the Exile Queen's mountain, waiting for us by the Ring."

"Hmm. I will speak to the Queen. She'll know," Merry-Weather responded.

"Beware: Talia set strong Wards on that Ring."

"The Queen will know," Merry-Weather said again, in a softer tone this time. She stepped closer to the bars. "I understand the tragedies all of you have been through. My heart breaks for all those Sisters who died." She put her hand on Shatter's. "I will return." Merry-Weather turned, and left, shutting the door firmly behind her. Shatter heard the bar slide home.

She turned to the others.

"What did she Send?" Min asked.

Shatter smiled. "She Sent that the Queen would see us after nightfall. There's no danger of us losing our wings." Min and Raven sat back, making the Sign of the Three in relief. "And there's no sign of Talia and Elanor."

"That's unexpected good news," Steel said.

"Yes," Shatter agreed. "I just hope they don't do anything rash. Merry-Weather also Sent that a capture order for them has been Sent to all Fairy towns, cities, and Embassies throughout the Realm. With a note adding that they're quite dangerous, and a threat to the Realm."

In the sudden silence, Min asked, "What does that mean?"

Steel answered, when Shatter did not. "The use of lethal force is allowed, if they don't surrender."

Flora sat on the floor. She was surrounded by her herbs and bandages. There was a cold cup of tea at her elbow. She didn't want to leave the Ring to heat it up.

"Here I am again, waiting," she said out loud. "Always waiting. I waited for them to come home during the last Human War. I waited for them all. Some never came back. 'Returned,'" she said with some bitterness. "Returned to the Cycle. Where does that leave me? Here, waiting for them to return yet again. Curse them." She knocked over her tea. The liquid threatened her bundle of clotting herbs, so she grabbed it out of the way. "Curse them," she said again.

"Good to know you still talk to yourself."

Flora turned to the Ring. Luna was standing inside it. Behind her, her hands on Luna's shoulders, stood Paramount Miranda.

"Sister," Flora said, her joy turning to fear in an instant. "The Wards!"

"Are contained," Miranda assured her. "But I don't know for how long. She's strong. It took me a while to get this far."

"Sister," Luna pleaded, "come home."

Miranda made a parting motion with her hands. The shimmer of the Wards moved aside. Luna held out her hand.

"She attacked the King's child," Luna informed Flora. "With Power that could only come from Blood Magic. A death curse. The others have been captured. Talia and Elanor escaped."

"I cannot hold the Wards back much longer," Miranda warned, the strain evident on her face. "Decide. Come with us, or stay."

"I can't leave her," Flora said, her voice torn.

"She left you," Luna countered. "She has betrayed everything we taught her. Everything she is. She has no hold on you. Come home. She'll be the death of you otherwise."

"Flora," Miranda added, "your mother misses you."

Flora decided. She set aside the child she wished Talia still were, and saw instead the woman she had become. Taking Luna's hand, she found herself pulled into the Ring. The Wards snapped shut behind her.

Leaving the library lifeless.

☾ ⩳ ☼

"So, this was her workspace," Elanor remarked, turning back to Talia.

"Yes. All her books and scrolls are here. There are years of her notes on Magic. Things that haven't been thought of since her time."

"This is where that Weave came from, then?" Elanor asked, leaning against the wall. Talia remained on the floor. She was still unable to Heal, but her concentration was back. The pain was barricaded away.

"Yes," Talia replied.

"How did you get here?"

"The Ephemeral Rings Holly gave me brought me here. They must have been hers, too. Holly said they were old, and had minds of their own."

"I can't feel the Ring." Elanor gestured to where it lay on the floor. Talia was still sitting half on it.

Talia took a deep breath. "I think the two are linked somehow. I left the Ephemeral Ring in my room. Only I can use it."

"How did we get here, then?" Elanor asked. "I intended to go straight to the library."

Talia only shrugged. "The backlash, maybe. Or interference from the Exile Queen. Or maybe just bad luck."

"But we're stuck here until your Power comes back."

"Seems that way."

Elanor sat down. "What do you think happened?"

"It was a backlash. From what, I don't know." Her frustration came out. "I felt nothing about the child. Did you?"

"I was too occupied dealing with the soldiers. I thought you had accounted for everything," Elanor accused.

"I did," Talia snapped back. She winced. "Everything was perfect. The three parts merged together as one." She shook her head. "I don't understand."

"Something deeper," Elanor thought out loud. "Maybe something the Goddess willed."

"Fool," Talia sneered. "If the Goddess willed something, why was it to protect that bastard? Why didn't She protect my child?"

"The child was an innocent."

"You never complained about that when we were creating the Weave," Talia reminded her. "This is the wrong time to bring it up. Now your conscience comes back."

"But she was," Elanor started, before Talia stopped her with a gesture.

"No one is innocent. The child was the product of a cruel man. Her path is attached to his. His decision led to this. It's his fault."

'You're trying to rationalize it,' Elanor thought. She leaned back. Her conscience began to prick at her. Was this the right thing to do? She didn't give voice to her worries, though. Fighting here, trapped in a small space, would not be productive.

"So where is this place?" Elanor asked instead.

"I don't know. The stone feels different from the mountain, but I can't say for sure. If Nova were here. . . . "

"Don't say her name," Elanor snapped, her emotions suddenly pouring out of her.

Talia started to reply, but caught herself, and remained silent.

A few moments later, Talia gestured to her ruined dress. "Can you help me out of this?"

Elanor stood, and walked over to her. "Where's the knife?"

Talia clapped her hand to her side, where the knife had rested. It was gone. "I must have dropped it, or it was consumed by the fire." She sighed. It had been the only thing left of Sunrise. She shoved her grief and sorrow away.

Elanor examined the dress. The back was burnt, and ruined. She winced as she looked at Talia's back: some of the buttons and clasps of the dress had melted, and were fused to the burns and scabs forming on her skin.

Talia heard her sharp intake of breath. "Well, what do you see?"

"This will hurt. It's melted to your back. I might have to cut it off."

Talia winced, but steeled herself. "Do it."

"Maybe we should wait," Elanor reasoned, unwilling to touch the damaged skin. "Till you're better able to Heal. And we can get Flora's help."

"No. Do it now. Give me more of the root." She gestured to the table. Nothing happened. Talia grunted in frustration. "There are other things. I think there's some clotting powder, too. We can use the front of the dress for bandages. There are knives on the table."

"I don't know," Elanor waffled. "You can't see this. It's bad. I would feel better if we waited."

"Maybe it's something in the cloth that's preventing my Power from working. Get it off me." Talia turned her head. "You always want me to beg you to take my clothes off. Now's the time."

"Now isn't the time to think of that."

"Exactly. Now's the time for you to act. I can bear it."

Elanor sighed. She went to the table, and located what she would need. She also found a bottle of strong wine. She picked it up. Elanor pushed the chair closer to Talia, so she could put her arms and head on the seat.

"Wine?" Elanor offered, as she gave Talia more painkiller root.

"No. Doesn't mix well with the root."

Elanor took a drink. "Well, I need some."

"Don't waste it all."

Elanor began to cut at the front of Talia's dress. Talia smiled again as her chest emerged. "We should do this when I'm better." She shivered. "The sharpness near my skin is exciting."

Elanor sat back on her heels. "Stop it. This is serious. I'll have to cut you to get this off." She gestured to the cloth that bound Talia's breasts. "This is burned, too. Melted to the dress in back." Elanor pulled back the knife. "Stop flirting."

"I thought you wanted me to be more forward." Talia reached out for her. "I was just thinking about later."

"What's wrong with you?" Elanor evaded her hand. "Is it the root? Your body is burned, and your Power is dormant. And you're thinking of pleasure!"

"Would you rather I scream and cry about it?" Talia shrugged. "This is the reality. I can't do anything but deal with it. I was just trying to lighten the mood. If I start crying, I won't stop. I need to be strong. Teasing you keeps the terror away."

"I'm just not in the mood," Elanor said, starting to cut around Talia's arms, and down her side.

"That's something I never thought I'd hear you say."

"Well, this is a rare day. Raise your arm." Elanor cut the seam down one side of Talia's dress, then moved to the other.

"At least it's warm in here," Talia commented as the dress fell away. Elanor removed as much as she could. The burns stopped at Talia's waist. Elanor began to cut the intact fabric into strips.

"Hand me a few of those," Talia ordered. "I want to knot them together, so I have something to bite down on."

Elanor finished her work, and took in the pile of improvised bandages. She looked at Talia, sitting mostly naked on the floor, her hands busy with fabric strips. 'Goddess,' she thought, 'if this situation weren't so horrible, I'd be teasing her, too.' But she felt no desire. Not just because of the ruin that was Talia's back, but because something between them had changed. 'She's changed,' Elanor finally began to admit to herself. 'Can we go on as before, after all this?' she wondered.

Elanor shook herself out of her unproductive thoughts. Talia had finished her gag, and was about to put it in her mouth.

"I'm ready," she said.

"If you need me to stop."

"You'll finish, regardless of what I do," Talia ordered her. "Get the fabric out of my wounds, and get them clean. If I pass out, that's better." She settled herself into the chair, wedging her legs under it. She spit out a chunk of root, and took another one. "Now." She stuffed the rags into her mouth, and gripped the chair firmly.

"Goddess Mother," Elanor whispered, "help me." She began to cut. She was only halfway down the left side when the volume of Talia's muffled screams rose. Elanor was almost done with that side when Talia finally passed out. The work was easier after that. Elanor poured wine on the wounds, and cleaned them. Then she poured on the clotting powder, and bound the left side.

She sat back, sighed, and started on the right side.

☾ ෴ ☼

The Queen of the Human Realm returned to her quarters. Her lady's maids were waiting there. The younger one made noises of consideration and sympathy, while the older one brought her tea with something strong in it.

She couldn't sit. She paced the room as the maids tried to get her out of her gown.

"You must stand still, My Lady," the older maid chastised her. "I can't get the buttons with you moving so."

"Oh, what a horrible thing," the younger one was prattling on. "That horrible Fairy. Why did we even let them in?"

The Queen wanted them both to stop talking. She turned abruptly, and faced the older maid. "Anne, do you know any Thorn Brothers?"

Anne narrowed her eyes. She looked at the other maid. "Sela, would you go and fetch Her Majesty something to eat? Soup, and some of those sandwiches the cook makes, perhaps." Her stern gazed finally penetrated Sela's prattle. "And make sure they make them the way the Queen likes them. Stay with them, and take your time. Knock before you enter when you return. Her Ladyship might decide she needs to sleep."

"But if she wants to sleep, why bring food?" Sela asked, totally missing the subtext of her elder's instructions.

"Just go, girl. Make sure everything's perfect."

Sela finally left.

"I don't know what you mean, My Lady." Anne finally responded to the Queen's question, taking advantage of the woman's stillness to undo her dress as she did so.

"Don't play the fool, Anne." The Queen turned out of the dress. "I know you know who I mean."

Anne held the dress. She looked at her Queen. "With all due respect, My Lady, you've been playing the fool for quite some time."

"Yes, but the fog has lifted a bit. I see things more clearly than I ever have now."

"They're dangerous," Anne warned her, as she put the dress away. "What would you want a Thorn Brother for?"

"As an escort, for a journey."

Anne considered. She got close to the Queen, and began to unwind her undergarments. "I think I know someone," she admitted in a low voice.

"Your Majesty?"

"What is it, Phillip?"

Phillip entered King Bastile's private room. An empty bottle of wine rolled under his foot. He looked around, and saw more bottles on the tables and chairs. Some had spilled on the floor, but most were empty. Phillip glanced behind him. The King's Guardsmen were further down the hall. Further back than Phillip would have liked, really, but seeing what the King's room looked like, it was probably best for them to be out of earshot. Phillip pushed the errant bottle away with his foot, and closed the door behind him.

"The Queen has gone to her quarters. Her maids are keeping her calm." Phillip took a deep breath. Bastile had not looked up. He was still staring into his cup. His other hand held an almost-empty bottle.

"The Priests have commanded that the Great Hall needs to be purified. There can be no one in or out for a month. I thought the High Priest would burst something, he was so angry." Phillip looked at Bastile, expecting a response. The King and the High Priest had butted heads over Fairies ever since Bastile had returned from the Fairy Realm. But Bastile didn't even look up. He just poured the remainder of the wine into his cup.

"Take care of it, Phillip," Bastile ordered simply. He looked around, and a look of drunken concern filled his face. "There's no more wine."

Phillip sighed, and glanced about the room. He headed to the sideboard. "There's only your father's brandy left." He picked up an old bottle.

Bastile frowned, draining the cup in his hand. "Bring it here." He motioned. "You can drink it with me."

Phillip picked up a cup, and went to sit beside Bastile. He had to clear numerous empty bottles from the chair. Phillip poured a hefty portion for the King, and then filled his own cup. He raised his cup to Bastile, who only slightly nodded in acknowledgment before draining his generous allotment.

Bastile grimaced. "I hate that stuff." He set his cup down.

"So do I," Phillip agreed, setting his cup down after only a swallow.

"But he made us both drink it with him."

"He was the King," Phillip replied, pressing his fist to his heart.

Bastile stared off into the room. His eyes lost focus, and he let go of his cup. His hands worried in front of his face, clenching and unclenching, folding together, then coming apart. Bastile finally thrust his right hand into the pocket of his coat.

Phillip could see his fingers moving through the fabric. Phillip opened his mouth to speak, but didn't know what to say, so he shut his mouth.

"So, I had a daughter," Bastile said after a moment. He pulled his right hand out of his pocket, and folded it with the other in front of himself again.

"My son and daughter," he said quietly, "are both dead because of me. She's right."

Phillip looked at Bastile, puzzled. "Your son?"

Bastile, through long practice, was able to reply through the fog of wine. "My Sun. Aurora was my sun. She was to be a bright spot in our Realm." He put his head in his hands. "And now she's gone."

"We don't know that she's dead," Phillip admonished him. "Wingless and his men," contempt and distaste filled Phillip's voice, "might yet be able to find her. Do not lose hope, My King."

"Why didn't you tell me?" Bastile's head came up. He fixed Phillip with a hard, though slightly wavering, stare. "Why didn't you tell me Ta . . . she was having a child?"

Phillip sat back. He gave himself a moment to think, by taking another sip of the horrible brandy. "There were only rumors. With the borders closed, we couldn't find out the truth. And I don't trust the Three Sisters. They only tell us what they think we should know. You know Fairies." Phillip tried to change the path of the conversation. "They're in so many beds, it can never be said with certainty who the father of any child is."

Bastile's head came up. There was fury in his eyes. "She wasn't like that!" He defended his former love.

"Yes, she was," Phillip shot back. "And you know it. You knew it before you started," Phillip waved his hands, trying to find the right words, "giving her dresses, and going to her Garden. You told Simon, 'It'll be an easy trip to her bed.'"

Bastile started an angry retort, but the truth in Phillip's words penetrated his drunken stupor, and he stopped. He picked up his cup, and thrust it at Phillip.

"You should have told me," Bastile said numbly, as Phillip poured more brandy.

"The Council of Clans," Phillip said firmly, "decided that you didn't need to know. It was only a rumor. And it would have pulled your focus." Phillip's voice softened. "And the Queen was having trouble conceiving an heir."

"The Council," Bastile muttered around a swallow. "They do too much, keep too much from me." He set the cup down with a bang. "I must know everything. I'm the King!"

"You gave them too much power," Phillip informed him, "as part of the deal for your marriage." Phillip paused. He didn't know how Bastile would react, but this might be the best time to broach a difficult topic. His words might actually get through to Bastile now. "And passively, you've given them much more. They've taken power you should have, because you won't tell them no."

"I am the King," Bastile stated again. He sat up straighter. "I will see that they understand that." Then he seemed to shrink. He sank back into his chair. "But after today, what can I do? Fairies came into our Great Hall. Cursed my Heir. Took her. I look weak. They'll use that." His voice got even lower. "I'm still trapped. Still trapped."

"Your Majesty," Phillip tried again, leaning forward, "there's still much we can do. All is not lost. You can have another child. Another Heir. A son." He wanted to shake the King, pull him out of this blackness that had been brought on by the wine. "You can still be a great King. You have the necessary support."

"Go, Phillip," Bastile commanded. "I wish to be alone now. I've lost my Heir, and I will not give my wife more grief."

"But, Bastile," Phillip urged.

"Go!" Bastile shouted. "Or I will throw you out."

Phillip stood. Bowed. And walked proudly to the door.

"Your Majesty." He took his leave. Bastile didn't even look up.

Phillip exited, and closed the door behind him. He stopped outside to gather himself. Behind him, through the door, he could hear Bastile shout, "Damn you!" followed by the sound of a glass bottle hitting the wall and shattering.

Phillip looked down the hall. The guards didn't move, though they had clearly heard the noise.

Lord Phillip sighed. He nodded to the guards as he left. Walking down the hall, toward his quarters, he wondered if he should stay, or if it wouldn't be better for him to go far away for a while. The fields close to the Exile Woods might need his direct hand. The production of grapes there had fallen. And his children were there. He might even have another grandchild by this time. Phillip smiled. He stopped, and spit the aftertaste of the prior King's brandy into a cloth. 'Yes. I'll go. My family needs me,' he thought. With renewed determination, he walked toward his quarters. Tomorrow, they would pack up. His wife would be glad to return to the north. She loved the lakes around which his vineyards grew.

Chapter Twenty-Seven
Walls

"Nothing?"

"Nothing," came Talia's frustrated response.

Elanor sighed. "And our Torcs won't work, either."

"No. This place is Warded too strongly. The only way out is this Ring." Talia gestured to the floor.

Elanor sat back against a bookcase, and pulled her knees to her chest. "Then we're trapped here."

Talia started to reply, but laid her head back down and remained silent instead.

She lay on her stomach. Her back was a maze of torn fabric strips from her dress and gobs of the healing ointments Elanor had smeared on the wounds. Elanor had tried to wrap her wings as well, but they had proven too sensitive.

"We need to figure out what went wrong," Talia said into her arm. "If we know that, we can fix whatever's wrong with my Power."

"We're cursed," Elanor said simply. "We did something we never should have done, and we're being punished for it."

"We're not being punished," Talia disagreed. "It was just some reaction that I didn't plan for. There is an answer." She pointed. "That book — bring it here."

"She was an innocent," Elanor said, not listening. "We worked to kill her."

"I killed her," Talia stressed. "I created the Weave, and I cast it. You only created a small part."

"That doesn't matter. I'm at fault, just as much as you are."

"Min isn't here with us, so this can't be a punishment," Talia reasoned. "Now, bring me that book."

Elanor looked up. She could see sunlight starting to make its way down the shaft. "It's another day." She leaned her head further back. "It seems like we've been here forever."

"We will be, if you don't help me," Talia snapped. "Bring me that book. I need to study it, and find an answer."

"Maybe it's better that we be here forever. Trapped. Lost. We won't Return to the Cycle." Elanor closed her eyes and hugged herself. "Maybe that will be better. We did something horrible. We won't take this corruption to another life. It'll end here."

Talia wanted to throw something at Elanor, but there was nothing suitable within reach. She wanted to scream, and threaten someone. She tried again to access her Power, but there was nothing. Nothing at all. It simply wasn't there. Not weak, not Warded off. Just gone. She might as well be a Human — a Human with twisted wings. She wanted to beat her head on the stone, to shake something loose. She wanted to beat Elanor's head against the floor. Talia tried to pull herself forward, but any movement threatened to re-open the wounds on her back, and she couldn't take any more pain just now.

"Elanor," Talia called sharply. "Elanor." She lowered her voice. "Love, please. I need you."

Elanor returned her focus to Talia. "You always use that tone when you need something, but never when I do."

"Elanor, I cannot do this alone. I need your help." Talia began to cry. All of the hot tears that had built up since Sunrise's death threatened to emerge at once. "I need you. Help me. I love you. Please help me — I cannot do this alone." Tears ran down her face. Talia laid her forehead on the floor.

"You've been doing everything alone, ever since she died. You did nothing when we needed you. But now that you're wounded and helpless, you need me. And I must help." Elanor spoke in a firm voice.

"You cursed, selfish, hurt fool," Talia snapped, looking up. Her hot tears were still falling, but she spoke through them. "You want me. But when I don't bow to your every whim and desire, you act like a hurt child. 'No pleasure for you.'" She waved a hand at Elanor. "Sit there and be hurt. Sit there and stew in your resentment. I'll lie here in my blood and pain. We can both starve. Will that satisfy you? Will that make it better?" Her head sank back down, and her voice got softer. "I love you. I've told you that. I thought we had decided: it's you and me, always. I cannot see a life that doesn't have you by my side. My Second. My Lady. Always."

"Maybe that isn't enough anymore."

"Then decide," Talia said, exhausted. "Make up your mind. I can't do this anymore. I told you how I feel. Nothing will change that." She beat her hands on the floor. "I can't use my Power. It's gone. Curse it all. Everything is destroyed."

"You destroyed it," Elanor stated. "You used your Power for evil, and now it's gone. Goddess's mercy. How much clearer can it be?" She leaned forward. "You call me a foolish child. That fits more with you." Elanor hugged herself. "I love you. I want you. How is that wrong? You're the only one I trust. The only one I can even think about being with without panic and fear flooding my mind. I want to be in your bed. I want to be by your side. I want more than the scraps you toss off. I want to be with you when I want to, not just when you find it convenient."

"That isn't my life," Talia explained. Anger and sadness fought in her voice. "I can't be that kind of partner for you. I'm the Heir. Do you not understand that? My life — our life — will always be stolen moments. Little looks, clasped hands. Quick pleasure at the end of the day. I can't give you more, because I have no more to give."

"I've been deluding myself all this time." Elanor stood up. "I feel resentment toward you because I resent myself. I have been a foolish child: it can never be." She crossed to the bookshelf, and pulled the book Talia had been gesturing at.

"Is this the one?"

Talia nodded. She tried to speak, and it came out broken. "Elanor, I. . . ."

"No." Elanor shook her head. "I must decide. But not here." She sat down in front of Talia's prone body. She opened the book, and set it so it leaned back against her knees. "We have to get out of here. Find the answer." Elanor closed her eyes.

Talia wiped away her tears. Her walls began to rise back up to enclose her emotions. She reached out, and began to flip pages. "I'll find an answer. Will you help me?"

"I will." Elanor didn't open her eyes, or look down. She just stared over Talia's head, to the bookshelf beyond. "It's my duty to My Lady, the Heir to the Fairy Realm."

Despite her walled emotions, Talia's heart sank at the finality of those words.

☾ 〰 ☼

"What do you see when you look at me?" Talia asked later.

They had endured hours of silence, broken only by Talia's requests for other books.

"I see the Heir to the Fairy Realm, splayed out on the floor, with twisted wings, and a burnt back."

The words hurt, but Talia pushed them aside. "No, See. With your Sight. What do you See? My aura, my being. Can you See anything?"

Elanor opened her Sight. She Looked hard at Talia.

"Well?" Talia asked impatiently.

"It's . . . odd."

Keeping her temper under tight control, Talia asked, "How is it odd?"

"I can See you." Elanor lost some of her bitterness and anger as she tried to puzzle it out. "But it's as though I'm Looking at you through a curtain. I can See you beyond, but I can't Touch you. You're there, but behind this veil. Layers of Wards, layers of memories and experiences. Everything. But it might as well be a stone wall: I can't Reach you."

"That's what I'm reading about." Talia gestured to the book in front of her. "A Paramount, treating someone who's lost her Power. But he doesn't say why. He assumes you know, or else the notes are lost. Listen to this: 'Her Power is there, but as inaccessible as the moon. Behind a gauzy wall, like my wife's night dress.'" Talia stopped. "Men. Always thinking of pleasure."

"Says the woman who wanted me as I cut off her clothes to treat her wounds."

"It was the root," Talia said primly. "Curse you," she addressed both the book and the Paramount who had written in the distant past, "tell me why!"

"How did he treat her?" Elanor asked. "That's the important thing."

Talia flipped pages. "He goes on for pages, musing about why, and how, this condition relates to the root of the trauma. What is the trauma, you pretentious prick?"

"How did he treat her?" Elanor's voice rose. "Maybe his spirit has Returned by now, and we can find him in his new life, but only if you can knock down this wall."

Talia stopped. "He doesn't say. Just that he had to consult with others." She closed the book. Her head sank. "I get the impression that was something that was known, but not spoken of. Something taboo. Something. . . ." She stopped.

"Evil," Elanor filled in. "Tainted."

"We can debate that later." Talia pounded the book. "I need to get around it."

"Maybe you just need to accept it," Elanor countered. "Acknowledge it, and maybe the wall will fall."

"Acknowledge what?" Talia snapped. "What have I done?"

"Killed a child!" Elanor snarled. "You killed another woman's child."

"I dispensed justice. I didn't kill her." Talia shook her head. "She's still alive. And she will be, for sixteen years."

"You still killed her. Whether it's today or tomorrow." Elanor pointed, for emphasis. "You set it in motion."

Talia didn't respond.

"You've done to another woman, what was done to you."

"A Human."

"That's what your Aunts would say." Elanor warred internally with her own frustration and anger. Once she got herself under control, she laid out the logical argument to Talia. "She bore her child, like you did yours. She gave birth to her baby, like you did yours. And you took her daughter away. As yours was taken from you."

"He took her away," Talia returned. "He killed her. I just evened the scales."

"Maybe that wasn't your decision to make."

Talia wanted to argue more — wanted to make Elanor understand the difference. Talia needed her to understand, but she pushed that aside.

300

"It doesn't matter what caused it. We need to break this wall."

"You've found no answers." Elanor stood up. "I need to walk."

Talia watched Elanor pace the small room, going around and around in a circle. No more than ten paces, and she was back to where she'd started. Then she'd continue, around and around, again and again.

Talia began to get dizzy. She put her head down. She could still hear Elanor's feet on the floor. She tried again, reaching into the place within herself that had been there since she was a child. Instead of the warmth of Power, now there was nothing but a blank wall. In her mind, she moved her hands up and down the wall, looking for cracks, holes — anything. There was nothing. What had always been there, was now gone. Talia gave up. She lay her head in her hands, and listened to Elanor's steps. The rhythm lulled her to sleep.

☾ ♒ ☼

"It's the only thing I can see working."

"No. I won't."

Talia was finally able to sit up. She still couldn't turn her waist, or move her arms too much, but it was an improvement anyway. Elanor remained unable to Heal her. Her Power sparked with backlash when she tried.

"The blood will give me the Power to knock down this wall," Talia argued. "Then, I'll be able to use the Ring, and we can escape."

"Maybe the blood is the reason you can't use your Power," Elanor countered.

"Holly never mentioned anything like that."

"If she was in half the state you described, she could have forgotten about it, or deliberately misled you."

"She wouldn't dare," Talia snarled, then winced as her movements pulled at a scab. "How could she forget something as catastrophic as this?"

"I don't know, but I won't give you any more of my blood, and I won't take any of yours." Elanor looked at her hands, then tucked them under her arms.

"Then you will curse us to die in here," Talia pronounced, with bitterness and anger.

"Let me think," Elanor pleaded, and began to pace again.

"Please don't do that," Talia asked. "I can't turn to follow you, and you're making me dizzy."

Elanor stopped behind Talia. "Is that an order, My Lady?"

"Elanor, I am tired and hungry. Do what you will."

Elanor resumed her pacing.

Talia closed her eyes. Without the benefit of her Power, it was harder to gain a meditative state, but she still had her discipline. Soon, Talia found herself floating in a pool of calm. Below her, she could see the swirl of her emotions: the dark red, the bright red, blue, and black. She reached up — into the silver and moon-white light above her. She sought that light.

"Talia." Elanor's voice broke her out of her calm. She plummeted back into the stormy sea of her emotions. She pushed at them, forcing them behind her ice wall. She fought back tears. She took a deep breath, and opened her eyes.

Elanor was kneeling in front of her. Her face was torn, vacillating between amazement and sadness.

"Your aura lit up," she said. "For the first time since we got here, I could See you. I could See the chaos of your mind, and how you put it all behind a wall."

Talia wanted to yell at her — tell her that the wall was the only thing keeping her sane — but she was too tired. She just wanted to rest, free of pain. In her body, and in her mind. "How does that matter?"

"You rose above the barrier between you and your Power. I could See it."

Talia brightened. "But how? I was just meditating."

"I don't know, but I think if we Joined in a Circle, I could lead you, and free you from the barrier. Maybe not completely, but enough to get out."

Talia began to hope, but then anxiety crashed down on her. "You would See everything," she whispered. "Everything I've tried to keep inside my wall. Everything."

"I know you." Elanor took her hand. "I understand you. Nothing could hurt me more than your lying about Wingless did. What else can there be?"

"I didn't lie," Talia objected.

"Keeping the truth from a loved one is a lie," Elanor informed her.

After a few long moments of staring into Elanor's eyes, she began to finally understand the repercussions of her actions. Talia nodded her head, but was still unable to say, 'I'm sorry.'

"I understand you, and why you did it." Elanor put both her hands on Talia's face. "I've trusted you. Now, you must trust me."

"I don't know if I can," Talia admitted brokenly.

"You can. Just trust me, my love."

Talia nodded. Elanor kissed her quickly, then settled into a cross-legged position, and took Talia's hands in hers.

"If this works," she grinned, "you'll give me what I want, when I want it."

"You'll have earned it," Talia replied, a twinkle returning to her eye. "If this works."

"Enter your meditative state first. I'll follow."

Talia closed her eyes. She slipped into her meditation, more easily this time.

Elanor opened her Sight, and Watched Talia's spirit form rise above the storm of her pain and other emotions. Elanor slipped into her own meditative state, and emerged beneath Talia. Winds of pain and loss buffeted her, driving her spirit form toward rocks of grief and fear. Elanor stood firm. She held the time they had spent together on the mountaintop, above the timberline, in front of her as a shield. She clung to the joy they had shared, and the understanding they had come to that day. All the pain and doubt that filled Talia's mind, also filled hers, though. Elanor began to falter; her wings couldn't support her. Then she remembered the full moon before Sunrise was born. It had been still on the cliff, in the cool night air. The grief rose up, but Elanor fought it down. She forced it back with her determination to stay by Talia's side, with her fierce love for her, her strong desire — more than she had ever had for any other person. She countered all the darkness with this amazing light.

Suddenly, they were floating in the light of both the moon and the sun, wings out, as if they were hovering. Talia took Elanor's hands. She took the blinding light of Elanor's love, trust, and desire, and wrapped it all around herself. Talia smiled, as the barrier to her Power fell away. She felt the Ring underneath her, and activated it. She felt them travel to her little room off the library at the Exile Queen's mountain. When she felt her bare legs touch the fabric of the Ephemeral Ring, she opened her eyes. Elanor stood there with her.

Talia's elation grew. Her Sight opened, and she began to Heal. She gasped, as the wounds closed, and the scabs fell away. She could feel the energy flowing from Elanor to her. Felt her body returning to normal.

'I will make you suffer,' Talia thought, as she became suddenly able to straighten her back again. 'Soon, I will regain my strength, and I will destroy you.'

When she thought those words, the barrier slammed down again. Her Sight disappeared. Elanor screamed, as her connection to Talia was severed. She fell to the floor, senseless.

Talia was hit by another wave of pain. She doubled over, her wings hitting the wall. Screaming, she fell into darkness.

☾ ∿ ☼

Night fell. Shatter, Min, Steel, and Raven pushed aside their dinner plates. The Sergeant had returned earlier with tea and water. She had also brought blankets, and bed rolls. She even offered to bring in more cots, but Shatter refused. Min would take one, and Raven the other. Raven had lost the toss, and was forced to take the cot. Steel and Shatter would be fine on the floor.

Later, a larger meal was brought. Shatter could almost pretend she was back home, but then the jingles of her bonds would remind her where she really was.

That evening, Raven had even gotten Min to smile and laugh a few times with her banter. Steel still sat apart, huddling in her corner. Shatter wondered what would become of them. She would lose her position, of course — that she was sure of. Would she be able to stay in the palace, or even the castle? She wished she could go back to the seashore, but grief barred the way.

"Goddess will show me the path," she muttered. She looked out the cell's single window, and began to count the stars.

Another Sergeant arrived to remove the remains of their dinner. She got close to Shatter, and whispered, "I support you, Captain — and the Heir."

Shatter gripped her arm in silent thanks.

After that, it was quiet. Min lay on her cot, and stared at the wall. Raven had formed something into balls, and was trying to juggle with her bound hands. The balls kept bouncing away. Most of the time, they rolled to Steel. It quickly became a game: Raven would lose the balls, and Steel would toss them back. It evolved into a soothing rhythm. Shatter skirted them, and sat down beside Min.

"How are you, Sister?"

"I'm full," Min replied.

"Good. We haven't been that in a long time."

"No, we have not," Min agreed.

Shatter put a hand on Min's side, and they sat in companionable silence. They both smiled at Raven and Steel.

The moon was rising when Shatter's head snapped up. "I know those boots," she remarked. "Raven, Steel," she called in her command voice. They stopped their game, and moved to the bars. "Get up, Min," Shatter urged her. "We're about to have company." She helped Min up, and they all lined up. Shatter stood in the middle, with Steel on her left, and Min and Raven to her right.

They heard voices outside the door. It opened, and in marched four soldiers in the silver of the Queen's Guard. They set themselves in a line across from the cell. Next came Captain Shattersteel of the Queen's Guard, and Lord Oberon. Behind him came a young Feather-wing aide, juggling a writing pad and a rolled Ephemeral Ring. He moved to set the Ring down, but Oberon shook his head. He tried to figure out what to do with his two burdens, until the nearest soldier took pity on him and grabbed the rolled Ephemeral Ring from him. He mouthed a thanks, then moved to get his writing pad into both hands and ready.

Shattersteel moved closer to the four in the cell.

"Sister," he said in a deep voice.

"Brother," Shatter replied.

"I need to know: did they die with honor?"

"They did," Shatter confirmed.

"Did they die so that others could live?"

"Yes, Captain."

"Did their deaths have meaning?"

Shatter heard the scratching of the young Fairy's pen stop. The image of Harpoon, full of bolts, dead after killing the last crossbowman, leapt to her mind. "To a Sister."

Shattersteel looked satisfied. He moved closer. "By what I hear, you've acted with honor. You took soldiers and court flowers," he nodded to Min, "and formed a company to rival my own. You did well. I grieve with you at the loss of so many brave Sisters. May the Goddess guide them to Return soon."

"Goddess grant," the soldiers echoed.

"Goddess grant them mercy," Shatter said. Raven and Steel didn't speak, though Min lowered her head.

Captain Shattersteel stood, waiting.

Shatter took the cue. "About the rest of my company. Is there any news?"

"Regrettably, no." Min gripped Raven's hand tight. "I spoke to the Fairies who were outside the Hall. The last soldier of Air reported that the Humans were attacking a tower near the Hall. He saw the top explode in Silverfire, then collapse."

Min made a muffled cry, and buried her face in Raven's side. The Captain paused, as Raven led Min back to her cot and helped her lay down. Min covered her face, and wrapped her wings around herself. Raven returned to the cell bars.

"Spearhead was her soldier?" Shattersteel guessed.

"No. There was another with her, with whom Min was quite close. An Elenite." Shattersteel's eyes went up. "It's a long story," Shatter told him, "but he was important to her, and to all of us. I'm sorry to hear they're dead." 'Someone else I have led to their death,' Shatter thought, with bitterness.

"Spear was holding the escape Ring?" Shattersteel surmised.

"Yes," Shatter confirmed.

"She and the other might have escaped. The explosion could have just been the Ring being destroyed."

"Goddess's mercy, we can hope," Raven said. "But where would they have gone?"

"They weren't at the Exile Queen's mountain," Captain Shattersteel started, but Oberon cleared his throat.

"I'm sorry, Lord." He turned back. "Not part of my story." He folded his arms. "I'm glad you're back. You've come in such a state, and with such bad news, though. I'm concerned for what you've done." He held the eyes of his Bre-Sister. "In time, we'll be able to talk." He stepped back.

Lord Oberon stepped forward. "I need to know," he said with absolute command. He pinned Shatter and Steel with his gaze. "Were you an active participant in the use of Blood Magic? Were you forced by the Heir?"

Shatter and Steel both started to say that they were active, but Oberon raised his hand. "And I will have none of that 'an honorable soldier takes the blame for her commander' folderol. I need the truth."

Shatter and Steel looked at each other. Finally, Shatter spoke. "We weren't asked. She just assumed that we would do whatever she required. We complied. We didn't refuse, My Lord."

"And you, soldier?" Oberon gestured to Raven.

"I neither gave my blood, nor used Blood Magic, My Lord," Raven replied.

"And her?" He gestured to the huddled Min.

"She should speak for herself, My Lord, when she's able," Shatter said. Oberon did not look pleased. "But," Shatter put in, "I didn't witness her use Blood Magic, or give her blood."

"Careful answers to hard questions," Oberon considered. "But I hear truth in your words. This is a difficult time. Many things, both in and out of our control, are moving at once. I honestly don't know what to do with you." He sighed. "It is good that I don't have to make that decision.

"What I need from all of you," he gestured to the whole room, "is your Oath, as soldiers, and Servants of the Moon and Sun, that you will not speak of this outside this room, or with any others who aren't here. I will not hear idle gossip about the Heir. If I do, I will make sure that you regret every word."

"Yes, Lord Oberon," the four Queen's Guard soldiers said in unison.

"Yes, Lord Oberon," Raven and Steel said together.

Shatter waited a beat, but also agreed. Oberon looked to Min. Raven went over, and bent down to whisper with her for a moment. There was a brief nod of her head after.

"She agrees," Raven confirmed, returning to the bars.

"What do you intend to do about Lady Talia?" Shatter asked.

"We want her to come home," Oberon answered honestly. "She's a danger, both to herself, and to all the Realm, right now. What she did at the Humans' Presentation destroyed all the work we've been doing to prevent another war."

"She'll be going after the King and the Blood Cultists," Steel offered, speaking for the first time. "We should help her."

Oberon looked at Shattersteel. "Others have said that as well."

Steel began to speak, but Oberon held up his hand. "Nothing has been decided. As I said, I will not be making this decision. Now," he turned, "I will leave you. Captain, leave one of your soldiers outside the door. What comes next is to be a private meeting." He gestured to his young aide. The young Fairy tucked the notes he had been taking under his arm, and spread the Ephemeral Ring the soldier had been holding for him on the floor. Oberon touched the crystal pendant around his neck.

He waited until the Queen's Guard and his aide had left. At the door, he paused. "I'm proud of all of you, too," he said. "I just wish she had made better decisions." With that, he closed the door.

Chapter Twenty-Eight
Reunion

The door shut. A breath later, two Fairies appeared in the Ring, wearing the hoods and robes of Shrinekeepers. They moved off the Ring, and threw back their hoods.

"Goldberry!" Shatter called. "Shield!"

They both looked older — far older than they had been just days before. Goldberry's bright hair was now dull, and Shield looked as though she'd been fasting.

"Shatterstaff," Goldberry greeted. "Raven, Steel." She looked behind them. "Min?" She looked to Raven. "Is she hurt?"

"Just in the heart," Raven said. She went to Min, and whispered. Min withdrew her wings and sat up. Goldberry moved closer.

"Sister," she called.

"Sister," Min answered. "It is good to see you." She turned to Raven. "I can't," she said, and turned back to the wall.

Goldberry turned to Shatter. "Where's Spear?"

Shatter looked her right in the eye. She didn't hesitate or hold back: this was her responsibility, too. "She didn't return."

Goldberry stumbled, and Shield grabbed her, supporting her. Shatter could only look on, with pain in her eyes and heart.

"Why didn't she come with us?" Goldberry asked. "Goddess's mercy. I knew this would happen." She looked at Shatter. "This is your fault."

"She made her decision, as you made yours," Steel interjected, stepping to the bars. "She did her duty."

"Her duty got her killed," Goldberry returned angrily.

"We don't know that," Raven offered, trying to help. "We don't know."

"We may never know," Shatter added pointedly.

Goldberry turned away. Shield let her go, then stepped up to Shatter.

"Goddess's mercy, but you look awful," Raven said, trying to banter.

"I've been trying to find myself," Shield said with a shrug. "I haven't been very successful."

"So, you're a Shrinekeeper now?" Shatter asked.

"I don't know yet what I'll be. Right now, Goldberry and her family are trying to guide me. I'm not the best at being guided, though, I'm afraid." Shield gestured to her cloak, and shrugged.

"You're no longer a soldier, then?" Shatter asked.

"I gave my sword to Nova's family. Told them to do whatever they wanted with it. Break it, melt it. Keep it. I failed her; failed to protect her."

"I would tell you that you didn't fail her," Shatter said, "but you wouldn't listen. One day, though, you will. I hope they have the wisdom to keep it for you until then."

"I'm sorry," Shield said. "I just wanted to see you, and make sure you were all right." She moved to the Ring.

"Where is she?" Goldberry asked, her back still turned.

"She escaped," Shatter told her. "She could be anywhere by now."

"I told you she would sell your lives cheap." Goldberry's bitterness burned the air.

"Such words from a Shrinekeeper," Steel taunted.

Shatter wheeled on her. "Silence."

Steel held her ground. "You aren't my Captain anymore."

"But you're still in this cell with me," Shatter threatened, stepping forward.

Raven moved to get between them.

"Children. Please don't fight," came a new voice.

Everyone turned to see Flora stepping out of the Ring.

"You, who have been through so much together, should not be fighting. In fact, I forbid it." Flora strode to the cell door.

Steel and Shatter backed away from each other. Raven smiled broadly.

"What's wrong with Min?" Flora asked. Min hadn't moved on her cot.

"Canin is missing," Shatter informed her. "With Spear. We don't know if they're alive or dead."

Goldberry turned. "Canin?" she asked, confused.

"The Elenite boy we helped find his father," Flora reminded her. "We found him, or rather, he found us. Min took right back up with him, as though no time had passed."

She went to the door, and banged on it. "Soldier! Come in here, and unlock this cell. One of my Ladies is in pain, and I can't comfort her from outside."

The door opened, and the soldier on guard stepped in. He was visibly torn.

"You'd better do as she asks," Goldberry advised him. "Or she'll just talk, and beg, and then threaten, till you do." He looked from face to face, and saw that Goldberry's words were true.

"Longstride," Shield said, "you know me. I swear, by the Goddess and that," she looked him up and down, "quick bit of Healing I did for you, that we're not going to let them escape."

"Goddess. Not at all," Goldberry said, going to the Ring and standing in front of it, her arms crossed.

"I need your word of honor," Longstride said, looking at Shatter.

"You have it," she swore.

Longstride shut the outer door firmly behind him. He went to the cell door, and opened it. He jumped out of the way, as Flora barged through, and gathered Min into her arms. The younger Fairy began to cry again.

The male soldier looked from face to face around him, at a bit of a loss as to how to proceed. Shatter gestured for him to go. He exited the room quickly, and with obvious relief.

Shield approached Goldberry, who was still standing by the Ring, and whispered in her ear. Goldberry's eyes narrowed, but she rushed toward the cell. She stopped at its door, locking eyes with Steel. The soldier lowered her gaze first. Goldberry entered the cell, and joined Flora in embracing Min.

Steel went back to her corner, and Raven sat down on the other cot, looking helplessly at Min. Shatter just stood at the cell door, leaning on the frame. The room was quiet, except for Min's quiet sobs, and Flora's comforting words.

311

☾ ⌇⌇⌇ ☼

When Elanor woke, she felt weak. Her head hurt, and she was very thirsty. As her eyes began to focus, she realized that she was in the library, lying on a cot. Her eyes cleared, and she saw Talia, sitting in a chair beside her.

"Here." Talia passed her a cup. The water inside was better than anything she had ever tasted. Elanor finished it, and passed the cup back.

"More," she requested, through a scratchy throat.

Talia smiled, and poured her more.

Elanor finished that cup as well, then began to look around. The library was empty.

"Where is everyone?"

"Shatter and the others were captured," Talia informed her. "Spear and Canin never returned." She stopped. Her fists clenched. "And Flora left us."

"How do you know?"

Talia stood up. She was dressed again, but her wings were still a blackened, twisted ruin. She began to pace.

"Someone broke through my Wards," she spat. "And either took Flora, or persuaded her to leave." She stopped at the foot of Elanor's cot. "No matter. I've strengthened the Wards. Whoever it was, they won't do that again."

"How?" Elanor asked. The pain in her head worsened. "I felt your barrier go back up. You shouldn't be able to do anything. I. . . ." She stopped, as she opened her Sight.

"I told you what I needed," Talia reminded her, "but you wouldn't give it."

Elanor looked at her arm. There was a new cut, just Healed. She shrank back in the bed.

"I will not give it again."

"You'll have to, if you ever want to leave this place," Talia said matter-of-factly, as she resumed her pacing. Elanor followed her, both with her eyes and with her Sight. Talia's aura glowed red.

"I've locked the Ring," Talia continued. "As well as the door leading below. Only I can use them." She rubbed her arm. "You will make me one of those bracelets like Canin has."

"Min made it. I only assisted," Elanor protested.

"I'm sure you can figure it out. If not, we'll be trapped here."

"I won't." Elanor swung her legs off the cot. A wave of dizziness hit her, and she almost fell. She gripped the side of the cot. "I will give you nothing. We'll be trapped here, then."

Talia stopped in front of her. Elanor started to slide back, but restrained herself, and crossed her arms instead. The calm look on Talia's face made Elanor's stomach clench.

"You will," Talia said. She pulled out a knife. "Give me your arm."

As if it were another person's, Elanor's arm went up.

"How?" she gasped, trying to pull it back. It wouldn't move. Talia gripped it with her free hand.

"I've put controls in your mind," Talia said. "Wingless gave me the idea. It's what he did to Willow. You cannot deny me." She drew her blade across Elanor's arm.

Elanor watched in horror as the blood flowed into a vial Talia held. She Pressed, with all the strength of her Power, but she couldn't move her arm.

"Curse you," she said. "How could you do that to me?"

"It was easy," Talia said lightly. "You have something I need. I'll do anything to get it. Sleep now." She made a pushing gesture, and Elanor collapsed onto the bed. Talia moved her legs back onto the cot. She ran her finger over the wound she had made, collecting the last of the blood, and Healing the cut. She rubbed the blood into her fingers. "Sleep," she said again. "I need to find a more secure place for us."

Talia spread her Ephemeral Ring on the floor. "I must find where that workroom is." She stepped onto the Ring, and disappeared.

"Are you quite done?" Luna Sent.

"Min needed me. I had to comfort her."

"How is the child?"

"She'll heal, but this cut is deep. I don't understand, but there's something about this boy."

"He was handsome."

"Is handsome," Flora corrected. "He isn't dead."

"We must face facts: he probably is."

"Goddess only knows."

"There's something else."

Flora tried to guard her thoughts, but she was out of practice, and her twin was quick.

"She did not."

"She did, or at least I think she did."

"A Ward cannot be removed without the consent of the woman. Or bypassed."

"It has happened before."

"Why is this never easy?"

"I don't know."

"So, are you ready? Our Queen is getting impatient."

"Yes. She may come."

"I will tell her you give your permission."

Flora only smiled.

☾ ♒ ☼

Min had recovered enough that she could sit up. Goldberry sat on one side of her, and Flora, the other. Flora was feeding her tea.

"We're getting another guest," Flora announced, turning to the Ring.

All eyes turned, and Shield stepped back. Zellandine materialized in the Ring. She stepped out. The soldiers went to one knee. Flora and the Ladies bowed their heads.

The Queen flowed into the room. Behind her, Luna and Merry-Weather came through the Ring. Luna went straight for Min, kneeling, and putting her hand on her belly. Min looked confused. She turned to Flora, who nodded.

"No," Min said with disbelief. "How?"

"I don't know."

"But my Ward?"

"The boy breached it somehow, or you let it fall," Luna said, settling back. "I must meet this young man."

Min looked like she was going to cry again. Instead, she screamed, "Curse you! Curse you! I just found him, and you took him. Curse you!" Her wings expanded out, pushing Goldberry and Flora off the cot. She wrapped herself in an iridescent cocoon.

Flora reached out to her.

"Let the child be," the Queen said. "All of you, please come here."

Everyone but Min moved into the room outside the cell.

"I want you all to Join in a Circle with me. Would you rather stand, or sit?" she asked.

"I'm old, My Queen," Flora said. "I'll sit."

"You kept up with us," Shatter reminded her. "You aren't that old."

The Queen smiled. "For Flora, let us all sit." She floated into a sitting position on the floor.

"What of Lady Min?" Merry-Weather asked.

"Sit with her," the Queen replied. "I'll go to her when I'm done here. She needs some time."

Merry-Weather grumbled, but went and sat close to, though not touching, Min.

"Now," the Queen said, as they all settled into a circle. Goldberry hadn't joined them. "Lady Goldberry, will you remove their bonds until the Circle is over?"

Goldberry looked like she was going to refuse, but bowed her head, and went to each of the prisoners and removed their bonds. Steel smiled broadly as Gold removed hers, at least until she saw the stern look the Queen was giving her, at which point she dropped her eyes guiltily.

"Lady Goldberry, I would like you to join us," the Queen requested, once everyone had been freed. "I need to know everyone's stories."

"With due respect, My Queen, you know my story. We've Joined."

"I would See it all together." Her eyes went hard. "I insist."

"Yes, My Queen," Goldberry relented, sitting down between Shield and Flora.

"Now," the Queen said again. "Join hands. I want you to lower your Wards. Keep nothing back. I know this will be hard, but I need to know everything. No matter how small, or how painful, the memory is."

There was a murmur of assent around the Ring.

"We will start at the dance."

((ᗰ ☼

Shatter watched from afar as her whole life with Talia was played back. From their first meeting, in the hallway outside the Queen's quarters, to her last view of her: standing, wings blackened, in the Humans' Great Hall. The Queen seemed to focus on her more personal conversations with Talia. For instance, she picked out the time after Canin's father had denied him, when Talia had worried about the place her own child would have in the Realm. Then, there was the time on the ride, when she had counseled Talia not to get too close to the others, because she might have to send one of them to her death one day. She felt pride at her execution of Talia's plan at the plantation. Grief, at the loss of her Sisters at the Crafthouse. Fear, and admiration, as she killed the Elenites of the Blood Cult in the woods, and was wounded. Pride, again, at the home they had built for themselves on the cliff. Bone-deep horror and sorrow, when that home was destroyed, and Sunrise and so many of her Sisters were killed. Shame, at her actions after.

And when the Queen was done, Shatter floated, her emotions subdued.

((ᗰ ☼

"Thank you, all of you," the Queen said, as she released the Circle. "I know that was hard, but this has given me greater insight into everything that has happened." She stood up, and went into the cell.

"Merry-Weather," she asked, sitting down beside Min, "would you replace their bonds, please?"

Merry-Weather grunted in assent, and got up.

"Lady Min," the Queen called. She put her hand on Min's wing.

Min startled, and unfolded her wings. "My Queen," she said, surprised, and embarrassed. She tried to rise, but the Queen took her arm, and kept her sitting.

"I'm sorry to do this to you, but I must Join with you, and See everything that has happened since this whole incident began."

"Yes, My Queen," Min agreed, bowing her head.

The Queen took her hands, and eased her into a Circle.

"I can distance you from your emotions," the Queen offered. "I remember what a loss is like. I would not put you through more pain."

"Thank you, but I've distanced myself for too long already. I will allow you to See everything you need."

To Min, the memories flashed by quickly, from the dance, to the Crafthouse, to the Garden, and on to the horrors of the plantation. Then, she was sitting again in the inn, watching Shatter bring Canin over to her table.

"He's a handsome young man," the Queen commented, breaking the flow of memories. "I can see why you were drawn to him."

"It wasn't just that." Min struggled with words, and still-nebulous concepts. "There was something about him — something intangible, but real. I couldn't look away. Nothing in the Realm could have prevented me from taking him to bed. Nothing. I can't explain any of it. His story was tragic, and he was so broken. And so innocent. I couldn't help myself. It sounds horrible, but that's how I felt."

"Who we are drawn to is never easy to understand."

"Oh, I understood: he was who I needed to be with. Both as a partner in pleasure, and in life." Her emotions threatened to overwhelm her, and disrupt the Circle. The Queen wrapped her in a calming wave.

"Peace, child. Live in that moment: find peace in the blush of new love. I'll Watch the rest of your memories, and return when I'm done."

317

"I had to show him almost everything," Min muttered, as the Queen gave her the peace she had promised. The Queen couldn't help but smile.

The Queen finished her Viewing of Min's memories, finding much of interest. She was glad when Min hesitated to give Talia her blood on the mountaintop, but disturbed at Talia's drive to use this new power.

She didn't want to take Min from her memory of the night when she had first met Canin, but she had to. With a careful hand, she Pulled Min back from that night.

"I'm sorry, but we must end our Circle."

"Thank you, My Queen. I'm glad to have those memories, uncolored by the grief of today."

"You're welcome, Lady Min. I was young and in love once, too, you know."

"I just don't understand. How did my Ward fall? I didn't remove it."

"Sometimes our unconscious mind knows better what we want than we do, and acts on it. You did say that you would have his child if you were ever reunited."

"I did, but I never allowed myself that hope. I didn't know if we would survive."

"Maybe that's it. He seems a rather remarkable man. His story and history are beyond my knowledge. The mere idea of the spirit of the Exile Queen, in a forest near the Human Realm, taking in women and children, and protecting them from their abusers. It's a fantastic story."

"He was remarkable," Min said with resignation.

"Do not give up hope, child. The Goddess and his Mother Goddess might have more to say on this yet." She sighed. "At least you will have the child, so some of him will live on."

Min's silent thanks were all she needed.

The Queen broke the Circle, and stood. Merry-Weather was standing beside them, ready to replace Min's bonds.

"I must go," the Queen said.

"My Queen," Shatter asked, as Zellandine exited the cell, "what will become of us?"

As Luna herded the other three prisoners back into the cell, the Queen considered her words. She spoke only after the door was closed. "I understand the difficulty of this situation, but you participated in the attack on the Human King, and I cannot let that go unpunished. The Humans are calling for your heads."

Shatter looked concerned. Flora moved to speak, but Merry-Weather stopped her.

"I will not turn you over to them," the Queen assured the prisoners. "But I can't let you go, either. So, you will stay here, in as much comfort as can be managed, until a compromise can be reached." Her face softened. "We are Servants of the Moon and Sun. The Goddess will lead us on the path. We must allow ourselves to see it."

"Thank you, My Queen," Shatter said. "We shall await your wisdom and mercy."

The Queen smiled. She turned to the others standing outside the cell.

"Lady Goldberry and Lady Shieldbreaker, please take the Ephemeral Ring to Lord Oberon. Then, I want you both to see the Keeper. I am concerned about each of you. Speak to her, and listen."

"Yes, My Queen," Shield acknowledged with a bow. Goldberry didn't speak, but only bowed, and rolled up the Ephemeral Ring. She gave one more bow, then left, with Shield on her heels.

"Merry-Weather, Flora, Luna: please precede me to my quarters," Zellandine requested.

"By your leave," Flora said, "I would like a few words with them before I go."

"Only a few," the Queen admonished her. "We have much to talk about." 'Most importantly,' she thought to herself, 'the location of my daughter, and what she might do next.'

"Yes, my Queen," Flora agreed, with a bow.

Zellandine gestured to Merry-Weather and Luna, who joined hands and disappeared. With one more stern look at Flora, the Queen herself disappeared.

Flora put her hands on her hips. "You lot: behave yourselves. More than the Humans are calling for your heads. Some of the factions of Fairies are, too. Keep your heads down, and your wings ready."

"We will, Mum," Shatter assured her.

"And take care of Min." She pointed to Raven.

"I will," Raven promised. She had sat down beside Min, and linked hands with her. Min had smiled softly at her.

Addressing Flora, Min said, "I'll do my best, Mum. I'll need your teas." Her hand drifted to her belly.

"I'll bring some."

Flora smiled, and brushed away a tear. She touched her Torc, and disappeared.

Chapter Twenty-Nine
Arrangements

Talia stood in what she had begun to call her workspace. She reached out with her blood-aided Power, and Felt the stone around her. It didn't Feel like the stone of the Exile Queen's mountain. She looked up the narrow shaft, and could see only a small circle of sky. It was daylight, but that was all she could tell.

Frustration built within her. It must have been Miranda who slipped through her Wards. Only she had both the skill and the audacity to do so. The Exile Queen's mountain was no longer safe. She had to find another haven. She considered the ruins, but her mother knew them, and her grief wouldn't allow her to consider the area safe anymore.

"Where is this place?" she asked. She thumped the floor with her foot. "Answer me," she demanded.

Nothing came to her.

She could feel her Power begin to dim, as Elanor's blood wore off. She stepped on the Ring. "Curse your secrets," she said dismissively, as she traveled back to the Exile Queen's mountain. Elanor was still asleep on the bed.

Talia sat down on the Ephemeral Ring, as exhaustion overtook her without warning. Her Power disappeared, as the last of Elanor's blood dissipated within her. She wanted to go to Elanor and take more, but she couldn't stand.

"I will meditate," she announced. Her eyes drooped, and she fell asleep, sliding onto her side.

She dreamed.

Water covered her feet, and spray hit her arms and face. The stone under her feet was cold. Mountain wind rippled through her ruined wings.

"Beginning, to the end, and around to again," a voice chanted.

"Time and water wash away memory.

Stone carries hope and death.
Water carries sorrow, and the door is there.
Past is here; tomorrow is for you —
Water runs through both."

"Have the arrangements been made?"
"Yes. The Humans are ready to attack."
"Not too close, and not too far away?"
"They've chosen a place between two Elen towns. In a force big enough to be a threat, but insufficient to hold either town."
"See to it that they make enough noise that she sends Oberon and most of her Guard."
"I'll make sure of it."
"Are you dealing with Wingless Bastard?"
"No — another one of his people. Also, another wingless Fairy. Tales tell, he had a falling out with the King, and Bastile now refuses to speak with him."
"I wish I didn't have to speak with the bastard, either."
"Indeed."
"There's another condition from the Humans."
"What is it?"
"They want the heads of those who attacked their Great Hall."
He laughed. "I thought they might want something hard."
"Take care of it yourself, Captain Hooklance."
"Yes, Lady Tra. With pleasure."

"Wake up!"
Elanor sat up, and Talia pushed a bowl into her hands.
"Eat," she ordered. "You need your strength."
Elanor took a bite. It was cold and tasteless. She ate it anyway. Her body felt used, her mind, foggy. She started to attempt to use her

Power, but stopped. She kept eating, forcing the food down her throat. She glanced over, and saw that Talia was also eating, emotionlessly.

Talia saw her watching, and put down her bowl. "What do you need for the Ring bracelet?"

"Metal of some kind," Elanor replied flatly. "I was only a small part of the making."

"I'll find something." Talia got up, and walked toward the exit. "Stay in the library," she ordered, over her shoulder.

Elanor listened for Talia to start down the stairs. When her footsteps had faded away, Elanor stood, on shaking legs. She felt for the amulet her mother had made. It was gone. She went to the Ring. She couldn't hear its Song; Talia had Warded it away from her. A thought occurred to her — the Ephemeral Rings. Talia had destroyed one while escaping, and another was with Spear and Canin, who hadn't returned. It hit her, then, that she hadn't even thought about those two. That poor, broken young man, who had begun healing under Min's touch, was gone. Another of our Sisters was gone as well. She struggled against the fresh grief, and resumed looking for the Rings.

There should still be another of those Canin had made, plus the second one Talia had gotten from Holly. She took a breath, and pressed her feelings aside for later. She looked through the supplies. She found Holly's old Ephemeral Ring, rolled up in a pack. She pulled it out, and listened to its strange Song, which became disharmonious as she ran her fingers over the fabric.

"Curse you," she muttered. It wouldn't work for her. Another strange, useless item from the crazy Paramount. She put it away, as she could feel Talia returning. She went to the cold pot of stew that Flora had left. She touched the warming stone, and heat began to flow. Her Power felt thin, and was barely sufficient to heat the stone.

Talia came up behind her, and tossed a bag at her. "I found some jewelry. See what you can do."

Elanor looked up at her. Talia's face was drawn, and her cheekbones stood out. "You're the one who needs sleep."

"Can you do it, or not?" Talia demanded.

"I need sunlight. My Power feels drained."

Talia gestured at the dome. Sunlight made a few spots on floor. "The sun's coming in now."

"I need real light," Elanor replied. "If Holly is right, we need exposure to the sun. If I'm to do what you want, I need the sun."

"You just want to escape," Talia accused.

"The controls you put in my mind make that impossible." She turned away. "Suit yourself. Though it could be days at this rate."

Elanor could hear Talia grind her teeth in frustration. Elanor's shoulders tensed, as she expected Talia to scream at her, but she didn't turn back to face her.

"Where shall we go?" Talia finally asked, with calm anger.

"That's up to you, My Lady."

Talia narrowed her eyes at her. "Then we will go to the broken tower Ring. There's nothing around there." She pulled a bottle from her belt. Elanor watched, as Talia dipped a finger into its contents, and rubbed her stolen blood around on her fingers. Talia's face changed. She stood up straighter, and smiled.

"Let's go, then." She led the way to the Ring, and Elanor followed. Instead of taking her hands, though, Talia turned her around, and grasped her at the base of the neck, the way Nesa used to scruff her kittens when they misbehaved. "Remember: I can make you do anything."

"Yes," Elanor said, fear rising in her stomach. Only days ago, she would have enjoyed Talia's touch, but now, she wanted to slide away from it. Elanor's mind went blank, as Talia took control, and moved them through the Ring.

Elanor returned to consciousness when she smelled the sea. Even under the earth, the scent of water and salt penetrated. It brought conflicting memories: grief, and elation. She was paralyzed for a moment, but pushed through it, and moved to the broken stairs leading upward.

Behind her, Talia didn't move.

Elanor turned, when she didn't hear Talia following her.

"I will stay here," she pronounced. "When will the sun set?"

Elanor reached out. "A few hours."

"Come back then," Talia ordered, and Elanor felt the controls move in her mind. "Do not go beyond the beach."

"Sun would do you good," Elanor urged.

"I will stay here," Talia declared again, as she sat down on the floor.

Elanor shrugged, and began to climb the stairs. She reached the Wards and Illusions that concealed the entrance, and pushed through them. The bright sun, and the clean air, touched her. She closed her eyes, and felt the sunlight touch her skin. Joy filled her mind, as the sun filled her spirit. The bad memories were pushed away by the pure ecstasy of being in the sun again. The sound of the surf filled her ears. She stood in the circle of the foundation of the ancient watchtower. Behind her, the faint outline of the fallen tower could be seen under the dune grass and sand. Elanor walked down a slight slope to the beach.

She sat down, and buried her hands in the sand. As the warmth and grit ran through her fingers, she felt her Power return. After a while, she began to test the controls Talia had put on her. They were wrapped, like black wire, throughout her mind. There seemed to be no end, and no gaps. She dared not even touch the working, for fear of what Talia would do to her if she saw signs of tampering. Elanor just watched the Weave. Her fear began to turn to sadness, as she realized the lengths to which Talia had felt she was being forced to get her way. With a sigh, she withdrew from her own mind, and spread her wings to the sun. She blanked her thoughts, and just sat in the golden rays.

$$\left(\approx \diamond \right.$$

When she heard Elanor reach the top of the stairs, Talia allowed her head to sink to the floor. Her fingers clawed at the dirt and stones beneath her. It all crashed back on her: the smell of the ocean, the sound of the waves, the feeling of being down low, after the great elevation of the mountain. All of it threatened to smash her wall, and send waves of pain crashing down around her. She tried to control her breathing, but it got faster and faster. She was on the cliff, overlooking the waves. The sound filled her mind. She could feel the bundle of bones in her lap. Her right hand struck a stone, and she gripped it; pain ran up her arm, as the tips of her nails snapped off.

She wanted to call Elanor back, command her, but activating the Ring had taken all her Power, and she had nothing left. She wanted to reach for the bottle, but her hand wouldn't release the stone. Talia tried to straighten, but her back locked, and she couldn't raise her forehead from the floor. Out of habit, she fanned her wings to pull herself up, but the blackened masses on her back were useless.

She screamed into the dirt, tasting sand and blood.

Her ice wall was melting, but the barrier to her Power remained strong. With tremendous willpower, she straightened her arms, and pushed herself up. The stone was still in her right hand. With her left, she pried the fingers open, and dropped the stone. Her nails were bloody and broken. She pressed her hand to her belly.

"There, I carried you," a calm voice spoke in her mind. "There, you lived, and your potential grew. New wonders every day." Talia didn't recognize the voice.

"And he took you away!" she screamed back. "He took you. I failed. I should have protected you, but I failed." With her twitching hand, she pulled the bottle out, and poured all the blood remaining within it onto her arms. She rubbed it in, the warmth spreading, taking away the pain, and the memories. She was able to push everything the sea had meant to her away. Far away. The warmth now filled her body. Red colored her vision. She lifted her hands, and conjured fire in each palm. Red flames bloomed to life. She smiled, without joy.

Talia wanted to destroy the room — expand a huge ball of flame, with her in the center, obliterating both the walls surrounding her and the ruins above her, and opening the whole room to the sky.

"But then you would have to actually see the sky," another voice, stern and formal, reminded her. "It is the skin of the Goddess, and the sun is her eye. She will see you. You cannot hide."

Talia's hands clenched, shrinking the fire. She grabbed a stone out of the dirt, and pushed the fire into it, Weaving the fire to the stone. Then, she grabbed another, and another.

By the time the Blood Magic ebbed, she was surrounded by stones, and hard-packed balls of sand, each glowing a dull red. She had finally pushed the pain and panic away. Her mind sank into exhaustion. She carefully leaned back against the stone wall, and watched the bottom of the stairs. Her eyelids drooped, and she fell into a dreamless sleep.

As the sun set, the controls in her mind began to pull at her. Elanor fought them. She concentrated on keeping her legs folded, when they wanted to straighten and push her up. They began to tremble, and a new pain throbbed to life behind her left eye. She gripped her arms, and kept them in front of her. More pain bloomed, in the back of her head this time, and traveled across her skull to her right eye. Blurry lines began to form in the bottom of her vision as the sun disappeared into the water.

Elanor let go of her resistance. Her body snapped upright, and she ran to the tower entrance. She descended the stairs into the Ring chamber.

It was dark. She conjured a Light. She saw piles of dully glowing stones all around the room. She didn't see Talia at first, but then she spotted her in the shadows of the wall.

Her eyes were closed, and her head was resting on her chest. Elanor wanted to run to the Ring, but her legs wouldn't allow it. She put all her might into the effort, and managed to make two steps in that direction, but then her knees betrayed her, and she fell to the rocky floor. Talia still didn't move. Her breathing was slow and steady. A sudden fear ate at Elanor's mind: what if she never woke up? What if, somehow, Talia was mindlost? She would be trapped in her own body till she died. Elanor grabbed the black Weave around her mind. Sparks filled her vision, and she fell flat, her left wing trapped, painfully, underneath her.

"Talia," Elanor called, mouth half in the dirt. "Talia!" she called again, more loudly.

Talia's head shot up, and her eyes opened. It took her a moment to focus. She rubbed her face.

"I see you tried to get away."

"I was just trying to walk," Elanor protested. "Your controls are too harsh."

"They have to be," Talia said flatly, standing up. She walked over to Elanor. "I must be harsh." She pulled out a knife, and without another word, cut Elanor's arm. She pressed her hand to the wound, and drank in the blood.

Elanor got suddenly, and terrifyingly, lightheaded. Her vision swam, and she wondered if Talia would take too much.

But Talia stopped, and Healed the wound, before Pulling Elanor to her feet with her Power.

"Gather the stones," she commanded. Elanor complied, making a basket with her skirt. Then, Talia grabbed her by the back of the neck, and walked her into the Ring.

"We will never come back here again," Talia hissed into Elanor's ear. "You knew what would happen. Never again."

Elanor's conscious mind went to sleep, as they returned to the library.

$$\left(\begin{array}{c} \approx \ \Diamond \end{array} \right)$$

When Talia was done, she left Elanor under a blanket on the floor. She pulled on a clean dress, and pushed the stopper into the bottle. She dropped it into a pocket, and heard it clink against the others of its kind. She stepped over the stones and balls of sand that had rolled across the floor when she had pushed Elanor out of the Ring.

Talia looked back at Elanor, senseless as a doll on the floor.

"You're betraying your Oath," a voice that sounded like Flora said. "You shouldn't treat her so."

"I am the Heir," she retorted. "I will treat her as I see fit." She walked across the library, toward her small room. Something caught her eye, and she turned to the door of the room that had been Min

328

and Canin's. Smiling, she pushed it open. The small bed was unmade. There was a scroll on the pillow, tied with silver string.

She picked it up, and unrolled it.

> I know there's a chance that I won't return, so I wanted to leave you this message.
>
> I love you. You have become my life. I'm not the person I was before I met you. I wanted to find out who I am with you.
>
> I'm glad for the time we had together, and I'm jealous for the time we've been denied. If I am forced to return to the cycle of death and rebirth, I will see you again, though sun, moon, and the Mother bar the way.
>
> Kiss the rest of our Sisters for me.
>
> Love you

Talia could hear Canin's voice as she read. She could see his earnest face as he wrote these romantic last words to his love. She could see Min's tears as she read them.

"Only Min," she mocked. Redfire burst from her hand, and the paper disintegrated into ashes.

Talia grabbed one of the discarded shirts from the floor. She sniffed it. "Good," she remarked. "It doesn't smell of him." She turned, and left.

For the prisoners, each day was pretty much the same. With sunrise came a chance to bathe, then a meal. Flora brought it the first day, and sat with Min while she ate. They talked about what she would be going through.

After a while, Min reminded her, "Mum, I was alongside Talia all through her pregnancy. I know what to expect."

"Knowing, and actually experiencing it, are different things," Flora stressed. "I thought I knew what would happen my first time, but I wasn't ready for the reality."

"But you'll be with me." Min put her hand on Flora's arm.

"I hope so," was Flora's only response.

Flora left at mid-day, leaving them to fill the hours until their next meal. They exercised, as best as they could with their bonds. Steel showed Min the patterns for pregnant soldiers, and taught her how to adapt them as she grew. Steel talked and talked, until Min had to demand that she stop.

"I'm overwhelmed with all this," she admitted. "I just found him, and now I'm planning to birth his child. Without him. It's too much. I need peace." She went off to sit on her cot alone.

A meal was brought near sunset, and Flora returned.

"What can you tell us, Mum?" Shatter asked, as they ate.

"Not much. There are rumors all over, but nothing that's worth anything. There's been no sign of Talia or Elanor. Or Spear and Canin," she told Min gently, worried that she would react badly. But Min only smiled sadly, and went back to her soup.

"I did hear a rumor that the King's child hasn't been seen since the attack. But, then, neither have the King or his Queen."

"That makes sense," Shatter said. "I would stay hidden, too."

"This is a little more than keeping his head down." Flora shook her head. "My source seemed to think they weren't even in the Human castle anymore."

"Again," Raven said, "that makes sense."

"Goddess, I know," Flora snapped, "but I feel that there's more to this than we know."

"Maybe they're running from Talia," Steel suggested. "I hope she finds him."

Shatter and Raven chuckled, but Flora gave them a disapproving look.

"I must go now," Flora announced suddenly, rising, and kissing each of them. "I'll be back in the morning."

She wasn't. There was a lot of commotion, and the sound of movement outside the cell, early in the morning. The soldier who brought their morning meal was new, and didn't talk. She simply set the meal down, and left.

While Flora didn't return that day, Shield did. She was only let in after much discussion, however.

"What's going on?" Shatter pressed her. Shield was looking better, but her face was still drawn. There was a hint of stubble on her skull.

"I can't tell you," she said. "I came here to talk to you." She gestured for Shatter to join her at the corner, away from the others.

Shatter joined her. They sat down, separated by the bars. Shatter waited, sensing that Shield would speak when she was ready.

"You tried to tell me that Nova wasn't my fault," she began. "That I did everything I could. That I saved her, by taking her arms. But I can't get out of my head, that she wished I had let her die." Shield bowed her head. "I told her family everything, and let them Share all the moments they could bear. Her father forgave me, and though her mother didn't say the words, I could see her understanding. Her sisters cursed me. Her brother," she smiled a little, "wanted to challenge me, but he's too young. I told him that, when he's grown, if he stills feels this way, I will give him the honor."

"You aren't to blame," Shatter told her again. "She made a decision. As hard as it was to watch, she walked to the Ring and triggered it herself. She did."

"But I've seen soldiers go through similar trauma. Seen them fall into the despair I saw in her eyes. I shouldn't have left her side. I could have stopped her."

"I don't know that you could have, Shield. She was determined."

Shield shook her head, but didn't dispute the assertion.

Shatter sighed. "There are things we can make up for, and things we just have to live with. You'll have to decide which this is. You're a good soldier, though. You've saved many lives, including mine. Don't walk away from everything you've been."

"I feel like I'm walking toward something, not away. I just don't know what it is yet," Shield admitted.

"Whatever that turns out to be, then, I'll support you," Shatter promised, in her best older sister voice. "I wish you would take the position the Queen offered you in the meantime, though."

Shield looked at her, surprised.

"Flora told me."

"I just can't think about putting on the uniform again. I see everyone looking at me. I just can't." She rubbed a hand over her head. She seemed surprised to feel the rough stubble.

"You must follow your path," Shatter said with resignation. "Goddess guide you."

"Thank you, Captain. I will remember everything you've said, and everything you taught me."

Shield stood, and left, with a crisp wave to the others.

The rest of the day went by, and the evening meal was brought. Flora still did not come. Another soldier brought their food, coming and going without a word. Shatter tried to question him, but he ignored her.

Min looked worried, but Shatter simply said, "She must be with her family."

The next morning, they were woken by loud voices in the hall. Shatter recognized Flora's voice through the door, but couldn't understand her words. After a few minutes of silence, the door opened, and another soldier entered. He was dressed in the blue uniform of Air. He motioned them back from the cell bars, and brought in the morning meal.

"What was that about?" Shatter asked. "Where's Flora?"

"No visitors," the soldier replied simply, setting down the tray.

"On whose orders?" Shatter demanded.

The soldier ignored her, shutting the cell door with a bang. He took a moment, looking at them, sizing them up. Steel stood, and joined Shatter at the cell door.

"Something interesting, soldier?" she asked.

His gaze went to Raven, who was also standing now. The atmosphere in the room became heavy with tension. His eyes moved to Min, who was still sitting on her cot. He got a small smile. Raven moved to block his eyeline.

"Soldier," Shatter said, in her most commanding voice. "We asked you a question."

Habit snapped him back to face Shatter. "You have no command here," he reminded her. "I'm following orders."

"Whose orders?" Steel stressed.

"The Captain's," he answered. Then, with a grin, he left, shutting the outer door loudly.

Steel and Shatter looked at each other. Min stood, and went to Raven's side.

"What was that all about?" she asked.

"Something's changed," Shatter announced. "I don't like it. That wasn't a soldier of the Queen's Guard. They've been the ones guarding us, until today."

"I didn't like his eyes," Min commented.

"We must eat," Shatter decreed. "And be ready. I don't like this." Steel and Raven nodded in agreement.

☾ ♒ ☼

They heard nothing — except the occasional sound from the changing of the guard outside — and saw no one, for the remainder of the day.

After sunset, they heard many feet outside. The door opened, and six soldiers of Air entered. A Sergeant — who was carrying a chest — and a Captain followed. The Captain sized them up. He gestured to the Sergeant.

"Get their bonds changed," he commanded.

"Captain Hooklance, what are you doing here?" Shatter asked, as one of the soldiers opened the cell door and pulled her out. "Where is Shattersteel?"

"He has business elsewhere," Hooklance replied. The Sergeant removed the bonds with the chain from Shatter and replaced them

333

with steel cuffs — from the chest he had been carrying — that held her wrists together in front of her. The others were brought out of the cell, and had their bonds changed as well.

Shatter could feel that the anti-Magic-Warding properties of their new cuffs were even stronger than the old ones. Anxiety rose in her belly. She looked at Steel, and could see the same thing on her face.

Min was last, and when she didn't stand quickly enough for the Sergeant, he grabbed her, and hauled her upright.

"Careful," Raven warned, moving toward him. She was stopped by a soldier of Air.

"I can stand," Min assured him, pulling out of his grasp.

Steel made a move toward her.

"Control your soldiers, Shatterstaff," Hooklance ordered.

"I'm not a Captain anymore," Shatter replied, but she motioned to Steel and Raven to stand down.

Min stared the Sergeant down. He hesitated, until Hooklance cleared his throat, at which time, the Sergeant finally moved to change her bonds. Then, they were lined up, a soldier of Air between each of them, and marched out of the room. Hooklance led them through empty halls, moving down through the bowels of the castle.

Shatter's anxiety grew into fear as she figured out where they were going. She glanced back, and saw that Steel and Raven had discerned their probable destination as well. They exchanged nods. Steel's fingers moved.

Finally, they reached a door. The Sergeant opened it, and they were led inside. The smell of running water was strong. The chamber was round, with a swift stream running through it. They were pushed to the edge of the water. The door closed behind them with a dead thunk.

Shatter and the others turned around. Each of the soldiers of Air, except Hooklance, was picking up a crossbow. Min uttered a cry of surprise.

"So, you've betrayed us," Shatter said calmly, hiding her fear.

"I haven't betrayed you. Your Queen betrayed us," Hooklance said. "She allowed the Humans in. Allowed those half-breeds to grow. Allowed her Heir to take up with a Human. She forced peace, when there should have been war. The new Queen will make sure the Humans are put in their place."

"And you'll be her Lord," Shatter stated.

"I will be the one who does what needs to be done." He gestured for his soldiers to raise their bows.

"At least give me the honor of a soldier's death," Shatter demanded. "Shattersteel said he beat you every time. Let me have a chance. I want to see if you're as weak as he said you were."

Hooklance curled his lip. "He lies. I never lost to him. Nor would I lose to you."

"If that's the lie you tell yourself." Shatter shrugged. "I hope your men can see your dishonor. Killing brave soldiers without a chance to defend themselves." She looked over the line of crossbow-wielding Air soldiers. "What kind of leader is that? What kind of Captain?"

"You waste your breath. They're loyal to me."

Shatter shrugged. "I just think you're afraid. You know I can beat you. You know it, and they know it." She shrugged again. Behind her, Shatter heard a splash. Hoping the Goddess was with her, she struck again. "I die knowing that I'm the better soldier. You'll never know."

Hooklance looked over his men. He saw a few raised eyes. Making a decision, he ordered, "Keep bows on them." He took off his sword belt, and handed it to the Sergeant. He pulled a knife.

"So, better soldier," he taunted, moving closer. Shatter stepped out of the line, and toward the center of the room. "You should be able to defeat me with your hands bound."

"You have no honor," Shatter spat. "But I'm sure I can."

Hooklance lunged, and Shatter blocked. She dodged a sweep from his leg, and kicked him in the side. Hooklance stumbled back.

"He was right. You are worse," Shatter taunted.

Hooklance yelled, and lunged, with his knife clenched in both fists. Shatter blocked the blow with her bound hands, then used her left hand to grab his fists.

As they struggled back and forth, Hooklance snarled in her face, "Fool! I'll order them to fire."

Shatter smiled. Her right arm disappeared. Shocked, and off balance, Hooklance was pulled forward. Her right arm reappeared, free of its bond, and she hammered him in the chest twice. Still moving forward, Hooklance lost his knife, as Shatter used all her anger to strike him with both hands on the back of his neck. He went down, with a grunt.

The soldiers were slow to react. Behind them, fists hammered at the door.

"Open, in the name of the Queen!" a strong voice called.

A form exploded out of the water. A wave of Power swept through the room at waist level. With multiple clangs, the prisoners' bonds hit the floor.

"Shield!" Min yelled, conjuring one right in front of the soldiers of Air. Three fired. The bolts shattered on the Shield, and threw splinters back in the archers' faces. Steel and Raven charged two who hadn't fired, throwing them against the wall. Min gestured the last soldier of Air's crossbow out of his hands. She used it to knock the Sergeant — who was belatedly moving to help his Captain — to the floor. Shatter kept Hooklance from rising by driving her knee into his back.

The door burst open, and Halfwing, his sons, and several other soldier Fairies rushed in, took down the remaining soldiers of Air, and disarmed them. Halfwing nodded as he saw Shatter rise.

Raven turned, and saw Shieldbreaker standing in the water behind her, dripping. She smiled, and helped Shield out of the stream.

"How?" Shatter asked as she gripped arms with Halfwing.

"It was all Flora." He gestured to the door as Flora entered, flanked by Goldberry and another soldier in the silver of the Queen's Guard.

"When I couldn't get to you," Flora said, "I went to Halfwing. He told me Lord Oberon and Captain Shattersteel had been sent away because of an attack by the Humans, and that soldiers of Air were now guarding you."

"I never trusted this bastard." Halfwing kicked the prone Hooklance. "He was too close to the Three Sisters. So, I left watchers." He smiled at his young son. "When this one saw where they were taking all of you, I knew. A quick message to Flora, and here we are."

"It's a good thing I used to play in these tunnels," Shield said, shaking her wings. "I know how to get around."

"I fear for the Queen," Shatter said. "He said something about a new Queen."

The other soldiers were binding — and stripping weapons from — the soldiers of Air. Steel wrenched Hooklance's head up from the floor. "What are you planning?" she demanded.

Hooklance spit on her. Steel hit his head on the ground until he was unconscious.

"We'd better get to the Queen's quarters," Flora said.

"Can you take me?" Shatter asked, as she put on Hooklance's sword.

"Yes," Flora agreed, taking her arm.

"We'll take the others," Goldberry said. "I can bring Steel and Raven. Shield, bring Min."

There were nods all around as everyone re-armed themselves.

"I'll alert the castle," Halfwing offered. "Who knows how far this goes, and who can be trusted."

Shatter gripped her father's arm. "Goddess guide you," she beseeched.

"And you, too," he replied.

Shatter looked around, and saw that everyone was ready. She took Flora's hand, and they disappeared.

Chapter Thirty
Through the Rings

"Drop the Ward on the door!" Gren demanded.

"No," the Queen responded defiantly.

Gren held a blacksilk blade closer to her eldest sister's face. "You know what this can do."

"I do," Zellandine confirmed calmly, "but I cannot release the Ward."

Gren's frustration was evident. She moved the blade closer to her sister's neck.

"She cannot release the Ward alone," Miranda confirmed from her chair. "It's anchored into the stone of the castle. Once triggered, it takes all three of us to release." She gestured to Lady Titania, who sat in a chair beside her. "And we will not allow that to happen."

Gren growled in frustration, and stepped away from the Queen. "Make sure their bonds are tight," she ordered the two soldiers of Air who stood behind the Paramount and the Lady. "There must be another way out."

"There isn't," the Queen said flatly. "My Ring is locked. That is the only door in or out. You're trapped, Sister. Let Us go, and We will grant you mercy."

Gren and her soldiers had stormed into the Queen's chambers. The Queen's Guard had reacted quickly, but found themselves no match for the blacksilk bolts of Gren's soldiers. Only one had lived through the first barrage. She had managed to kill two of Gren's soldiers before succumbing to multiple hits.

Titania and Miranda had also reacted quickly: Miranda had triggered the Ward on the door, while Titania had struck down two more soldiers of Air with Silverfire.

Gren had been too quick, however, and had the Queen at blacksilk bladepoint in an instant. Seeing their Queen in danger, the other two had allowed themselves to be bound.

Now, trapped, Gren paced the room, kicking at the bodies of the fallen Queen's Guard soldiers.

"You can't win," the Queen proclaimed. "No matter how many soldiers of Air you've corrupted, the rest of my Guard will return soon. Your coup will be short-lived."

"You put too much faith in Lord Oberon and Captain Shattersteel. We have plans for them."

"Curse you," Titania said, struggling in her bonds. "If you hurt him. . . ."

"You are in no position to curse," Gren retorted, approaching Titania and setting the point of the blacksilk blade against her chest. Titania's eyes grew in fear, but she didn't move.

"All you have to do, Sister," Gren said, her eyes not leaving Titania's, "is release the door and go out with us. We will allow you to step down, and go into exile."

She turned, and continued, "Then, we will rule this Realm, as it should be ruled."

"There's only room on the throne for one," Zellandine reminded her. "I don't think Tra or Dina will let you sit on it. Your only chance is to put down your weapon, and release Us. You might even keep your wings."

Gren moved to stand over Miranda. She hovered the blade over her fingers. "You said it takes all three of you. Well, I know these blades kill, but how fast, I wonder, if I start removing fingers?" She giggled. "How much pain can you withstand until you break?"

"I will never betray my Queen," Miranda swore.

Gren stepped back. Her expression changed, as a thought occurred to her.

"Yes. Your Queen. How much would you do to protect your Queen?" Gren went over and pushed Zellandine into a chair. Her blade hovered over the Queen's hand. "How much?"

"Get away from her, you foul creature!"

Gren turned, and saw Shatter and Flora standing by the Ring. Shatter drew her sword, and Flora picked up a fallen blade. Together, they advanced on Gren.

"Hold them!" Gren cried, dodging behind the Queen, her blade diving to Zellandine's neck. The soldiers of Air holding Miranda and Titania did the same with their captives.

"Do not come any closer," Gren warned, "or their blood will flow."
Shatter took another step.

"Foul thing," Flora growled. "I should have strangled you when you were a baby."

"But you didn't, Mum," Gren mocked. She twitched the blade. Zellandine sat very still.

Shatter addressed the other soldiers. "You're betraying the Queen. What of your Oath?"

Behind Shatter, Steel and Goldberry appeared in the Ring. Steel sized up the situation swiftly and drew her sword. Gren tightened her grip on the Queen.

"Don't bring any more through," she threatened, "or I'll kill her."

"Then you'll have no shield," Steel grunted. She moved closer to the soldiers of Air holding Miranda and Titania.

Silverfire danced over Goldberry's hands. "I can smell your corruption." She moved to shield Flora. "Goddess curse you."

"Curse you, foolish girl. Looks like Hooklance can't be relied upon to perform even a simple task." Gren looked at the two soldiers of Air. "Whoever kills the most can be Captain."

They looked at each other. The one holding Miranda smiled, and raised his blade. But his arm suddenly reversed, and the blade plunged into his own chest. Raven appeared out of a Shadow, and kicked the other soldier firmly away from Titania. Steel pounced on him, kicking his blade away, and rendering him unconscious with a second powerful kick.

"No!" Gren yelled as Shatter moved closer. "Curse you, Sister," she whispered, as she drove her blade into Zellandine's shoulder. She then kicked the chair over, and dodged a line of Silverfire from Goldberry.

Crying out incoherently, Goldberry cast again. Gren, giggling, put up a Shield, and locked eyes with Flora, who was standing still in shock. "Goodbye." She waved, touched her Torc, and disappeared.

Raven cut Miranda and Titania loose, and Miranda ran straight to the Queen. Flora was already there.

"We must remove the blade," Flora advised the Paramount, "or corruption will flow into her."

Miranda wrapped her hands in cloth and pulled the blade out. The Queen gasped. Flora pushed more cloth into the wound, sending Healing into the Queen with it.

Min and Shield appeared in the Ring. Shield ran to help Flora and Miranda with the Queen. Titania motioned to Shatter.

"Captain," she said. "I sense more of the rebels outside. They're trying to break the Ward on the door."

"Where can we go, My Lady?" Shatter motioned for Steel to bind the other soldier of Air.

"We don't know how far the corruption goes. All the Rings are suspect. We need a place unknown to the Three Sisters."

"The Exile Queen's mountain," Min suggested, as she helped Raven move the body of the soldier of Air she had killed. "The Three Sisters don't know that Ring."

"That Ring is heavily Warded, and will be stronger than when I was last there, though," Miranda cautioned from the floor. She was pouring her own Healing into the Queen, alongside Flora and Shield.

"You did it before. You can do it again," Flora said confidently.

"I don't know," Miranda replied doubtfully. "Talia's strong, and if she's fallen to the blood, she might have made the Wards lethal."

"What about the ruins?" Steel suggested.

"Same problem," Shatter reminded them. "Talia might have increased the power of the Wards there as well."

Zellandine grabbed Flora, and pulled her close. "My Geode," she whispered.

Flora hesitated. A bang from outside the door echoed through the room.

"Those Wards won't hold much longer," Titania warned.

"Go," Miranda urged Flora. "I can hold the Healing."

Flora stood, and ran to the Queen's bedchamber.

"We're going to need more supplies," Talia announced. She was sitting across from Elanor, who was still working on a Ring bracelet for her. Her eyes narrowed.

"We can't go to Realm's End," Talia continued, "so we must find other Rings to use." She looked at Elanor, expecting a response.

Elanor dropped the half-completed length of chain to the table. "You control my body, and my Power. If you need me to have conversations with you, and help plan your next move, you'll have to put more controls in my mind. Or rip the information out." She brushed a hand over her eyes. "Maybe that would be better: you might kill me, and that would be preferable to living with the person you've become."

Talia stood up. "How dare you!" she started, but then, she suddenly stopped, and went still. Elanor could see the tiny flickers of her aura. Taking a risk, she got closer, and touched Talia's arm. She fell into a Send being transmitted through a Geode Web.

"Talia, we need your help," the Queen begged. Elanor could see the darkness in Zellandine's aura: it was spreading from her shoulder.

"We're trapped, and none of our Rings are safe. Yours is the only one we can trust."

"You're trying to trick me," Talia accused. "You want me to drop my Wards, and then you'll come and capture me. I will not."

The Send was wrenched away from the Queen, and Miranda's powerful presence filled the Web in her place. *"Your mother is severely wounded, and may be dying,"* she advised Talia. She pulled Talia and Elanor's Sight to her. *"Look around."* Miranda Showed them the ruins of the Queen's chamber: the dead Queen's Guards, and the dead Air soldiers. Miranda opened her Sight, and Showed Talia the door, and the strong Wards being assaulted from the outside. *"We need to escape. If you don't do this, we'll all die. Your mother will die. Flora, and all the others, will die."* She Showed Shatter, Min, and the others, all ready for whatever came next. *"I understand your pain and reluctance, but you must put them away now. Your Aunts are trying to kidnap or kill the Queen and take over the Realm. We must not let them. They're using blackblades."*

Talia hesitated. Doubt and fear warred in her mind. Miranda was powerful enough to make such Illusions: this could still be a trick.

"But it isn't," Elanor argued. "Look: I can See the aura of Shatter's arm. Miranda wouldn't know to fake that. They're in danger! We must help."

"Get out of my mind," Talia snarled, as she tried to Push Elanor out. She was too weak, though.

"What's wrong?" Miranda asked, sensing Talia's lack of Power.

"There's a barrier in my mind, keeping me from my Power," Talia admitted. "Must've come from the backlash. Only blood allows me to get around it."

"Barrier, backlash," Miranda thought quickly. "Talia, I know what it could be."

Talia brightened. *"Tell me."*

"Let us through, and I will," Miranda promised.

"Curse you," Talia said. "You deny me again."

"I will tell you all I know, but we must escape first." Miranda's voice hardened. "Allow us to die, or be captured, and you'll be trapped forever in the cycle of blood lust. You'll never be free. I can help you."

"Please, Talia," the Queen's voice begged, low and full of pain. *"I need you."* Talia could See the darkness creeping into her mother's wings.

Talia couldn't think. Her wall loomed up even larger in her mind, and threatened to crush her. Pain, grief, and the memory of all her horrible deeds hovered over her.

A gasp of pain made Talia open her eyes. Elanor had ripped her hand open on the edge of the table, and was wiping her blood on Talia's arm.

"I do this of my own free will," Elanor informed her. "To save my Sisters."

Talia felt the warmth flowing through her. The wall retreated, and she began to glow.

"The Ward will be down in a moment," she Sent to Miranda. "Do not betray me."

Talia stood up, and moved to the Ring. She held up her hands, and began to alter the Weave of the Wards.

☾ ཥྀ ☼

Miranda looked up. She could sense that Talia would honor her words.

"Everyone!" she shouted. "Join hands. I must Give you the Frequency of the Ring."

"Only Lady Titania needs it," Shatter said. "The rest of us already have it."

"What of my sister and mother, and everyone else?" Flora asked, her worry for her family evident in her shaky voice.

"We can only hope that they have escaped," Miranda replied, in an attempt to comfort her. She felt more strikes on the Ward. "We must hurry. Goddess guide them to safety."

Flora looked stricken, but helped Shatter pick up the Queen and carry her to the Ring.

"I will go first," Steel volunteered. "Just in case."

"No, I will go first," the Queen countered. "With the help of your brave Captain." Weakly, she grabbed Flora's hand. "And you, too, Mum."

Not waiting for Flora to respond, Shatter pushed them into the Ring, and took them through.

Min grabbed the dropped Geode, and moved to the Ring with Raven.

Miranda moved up behind Titania, who was holding the Ward.

"It won't be long now. I can feel the Three Sisters all beating on the Wards together." Titania looked at Miranda. "I don't know if it will hold long enough for us to travel."

Miranda kissed her on the cheek. "I'll hold it. Go." She gestured to the Ring. Steel and Goldberry had just disappeared.

"No. We can't lose you. We need your wisdom. We need your Power. I need your counsel."

"You know I'm the only one who can hold them long enough." She kissed Titania's forehead. "Your children are safe. They were evacuated through the Tower of Learning. They're in your secret place."

"Miranda, I can't leave you," Titania said again. "They'll do horrible things to you."

"No, they won't," Miranda contradicted. "Go. As the student you once were, obey me. Escape." Miranda took the controls of the Wards from Titania, and gave her a Push with her Power. "Go. Tell Oberon."

Titania kissed her cheek, and ran for the Ring.

"Attention all Fairies," Miranda Sent as widely and as strongly as she could. "Those Loyal to Queen Zellandine should escape any way they can. The Three Sisters of the Queen seek to depose her. They are Blood Cult members, and pervert our ways. Flee, and resist."

Titania Saw the Wards begin to crack. Miranda stood firm. Titania felt something building.

"Goodbye," she said softly, and disappeared.

Miranda felt Titania leave, and stepped back to the Ring. She took the Weave in her Power. She twisted and pulled, yanking it from the Realm. The door opened. The Three Sisters entered, flanked by soldiers of Air.

"We have you now," Dina gloated.

"No, you don't," Miranda disagreed placidly. She took every scrap of Power and potential within herself, and smashed them into the broken Weave of the Ring.

The Three Sisters screamed, running for cover and attempting to conjure Shields.

The room exploded in Silverfire and backlash from the powerful Paramount's sacrifice.

☾ ♒ ☼

Titania stumbled out of the Ring, and fell to her knees.

"Where's Miranda?" Talia demanded, pulling the Queen's Justice up. "Where is she?"

Titania could only shake her head. Tears began to flow.

"Where?" Talia asked again, but she let her uncle's wife go without waiting for a response. Instead, she went to the Ring, and searched for the Queen's Ring. It was gone.

Talia whirled. Titania was being helped to a seat by Raven.

"Where is she?" Talia shouted. "She promised me."

"She's gone!" Titania shouted back. "She sacrificed herself for us. For you!" She pointed at Talia.

Talia moved toward Titania, fire in her eyes, her aura glowing red.

"Talia," Flora called. "Your mother." Talia didn't move. "She needs you," Flora called again.

Talia turned. The Queen lay on the floor, not far from the Ring. Her hair was spread out like a pool around her. Shield, Min, and Goldberry were lined up on one side, all deep in a Circle, pouring Healing into her. Flora sat, holding Zellandine's head.

Talia knelt. The Queen's eyes opened. They were pale, paler than Talia remembered.

"She's . . .," Flora started.

"I'm dying," Zellandine finished. She made a motion. "Children, there is nothing more you can do." Min looked at Flora, who nodded. Min, Shield, and Goldberry stood up, and left Flora and Talia alone with the Queen.

"Daughter," Zellandine said, weakly. "I can feel the darkness overtaking me. I cannot fight it. I wish we had more time." She stopped, grimacing.

"No," Talia said. "I have the strength: we can fight this." She grabbed her mother's hand. "I cannot lose you."

"There is no strength in the Realm that can stop this," the Queen said, her voice becoming thinner. "The Goddess calls me back to the Cycle. I must go."

"No," Talia cried. "No! I'm sorry, so sorry." She cried.

"Talia, Daughter." Zellandine reached out with her free hand to touch Talia's face. "Let go of your pain. Let go of this wall in your mind. These ladies will help you. You can face it. Let go."

The Queen's hand fell away, and Talia felt her spirit depart.

Talia heard Flora begin to cry, and heard the others fall to their knees and cry or sob. Talia just sat, holding onto Zellandine's quickly cooling hand. She was gone.

Talia crossed her mother's hands over her still chest. With a practiced motion, Talia pushed this new pain and grief behind her wall. Her anger, however, she kept. She rose.

No one else was standing. Talia looked over the group, taking stock of those who remained. Then she strode over to Steel. She grabbed her chin, and forced it up.

"Who?"

Steel looked confused; her eyes were filled with tears.

"Who killed her?" Talia clarified.

"Gren." Steel began to stand after answering.

"No," Talia said, pushing her back down. "I will go alone."

Talia strode to the Ring. From behind, she heard her name, but she neither stopped nor turned. As she crossed the line of the Ring, her hand reached out, and Shatter's fallen sword flew to it. Then, she disappeared.

Chapter Thirty-One
Resentment

Talia appeared in the Heir's Garden at Fae-Treval. She cast a Shadow, and darted to the side. She scanned, trying to determine whether anyone had seen her arrive.

Nothing.

After a moment, she relaxed, and stepped back onto the path. The flowers and plants were overgrown, and ill-kept. There was barely a path through the underbrush, which had run wild.

'The Twins would cry if they could see this,' a voice said in her mind.

"I wish they could see it," Talia replied out loud.

The voice faded into the background.

Talia moved toward the wall. She reached out. There were many Fairies moving around both the castle and the palace, but none were near the Garden. She reached the door, and opened it carefully. The hall beyond was dark. She could hear voices — and fighting — further down to the left, but nothing to the right. She exited, making sure to close the door firmly behind her.

'The main Hall,' she thought. 'That's where they'll be. Reveling in their victory.' Her hand tightened on the hilt of Shatter's sword.

She turned a corner, and bumped into a group of Leather- and Feather-wings. They were all armed, and blood-spattered.

The Leather-wing in the lead started back, his face broadcasting his horror at her twisted wings.

Talia took the initiative. "Who do you serve?" she demanded.

After a small hesitation, he said, "The true Queens. The Three Sisters."

"Good." Talia smiled. She called on everything she had learned from Halfwing, Shatter, Steel, and all her other teachers. She pulled it all into a Weave of brutality and Power with the blade. She surrendered herself to the Weave. "I only need one," she said, as the Power took over.

Talia didn't know how long it took — a three-count, or a 10,000 count — but when the Weave ended, she was the only one still standing. The leader was slumped against the wall, his handless arms held out in front of him. They spurted blood as he waved them at her helplessly. His wings were gone, buried under the bodies surrounding them.

Talia approached him. She stuck her sword upright into the body of another Leather-wing as a temporary scabbard. She grabbed the leader's arms, and covered the wounds with her hands, both Healing him and taking in his blood. Power flowed back into her, replacing all that she had used.

In a moment, he settled down, and looked at her with glazed eyes.

"Where are they?" she asked, while she penetrated his mind, looking for all the information she could find. She also set controls, as he struggled to speak.

"They're in the room past the throne," he told her.

"Good," she said. Talia contemplated killing him, but decided she might need more blood.

"Stand up," she commanded.

He struggled to his feet.

Talia retrieved her borrowed sword. A sound behind her made her turn.

"I guess you paid more attention than I gave you credit for."

Halfwing, several soldiers, and a handful of other Fairy citizens of the castle were standing in the hallway. Shock and horror were evident on most faces, even those of the experienced soldiers. Halfwing looked both shocked and proud.

"Who do you serve?" Talia demanded. She raised her sword. Most retreated, but Halfwing stood his ground as Talia approached.

"The one true Queen: Zellandine."

Talia lowered her sword. She looked over the Fairies Halfwing had gathered. They all looked scared. Talia bent down, and ripped a large button from the uniform of one of the dead Fairies. She pushed a small Weave into it.

"Here," she said, pushing it into her old teacher's hand. "This will allow you through the door into my Garden." She Sent to him, *"That's the Frequency of a safe Ring. Take as many as you can there. But be careful: no traitors will be allowed in."*

"As you say, My Lady," Halfwing said with a short bow.

Talia turned to go.

"My son can guide you," Halfwing offered, calling Dougal up.

"No. I have a guide. You'll need him, and I will not be responsible for another life."

Halfwing considered her. "I taught you well, but not that well. It may be, Lady, that there is more to you than I yet understand."

"Just take them, and go. I need to find my Aunts."

"Merry-Weather and Luna are with them," Halfwing informed her. "Go with the Goddess."

"Keep your sword ready," Talia reminded him. She turned, grabbing the handless Leather-wing and pushing him forward.

Halfwing watched her go. His son looked at him. "Was that the Heir?"

"I'm not sure," Halfwing replied honestly. "But we need to get these Fairies out. Come on." He gestured to the others. "We have an escape now."

"Praise the Goddess," came the relieved response.

$$\left(\!\!\begin{smallmatrix}\\\end{smallmatrix}\right.\;\mathrm{\approx}\;\mathrm{\diamond}$$

Talia approached the door to the Queen's relaxation chamber behind the throne room. She and her guide had moved around the perimeter under a Shadow. There were several Fairies, mostly soldiers in the Air uniform, milling about. They had found some wine, and were drinking. Arguments, and even a few actual fights, were starting to break out.

Dead soldiers of the Queen's Guard — some hacked apart, but most filled with crossbow bolts — lay everywhere, like the horrible pin dolls that Flora used to make. Talia didn't look too closely, as she knew that some of the faces would be familiar, and it brought back images of Harpoon, Helm, and Honor to her mind. She pushed those images back. She could still see black wings everywhere.

There were four guards at the door. Talia remembered that there was an anteroom before the Queen's main rest area. She hoped her Aunts would be in the second room.

She looked around. There were too many soldiers about; she couldn't strike them all down. With a whispered, "Stay," to her guide, she crept to one of the dead. Avoiding the face, she pulled several bolts from the fallen soldier's body. She was glad to see that they weren't tipped with blackblades. She gathered them into one hand, shoved her sword through her belt, and returned to the handless soldier, still standing where she had left him.

'Something more subtle, perhaps?' a voice suggested.

Talia smiled. She cast an Illusion over herself. Her blood-splattered clothes became the blue of Air. Her wings became feathered, and full. As a last touch, her hair turned to red, and flowed in full waves down both her back and front.

'How you would fly or fight with all that,' the voice commented, 'I do not know.'

'It's only to get through the door,' she replied. Then, with all her confidence and arrogance on ready display, she pushed her prisoner up to the door.

"I have someone for the Three Sisters," she announced to the guards.

They looked at her, bored. The only woman looked at her with a side eye.

"What is he worth to them?" she asked.

"And what about his hands?" another laughed.

"He was trying to escape in an Air uniform," she told them. "I think he knows where some of the old Queen's people are hiding. Maybe even that Halfwing bastard." She grinned at the woman. "He tried to bluff past me. Put his hands where he shouldn't have."

"He'll never do that again," the woman laughed in return. She took a long look at him. Talia became nervous. If the soldier knew her guide, she would be in trouble.

"Too bad," the soldier finally said. "He's not too bad to look at. But now he's of no use to me."

Talia returned the laugh. "So, can I take him in?"

"The Sisters are having fun with some others now, but yeah." She gestured. "Go on in."

One of the male soldiers opened the door, and gestured her into the anteroom.

"Thank you," Talia said, pushing her guide in before her. The door closed behind her, and she cast a quick Lock Spell on it.

Inside were two more soldiers. They were not amused. Both were large, and battle-scarred. They approached, keeping to Talia's right and left.

"Who are you, and who's this?" the one on the left asked.

"I am your doom," Talia proclaimed, propelling the bolts she held in her hand into their heads with a flick. She followed with a quick Silence Spell to cover their falls to the floor.

Talia released her Illusion, and took in the room. It was largely as she remembered, but full of broken chairs and bottles now. Two more of the Queen's Guard lay by the door. They had given a better account of themselves: both their swords were covered in blood and feathers. But they were still dead.

"Sit down," she instructed her prisoner, directing him to sit with his back to the outer door. She grabbed a silver tray from a stand along the wall. She put the tray in his lap, and set several stones holding Redfire on it.

"Don't move," she ordered him, waving her hand over the stones, altering the Weave to trigger if they were disturbed. "You've been helpful," she told him. She nicked his arm with her last arrow, and rubbed the blood over her arms and face. She felt a sun come to life in her body. She nicked her prisoner's other arm, and left him to bleed.

Full of Power, she moved to the inner door. Dispelling the Silence, she put her ear to the wood.

"Where are they?" a voice yelled. Dina.

"Give me the Frequency!" Tra.

"I will not." This came from Merry-Weather.

"She only has a few more fingers," Gren taunted. "She will no longer make pretty things for the Queen."

"Goddess, but you're monsters," Merry-Weather cursed. "You hid it well, but now it comes out. Curse you."

"Poor Luna," Gren chortled with glee. "She passed out again."

"She can only last so long," Dina warned.

"Why don't you bring out the blacksilk blade, Sister?" Tra suggested, cold filling her voice. "That will force her to hurry up and make a decision: see her daughter die, or tell us what we need to know."

"Goddess curse you to a deep dirt grave," Merry-Weather spat. "Foul and evil. I will not."

"Then you will watch her die," Tra decreed. "And then we will start on the rest of your family."

"Wake her up," Dina commanded. "I want her to see her mother's eyes as she dies."

Gren giggled again. Talia heard a violent slap.

"Curse you!" Merry-Weather cried again.

Talia gathered all her Power, and flung the door open. She burst into the room, Redfire crackling on her fingers.

In the middle of the room, Luna sat slumped in a chair, with Gren standing over her. To her right stood Merry-Weather, flanked by Dina and Tra. A blood-stained knife lay in Gren's hand. The side of her head was wrapped in a bloody bandage. Dina's hands were also wrapped, and both of Tra's eyes were covered.

With a cry of pain and anger, Talia cast Redfire at Gren, striking her on the shoulder, and throwing her against the far wall. Talia cast again, but Gren's Shield stopped the Spell, the fire parting and flowing away innocuously.

Merry-Weather grabbed Tra's arm, and pulled her into Dina, knocking them both down. She then ran to Luna, pulling her out of the chair, and out of the way of Talia's fire.

Dina took one look at the fury on Talia's face. Without a word, she grabbed Tra's hand, touched her neck, and disappeared.

Talia stepped closer to Gren, who was huddled behind her Shield. Talia poured more fire at it, but it didn't break.

"She anchored it to the floor," Merry-Weather offered, standing. She was helping Luna stand, and wrapping the bloody remains of her hands as she did so.

"I'm better than you," Gren taunted. "It will last long enough for my sisters to return."

Talia looked around, and saw a blackblade on the floor. She wrapped her hand, and picked it up. The darkness and corruption screamed in her mind. She walked up to Gren's Shield, and began to run the blade over the iridescent surface. Sparks began to rain down.

Gren began to panic.

"You killed my mother," Talia said, calmly running the blade over the surface again. "You'll pay for that."

"You can't kill me," Gren gloated. "Don't you know? The ancient Fairies made it a curse to hurt our family. You will be. . . ." She lost her words to the screech of the blade on her Shield.

"That's a lie. You killed your own sister." She set the point of the blackblade on the Shield, and began to push. The Shield sparked, and began to bend.

"I didn't kill her," Gren countered, now grinning. "The blade killed her. That blade."

Talia stopped. She looked at the blade in her hand. "I will punish you for your crimes. You killed my mother. You acted to kill my daughter. Any punishment will be well worth it if I kill you."

"Looks like you've already been punished," Gren taunted. "Backlash for something?"

"Foul creature," Merry-Weather cursed. "Talia, we need to escape. They'll be back."

"Not until I get justice, both for the Queen and for my daughter."

Something changed in Gren. "Oh, you will be so disappointed," she said, an evil light in her eye. "We didn't kill your daughter."

"Wingless killed her," Talia interrupted. "He's your plaything and tool. You gave the orders."

"No," Gren crowed. "I wanted to, but they had other ideas." Her smile became lopsided. "They put controls in my mind. I can't tell you that she's alive, and that we gave. . . ." Gren's confession ended in a gurgle, as her body twitched, and blood poured from her mouth.

"Curse!" Talia swore, reaching for the body, as the Shield fell with Gren's death. Talia grabbed the dead woman's hair, and forced her way into her Aunt's mind. Too late: Gren's mind was gone, and whatever she had been trying to say was gone with it.

Crying in frustration, Talia slammed Gren's head against the wall. She felt the skull crack. Another blow, and the head collapsed like a rotten fruit. Talia finally let go, and stood up. She turned around.

Merry-Weather was staring at her, with a mixture of horror and fear. "Alive? She's alive?" The horror of what had happened filled her voice. "Then it was all for nothing. All this," she gestured to the destroyed room. The blood. "All of this, for a deception. A horrible game, arranged by these evil, corrupt Fairies."

Talia began to rub her Aunt's blood and brains from her hands. She felt a sense of calm. "They would have attacked the Queen eventually. This was just an excuse. An extension of their resentment."

"Resentment!" Merry-Weather cried. "The palace and the castle are covered in the blood of Fairy killing Fairy. And all for 'resentment.' Goddess's mercy, what has become of you? I don't know you anymore. How can you just stand there? Your mother is dead. Her Realm is in chaos."

"Her killer is dead," Talia reminded Merry-Weather. She cocked her head. "They're getting ready to come in the first door. I left a surprise, but that won't keep them for long.

"Another army is on the way," Merry-Weather announced, breaking herself free from the horror of the situation with obvious difficulty. "One that supports the Three Sisters. We must flee."

Talia offered her hand. It was still sticky with blood. Merry-Weather stared at it. "Do you want the key to my Garden Ring, and the Frequency to the Exile Queen's mountain Ring? The others are there."

With evident distaste, Merry-Weather took her hand. Talia Sent her the information. "Go. I'll follow." With a gesture, a torc flew from a table into her hand. She passed it to Merry-Weather, who took a moment to wipe the blood off before settling it on her neck.

"Talia," Merry-Weather started, but Luna moaned, and she had to hold her still.

"I'll be along soon. Take her to her sister."

Merry-Weather nodded, and touched her neck. She and Luna disappeared.

Talia waited a moment, listening to the sounds of the outer door being breached. She sighed happily as she felt the Redfire flash through the approaching Fairies. She touched her Torc, and disappeared, just as the flames burst through the inner door.

☾ ⌇⌇⌇ ☼

The peace of the Secret Tower enveloped Talia. The noise receded. She could hear nothing beyond her own breathing.

The smell of age brought back memories, but no pain — only a bittersweet ache. 'This was the last place of happiness,' she thought. 'The last happiness of my old life.'

"She's alive," Talia said to the picture. "She's alive." Talia went to the picture, and put her hand on the painting itself.

"You've been in front of me all this time." She looked into the painted eyes of the Exile Queen. "You led me on this path. Now where do I go?" she demanded. "Where do I go? What will make all of this make sense? Where's the path for me?"

The painting didn't respond. Only aged silence remained in the room.

"Answer me!" Talia cried, pushing both her palms into the paint. "You've been leaving messages through time. Now, I need you, and you're silent. Curse you." Her fingers clutched at the painting, but couldn't gain purchase.

With another curse, she stepped back. Redfire bloomed in her hands. She held them up, with every intention of burning the painting, and maybe the whole tower. But then she stopped. Talia's eyes moved, following symbols that had become visible in the red light. Symbols that she had seen before. Symbols that she had found in the ancient scroll that had led her here. They circled the painting, and moved up to the ceiling. Talia raised her hands, following them. The Frequency of a new Ring became clear in her mind.

She clapped her hands together in glee, and extinguished the fire. "Thank you, Ancestor," she said reverently to the painting. "I understand. This is the beginning of another path. I'm like you: I'm a Servant of the Stars."

Moving with renewed purpose, she strode to the Ring. Fire bloomed again as she faced the bed, unmade and untouched since she and Bastile had lain there together. She wanted to burn it. Wanted to remove this reminder of her mistake.

'But then you wouldn't have Sunrise,' a voice reminded her.

Talia extinguished her flame. "You're right. I need to find her."

With a short bow to the painting, Talia disappeared.

Chapter Thirty-Two
The Queen's Pyre

Talia appeared in the library to controlled chaos. There were cries of pain and grief. Cries of despair, and cries of happiness.

Lady Titania ran up to Talia as she exited the Ring.

"My Queen, we need you."

"I am not your Queen," Talia said, trying to brush past her.

"But you are," Titania contradicted, grabbing Talia's arm. "There are decisions that must be made. Lord Oberon has contacted me. He has escaped, with most of his force. He has found sanctuary in one of the Elen towns. We need to strike back."

Talia pulled her arm out of Titania's grasp. "I can't make those decisions. You're the most senior person here. You can make them."

"Your people need their Queen," Titania said, gesturing to all the Fairies in the room. The level of noise decreased, as everyone noticed that Talia had returned. There was a quiet murmur at the appearance of her twisted wings and her blood-covered clothes.

"I am not the Queen they need," Talia declared. "Let me pass."

Titania stepped in front of her. Talia raised her hands. Titania did so, too, a Shield ready.

"I am not afraid of you," Titania informed Talia, her voice going harsh. "I know what you are, and what you're becoming."

Redfire danced on Talia's hands. Silence fell. Flora looked up from tending Luna. Fear filled her face.

Titania noted how far Talia had fallen. "You can't even summon Silverfire." Her voice softened. "Let go. We've all lost. Hate isn't what we need right now." She dropped her hands. "We need our Queen."

Talia looked over all the faces watching her. All that was left of her Ladies. Shatter and the few other survivors of The Nine. Familiar faces from the palace. Strangers. Children.

She closed her fists. The fire went out.

"Lady Titania," she said formally. "You have been by my mother's side longer than I have been alive. You have my complete trust. Will you help me guide our Fairies through this horrible time?"

Titania looked from Talia to the others, standing, sitting, and lying on the floor. "I would be honored, My Lady." She gripped Talia's arm.

A small cheer went up from those present who were still capable of such a thing. Talia caught Flora's eye. The maid smiled sadly.

"Mistress?"

Talia opened her eyes. She had been in meditation. Sleep was evading her again. Most days, meditation was enough. Flora was standing in the door.

"If you've come to talk to me about being Queen, you can go."

"I didn't," Flora said, coming in and sitting down across from her. "Luna made me come."

"I didn't realize she had that much influence on you."

"She doesn't, but she saw me watching your door, and told me to come speak to you."

Talia sighed. "If you're here to ask my forgiveness for leaving, you have it. I understand."

"No. That's not it." Flora reached out, but Talia kept her hands in her lap. After a long moment, Flora dropped hers.

"I," she started. "I wanted to see you. Wanted to know." She stopped again, overcome. She wrung her hands. "I want my daughter back," she finally sobbed. "I want the little girl I helped learn to fly. I want to see the girl who brought me that tiny, wounded bird and begged me to help it again. I want to see the young woman who came to me after her first kiss. And who needed me to check her Ward. I want to see again the woman who stood proudly at her mother's side. I want to be with the woman who defended her Ladies. The woman who comforted her best friend when she was hurt so badly. Where is she?" Flora reached out her hand to Talia again. Tears fell from her eyes.

Talia didn't move. "I don't know if she exists anymore," she admitted after a moment.

"Why?" Flora implored. "I know she's within you. Let her out. Let go of the anger. Let go of this quest for justice."

"I can't."

"Why?" Flora asked again.

"Because I can't face her."

Flora looked stricken.

"I can't face her," Talia continued. "After what I've done? I can't show her it was all for nothing. I must find my daughter. Only then will it have been worth it."

"You can't do this alone," Flora cautioned, trying to get through to her former charge. "If she's out there, we can help you find her." She made the Sign of the Three. "Goddess will guide us."

"No. You've all paid too much for my mistakes already. Too much for my arrogance. Too much for my trust of a man." Talia clenched her fists. "I will find her." 'If I have to kill every Human to do it,' she finished in her mind.

'And you might have to,' a voice answered.

"No. I will not let you leave again," Flora implored, reaching for Talia again.

Talia stood, avoiding her maid's grasping hands. "Flora, would you ask Lady Titania to join me before we go up to the Vigil for my mother?"

Flora sank back into herself. "Yes, My Lady," she whispered, standing.

$$\text{\char"263D} \approx \text{\char"263C}$$

The Vigil for Zellandine, Queen of the Fairies, was held on the summit of the Exile Queen's mountain. Talia stood at her head, still and silent, all night. She watched the moon rise, and the stars twinkle. The spot was narrow, and only a few could stand near, but all who were able either sat or stood with her throughout the long night.

Elanor, Goldberry, and Min stood, arm in arm, in a small bowl lined with moss. They watched Talia. Watched the moonlight play over her face. Saw her wings absorb the light, and give off only darkness. Watched for any change, any emotion at all. There was none. Elanor cried, remembering the last time she had been on this mountaintop.

Min cried for her missing love, and the knowledge that he might be lost forever.

Goldberry didn't cry: her Goddess Sight burned away any tears she produced, as she watched Talia under the moon and stars.

Flora, Luna, and Merry-Weather stood together, mourning the loss of the woman they had served for virtually all their lives. The one who had brought so much love into their lives. A powerful Queen, a loving partner, and a mother who had always tried to do the best for her Heir.

Shatter, Steel, Raven, and Shield stood, wings outstretched, at the corners of the Queen's litter, as silent guards for the Vigil.

Others came and went as they were able. Halfwing and his soldiers helped those who were too weak, but still wanted to pay a last tribute to their Queen.

As the moon sank, Titania arrived, and stood at Talia's shoulder. She had donned a Keeper's cloak. The Keeper hadn't made it to the Exile Queen's mountain. Her fate — like that of her Shrinekeepers — was unknown.

As the sun rose, the survivors came to the mountaintop: some on their wings, and others with the help of their Sisters and Brothers. No one was left behind.

Titania looked out over all the faces before her. She raised her arms, and the murmur of the crowd ceased.

"Servants of the Moon and Sun," she started, but her voice broke. She couldn't continue. Grief, and fear — both for her husband, and for her people — suddenly overwhelmed her. Goldberry rushed to her side, and supported her when she would have fallen. Goldberry looked at Talia, silently asking if she should take over.

Talia remained still. The moment stretched.

"Servants of the Moon and Sun," Talia finally said, in a strong voice that reached everyone. "We are here to Return our Queen, my mother, to the Cycle." Her voice remained strong, and did not break. "We beg the Goddess's mercy, that her spirit be received, and that she Return swiftly as a Servant. Mother of Waves, hear us. Zellandine was your Servant."

"Zellandine!" The cry arose from the lips of each of the gathered Fairies.

"Our Queen is gone," Talia said, her voice finally breaking. "She will Return."

She stepped back. All those around the Queen did so, too.

"Servants of the Moon and Sun, speed our Queen on her journey."

Red-gold flames leapt from the Queen's body, and billowed up into the air. The Power of all the Fairies Joined, and added to the pillar of flame. It rose high into the air, so high that it disappeared into the rising sun.

Then, with a snap, it was gone. The Queen's body was gone as well. Only a charred black circle marked the stone.

Into the quiet that covered the mountaintop, Talia spoke.

"I have asked Lady Titania to be my Regent. She will guide you through the trials to come. Her wisdom and strength will lead you to fight the corruption of the Three Sisters. Fight their evil. She will stand with you. With the mercy of the Goddess, we will prevail. I am not the Queen you need right now. When I return, I will be."

Talia walked off, to the stunned silence of the Fairies.

☾ ♒ ☼

The next day, Talia emerged from her small room. She bore a pack of supplies and food, and the sword she had taken to the palace was sheathed at her side. In the pack were the two Ephemeral Rings from Paramount Holly.

The survivors of her company stood around the Ring. Flora, Luna, and Merry-Weather were gathered off to the side. Regent Titania had departed after the Pyre, with Halfwing and a company of soldiers as escort. They planned to go first to Lord Oberon, and then on to other places, to find more loyal Fairies, and spread the word of the resistance to the Three Sisters.

"So, you're leaving," Min observed.

"Yes. I must find my daughter," Talia replied. She looked at Elanor. "Come. We must go."

Elanor didn't move.

"We removed your controls," Min informed her. Her anger and betrayal were clear. "She's free again."

Talia's expression didn't change. "I had hoped you would come with me anyway."

"No," Elanor said, her voice flat. "Not this time." Her hand gripped the amulet Celia had made. Goldberry had found it, simply tossed aside in a corner.

Talia's heart fell. She had really thought that Elanor would still follow her. Her face didn't betray her feelings, though. 'You really expected her to follow you again?' an internal voice said with contempt. She stepped into the Ring.

"I'll be going with you," Goldberry announced. She stepped forward, dressed for the road. She had a sword at her side, and a bow over her shoulder.

"I thought you hated me," Talia said, surprised and amused.

"I do, but Spear is out there, too," Goldberry said with obvious distaste, but also resignation. "The Goddess has made it clear that my path is with you."

Talia stared at Goldberry for a long time.

"I will never forgive you," Goldberry stated into the silence.

"I won't either," Talia said, her mind unclear as to who she was to forgive.

"Take this, Sister," Elanor offered, handing Goldberry her father's spear. "You might need it."

Goldberry nodded. She stepped up to join Talia.

Raven stepped forward. Min grabbed her arm, shaking her head no.

"If you find Spear," Raven conjectured, "Canin might be near." She turned to Min. "I will find him for you."

"Then I'll go, too," Min said.

"No," Talia and Raven objected together.

"I will not risk another child," Talia swore.

"This is too dangerous," Raven told her.

"I am not a Human, to be set aside while I grow a child," Min reminded her. "I'm a powerful Fairy."

"I know you are," Raven agreed, taking her hands. "But you still can't go. You're needed here. I'll tie you up, if I have to," Raven said, with the hint of a smile.

"Promise?" Min replied, with a similar twinkle. "Goddess grant you a swift journey," she said with resignation. She reached her hand out, and a rolled Ephemeral Ring flew to it. She handed it to Raven.

"This is the first one he made here. It might guide you to him," she said, fighting back tears.

Raven took it gravely, and kissed her. "I will return. And he'll be with me."

Min stepped back into Elanor's embrace.

"Protect the child," Goldberry advised. "She's important."

"We will," Elanor and Flora promised together.

"If that's all," Talia said tartly, "we must go."

Raven and Goldberry took their places at her side.

"Mother of Waves guide you, Mistress," Flora called out.

Talia simply nodded in her direction.

"We're traveling blind," Talia warned her companions. "It's dangerous."

"I won't give you any blood," Goldberry stated.

"I didn't ask for any," Talia replied. "I have just enough Power for this." She put her hands on their arms.

"Ready?" she asked, and without a pause for an answer, they disappeared.

Epilogue

The Queen of the Human Realm stood in the Great Hall.

The Priests of the Father had declared the room corrupted by the Fairies, and thus, it had needed to be purified. No one had entered since that horrible day.

The Queen walked across the floor. She looked up to where she had stood with Aurora in her arms. Tears began to sting her eyes.

She brushed them away. Her foot landed on something. She bent down.

It was a small knife. The blade was black, and twisted, as if it had been in a fire. The hilt was still intact. She picked it up.

"This was where she was standing," the Queen remarked to the empty room. "Maybe it will lead me to her." She wrapped the knife, and tucked it under her coat.

"Maybe I can make her understand that Aurora isn't her enemy. Maybe she'll remove her curse," the Queen mused with mounting hope.

"Mistress," Anne called in a whisper from the side of the Hall.

"Yes?" the Queen replied, wincing at the sound of her voice in the empty room. She hurried over to her senior lady's maid.

"I've been looking for you," Anne told her. "What are you doing in this place? Too much evil has happened here."

"I just needed to see it again," the Queen said.

"You're getting strange ideas, Mistress Rose." Anne motioned her through the door. "Come. I've found the man you were asking about."

The Queen, Rose of the Briar Clan, smiled. "Good. Where is he? The Father has guided me to this day."

Anne could only shake her head. She took her Mistress's arm, and led her away.

They arrived to the sound of falling water, and wet feet.

They looked around. Behind them, a thin waterfall trickled down a rock wall to the pool they were standing in. The water flowed past them, to fall — thunderously — over the cliff face in front of them.

"Outside, and in the water," Goldberry said, walking out of the shallow water covering the Ring. "This was very dangerous."

"I told you it was," Talia replied, "but you still came." She knelt, putting her hand on the submerged Ring. Shaking her head in frustration, she grabbed Raven's hand. "Tell me what you Feel."

"Just that this Ring hasn't been used in a long time," Raven replied. "It's glad to be in use again."

"The stone," Talia pressed. "What about the stone?" A pressure started behind her eyes. She had a small vial in her pocket, but she didn't want Goldberry's eyes on her when she used it. 'Best to save it,' she thought.

'Where will you get more?' a voice worried.

"I don't know what you mean," Raven said, her confusion evident.

Talia almost screamed in frustration. The barrier between her and her Power was strong. "Go look around," she finally said, gesturing the soldier away impatiently.

Raven moved off to the right, where the ledge bent around the mountainside. Goldberry walked to the edge of the cliff, and looked down. Below, a vast, green valley spread out from one set of mountains to another. She could see shapes moving on the green, but couldn't tell what they were. In the distance, she could see smoke rising.

Talia turned, and headed deeper into the pool, toward the rock wall. Carefully, she removed the vial from her pocket, and rubbed a drop of its contents between her fingers. With a sigh, she knelt, and laid her hands on the stone. Warmth filled her. She pressed into the stone, seeking their location.

"Talia! Goldberry!" Raven called from behind.

Talia rose, a smile of triumph and understanding on her face. Goldberry looked concerned, as Raven came running back toward them.

"What is it?" Goldberry asked.

"You must see," Raven said, motioning for them to follow. Goldberry looked at Talia. Talia smiled, and motioned for her Lady to go first.

They followed the mountainside until it stopped.

Below them, a castle sat in the arms of the mountain. Towers dotted the walls. A large hall and palace stood in the center. Figures moved about, both on the walls and around the grounds.

"It looks like our castle," Goldberry noted, "but." She stopped.

"No, it isn't," Talia said with triumph. "It was ours, but they stole it."

"What do you mean?" Goldberry asked, annoyance filling her voice, as she hated not understanding what she was seeing.

"That's the Human castle," Raven said. She pointed. "There's the tower we used. It collapsed. We're in the Human Realm."

"It used to be ours," Talia said again. "This was the first castle and palace of the Fairy Queens. I thought I felt something when I was in their Great Hall. Our ancestors built this. The Humans took it from us."

Talia looked out over the castle below her. "The Exile Queen wanted me to discover this. Our path starts here."

☾ ⌇⌇ ☼

They landed, with a thump, in wet grass.

"Motherless," Canin swore, rubbing at his bracelet. The skin around his wrist was white with cold. His hand hit the metal, and it shattered into four pieces, falling to the ground.

"Mother curse," he swore again, gathering the pieces. "Now what do I do?"

He looked around. The sun was just beginning to go down. He smelled a familiar scent.

"Spear," he remembered, sitting fully up.

She lay beside him, on her back, with her wings wrapped around herself. White frost covered her.

"Spear," he called again, crawling to her. He felt her face, looking for breath. Her skin was cold, but he could feel her breathing.

"Spear," he called again, this time directly in her ear. He pulled at her wings, sudden panic filling him, because he didn't see the child.

She made a noise, and her eyes opened. She raised her head. Her wings began to unfold. With a horrible crack, the outer edge of each wing shattered like glass and fell away. Canin, still holding a part of one wing, gripped it in shock as it came away in his hands. Her eyes widened in the most profound display of shock Canin had ever seen on a person. She tried to speak — or scream — but fell back to the ground, unconscious, instead.

Canin carefully set down the shard of wing he was still holding. He laid a hand on her throat, to confirm that she was still breathing. "Mother's mercy," he breathed. Then, he remembered that he had been looking for the child. He saw the wrappings, still held in her arms. Carefully, he eased the bundle out of her embrace. When it was free, he sat back, and began to unwrap it.

The girl's golden hair emerged, and Canin felt her breathing. It was steady and slow. She was still asleep.

Canin sighed in relief. "Mother, thank you," he whispered fervently, cradling the child. Tears began to flow from somewhere deep inside him. The wet splotches dropped onto her face. She yawned, opened her eyes, and looked up at him. Canin felt his path shift.

Most people have just one of these moments in their lives. In Canin's young life, he'd now had three. The first was when he had stood over the body of the abused woman who, through his impatience and arrogance, he had gotten killed. His path had shifted again when he'd gripped Min's hand across the table at the inn at Bell-Oak. And now, the child of a Human King lay in his lap. The child he had stolen — or maybe rescued — from Blood Cultists and vengeance-seeking Fairies. Canin began to laugh through his tears. The baby smiled at him.

She was quiet for a while, but soon, she began to whimper. Canin, knowing little about children, began to look around. What he was looking for, he didn't really know. Maybe another Mother-granted miracle. He looked into Spear's open eyes.

She struggled to a sitting position.

Canin looked at her, shocked. "Spear, your wings," he said, unable to say anything else.

"They're Healing," she announced matter-of-factly. "She's hungry. Give her to me," she ordered, holding out her hands.

"But," he stuttered.

"She's hungry," Spear said again, with an edge to her voice. "Give her to me."

Canin handed the fussing infant over. Spear took her. Her face changed, taking on a look of reverence and satisfaction. She held the baby to her chest.

"Help me undo the ties," she said. "My Power is too weak."

Canin looked at her, confused.

"The ties on my ringmail," she clarified, gesturing — with her chin — to her back.

Canin went behind her. Avoiding the raw edges of her wings, which were Healing as he watched, he undid the ties of the ringmail that went down her back, and under her wings.

"I have to set you down," Spear told the child, gently setting her on the grass. "Don't cry: it will only be a moment." Spear raised her arms, so Canin could pull the ringmail shirt over her head. She winced as it brushed her wounds. She began to unlace the front of her shirt.

"What are you doing?" Canin asked, as she bared her chest. He turned away in embarrassment.

"She must be fed," Spear answered, picking the child up again. "I never picked a name for you, all those years ago. Now, we must find something to call you," she said in a sing-song voice. "Maybe Aurora? She'll be my new dawn. What do you think, Canin?"

"I don't know," he replied, lost in confusion.

"He isn't that bright," Spear confided to Aurora, "but he did help us escape from those horrible Humans. Ah," she sighed. "Is that better? Drink up."

Canin turned to see Spear nursing the child, now known as Aurora. Just another step in the insanity that was now his life. Canin sat down heavily on the grass. "How?" he asked, waving his hands about in the air. "How are you feeding her?"

369

"We Fairies have complete control over our bodies. You've seen us Heal, and throw Silverfire." She smiled over at him. "And you think a little thing like making milk is beyond understanding?" She got a faraway look in her eyes. "I couldn't before, but now I can. I must make up for what I did. How I failed." She brushed Aurora's hair. "I failed you once. I won't again. The Goddess has given me another chance." Spear closed her eyes, lost in the joy of this child nursing.

"Mother's mercy," Canin said. He could see the break in her eyes. He had seen it as she killed all the Cultists in the Blood Ring room. He felt afraid. He didn't know what she would do to anyone who threatened "her" child.

The blanket Aurora had been wrapped in was slipping. Canin reached out to pull it up.

"She has two scars on her back," he said, tracing them with his finger. They ran downward, and started just below her shoulder blades.

"Horrible Humans," Spear cursed. "The Goddess led me to you."

Canin got up. "I'll try to find some water. Maybe I can find out where we are."

Spear didn't respond.

Canin walked a little way away. He thought about what had happened. All he remembered was panicking, and wanting to escape. Then, he had been in the nothingness. Cold. It might have been years, there in the cold. Then, he and Spear had been here.

"And where exactly is that?" he asked. "And what is that smell?" he said, looking around. He looked to the west. He could see the sun continuing to dip, falling into the trees of a huge forest in front of him. He saw the sun glint on the thorns covering the trees.

Canin fell to his knees. He thrust his hands into the pungent flowers of the redberry bushes that surrounded him. The same bushes he had picked berries from as a child. The bushes outside the borders of the Exile Forest.

He had come home.

Like what you've read so far? Eager for news regarding the upcoming release of Book Three, and the further adventures of Spear, Canin, and Rose of the Briar Clan, *et al.*? Please remember to sign up for the email list at ServantsoftheMoonandSun.com, and review this book at Amazon.com or your preferred recommendation platform.

Author Bio

Joel C. Flanagan-Grannemann has a B.A. in writing from the University of Pittsburgh at Bradford in Bradford, PA. He has lived in Columbia, SC for more than twenty years with his wife and editor, Jay-Jay Flanagan-Grannemann, and a coterie of cats. Joel's day job is Claims Supervisor at a major national retail chain. For more information, please visit www.ServantsoftheMoonandSun.com.

www.ingramcontent.com/pod-product-compliance
Lightning Source LLC
Chambersburg PA
CBHW050028030726
47506CB00001B/172